HA'PENNY SCHEMES

In 1920s inner-city Dublin tenements, Ivy Rose Murphy struggles to survive in the harsh poverty-stricken environment she was born into. She is trying to adapt to her new role as a married woman. There are those jealous of the improvements she has managed to make in her life. To Ivy it seems everyone wants a piece of her. Ivy's friends gather around to offer support but somehow Ivy is the one who gives hope to them.

Ivy's old enemy Father Leary keeps a close watch on her comings and goings. Ivy's husband, Jem Ryan, is a forward-thinking man, but can he protect Ivy when her enemies begin to close in?

GEMMA JACKSON

HA'PENNY
SCHEMES

Complete and Unabridged

MAGNA
Leicester

First published in Great Britain in 2017 by
Poolbeg Press Ltd
Dublin

First Ulverscroft Edition
published 2020
by arrangement with
Poolbeg Group Services
Dublin

A catalogue record for this book is available
from the British Library.

ISBN 978-0-7505-4759-8

Published by
Ulverscroft Limited
Anstey, Leicestershire

Set by Words & Graphics Ltd.
Anstey, Leicestershire
Printed and bound in Great Britain by
T. J. International Ltd., Padstow, Cornwall

Dedication

To my parents Rose and Paddy Jackson — both gone now but never forgotten. They were true Dubs — no matter how tough the going got they smiled and shared what little they had. I never told them how fortunate I was to be their daughter.

Acknowledgements

To Jewel Gore — my first rabid fan, now a friend — who berates me, loudly, if I allow something to happen to Ivy that she doesn't like.

To my daughter Astrid — thanks for the constant supply of life-giving tea and for sweeping around me as I escape into another world. I'd be buried in dust and dog hair but for you.

To my readers who have taken the time to share their enjoyment of my books with the world — thank you.

To Poolbeg Press — I thank you for allowing me to fulfil my dream of being a published author. Paula Campbell and Gaye Shortland — two ladies who work hard to make my books the best that they can be — I've learned so much from you both.

1

'Ivy . . . '

'*Shhh*, go back to sleep.'

She hated to move away from her husband Jem's warm flesh but needs must when the devil drives. She had things to do. She crept almost silently from the warm nest of the bed. She pulled the old army greatcoat from the foot of the bed, wrapping it around her shivering body with speed. She needed no light in the dark room. She grabbed her boots and left the room, closing the door at her back.

The bedroom was one of two large rooms that opened directly onto the long wide kitchen. Ivy had set the other room up as her workroom. The still-glowing embers in the black range nestled into the chimney breast gave enough light to guide her around her kitchen.

In moves that were automatic, she took the long, knotted strip of newspaper she'd prepared the night before from on top of her kindling box which was kept close to the range. She removed the glass domes from the wall-mounted gas lamps. 'These domes could do with a wash,' she whispered before turning to light the paper from the embers in the range.

Over the years, Ivy had developed the habit of talking aloud to herself — and sometimes to her dead father — when alone in her rooms. Having a husband now hadn't broken her of the habit.

She swiftly turned the knob on the nearest lamp to release the gas. The blue flame hissed and danced when she touched the flaming paper to the gas. She repeated the action with the second lamp before dropping the burning paper into the range.

'My kingdom for a pot of tea!'

She felt the familiar frisson of joy shiver down her spine while she filled her small metal teapot directly from her kitchen tap. No more standing in line at the outdoor community tap for her. No more hauling buckets of water until your arms ached and your fingers bent. The novelty of indoor plumbing was delightful.

She lit one of the four gas rings on her new freestanding stove and put the battered pot onto the ring with a satisfied sigh. Would she ever take the touches of luxury Jem had brought into her life for granted?

I'm glad Emmy isn't here this morning, she thought while raking the still glowing fire in the range. When their adopted 'niece' stayed over, Ivy was afraid to move around the kitchen. It didn't take much to wake the little girl. She shovelled the hot ash from the grate into a tin biscuit box. She'd save the ash for Jem to use in their back garden. She dropped kindling made from broken boxes and fresh nuggets of coal onto the glowing embers.

'You little beauty!' Ivy jumped to tend to the spitting teapot on her stove.

She still couldn't believe the speed the gas boiled up the water for her tea. It was a blessing on a cold dark morning. She removed the metal lid and poured tea leaves into the bubbling water. Then she turned off the gas and set the teapot on top of the warm range, leaving the tea to brew.

Without removing her coat, she began to dress. She'd left her clothes draped over two kitchen chairs pulled close to the range overnight. Sitting on one of the chairs, she wiped her hand briskly over the soles of her bare feet before pulling long knitted stockings up her legs. She pulled the boys' tweed trousers, which she'd taken to wearing to keep the cold wind from freezing her nether regions, up her slim legs. She pushed her feet into her well-worn boys' work boots.

'I'll have me first cup of tea before going any further.'

She washed her hands and face in cold water before taking the metal milk jug from the cold cupboard and putting it on the oilcloth-covered kitchen table. Then she selected a matching cup and saucer from the freestanding cupboard.

With her first cup of tea inside her, she dropped the heavy coat onto a kitchen chair pulled close to the table. Shivering, she pulled a man's long-sleeved vest over her head and down her body. A long black skirt came next, over the tweed trousers. A youth's linen work shirt and a heavy knit jumper completed the outfit. She pushed the two chairs back under the kitchen table and poured another cup of tea.

She felt guilty taking the time to just sit sipping her tea. There was work and plenty of it to be done in the kitchen. She sighed and leaned over to take out the notebook she kept in one of the deep pockets of her coat. She'd packed her pram the night before. It was sitting waiting for her in one of the four sheds that ran along her garden wall. She wanted to make a note of the people she needed to visit this morning. No point in running around Smithfield Market like a headless chicken.

'I hate to offer Sally those two lace dresses.' Sally, a stallholder at the market, and her daughters would use the material in the dresses to produce collars and cuffs to smarten up worn dresses. There was money to be made there. 'I haven't the time to alter them meself but I won't let her have them unless I can get a good price.'

Ivy was finding it difficult to stay on top of her business. She'd only two hands. When she'd lived alone she'd had nothing but time. As a married woman, time was something she never seemed to have enough of. Her husband — a man in a million — wanted to spend time with her. Jem liked to take her out on the town and she'd be lying if she said she didn't enjoy their outings.

'I've all those shoes that need cleaning. I'll not sell them on dusty.' She pushed to her feet to fetch another cup of tea. 'I'm annoying meself with me moaning. It's time to get on the road, Ivy, and stop yer bloody complaining. There's many a one would swap places with yeh.'

She stood and carried her cup and saucer over to the sink. She pulled on the old overcoat, pushing her keys and notebook into the deep pockets. She took her black knitted shawl from the hook at the back of the kitchen door, pulling it over her shoulders. She blew out the gas lamps and stood for a moment, checking by the light from the fire she'd left blazing for Jem that she'd left everything in order.

'The place needs a good going over,' she remarked. 'Still, I've only the one pair of hands. It'll have to wait.'

She pulled the kitchen door open and stepped out into the freezing-cold dark Dublin morning. She navigated her way by feel down to the shed nearest to the door that led from the garden into the lane that ran along the back of the terrace. She unlocked the shed, grabbed her laden pram by the handle and pulled it out before locking the shed door again.

'I feel like a prison warden with all these bloody locks,' she muttered, unlocking the wooden door in the brick wall.

She pushed her pram through, stepped out and locked the door at her back. She pushed the pram at speed around the side of the house towards the gas-lamp-lit, square, cobbled court-yard of The Lane.

'Watch it!' a male voice barked.

Her pram was brought to a sudden halt.

'You'll run someone over!'

'Name of God, Mike Connelly, you nearly gave me a heart attack!' Ivy stared at the well-set-up young man holding her pram in place. 'I thought I'd be the only sinner out and about at this hour of the morning.'

'You're not usually out and about this early yerself, Mrs Ryan.' Una Connelly was standing

5

at her brother's side, so wrapped up in odd bits of clothing only her eyes were showing.

'I've things to do.' Ivy turned her pram in the direction of the Stephen's Lane exit from the enclave of poverty the inhabitants called The Lane.

The other two fell into step alongside her. At one time there had been only one way in and out of The Lane — the urine-soaked exit that bordered the local public house — but, since the discovery of other openings, the people of The Lane avoided it.

'Where are the pair of yez off to at this hour of the morning?' Ivy asked as the threesome made their way along the exit tunnel onto Stephen's Lane and turned right in the direction of Merrion Square.

'Me and Mike are off to enjoy the pleasure of gutting fish,' Úna said.

'Are the pair of yez working at the fish factory now?' Ivy didn't wait for an answer. 'Would you not rather be working at the livery with yer brother Conn, Mike?' Conn Connelly, the eldest Connelly brother, worked at the livery with Jem.

'Me little brother is a martyr to his lungs.' Úna pushed her shoulder against her tall brother's chest affectionately. 'He has only to step into the livery to start wheezing like an old man. Our Liam's dogs do the same thing to him — poor lad.' Liam Connelly and his sister Vera had a dog act that was gaining renown on the Dublin stage.

'I've no tongue in me head either by the looks of things, what with me big sister doing all me talking for me.' Mike put his arm around his

6

sister's shoulders and covered her mouth with his hand. 'Come on, mouthy, or we'll be late. We'll love yeh and leave yeh, Mrs Ryan.'

The two turned towards a side street that would take them directly to the fish factory on the Dublin docks.

'Mike!' Ivy's shout stopped them in their tracks.

They turned and waited.

'Come see me this afternoon, will you, please?' Ivy wasn't sure what she wanted with the lad but she'd a thought tickling at the back of her mind.

'I'll do that, Mrs Ryan, but we have to go now.' He pulled his sister along with him as they ran off. It didn't do to be late as the overseer was a man very fond of docking wages.

Ivy didn't stay to watch the pair. She pushed her pram along the sleeping streets.

'Is that yerself, Mary?' Ivy didn't slow her fast pace when she caught sight of the shadowed figure on the other side of Kildare Street. She'd guessed the identity of the other woman by the shape of the pram she was pushing.

'Yer out before the corporation cart this morning, Ivy.' Mary pushed her pram into the deserted street.

There was no sign of the horse-drawn corporation water cart that washed the Dublin streets every morning.

'It would freeze the hair off a monkey this morning.'

The first month of January 1927 had been wet and miserable. It seemed February was going to match it.

'I wanted to get down to the market early,' Ivy said when Mary joined her.

The two women, shrouded in dark clothing from neck to ankles, shawls covering their heads and shoulders, pushed their prams through the gas-lit streets.

'I thought, with all them farmers making their way to Dublin for the Farmers Conference,' Ivy said, 'that some of their women would be down the market with their jams, butter and cheese.'

The first Irish Farmers Conference was attracting a lot of attention in the newspapers. She was hoping to pick up fresh produce for her friends and family.

'What about yerself — a bit early yet for you, isn't it?'

'My fella said the orange boats are in.' Mary was hoping to find a sailor with a box of oranges that 'fell off the boat' into his arms. Mary sold produce from her pram on street corners.

'Oh, lovely,' Ivy said. 'If I see yeh on me travels I'll have some off yeh.' The Garda moved on the street traders so Mary could be on any street corner.

The two women separated when they reached the Dublin docks. Ivy hurried along the empty streets, making mental lists of everything she needed to achieve today. She stifled a sigh — there never seemed to be enough hours in the day to get everything done.

2

'Well, would yeh look at that? '*The dead arose and appeared to many*'! I thought you were too high-falutin' to come down here these days, Ivy Murphy.'

Hopalong's tea stall was right inside the main entrance to Smithfield Market. He served tea and fried sandwiches to anyone who could pay for them. The stall was a gathering place for everybody who passed through the market — stallholders and customers alike.

'Give us a mug of tea, Hopalong.' Ivy didn't bother to mention that she'd been Mrs Ryan for the last nine months. She'd be dead and buried before the people she'd grown up around remembered her married name.

'Here, Ivy — ' Hopalong looked around carefully before almost whispering as he attended to putting his enamel mugs on his counter. 'Do you know Iris Walker?'

'Her whose husband was gassed in the Great War?'

'That's the one.' Hopalong leaned forward. 'She's been asking about yeh. I think she's looking for a bit of work with them dolls of yours.'

'Send her up to me.' Ivy produced a series of dolls under the name 'Ivy Rose'. She had a team of women who dressed the dolls for her in their own homes.

'The poor woman doesn't like to leave her husband.' Hopalong filled one of the big black pans he kept on top of his freestanding gas stove with sausages. 'Poor aul' Seb — he left home a broth of a lad and came back a wreck. He can't take two steps without gasping. Iris won't leave his side — devoted to him she is.'

'I'll fix something up.' She hadn't a clue right now where she'd find the time. She took her notebook from the deep pocket of her greatcoat. 'Give me her address.'

'Bless you,' he said when she'd written down the address. 'Sure if we don't help each other, who will?'

Ivy looked at the address. It would be only a few minutes out of her way to pass by Henrietta Street — but not today. She simply didn't have the time.

'Is that yerself, Ivy Murphy?' came a shout.

Attracted by the smell of cooking sausages wafting around the market, a crowd of stallholders were gathering for a cup of tea, a sandwich and a gossip before the hard work of the day began. Friday was a busy day at Smithfield Market.

'We all saw your picture in the newspaper, Ivy!' Big Polly shouted as she walked up to Hopalong's stall. 'You and Jem Ryan attending a talking-picture premiere if you wouldn't be mindin'. You was the talk of the place, I can tell yeh.' The tall, heavily built woman pushed her way to Ivy's side. 'I almost didn't recognise yeh meself. Yeh looked just like a fillum star. Fair took me breath away.'

10

Hopalong was busy serving big mugs of piping hot tea. Ivy got out of the way as people reached for milk and sugar from the countertop.

'My missus almost fainted the first time she saw your Shay up there dancing and singing on the big screen.' Tony the greengrocer joined the group around Hopalong's stall. 'Them talking pictures is something to behold.' He shook his head, marvelling at the new technology that was being introduced into Dublin cinemas. 'The whole family has been back more than a couple of times to watch them short pictures with your Shay in them. I puff out me chest when I tell the people around me in the picture house that I knew the big fancy star Douglas Joyce from the time he was knee-high to a grasshopper.'

'They're saying them talkies is the way of the future — that soon they'll be making long pictures that talk,' Big Polly gave her opinion. 'I hear Jem Ryan had a hand in bringing that lot to Dublin. There must be a queer few shillings to be made there.'

There was a murmur of agreement from the crowd.

Ivy sipped from an enamel mug of tea. 'Only time will tell if there is money to be made but, sure, nothing ventured, nothing gained.'

Ivy and her family had been a topic of conversation around the market for months. The coming of talking pictures had been big news at the tail end of 1926. The newspapers had covered the subject for ages. The crowds that paid to see this modern marvel were a source of income to the street traders, many of whom

11

shopped at the same wholesalers as the market traders. When the photographs of Ivy and Jem appeared in local newspapers, the dealers had begun a game of one-upmanship, each claiming to know Ivy and her family personally.

'You haven't got that outfit you wore to the film premiere in your pram for sale, have yeh?'

Big Polly's nudge almost sent Ivy flying. If Tony hadn't grabbed her arm to steady her she'd have landed face first in the straw around the stall.

'I must say, I was proud to say I knew yeh.' Hopalong was now busy making his sausage sandwiches and stacking them on the counter in front of him. Each person who grabbed one passed him cash. He never paused in his handling of his stall as he commented, 'You and Ann Marie did us proud — a proper pair of beauties. I almost wore me finger out pointing to yer picture in the newspaper and telling anyone who would listen that yez were customers of mine.'

Ivy's wealthy friend Ann Marie often accompanied her to the market.

There were murmurs of agreement and laughter from the stallholders. Each of them had gained a little bit of notoriety from their association with someone who had their picture in the dailies.

'Is your Shay going to stay out there in America?' Tony asked.

'According to me little brother Shay — now known as the film star Douglas Joyce if you wouldn't be minding,' Ivy said, 'there's money to be made in these new talking pictures. So he's staying in Hollywood.'

'We'll be able to say we knew him when he didn't have an arse in his trousers!' Hopalong laughed.

Ivy let the insult pass. She'd raised her three younger brothers after her mother deserted the family. She'd never let them leave the house with torn trousers.

'Polly, I have an outfit for you to look at when you have a minute — it would suit you a treat.' Ivy put her empty mug back on the stall. 'And, Sally, when *you* have a minute I've something for you to look at and all.'

She had filled her pram with the refashioned clothing that she created from the discards of the wealthy. Mondays and Wednesdays she pushed her pram around the back streets of Dublin, begging discards from the homes of the wealthy. Thursdays she stayed home washing and mending the items she received. Tuesdays and Fridays were market days where she sold the goods she had on offer.

Ivy walked away from the stall to see those who might have stayed at their own stalls. The market was a thriving spot. The people of Dublin did most of their shopping around the many markets dotted around the city. Friday, the women who could afford it did the weekend shopping.

For many years she'd had a set routine but lately she didn't know if she was coming or going. Still, she was determined to continue doing her round of the wealthy homes in her

13

neighbourhood. The money she made from their discards was her bread and butter. The visits to the market had become sporadic which strangely enough had improved her business.

She had come to the market early this morning, hoping to shift her goods to the stallholders before the market opened. She wanted an empty pram and cash in her hand when the farmers' wagons arrived.

★ ★ ★

'Ivy Murphy, yeh'll have me childer in the workhouse if I pay that much for them two dresses.' Sally eyed the beautiful lace dresses Ivy held out to her. 'Them dresses is damaged. I'd never be able to sell them on.' They'd been arguing about price but she had Ivy down to what she was willing to pay now. Still, it didn't do any harm to try and get them for a lower price.

'Sally, we both know them dresses have so much beautiful lace in them that you'll be able to retire on the money you make from them.' Ivy knew she had a sale.

'Chance would be a fine thing!' Sally searched in the leather bag she wore around her waist for the money to pay for the dresses. There was a quick exchange between the two women and the dresses disappeared under the counter of Sally's stall.

'Here, Ivy — ' Sally put out a hand to stop Ivy from moving on, 'do you know Molly Coyle — her that knits for the fancy shops?'

14

'I do indeed.' Ivy had bought several of the beautiful garments Molly produced for her own wardrobe.

'Well . . . ' Sally reached under the stall — she kept her special pieces wrapped in tissue paper out of reach of the public, 'Molly has a young one . . . ' the voice now came from under the stall where Sally searched for the items she'd stashed away, 'and she's a magician with a sewing needle.' She stood to place three carefully wrapped packages on top of the items on her stall. 'Look at these.' She held out a pencil for Ivy to use its end to move the delicate fabric around. Too much handling could dirty the garments.

'That's never lace from the tablecloth I sold yeh!' Ivy thought she recognised the birds and butterflies that had adorned the stained cloth she'd sold on months ago. She'd wanted to keep it but never found the time to touch it.

'It is,' Sally said, beaming.

'Honest to God, Sally, that's beautiful work. Does she make the lace join up herself?' Ivy could make lace and the delicate work she was admiring was first class. Old Granny Grunt, her teacher, couldn't have done better herself.

'The girl's fourteen — her name's Jennifer.' Sally ignored the question. She had to get on but, since she had Ivy here now, she wanted to do the girl a good turn. 'Her mother doesn't want to put her in a factory. It would be a crime for that young girl to sit all day in front of a sewing machine.'

Besides, if Jennifer went to work in a sweat

shop she'd never have time to do any work for Sally. Jennifer Coyle's work made Sally a lot of money. 'I thought, with you knowing the people in them fancy houses around you, you might hear of a seamstress job going.'

'The people in those big houses don't like to employ us Dubliners.' Ivy looked up from the work she'd been examining. She put on her posh voice and said, '*They simply refuse to learn their place, my dear!*' It was true that the people in service were mostly people from the country.

'Pity about them,' Sally laughed. 'Anyway, see what you can do for Jennifer, will you?'

'I'll keep me ears open.' Ivy grabbed the handle of her pram to continue on her way. She'd a few things left to shift. 'See yeh, Sally.'

'Take care, Ivy.'

The two women set about their business.

★ ★ ★

Ivy was delighted to be selling the last of her items when she heard the sound of heavy wagons crossing the cobbled streets. The street children appeared as if from nowhere to run alongside the wagons, hoping to be able to pinch something from the slow-moving vehicles. The farmers were wise to their ways and kept a sharp look out and their long whips at the ready.

Ivy pushed herself to the front of the crowd gathered around the farm wagons that had stopped by the market entrance.

'It's not all me own work, you understand.' An apple-cheeked farmer's wife was giving chapter

16

and verse about the neighbours whose goods she was offering for sale.

Ivy let the music of her voice pass over her head. She bought farmhouse cheese from her, after being offered a sample to taste. She watched milk and cream being ladled from tall churns into her screw-top cans. The woman's daughter used wooden paddles to cut butter into squares before wrapping it in greaseproof paper. After years of squeezing every penny until it wept, buying without thought as to cost was a secret delight. Eggs, cakes, bread and jams went into the depths of her pram. She'd serve cheese omelettes to her family this afternoon. Friday was a black fast day — no meat products.

With a wave and a friendly goodbye, she pushed her pram through the crowd.

★   ★   ★

Long before the market was open to the public, Ivy was making her way home. She kept her chin down and hurried along the familiar streets. She walked along the Liffey, avoiding Grafton Street altogether. She hurried along the streets filled with people going about their business. The Lane — the hidden enclave of poverty — was placed among the most expensive real estate in Dublin. The four entry tunnels that led from wide tree-lined streets into the cobbled square were deep and dark. It was impossible to see into The Lane from the main streets that surrounded it.

Ivy walked along Stephen's Street, her eyes on the tall spire of the church at its end. She'd use

17

the Stephen's Street tunnel to enter The Lane. The new home she'd recently moved to was steps away from the end of the tunnel. She quickened her pace. She could almost taste the tea and fried egg she'd been promising herself.

3

'Ivy, have yeh a minute?' The voice echoed down the Stephen's Street tunnel.

'In the name of God, missus, what are you doing out in this cold weather?' She wanted to scream *'No, I haven't a minute!'* She couldn't. Maisie Reynolds, the woman waiting to speak to her, had been Ivy's closest neighbour — occupying the two rooms over Ivy's basement home — from the day she was born until the day she moved from the tenements.

'I'm in a terrible state, Ivy.' Maisie pulled her black woollen shawl around her thin shivering body.

'So that's what you've been waiting for!' Marcella Wiggins, a woman who liked to know everything about everyone, appeared at the opening into the tunnel from The Lane.

'Mrs Wiggins!' Ivy wanted to kiss the nosy neighbour with the heart of gold. Perhaps she'd be able to escape into her own place and have that pot of tea she'd been promising herself.

'Lily Connelly is in my place making the tea,' Marcella said, referring to another long-time neighbour. 'I've a pound of broken biscuits I picked up from Jacob's factory.' Marcella took Maisie by the elbow and began to pull the woman after her. 'Ivy, you put that pram of yours away and come on over to mine. Maisie has been going around the place with a face as long as a wet week for long enough. Time we got to the bottom of this.'

A blushing Maisie was pulled across the wide cobbled courtyard that formed the central area of The Lane. Marcella was storming full steam ahead, heading towards the row of tenement buildings that ran along one side of the square, directly across from the long length of the livery building owned by Ivy's husband Jem Ryan. A row of two-storey double-front houses, so called because of the big windows that framed each side of the front door, stretched across the divide at one end of the square. One of those was Ivy's new home.

Ivy watched the powerhouse that was Mrs Wiggins pull poor Maisie along in her wake. There was no point in trying to get out of the demand to join the women. Mrs Wiggins was capable of coming and pulling her out of her own home if she disobeyed her orders. She sighed deeply before turning to walk around the side of her new home.

Ivy had come to love everything about her new place. She took the keys from her coat pocket and unlocked the door that led into her back garden. She put the pram back in its shed. Then, with a heavy sigh, she retraced her steps out into the courtyard.

'Ivy, where are you off to?' Jem Ryan stood in the double doorway of his livery building.

'I've been ordered to appear before Mrs Wiggins.' Ivy enjoyed the sight and sound of the man she'd married. You could still hear traces of his Sligo accent when he spoke — it sent pleasurable shivers down her spine.

Jem's long-legged stride ate up the distance between them. He was dressed as she loved to see him — wearing his work clothes of rough brown tweed trousers, thick linen work shirt and the green cable jumper she'd knit for him. The colour matched his gorgeous eyes. The wind whistled through his shining mahogany hair.

'You were out and about before the birds this morning.' He reached her side and stared down at her, worried that she was pushing herself too hard. He took her hand in his and squeezed her fingers. A kiss would have scandalised the neighbourhood. 'I was going to join you for a cup of tea. What does Mrs Wiggins want you for?'

'Something to do with Maisie Reynolds — I don't know exactly. I was just ordered to present myself.' She smiled when he grimaced.

'Jem Ryan, would you put your wife down and get about your business!' Marcella Wiggins stood in the open doorway of her tenement building. The granite steps leading up to the front door made the woman appear larger than life from their position down in the courtyard. 'Yer holding up proceedings.'

'I better go.' Ivy squeezed the fingers of the hand that still held hers.

'See you later, love.' Jem watched Ivy hurry over to climb the steps up to the open door.

The Wiggins family rented the front two rooms on the ground floor — a very desirable residence in this enclave of poverty.

21

★ ★ ★

'Right, Maisie, spit it out!' Marcella snapped when she had everything in her front room organised to her satisfaction. The teapot was steaming on the hearth of the low-burning open fire. The four women were seated around the long wooden table beneath the tall window that overlooked the courtyard. 'You've been going around the place with a face like Misery's Mother.'

'It's me boys.' Maisie pushed the mismatched cup and saucer away from its place in front of her. She put her elbows on the table and dropped her aching head into her hands.

'What's up with your sons?' Lily Connelly sat erect in her wooden kitchen chair. Mother of ten, Lily was tall for a woman and skinny rather than slim. Like most women she fed her children before she ate anything herself. Her once-blonde hair was completely grey now and pulled into a tight bun. She felt uncomfortable questioning her neighbour.

'They're in danger of being laid off!' Maisie almost wailed. The threat of unemployment was a constant cloud over the life of the working man.

'Nonsense!' Marcella slapped the table with her open hand. The china dishes danced on the rough surface. 'Your Petey has done his time and is a master fitter. Enda has been working for George Watson the blacksmith since he could toddle. The pair of them have never been out of work.'

22

'Pour the bloody tea, Marcella!' Lily glared at her best friend. It was plain to see poor Maisie was shaking.

'Petey punched his boss in the face.' Silver tears ran down Maisie's face.

'*What?*' Marcella was shocked. Petey had never been a thug.

'Mr Chippins told him he's going to lay off three of the young lads so he won't have to pay them a man's wage.' Maisie hiccupped as she told a familiar tale. Young men and women worked for years for little or no wages in order to learn a trade — only to be laid off days before their apprenticeship was complete.

'I'm surprised,' Marcella said. Mr Chippins — no one remembered his real name — was the leading shipwright on the docks. 'I've never heard anything bad said about Chippins. I thought young lads fought to get taken on with him?'

'Petey said as how times seemed to be getting harder for everyone down the docks.' Maisie was at her wits' end. How would she manage to feed and keep three grown men on one man's wage? 'Petey has had his wages docked and is on notice.'

The listening women sat as if frozen. They all understood the nightmare situation only too well.

Marcella, pushing herself slowly to her feet, broke the awkward silence. 'That aul' blacksmith can't be going to lay Enda off. George is almost crippled with that arthritis. He'd never manage without your Enda.' She put a chipped china bowl on the table for cold slops. Then she filled each china cup with dark tea. She pushed the milk jug and sugar bowl towards Maisie, proud of her table. The china might not match but it was better than most could offer company. The pretty china plate covered in broken biscuits sat prominently on the table top.

'George Watson told my Enda he was going to have to sell the blacksmith business.' Maisie sat back and stared at the tea in the cup in front of her as if she couldn't think what she should be doing with it. 'Mr Watson said as how he'd give my Enda first refusal.' She waited a moment to allow the ridiculous notion to sit. How would someone like her Enda — a man who lived from wage packet to wage packet — afford to buy a business?

'It's true what they say.' Lily Connelly sipped her tea. 'The rich are different.'

To the women at the table, a man with his own home and business was rich beyond their wildest dreams.

'Mr Watson did say that if my Enda were to marry his daughter Clara he'd let him have the business. Enda would only have to buy the tools.' Maisie was still staring into her cup.

'But your Enda has been walking out with Orla Bryce for years,' Ivy said. 'Orla has been filling her bottom drawer with stuff she buys off me when she has a few extra bob.'

'Still and all, one of us owning his own business . . . that's not to be sniffed at.' Lily Connelly thought of her own sons and was impressed by the chance being offered to a

24

young man she'd watched grow up.

Ivy sipped her tea and listened to the other three women as ways and means of making money were thrown around the place but nothing that would earn the amount of money needed.

'That clever aul' bastard!' Ivy lowered her empty cup into its saucer.

'Ivy Murphy, I'll thank you to mind your language when you're sitting at my table!' Marcella barked.

'Give us another cup of tea, missus.' Ivy ignored Marcella's insulted sniff and glare. She leaned across the table to take Maisie's cold shaking hands in hers. 'Tell me exactly what is being offered to Enda.'

'I was hoping you might be able to help,' Maisie said. 'I thought, what with you and Jem running your own business, you would be the best person to talk to.'

'What?' Marcella stood over the table, her teapot in her hand. 'You think this young whippersnapper knows more than us? We're not good enough for you now, Maisie Reynolds?'

'Whisht, Marcella!' Lily emptied the dregs from her cup into the slop bowl. 'Let's hear what Ivy has to say. It may be she does know more than you or me.'

'Does she indeed?' Marcella said. 'We've run a home on a string and a prayer. We've managed to raise families a woman can be proud of.'

Ivy looked at the three older women. She would hate to offend them by what she was sure they would see as showing off. 'Mrs Wiggins, I'm not for a moment being disrespectful.'

'Well, I have to say,' Marcella poured the tea, 'that George Watson isn't known for doing anyone a good turn. I'd forgotten that in me excitement at the thought of Maisie's Enda coming into a bit of good fortune.'

'Tell me again what your Enda said.' Ivy gulped at the fresh cup of tea.

'Mr Watson told him how he had to sell the blacksmith business. He said as how if Enda would marry his Clara it would be different. Enda need only buy the tools. Then he'd be set to inherit the house and everything George had. Clara is his only child, you know. She'll be worth a queer penny when her parents pass on.'

'That's not to be sniffed at, Ivy.' Marcella was sitting forward in her chair, waiting to see what would happen next.

'We really need to talk to Ann Marie when it comes to matters of money.' Ivy's friend was a familiar figure in The Lane and Marcella worked as Ann Marie's laundrywoman three days a week. 'The woman is a marvel when it comes to money.'

'Ivy,' Lily watched the younger woman push her fingers through her short black hair, 'tell us what you're thinking.'

'Enda would be selling his soul to the devil if he agreed to aul' George's terms.' Ivy jumped up to serve herself more tea. She'd almost inhaled that last cup.

'Make yerself at home, why don't yeh?' Marcella said.

'Sorry, missus, but me mind is running away

26

with me.' Ivy carried her full cup back to the table.

'Why did you say what you did, Ivy?' Maisie couldn't bear to wait.

'Aul' George can see to it,' Ivy said, 'and I wouldn't put it past the man — he can make sure that Enda never touches a penny of his money after George is dead and gone.'

'How?' Lily stared — everyone knew everything a married woman had belonged to her husband.

'I only know about this because Ann Marie explained it to me.' Ivy didn't want to present herself as any kind of expert. 'A new law was passed recently.' The law had come into effect in Britain but the Irish legal system was still following the British. Ann Marie had consulted a solicitor concerning a married woman's rights before her own marriage. The woman was nobody's fool when it came to protecting her money. 'A woman can protect her own inheritance from her husband these days.' She ignored the shocked gasps. 'I'll bet you any money that George Watson knows all about that. Your Enda would need to be careful if he decides to accept the offer aul' George made to him.'

4

'Honest to God, Jem, I thought we were going to have to hold Marcella back!' They were seated at the kitchen table, enjoying the omelette and chips Ivy had cooked for their midday meal. 'I swear the woman was ready to storm over to George Watson's house and box the man's ears.'

'It just goes to show you never know when something you've learned might come in handy.' Jem sipped from his mug of tea.

'I think Mrs Wiggins is going to ask Ann Marie all about that Married Woman Act,' Ivy laughed. 'The woman's not going to take my word for something so important.'

'The law only came into effect last year. Mrs Wiggins is probably put out that you knew something before she did.'

'All the same, Jem, imagine that Mr Watson trying to take advantage of Enda!' She stopped with her laden fork in mid-air. 'Here, why don't you ever use Watson as a farrier for the livery?'

'When it was only me and Rosie, I did the horseshoes for Rosie myself — but when my uncle was alive and we had more horses, he wouldn't have Watson around the place. He didn't like the way the man handled the horses.'

'That says a lot about the man's character.' Ivy stood to fetch more tea. Her small china cups were soon empty. 'Enda Reynolds has worked for the man since he was in short trousers. It's hard to believe the man was ready to cheat someone he's known for years.' She needed to let the subject drop. She couldn't take the worries of the world on her shoulders.

'Where is aul' Frank anyway?' Jem asked presently. 'He's usually in here cadging something to eat or a cup of tea.'

Ivy had bought the house they lived in from Frank Wilson. Frank used to rent out rooms in the large house and Ivy continued the practice. It was a good source of income and Frank handled all of the details.

'He's at the library looking for designs for his miniature furniture.'

Frank Wilson was a skilled carpenter. Ivy had talked the man into making and selling dollhouses and furniture. She sold his work through a Grafton Street toy shop.

'Gives us a bit of time to ourselves,' Jem said.

'You know, Jem, I was thinking — '

'Look out!'

'Would you stop that?' She refused to smile. Jem always said she was at her most dangerous when she was thinking. 'You got that fancy car of yours to start an automobile taxi service.'

'Yes,' he said, 'but you know I haven't the time what with one thing and another. I still think it's a good business to get into but there are only so many hours in the day.'

'It seems to me, and I could be mistaken, but Enda Reynolds was always mad about anything to do with combustion engines.' She laughed at a memory. 'He almost blew the windows out of the rooms over my head many a time, to hear Maisie tell it. I know he's kept that old banger the blacksmith drives around the place on the road.'

'Is that a fact?' Jem was surprised. Enda Reynolds was a man who walked around the place without passing comment to anyone. 'Hmm . . . it's something worth thinking about.'

'You said you wanted more than one automobile on the road. Enda would be good for looking after the engines. There's no doubt about that. But I don't know what he'd be like dealing with the customers.'

'I'll have to make time to talk to the man.' Jem finished his meal and pushed the plate away from him. 'I seem to recall that Petey Reynolds was good at school work. Didn't he win some kind of fancy scholarship at one time?'

'He did,' Ivy said after thinking about it for a moment. 'He couldn't take it, of course.' It went without saying that the Reynolds family couldn't afford the cost of uniform, travel and books. They needed their son bringing in a wage.

'I'll have a word with Pete.' Jem had no intention of calling a grown man 'Petey'. 'He might be just what I'm looking for — if he has a smart head on his shoulders. I need a manager for the livery.'

'What about Conn?' Ivy wouldn't allow Conn Connelly to be pushed aside for anyone. The lad had been working with Jem and herself since they first started to improve their lot in life.

'Conn will be twenty-one soon — a man grown.' Jem recognised that look in her eyes. She was ready for battle. 'I thought he might like to come work for us at the picture house.'

'Doing what?' Ivy was suspicious. Conn had been promised a managerial position at the livery.

'Learning to manage a talking-picture house.' His green eyes sparkled with silent laughter.

'Go way!'

'Conn is a good, reliable worker. He's willing to turn his hand to anything and he's a marvel at handling people. I want to give him the chance to better himself.'

'Being manager of the livery would be a big step-up for Conn.'

'It would.' Jem thought of Conn's brother and sister — Liam and Vera were making a name for themselves on the Dublin theatre scene. Conn was the eldest son. Jem sometimes thought the young man felt as if he was being left behind by his younger brother and sister. 'But I think Conn would love something more exciting out of life than being hidden behind high walls here in The Lane.'

'I can't say I'd blame him.' Ivy stood to remove their dirty dishes from the table. 'You and I weren't content to drift along. Why should Conn be? But I thought Armstrong had his own son being trained up to run the picture house?' Armstrong was Ivy's uncle, William Armstrong, her deceased father's brother — but she never referred to him as such.

'The other partners and I have been talking.' Jem had gone into the business of talking-picture houses with two other men. They called their company ARC for Armstrong, Ryan and Connor. The O'Connor in the company was Ann

31

Marie's husband Edward. 'We are not going to stop at only one talking-picture house.' His voice became animated when he talked of the modern marvel of talking pictures. Jem loved anything new and forward-thinking. He felt lucky to be given the chance to be part of something so thoroughly modern. 'Conn would have the chance to learn something that I believe will set him up for life.' Besides, he wanted someone of his own on the inside. Armstrong was the visible head of the new company. The man was a canny businessman, there was no denying it. However, Jem would feel more comfortable if he had someone he trusted keeping an eye on his investment. He didn't know Armstrong's son and it didn't pay to take your eye off the ball.

'You should talk to Conn about it.' She'd miss his smiling face around the place. 'He'd need a lot of fancy new clothes, wouldn't he?' She was mentally running through a list of items she might have to hand. She collected a lot of gent's superior apparel and trimmings on her round of the wealthy homes. It was amazing to her what the wealthy threw away.

'We'll send him to Mr Solomon,' Jem named a neighbour who was a master tailor. The old man made bespoke suits for the people of The Lane. The suits were expensive but they'd last a lifetime. They fetched a fine penny at the pawn too which was always a consideration in The Lane.

'Have you discussed any of this with John?'

John Lawless was recovering from a work accident that had almost crippled him for life.

The man was devoted to Jem and Ivy since the pair had rescued him and his family from the threat of the workhouse, employing not only him but also his daughter Clare in the livery.

'I haven't talked to anyone yet, missus,' Jem said. 'It's more than my life's worth to make decisions without the wife's approval.'

'Oh, go way, you!' She pushed at his shoulder while he laughed aloud. 'I bought a lovely fruit cake this morning. Do you want a slice to finish off the meal?'

'Go on, give us a bit.' Jem pushed his enamel mug across the table. 'I'll have it with me last cup of tea and then I'll have to get back across the way.'

Ivy busied herself cutting into the moist cake she'd bought from the farmer's wife. She'd sold the excess produce to the women of The Lane before coming home to start cooking her husband's meal — but she'd kept far more back than she'd sold.

★   ★   ★

'Mike, thanks for coming — come in.' Ivy smiled at the tall young man standing outside her door.

'I wasn't sure what time you wanted me to come over.' Mike stepped in at her invitation. 'I hope I'm not in your way.'

'No, this is fine.' Ivy walked ahead of him down the long hallway towards the door that opened off the main house into her kitchen. 'Sit yerself down.' She pointed to her oil-cloth-covered kitchen table. 'Are you hungry? Silly question — you're a growing lad. I expect you're always hungry.'

'So my mother tells me.' Mike was nervous. He couldn't imagine what this meeting was about.

'Do you like working at the fish factory?' Ivy filled her larger teapot from the black kettle she kept sitting on the range.

'I hate it but it's a job.' Mike watched while Ivy took bread from a breadbin and began slicing it.

'I bought a nice bit of ham straight off the farm this morning,' she said with her back to him. She'd thought about this meeting but she wanted to be sitting at the table with him before she started the discussion.

'That would be lovely, thank you.' Mike decided to sit back and wait to see what would happen.

Ivy sat down opposite the lad when she had a plate of ham sandwiches sitting in front of him and the tea poured.

'How would you like to come work for me?' she asked him.

Mike stared at her, startled. 'I couldn't give up me shift at the factory,' he said. He wished he was free to accept her offer. He would love anything that would get him out of that place where early each morning he had to stand in freezing-cold water for hours, surrounded by women, all of them gutting fish. The pay was miserable — they were paid by the weight of the fish they filleted. 'I have to walk our Una down there every morning. The streets aren't safe for a young woman alone at that hour.' He took a sandwich and put it on the side plate by his cup and saucer. He had to force himself not to attack the sandwich. He was starving. 'The gentry are rolling out of them fancy houses from their parties when we walk past. You know how they feel about our women.' He began to devour the sandwich.

'Sadly, I do — if I remember from when your sister used to work at the factory.' Vera had hated every minute of it and hadn't hesitated to let everyone know. Ivy knew that there was an element of the gentry who thought throwing a shining coin at a woman entitled them to take liberties. Úna was an attractive young woman — the Connellys were a good-looking family with their blond hair and light-coloured eyes. 'You finish your work early in the morning. You could come to work for me after your shift is finished.'

'Doing what?' Mike wanted to smack his lips in pleasure. He couldn't remember the last time he'd eaten ham.

'I need help around here.' Ivy stood to fetch the fruit cake and the teapot.

'I can't do housework.'

'I wouldn't ask you to!' Ivy laughed. 'I need help outside. I'm not even sure what the work would entail, to be honest with you. I just know that I need a warm body — preferably one with muscles — to help me handle some of the work that's going on.'

'I can't get the smell of fish off me.' Mike hated the smell but it was in everything he owned. He boiled a kettle on the fire and scrubbed himself every day but the smell lingered.

'That would be the least of your problems.' Ivy was pleased with his responses. She needed help and having a strong-looking lad around the place would help her in ways she didn't want to discuss yet. 'We have the indoor plumbing here.' She smiled, delighted with the fact. 'You could have a hot bath before you start work. I can easily sort out a couple of outfits from what I have on hand for you to wear to work.'

'I'd love to have something to do with me days.' He walked the streets and hung around corners after he finished his shift at the factory. It wasn't much of a life.

'I'm not sure exactly what I'll be asking you to do. We'd be learning together, Mike.' Ivy wanted to dance with joy. She'd have someone to help share the load of work that seemed to be growing bigger with each passing day.

5

'I asked Mike Connelly to come and work for me today.' Ivy sighed happily. All of the time she'd spent worrying and wondering about married life! Why hadn't anyone told her about the simple pleasure of sitting in your man's arms? She loved the times when it was just her and Jem. They happened so seldom. Such moments were doubly precious to her.

It was late in the day. Ivy was sitting on Jem's lap, snuggled in close to his muscled chest. They occupied one of their big overstuffed armchairs. Jem had pulled the chair close to the black range that heated the kitchen. They hadn't bothered to light the gas lamps. The dancing flames of the fire added a soft glow to the room. They had learned to ignore the noise from the comings and goings of the tenants in the rest of the house.

'Say what you like about Brian Connelly, he and Lily have raised a family to be proud of.' Jem rubbed his large workworn hand along Ivy's back, loving the chance to simply sit and be. No one was yelling for them. He had capable men working for him at the livery and for once his Ivy was content to simply sit.

'Aren't you going to say anything about me employing someone without talking it over with you first?' Ivy snuggled into Jem's neck, not really worried.

'It's your business.' Jem nuzzled his nose into the dark mass of curls that covered his wife's head. 'I'm glad you've got someone in to give you a hand.' He wondered about mentioning getting someone to help her with the housework. Ivy was trying to do too much. There were only so many hours in a day. It made more sense for her to concentrate on her work. That's what she enjoyed doing and where the money was. They could pay someone to do the housework. But he hated to bring the subject up. Ivy was very sensitive about what she saw as her failings as a housewife.

'There seems to be so much for me to do.' Ivy stared into the flames. She knew she should be up taking care of things that needed tending but she was a married woman now and her husband had the right to expect his wife to spend time with him. How did other women manage? 'I got a couple of names at the market this morning.'

'More women to dress your dolls?'

'One of them.' Ivy nestled in closer. She was getting sleepy. 'The other I don't know what to do about.' She gave him the details she had about Mrs Coyle's daughter.

'If you were impressed by her needlework, that's saying something. You're not a bad hand yourself at turning out beautiful lacework.'

'It would be a mortal sin for such a skilled worker to spend her days in a sweatshop. She's only young. Who knows what she could achieve if given a chance. I'll ask around the houses I visit on my round and see if anyone is looking for a seamstress. I won't hold me breath though.'

38

'Why don't you employ the girl yourself?' Jem suggested.

'Are you mad?' Ivy pushed away from his chest to stare into his beautiful green eyes. 'What would I do with a young one underneath me feet all day?'

'Think about it.' He gently moved her stiffened arm and pulled her back against his chest. 'You have all that stuff that needs altering. You know you haven't the time to do it.' He pressed a kiss into her hair. 'I'd a pain in my ears listening to you go on about those two lace dresses you didn't want to sell on.'

'Still . . . ' She didn't know the girl. What if she didn't like her for some reason? She felt as if she was surrounded by people as it was. Could she have someone under her feet all day long? She'd have to think about it — meet the girl.

'Ivy, a skilled seamstress would be a blessing to you.'

'But she'd be under me feet!' Ivy almost wailed into his chest.

'So will Mike Connelly.'

'All the people who say I'm getting too big for me boots will have a great time of it.' Ivy couldn't get her head around it. Imagine her, an employer. What was the world coming to? 'I don't know how to be a boss woman.'

'I don't think anyone cares about that, Ivy.' Jem hid his smile in her hair. She was one of the bossiest women he'd ever come across. 'The people you take on only care about the money they earn — people are glad of the chance to earn a few shillings, Ivy.'

'I suppose.'

'Come on.' He pushed her gently from his lap. 'It's getting late. Time for bed. We can discuss all of this in the morning when we are both fresh and rested.'

'Do you not want a cup of tea before bed?'

'No, I don't,' Jem put his hands on her waist and pushed her to her feet. He stood close to her side. 'I want to go to bed with my wife.'

'I know that look in your eyes, Jem Ryan.' Ivy lowered her thick black eyelashes over her violet eyes coyly. 'You can damp down the fire for the night.' She pushed him back into the armchair. 'The one in the grate, I mean,' and, with laughter pealing, she ran towards the bedroom.

'You're going in the right direction anyway, missus.' Jem pushed himself out of the depths of the chair. It wouldn't take him long to tend the fire.

He raked the fire and put damp nuggets of coal in a thick layer over the glowing embers before closing the door that covered the flames. The fire would stay on all night. He made a couple of long paper spills for whichever of them got up first in the morning to use. Then he washed his hands in cold running water over the kitchen sink.

With a last look around to make sure everything was in order he turned towards the bedroom. Now he'd tend to his wife.

'What are you lighting the lamps for?' Ivy stopped removing her clothes to ask.

'I want to see what I'm about,' Jem replied as he removed the second globe from the wall-mounted gas light in their bedroom.

'In the name of God, Jem Ryan!' Ivy pretended shock. 'You're not decent, you're not.'

She shrieked when he pushed her down onto the bed.

'I'm going to have my wicked way with you!' He leered down into her laughing face.

Ivy put the back of her hand to her forehead in a gesture she'd seen Mary Pickford use in one of her films. '*Helllp!*' she groaned dramatically.

'Ivy Murphy, you'll be the death of me.' Jem fell onto the bed beside her where they lay laughing hysterically.

The laughter soon ended and then the only sounds to be heard in the room for a long time were the sounds of sighs of pleasure. Jem and Ivy were young and in love. They ignored the church's teaching that it was wrong to enjoy the pleasures of the flesh.

'It's your turn to blow out the lamps.' Jem nudged Ivy who was draped across his chest.

Ivy was feeling like a limp wet rag. If they got much better at this loving stuff she'd be dead. But she'd die with a smile on her face.

'I'm not putting my feet on that cold floor, Jem Ryan.' She rolled over and snuggled into her pillow. 'You were the one who wanted the gas lamps on — you can be the one to blow them out.'

'Didn't you promise to love and obey me?' Jem had never intended that Ivy should blow out the lights. He pulled back the nest of blankets and stepped out quickly. He slammed the blankets back in place, not wanting the cold air to enter the warm bed. He needed to take care of the device he used to prevent conception. He kept a covered china dish filled with water under the bed for that purpose.

'I don't remember saying that. You must have been dreaming.' Ivy's voice was slurred with sleep. She waited only until he'd joined her in the bed before falling into a deep sleep.

'You're my dream, Ivy Murphy Ryan.' Jem pressed a kiss into her hair. He lay on his back, his softly snoring wife in his arms. 'I hope to God you won't kill me when I tell you that the rubber contraption broke.' He was using a device designed for young men going off to war to prevent unwanted babies. Ivy hadn't wanted to fall for a child too early in their marriage. He'd have to tell her in the morning. He didn't keep secrets from her — not when they concerned her more than him anyway. He sighed deeply, tightened his arms around her, tucked the blankets around their ears, then joined her in sleep.

6

Ivy stood in the first of the whitewashed sheds that ran along the freestanding wall of her garden. Jem had found a heavy old table that must once have graced the kitchen of a fine house for her. She stood behind this table now, a group of women forming an orderly queue in front of her, collecting up completed dressed dolls. The shelving unit at her back held orange boxes filled with naked dolls and supplies. She would hand out supplies and fill the boxes with dressed dolls through the day. It was a time-consuming business to inspect each doll, make a note in the ledger sitting open on the table, pass out supplies, then pay each woman for her work.

It was a familiar routine to the women now. They came to Ivy's soon after they got their men and youngsters out from under their feet. They parked their prams and carts in the lane that ran along the high walls of the expensive real estate that surrounded The Lane and the brick walls that ran along the back of this row of houses. There wasn't enough room in the garden for all of the prams. Young children ran back and forth — it was chaos and mayhem but the women had to bring their children with them.

'Now, ladies,' Mike Connelly appeared at the back of the crowd, a big smile on his handsome young face, 'is everyone here for the dolls or can

I help you with something else?'

'I've a few things you could help me with!' one of the women called. 'In fact, I've friends you could help and all — a big handsome lad like you!'

There was tittering and laughing along the standing crowd.

'Now, ladies, you'll be making me blush and me ma wouldn't like that.' Mike loved coming to give Ivy a hand. A laugh and a joke in the open air suited him down to the ground, after his shift at the fish factory.

'I want to pay a few pence off me wool!' one of the women shouted.

'I'm looking for something for me childer!' another voice said.

'I'm looking for woollens to unpick!'

'Give's a few minutes to wash the smell of fish off me,' Mike said. 'Then I'll be with yez. If the people not here with dolls would form a line over here,' he pointed to a spot on the grass, 'I'll see to yez.'

'Do you need a hand with washing yerself, son?' someone shouted. 'I'd be glad to scrub your back.'

'Keep that kind of talk to yerself! Can't yeh see yer making the poor lad blush — and me and all!'

'It would take a sight more than that to put you to the blush, yeh brazen hussy!'

Ivy ignored the crowd and continued to examine the dolls presented.

Sometime later Mrs McCabe approached Ivy with a load of dolls she and her daughters had completed. Their work was always excellent but Ivy couldn't afford to show favouritism. This lot would be on her in a minute if she passed someone else's dolls without checking every one. With Easter fast approaching, she needed as many dolls as she could produce for the shop in Grafton Street.

'I don't want no paper money,' Mrs McCabe leaned across the table to say under cover of the noise of the crowd.

'I know.' Ivy had a good working relationship with Mrs McCabe. She and her young daughters could get through a hundred of the small Alice dolls in days. They were some of her best workers. She wanted to keep them happy. 'I've shiny half crowns in me pocket for you.'

'Mrs Ryan,' Conn Connelly said as he strolled into the back garden, 'your husband has sent me to tell you to take a break. He's worried you'll turn into a block of ice standing out here.' He turned to the crowd with a smile. 'Morning, ladies.'

There were shouted ribald remarks which he ignored. The presence of the Connelly men was deliberate on Ivy's part. She didn't want anyone to think she stood out here with money in her pockets and no security.

'I'm back!' Mike Connelly stepped out of the house, making an obvious show of locking the kitchen door at his back. No one was allowed enter the house without invitation. He felt like a new man without the smell of fish clogging his nostrils, wearing clothes Ivy supplied for his use. 'I had a cup of tea and something to eat and all.'

'Yeh cheeky beggar, you haven't even started work yet!' someone yelled. 'It's all right for some people.'

'I'm a growing lad,' Mike laughed. 'I have to keep me strength up.' He walked over to the shed, grabbed a wooden chair and sat at the table. He pulled one of the ledgers on the table over. 'Right!' he shouted to the second queue of women that had formed. 'I'll take money from those that have it for stuff they've put to one side.' Ivy allowed the women to pay a little something off goods. When they had the goods they'd ordered paid for, only then would she allow them to take the items home with them.

'I want more of that yellow wool I put to one side . . . '

'I'm looking for a pair of lad's short trousers . . . '

'I want old woollens . . . '

Ivy ignored the shouted demands while completing her transaction with Mrs McCabe. She silently blessed the day she'd taken Mike on to help her. She didn't know how she'd managed without him. She stood pressing her hands into her back. It was awkward leaning over the table for hours. She didn't sit down when she worked with these women. She'd be jumping up and down every two seconds.

'Mrs McCabe, before you leave, can I ask if you know . . . ' She removed a piece of paper from her pocket and glanced at it. It had been over a week since Hopalong had given her the name but this was the first time she'd been able to do anything about it. 'Iris Walker . . . she lives

46

in Henrietta Street too according to this.'

The change in the mood of the crowd was startling. Every woman there closed her mouth and stared. Mike looked up from his ledger and looked around, wondering what had happened. These women chattered constantly it seemed to him.

'I'll bid you a good day, Ivy Murphy.' Mrs McCabe almost stormed from the shed.

Ivy was left open-mouthed, staring after her departing figure.

'In the name of God, anyone want to tell me what that was about?' Ivy, hands on hips, asked the crowd.

The crowd remained silent, the women looking at their feet. No one wanted to be singled out. No one offered an explanation.

'Right.' Ivy couldn't stand there all day. She'd have to get to the bottom of this later. 'If that's the way it is . . . *next*.'

The women pushed forward and the business of the day continued without the good-humoured chatter that usually accompanied it.

*   *   *

'That was strange.' Mike locked the gate in the brick wall of Ivy's garden. 'I've never seen the crowd react like that.'

'Neither have I.' Ivy intended to find out why the name of Iris Walker would have that effect on the women. She'd be having a word with Hopalong. He'd been the one to give her the woman's name after all. 'Bring those ledgers into the kitchen, Mike. I'm almost frozen solid.'

'It was a busy morning right enough.' Mike returned to the sheds. 'I'll tidy up a bit before I come in. I pulled that much stuff off the shelves I've left the place in a mess.'

'Good lad.' Ivy turned to walk towards the house. She took her keys from her coat pocket and unlocked the kitchen door.

Without stopping she walked through the house and out the front door — she wanted Jem. She needed his advice.

★   ★   ★

'This might take a while . . . ' Jem had listened intently to Ivy's words. He had immediately pulled her into the cubicle he'd been forced to build off his livery office for all the people wanting to use the telephone. 'You could wait in the house. I'll get you when your uncle telephones.' He had telephoned his business partner William Armstrong, Ivy's uncle. He'd left a message asking William to find out what he could of Iris Walker. William in his alter ego of Billy Flint would be able to find out all they needed to know. Billy Flint was a known and feared name in Dublin's underworld.

'I'm putting that call through to yez!' John Lawless shouted from his position in front of the livery main telephone board.

'That was quick.' Ivy rubbed her hands together before picking up the handset.

'What the hell have you been up to now?' the irate voice of her uncle barked in Ivy's ear. 'The

48

Walkers — I ask your sacred pardon — what have you done to bring yourself to their attention?'

'Nothing.' Ivy went on to explain the situation in detail.

'And you say Hopalong at the Smithfield market gave you the Walker name?'

'He thought I might be able to put a bit of work in Iris's way.'

'Ha, Iris Walker — Iris McCabe that was — doesn't fart without her husband's permission.'

Ivy jolted at the name. Was Iris one of her Mrs McCabe's girls? 'There is no need to be vulgar,' she said.

Jem rolled his eyes to the heavens. Ivy and her uncle — always biting into each other.

'I suppose you've never heard the like before, little girl?'

Ivy gasped in outrage.

'Listen to me carefully, Ivy — you've attracted the attention of a dangerous man. Iris is married to Seb Walker and he is an out-and-out gangster. He uses Iris to find his marks. Don't fret for her — she's no innocent — there's a pair of them in it.'

'I thought Iris's husband was an invalid — gassed in the war?'

'My eye — that fella is too fond of his own skin. I heard he was claiming a pension from the British — more power to him — but he was never gassed — he probably licked the officers' arses to keep himself out of the fighting.'

'But what has any of that to do with me?'

49

'You're becoming too successful. There is a certain class of person who would want to either take the business out of your hands or demand a share of the profit. I don't like that Walker thinks you're a soft mark.'

'What!'

'He didn't come after you himself — he was sending his missus in — must think you're a fool.' His sigh echoed down the phone lines. 'Leave this with me. I'll ask a few questions around town. You be on your guard, my girl — don't take any unnecessary risks.'

'He hung up!' Ivy stood with the phone in her hand, staring at Jem.

'What did he have to say?' Jem had been unable to hear all of the conversation.

Ivy repeated the information and saw the colour drain from his face.

He pulled her into his arms, holding her close, his mind frantically planning ways to protect her. No one was going to hurt his wife.

7

'Ivy Rose Murphy Ryan, what in the name of God are you up to now?' The voice echoed around the vast space of the livery building.

The whistling and shouts of the stable lads preparing horses and carriages quietened down.

'Oh-oh!' Ivy buried her nose in the thick black mane of the horse she'd been grooming. She'd thought by creeping in during the changeover of horses she'd have been safe enough.

She walked out of the stall to meet the fiery green eyes of her husband. God, he looked handsome in his tailored grey suit! She felt like a ragamuffin in her long black skirt and green woollen jumper. He stood in the aisle separating the horse stalls, his feet braced apart, hands on his hips, and glared at her.

'Jem, I thought you were away on cinema business.'

'I'm back.' He stated the obvious and waited for her to explain what she was doing. He ignored the men handling the changeover of horses for the next shift of his Dublin taxi service. 'Well,' he prompted, 'are you going to tell me what you're up to?'

'I thought me and Rosie,' she waved towards the horse watching them from her stall, 'could have a bit of a walk.'

It was the last Saturday in March. The day was promising to be a fine one. She wanted a break

51

from being surrounded by people demanding something of her. She wanted to breathe in the fresh clear air. She'd thought walking with Rosie alongside the grass verge of the nearby Grand Canal would give her time to breathe.

'Ivy . . . ' Jem closed his eyes and took a deep breath, 'Rosie is not a dog.'

'I know she's not a dog, Jem, but the poor old dear likes to get out and about.' Ivy didn't want to hear a lecture.

Rosie had been Jem's sole horse for a long time but had been retired when Jem decided to expand his business. Ivy liked to spend time with her, whispering in her flicking ear — Rosie made no demands and kept her opinions to herself.

'John!' Jem shouted to his shift manager and friend. 'We'll be in our place.' He took Ivy by the elbow and began walking towards the rear entrance of the livery.

'Ivy,' John Lawless put his head around the partition that hid the livery office from the stable area, 'would you have a word with my Sadie when you've a minute?'

'I'm not talking to you, John Lawless!' Ivy shouted over her shoulder. 'You've been telling tales on me. You think I don't know it was you told Jem I was up to something?'

'Ah now, Ivy!' John groaned.

'I'll change out of this fancy suit and be back, John.' Jem continued to tug his reluctant wife along, while being careful to avoid the horse manure that clogged the central aisle of the stable.

Their house was only steps away from the

gable end of the livery.

'Auntie Ivy, Auntie Ivy!' A whirling dervish slammed into Ivy's legs.

'Miss Emmy!' Ivy bent and picked the child up. She stared into green eyes that sparkled with mischief. She was surrounded by green-eyed people, it seemed. She spun in a circle, the laughing girl in her arms.

What a difference the arrival of this child had made in Jem and Ivy's lives. Emmy had been a catalyst for change. The accidental death of Emmy's guardian in a carriage driven by Jem had catapulted Emmy into their lives. Unable to contact any relatives, they had taken care of the little girl, pretending she was Jem's niece, until eventually they had found her father on his return from abroad.

'Ann Marie is feeling tired — I was getting under her feet.' Emmy didn't like to refer to the woman who had been a friend before marrying her beloved papa as her stepmother — step-mothers were almost always evil in her storybooks. The delightful giggle rang out again. 'So, I came over with Papa and Uncle Jem to spend some time with you.'

Jem garaged his precious automobile in Ann Marie's carriage house.

'Good day to you, Mrs Ryan.' Edward O'Connor stood slightly apart, putting the hat he'd raised in greeting back on his head. He was dressed in an exquisitely tailored stark-black Savile Row suit. The picture of an elegant gentleman about town — Ann Marie's husband, Jem's business partner and little Emmy's papa

53

— was a good-looking man.

'Mrs Ryan indeed!' Sheila Purcell almost spat. The woman had walked unnoticed out of the Stephen's Street tunnel at their backs. 'I doubt that hussy is wed. She was never churched. I know that for a fact.' Mrs Purcell scrubbed for the Parish Priest and reckoned that made her an expert on all matters religious.

'I attended the marriage ceremony, Mrs . . . ' Edward O'Connor was an aristocrat and it showed. He glared down his nose at the offensive individual.

'Did yeh now?' Sheila Purcell knew she had the Good Lord on her side. She need fear no man. 'I suppose you're another heathen like this lot.' She gave a disparaging sniff in Ivy's direction. 'Fit yeh better, Ivy Murphy, to be making babbies of your own instead of being out in the streets at all hours of the day and night.'

'This is Mrs Purcell, a neighbour, Edward.' Ivy clutched Emmy close to her chest, wishing the child could have missed this little scene. She wouldn't put the child down — Sheila was quick to box kids around the ears when they came within her reach. 'A beacon of happiness and delight to all who know her.'

'You're a godless heathen, Ivy Murphy, and everyone knows it.' Sheila Purcell was rooting in the pocket of the threadbare coat she wore. 'Father Leary never heard your marriage vows. I know that for a fact. You're a shameless fornicator. You're not fit to be around decent god-fearing Catholics!'

'I wouldn't throw that Holy Water you're

searching your pocket for over these men.' Ivy knew her neighbour. She was aware of Jem trying to pull her from the scene. As far as she was concerned Mrs Purcell was like a mad dog. It didn't do to show fear. 'They won't turn the other cheek, I can promise you. You might find yourself up in court for damaging their finery. You couldn't buy one of their hankies, much less pay for one of their suits!' Ivy was being a bitch and she knew it but Sheila Purcell was a dangerous bully.

'Mrs Purcell,' Jem moved in front of Ivy and Emmy, 'I believe you are overwrought. Perhaps you should go home and tend to your own family.' He heard his own words and wanted to laugh. He'd been hanging around the gentry too much.

'Look to your own, Jem Ryan!' Sheila Purcell spat before spinning on her heel. 'Produce and multiply, that's what the good book says. Where's your childer?' She pushed her way through the crowd that had gathered to watch the scene. '*Yez are all going to hell for consorting with this sinner!*' she roared wildly.

'That woman is dangerous.' Edward O'Connor had seen religious fanaticism before. That woman would kill without blinking for her god.

'Auntie Ivy,' Emmy released the choke hold she'd had around Ivy's neck, 'why doesn't that woman like you? I think you're wonderful.'

'We'll be more comfortable inside, I think.' Jem began to shepherd Ivy and Edward towards the house.

'*Ivy!*' Frank Wilson shouted from the open

window of his front room. He'd seen and heard everything. There was nothing anyone could say about Sheila Purcell. The woman was a cross they all had to bear. 'Have you a minute?'

'Not right now, Frank.' Jem used his key to open the front door.

8

Edward O'Connor stepped into the long hallway, removing his hat and revealing the raven-black hair he'd bequeathed to his daughter. He was aware that his daughter Emerald — he simply could not call her Emmy — was an inquisitive child who understood more than he was sometimes comfortable with. He did not intend to discuss the happenings in the street within her hearing. He had joined his daughter and Jem only in an effort to give Ann Marie time to rest. His daughter was a delightful child but did not seem to understand the concept of silence.

Ivy, holding Emmy's hand, walked down the long hallway leading to their rooms at the back of the house. The two men stopped to hang up their outer wear in the hall cupboard and then followed her to the kitchen.

'Edward, sit yourself down — you're making the place look untidy.' Jem gestured to the six wooden chairs pulled up to the kitchen table.

'I had not intended to stay,' Edward tried to protest.

'Sit yerself down — yer in yer granny's.' Ivy, removing Emmy's cherry-red coat, used an old Dublin expression of welcome.

Emmy laughed at her papa's expression. 'That means make yourself at home, Papa,' she said.

'Thank you, dear.' Edward did sometimes feel

57

as if he needed an interpreter around this couple.

'I'm going to change out of this suit.' Jem turned to walk towards the bedroom off the kitchen. 'I need to get over to the livery at some point today and I don't think a tailored suit is required attire for cleaning out stalls.' He looked over at Ivy who was putting Emmy's coat over the back of a chair. 'I can't believe I have to say this: put the kettle on, Ivy! And if there's anything to eat I'd be glad of it. My stomach thinks my throat's been cut.'

Ivy walked across the linoleum-covered floor to pick the black kettle up from its spot on top of the range. She filled her larger metal teapot from the kettle and put the pot on top of the gas stove. It wouldn't take a moment for the water to come to a brisk boil.

'Will you have something to eat, Edward?' Ivy asked as she checked the supply of food she had on hand. 'I don't need to ask Emmy — she's always ready to eat.'

'I don't like to impose,' he said.

'What's one more mouth to feed?' Ivy loved to feed people. It gave her such a feeling of accomplishment to be able to offer food to her guests after years of going without life's necessities.

'Edward will have whatever I'm having.' Jem stepped back into the kitchen, wearing his work clothes. 'We didn't take the time to stop and get anything to eat.' The two men had spent the morning involved in the affairs of their Dublin picture house.

'Sit yerself down.' Ivy bent in front of the cool cupboard Jem had built for her beside the sink. The thick marble slab he'd set into the cupboard kept her butter, milk and meat fresh. She removed the items she needed.

Grabbing two black, cast-iron frying pans from hooks over the range, she set sausages frying in a chunk of butcher's dripping in one pan. She'd wait to put rashers of bacon in the other when the sausages were almost cooked.

'Do you lot want egg and tomato with this?'

'Please,' three voices chorused together.

'The postman's been!' Frank Wilson shouted and knocked before pushing open the door that opened from the main house into the Ryan's kitchen. 'I had to sign for a registered letter and parcels from America for you, Ivy.' The smell of Ivy's cooking had wafted out into the hallway, tempting him to chance his arm for a free feed. 'Do you want me to bring them in?'

'Come in and sit down, Frank — I'll get the post later.' She'd open her post when she could take the time to sit down and examine everything. 'I put your name on the fry-up.'

Jem leaned over to explain to Edward when he saw the man's confusion. 'She means she made enough to include him.'

'I hope you've removed all the wood chip and sawdust from your clothes,' said Ivy.

Frank was a master carpenter. His work with wood meant he sometimes walked wood dust around Ivy's kitchen.

'I might have some small bits of wood about me person,' Frank said, his eyes twinkling. He

59

put his hands into the deep pockets of his well-worn work trousers. He removed his clenched fists from his pockets. With a mischievous smile for Emmy, he opened his hands. On one palm sat a beautifully detailed rocking horse. A tiny rocking chair sat proudly on his other hand.

'Granddad!' Emmy clapped her hands. She knew just where she would put these items in the doll's house he had made her as a Christmas gift.

Edward watched his child, bemused once more by the attachments she had formed in this enclave of poverty. Emerald had adopted a grandfather who built her toys that would delight any child. She'd adopted an aunt and uncle who loved and protected her. While he'd been mourning her loss, his child had found a family unlike any he had ever encountered.

'Look, Papa!' Emmy held her treasures out for her father to examine.

'These items are exquisite, Frank.' Edward examined the workmanship. 'I hope you take good care of these wonderful gifts, Emerald. The value of something like these is priceless.' He knew his daughter would treasure the items. He'd watched her play for hours with the dollhouse that took pride of place in the large bedroom Ann Marie had furnished for her. 'Have you ever thought of selling your work, Frank?'

'Oh, yer one over there,' he gave a jerk of his chin to where Ivy was lifting fried eggs from one of her big black pans, 'wouldn't let me rest until

I put a price on my work. But, of course, a man doesn't charge his first grand-baby.' He tenderly touched Emmy's rosy-red cheek.

'Jem, put those toys on the dresser,' said Ivy. 'The last thing we want to do is spill grease on Frank's masterpieces. Right, everybody, sit down — the food is served.'

Ivy had arranged the food on china chargers which she now placed on the table, next to the breadboard laden with sliced bread and a pretty china bowl holding curls of golden butter.

'Now, before I sit down, has everyone everything they need?' She stood with her steaming teapot in one hand and waited while the table was inspected.

'Would you just pour the tea, missus?' Jem was seated at the head of the table. 'If we need anything I'll get up and get it. Sit yourself down before we drown in the drool dripping from my chin. I'm starving.'

The meal was consumed with evident delight, much to the appreciation of the chef.

'That was a delicious meal, Ivy.' Edward used the thick napkin provided to pat his lips.

Ivy lowered her eyes, amused by the sight of this aristocratic gent sitting at her kitchen table, wiping his face with a napkin that originally had been a bleached flour sack.

'You always make the best stuff, Auntie Ivy.' Emmy used her napkin to remove all traces of food as she'd been taught. She'd eaten so much her tummy hurt. 'I'm glad it wasn't duck under the table!' Peals of childish laughter echoed, raising smiles on adult faces.

'What on earth do you mean, Emerald?' Edward stared at his child.

'That's an old Dublin expression,' Frank said when Ivy and Jem were too busy laughing to answer. 'It means there's nothing to eat in the house.'

'I see.' Edward quite plainly didn't. 'Emerald, we need to thank Mrs Ryan and get on our way, I'm afraid.'

'May I stay here and play outside with my friends, Papa?'

'I'm afraid not, darling — we must be on our way.'

Frank had enjoyed the meal. He'd listened to the conversations going on around him. He added his tuppence worth when he had something to add but was generally content just to be part of the group.

'I have to be out and about too.' Jem stood and began to clear the table. 'I told John I'd be over to the livery. I don't like to keep him waiting.'

'Leave those, Jem, I'll take care of them.' Ivy knew Jem wanted to allow John to leave and spend time with his family. The man worked long hours.

With a nod of appreciation, Jem left — but not before giving Emmy a big hug and kiss.

'We'll be off then, Ivy,' said Edward, standing away from the table. 'Come along, Emerald.'

'Frank, give me a few minutes to tidy the kitchen before you bring the post down,' Ivy said as she picked Emmy's coat up. 'I'll give yeh a shout when I've a fresh pot of tea made.' She then escorted her guests out.

9

Frank had gone to get the post by the time Ivy returned but she saw that he had carried the dirty dishes to the sink and wiped the table down. He liked to lend a hand.

Ivy rolled her sleeves up and prepared to restore order to her little kingdom. The rooms needed a good going-over, she knew, but she'd no idea where she was going to find the time. It shamed her when Jem started to help with the housework. That was her job as his wife.

'Look at me, washing me lovely matching dishes while looking out the window over me very own back garden.' She dried the dishes and returned them to the tall wooden dresser standing proudly against the wall that separated her kitchen from Frank's back room. The kitchen table and chairs sat away from the dresser with space enough to walk around them. She grabbed a sweeping brush and swept the linoleum. Then she beat the cushions of the two old armchairs sitting in front of the range.

When the kitchen was tidy and a fresh pot of tea was sitting on the range top she shouted down the hallway for Frank.

'I've the rent money and books for you to check over too, Ivy,' Frank said as he came through the door. 'There's a parcel from your Aunt Betty and a big envelope from your brother Shay. I don't know who the other parcel is from.'

He set the post on the table top, together with the leather-bound rent ledger. He was nervous about the registered letter. Those things didn't bring good news in his experience. He hoped no one was bringing bad news to Ivy. She'd enough to deal with. 'I got the cheque for Mrs Beauchalet's rent in the mail and all.'

'We could do with more tenants like her — someone who pays but is seldom around.' The woman — a travelling actress — rented the two rooms across the hall from Frank's.

'I doubt she'll be able to tour the country much longer — she's getting older like the rest of us.' He reached into the deep pockets of his trousers, removed the rent money and the cheque and put them on the table.

'Thanks.' Ivy let the subject of the absent tenant drop. The woman made her presence known when she was here. She would check the ledger later. She'd open the parcels then too. 'Sit down.' She gestured towards the soft chairs in front of the range.

'Maggie Frost is complaining about the smell of chemicals again.' Frank lowered his body into one of the fireside chairs. The tenants had no idea Ivy was now the owner of this house. They continued to pay their rent and carry their complaints to Frank. Maggie Frost and her two sons rented two upstairs rooms. She cleaned the WCs, bathrooms, stairs and hallways of the house for a reduction in rent. Ivy was happy with the arrangement — she had more than enough to do with her own day.

'I don't blame the woman,' she said. 'The

smell of those chemicals Milo uses is something awful.'

She passed an enamel mug of tea to Frank. The man complained about the small size of Ivy's precious china cups. She sat in the chair facing his with her own cup and saucer in hand.

Milo Norton, one of the upstairs tenants, was a street photographer. He had a nice little business taking photographs of courting couples on nearby O'Connell Bridge. He developed the photographs in one of his rooms.

'Maggie was wondering if you'd be willing to rent one of your sheds to Milo.' Frank knew the answer. 'She reckons the smell would be better out of doors.'

'In her dreams.' Ivy needed every inch of space for her own growing business concerns.

'So I told her,' Frank nodded.

'Maggie Frost is in well with next door — why doesn't she ask aul' Grumpy Gibson if Milo can use one of their back sheds? They have the same back garden as us.'

'I wouldn't ask that shower next door the time of day. They're an odd pair.' He smacked his lips together. 'It was different when Ria was there.'

'The cheek of you!' Ivy stood to take his mug. 'There was a time when you'd as soon box someone's ear as look at them.' Ivy hadn't had much to do with Valeria Gibson. The woman was a few years older than she and had married and moved to Kildare years ago. She'd been a big mountain of a young woman. Still, what could you expect when her grandmother was bigger

65

around than she was tall? It must run in the family.

'Your brother Eamo has a lot to answer for when it comes to poor Ria.'

'*What!*' Her cup and saucer almost fell from Ivy's hands. 'What do you mean?'

'I mean he took advantage of her.'

'No! Valeria Gibson is years older than our Eamo!' She hadn't had much in the way of looks either, the poor girl, pale as a ghost and covered in pimples.

'You wouldn't have heard — you were never one to listen to gossip about your brothers — but your da knew. Eamo and Valeria were caught doing what they shouldn't. She was married off right quick after that.'

'In the name of Jesus!' Ivy fell into the chair.

10

Valeria Gibson Hunter — Ria — ached in every bone in her body. She lay draped across the foul-smelling bed, feeling like a discarded rag. Her body was bruised and battered from her husband's loving attention. He was a clever bastard. She'd have to give him that. He never marked her where it could be seen by the public.

The door to the bedroom burst open.

'Still lying around — can't get enough of it — like all good bitches.' He fisted his hand in her hair and pulled her from the bed. Her naked body slammed onto the bare floorboards, a kick to her ribs an additional greeting. 'I'll be late to the estate party but they'll understand.' His hands went to the belt holding his trousers in place.

Ria didn't cringe, didn't cry out. She rolled into a ball and endured. The whistle of the belt rising and falling as she was lashed was the only sound to be heard. When his trousers dropped to his boots, she braced herself. She thanked God there was nothing in her stomach to throw up. She made no sound when he forced her to her knees and mashed her face in the soiled bedding. She was glad she didn't have to look at him.

'Putting the stallions to the mares!' His body rammed into hers.

She didn't hear his words — floating away from the pain.

'Stud work puts a man in a frisky mood.' He grunted as he withdrew and slammed back into her dry body.

She prayed that he would finish quickly. She endured his panting, sweating, and groping. His fists punched into her ribs when she didn't react to his loving attention. She wanted to cry out with relief when he reached his release after what felt like hours.

'You're the most useless piece of ass I've ever had!' He slapped her rear painfully before pulling out of her body. She collapsed back onto the floor. 'That's where you belong,' he kicked her again, 'in the dirt!'

Ria didn't move — didn't make a sound.

'That took the edge off at least.' Laughing, he walked out of the room.

Ria lay on the floor, listening to the man she'd married prepare himself for an evening of debauchery. He whistled while lowering himself into the bath she'd prepared for him earlier. She hoped the water was freezing. When there was no shout of outrage from her lord and master she crawled across the floor. She put her back to the wall beside the single bedroom window. She hugged her knees to her chest and lowered her aching head.

'He'll be eager to get to the party.' She hoped talking aloud to herself wasn't the first sign of madness.

The party at the stud barn was the social event of the season for the estate workers. The wealthy mingled with the workers. The gentry who had brought their mares to be bred by the proven stallions of the Kilbarrick Stud would be in the mood for what the Squire called a 'bit of fun'.

She remained on the floor, shivering. She prayed he wouldn't return to the bedroom. She'd pressed his suit, starched his white shirt and polished his good boots. She'd left everything close to hand. He'd only to step out of the bath and dress himself. Surely to God he could do that much for himself? She forced breath in and out of her lungs and waited.

'Clean the bathroom!' A fist shook the wooden door.

The sound of boots running down the uncarpeted wooden stairs brought tears to her eyes. She didn't move until she heard the slamming of the front door. She used the sturdy walls of the three-bedroom terrace house to support her as she stood and made her way to the indoor bathroom. The flickering flame on the gas water-heater over the bath glowed. The bathtub as she'd expected had a ring of scum around the sides.

'Well, I can look on it as a blessing, I suppose.' The water for her bath would be heating while she scrubbed the bath. She took cleaning supplies from the bathroom cupboard.

Later, in the bath, she scrubbed her flesh, ignoring the multi-coloured cuts and bruises.

Seven years is long enough, she thought. There is no knight on a white charger going to ride to my rescue. I'm on my own and if I don't get out of here that man is going to kill me someday.

She had to take this chance. She'd been

planning her escape for years. Tonight was the night.

In the smallest bedroom she knelt on the bare floor. She removed the false bottom from one of the leather chests she'd packed with such hope in what felt like another lifetime. When I think of how I looked down my nose at Ivy Murphy back in The Lane, she thought. I thought Ivy was such a fool for allowing the men in her family to order her about!

'How the mighty have fallen!'

She had spent years fashioning the garments hidden in the chest — needlecraft was something she excelled at — if she did say so herself.

When her husband had been revealed for the bully he was, she'd taken her concerns to the local magistrate. It had shocked her to be told what happened between man and wife was the man's business. She'd turned to anyone who might help her only to watch them turn away from her in disgust.

'Enough self-pity.' She pulled a man's vest and long johns from the chest. She'd fashioned the garments to fit her. She stood to pull the items over her damp shivering flesh.

'I've grown up and in since I came here,' she whispered absentmindedly.

The tweed trousers she pulled up her legs were heavy with golden sovereigns hidden in the seams and turn-ups. She had been careful when removing the sovereigns from Robert's hidden stash. She'd watched through the years, only taking one coin at a time when Robert threw the money inside his safe box in a golden shower without counting it. The times were few and far between. She'd watched and learned what she could and couldn't get away with.

She'd fashioned a liberty bodice to cover her meagre breasts. This garment too was heavy with hidden treasure. The bodice hung from her shoulders down to her hips. She hoped the weight of the coins would flatten her feminine figure and give her the appearance of a youth. She'd even covered sovereigns in fabric and attached them to the cap that would cover her shorn white hair. Robert hated the attention her long white-blonde hair had received from male admirers. He delighted in cutting her hair into straw-like tufts on a regular basis.

'Well, it's time, Ria.'

She stood in front of the mirror, staring at a stranger. To her eyes she looked like one of the estate lads out and about. She prayed her disguise would hold up amongst strangers. She shoved the cap she'd made into one of the trouser pockets. She covered everything up with one of the overlarge ugly dresses Robert procured for her. She'd no idea where he found the ancient garments but she was glad of them now. The black dress covered her from neck to ankle. He'd got rid of all the fashionable clothing she'd selected with such care. With shaking hands she restored order to the room then stood in the doorway examining it intently.

'That's it.'

She picked up a black bonnet and shawl and made her way down the stairs. The weight of her hidden stash was strange — she'd have to be

71

careful how she walked. The clothing rubbing against her cuts and bruises was a familiar pain.

She left the bonnet and shawl on the banisters and made her way to the kitchen. She walked towards the sink under the window. She almost screamed. A little face was pressed to the glass.

She unlocked the back door that opened directly into the kitchen. The child squeezed inside when the door was only partially open. Ria slammed the door closed and locked it.

'You frightened the life out of me, Stanley.'

'I saw him pass our house so I knew it was safe.' Stanley hobbled over to the kitchen table. 'He went early. My ma isn't ready to go yet.'

'Women take longer to get ready.' Ria didn't mention the new crop of bruises on his skinny legs or the black eye. They were fellow-sufferers and understood that talking changed nothing. 'You're in luck. He had a big fry-up before he went out. You can have the leftovers between two slices of bread.' She worried about leaving the young lad in this place but she couldn't take him with her. 'I was just going to make a pot of tea. We have fresh milk.' She filled the black kettle and put it on top of one of the gas rings. She needed something to do while waiting until the light left the sky. She needed the cover of darkness to make her escape.

'He'll batter yeh if I eat his food and we use his milk.'

'He won't be in a fit state to notice a thing by the time he gets back.'

Ria thought she'd throw up at the sight of the

greasy food she was making into a sandwich for the boy.

'Here.' She pulled out one of the four kitchen chairs. 'Sit yourself down out of the way.'

'Can I — '

They'd both heard the slam of the back-garden gate.

Stanley slipped into the cupboard under the kitchen window without a word.

'Is that little bastard in there?' A fist slammed against the window.

'He's not here! I'm alone — go away.' Ria prayed the window wouldn't break. If Titus Blackmoor got his hands on her he'd finish the job her husband started. Stanley's stepfather was a brute.

'Well, now, I'm alone too — the missus has gone up to the big house. Let's you and me look after each other.'

'My husband wouldn't like that.'

'Your bloody husband is too busy lifting my wife's skirts to care.' Titus slammed a giant open hand against the window. 'Let me in, bitch. I'll show you what a real man can do.'

Ria wondered if she was supposed to be overcome by the offer.

'Titus Blackmoor, you come out of there!' a feminine voice shouted.

'Ah now, Mrs Riordan, I'm only passing the time of day with me neighbour.' He turned to leave but not before softly growling to Ria, 'I'll be back! The party at the big house will be going on all week.'

Ria collapsed over the kitchen sink. She'd

73

been terrified. She watched the Widow Riordan stand in the lane that ran alongside the back gardens until Titus left. She waited another minute before walking along the lane to her own home. The man wouldn't dare to return while the older woman might be watching — Mrs Riordan had the Squire's ear. Ria had a reprieve but for how long?

'I'm going to feed you, Stanley.' Ria had to get away — today. 'Then I'll walk you up to your Uncle Rowley.' Rowley lived in a shanty deep in the woods. He wasn't really Stan's uncle but he'd protect the boy. It would serve her purpose to be seen leading the child towards Rowley's home. It wouldn't be the first time.

'Ah Ria,' Stan whined, 'can't I stay here with you?'

'No.' How could she explain to the child what his stepfather might do to her if he stayed.

Ria put the sandwich and a mug of tea on the table and pushed the boy into a chair.

He began to eat ravenously.

'Don't gulp your food, Stan. If you eat too fast it will only come back up again.'

When light left the sky — after what felt like a lifetime to Ria — she took the young lad by the hand. She walked through the house, her heart beating fit to burst. She barely glanced into the living room at the two overlarge fireside chairs. The gold sovereigns hidden in the safe boxes built into the arms of the chairs were safe from her pilfering fingers now. Robert Hunter didn't trust banks. He turned her dowry and the money he made gambling on horses into sovereigns and hid them. She put on the ugly black bonnet and black blanket shawl and led the child outside.

'Come along, Stanley, it's getting late,' Ria said for anyone who might be listening. She pulled the door to her husband's home closed with a bang. 'We must be on our way.'

11

On the first Wednesday in April Ivy took her usual route around the rear entrances of Fitzwilliam Square. She knocked on doors, accepted the discards and shared a laugh with the people she met, yet all the time she felt out of sorts with her world. She hadn't been to the market recently. The discarded clothing was mounting up and needed to be refurbished. She was spending so much time talking, thinking and worrying that nothing seemed to get done.

The small army of outworkers she employed to dress the dolls continued to churn out work. The Alice doll — the latest in her range — was proving very popular.

She'd passed out wool in the first week of January so outfits for the baby dolls were well in hand. She'd had plans to start her workers on a Little Red Riding Hood doll but as yet had done nothing about that. Then there was the paperwork. *Aagh!* She was going to kick her own arse if she didn't stop moaning and get something done!

She felt buried by the constant demands on her time and energy. Her kitchen had been invaded. It seemed a night didn't pass but that some crowd was clustered around her kitchen table discussing business. There seemed to be so many changes in the wind. Why had her kitchen become Grand Central Station, she'd like to know?

Pete Reynolds was a regular visitor. The man had a lot to learn about Jem's business. He worked hard in regular business hours. He kept a list of questions to put to Jem in the evenings. Conn too was a regular visitor in the evenings. The men were eager to learn all they could about Jem's business concerns. Enda Reynolds came to discuss his options frequently. The man was dithering about — afraid of taking a step into the unknown.

She wasn't much better. She seemed to be chasing her own tail these days. She pushed her pram to the next house on her round.

'Ivy!'

She'd left the last house on her round when someone grabbed her arm and pulled her to a stop. She turned with her fist raised, ready to punch out at whoever had dared to lay hands on her.

'My God, but you've got a cheek showing your face to me.' She refused to show the heartbreak she felt on seeing her eldest brother Eamo standing in front of her. He was the living image of their deceased father. 'Slumming it, aren't yeh?'

Eamo had left home to travel to England to live with their mother six years ago. He'd cut her completely out of his life. He'd returned to Dublin recently with his mother and their youngest brother — to live the life of a wealthy gent.

'I need to speak with you,' the man now known as Richard Williams since his mother's remarriage said, looking furtively around the shadow-deep lane. He could not afford to be recognised. 'I cannot believe you are still in the same rut I left you in. You've kept to your old routine, I see.' He sniffed disdainfully down at the old coat she wore — he recognised it as one of his own discards. 'I had nightmares for years about being dragged along these back yards at the side of your pram.'

'Pity about yeh!' Ivy forced the words past the lump in her throat. 'Yeh weren't too proud to take the money I earned from me rounds — were yeh?' How dare her brother look down his nose at her? 'If you want to talk to me you'll have to walk along with me. I've places to be.' She'd love to walk away without speaking to him but her curiosity would keep her awake nights.

'Don't be ridiculous!' her brother snapped. 'I can't afford to be seen in your company.'

She pulled the arm he still held free and made to walk away.

'I need you to do something for me.'

'I didn't think you were here for the pleasure of my company!' Ivy snapped. 'Got something to sell on, have you?'

'Hardly,' he bit out.

But she could almost see him thinking that selling on some of the gold he wore about his person might be a consideration. Eamo had always been very fond of having money in his hand.

'I simply need you to ask Valeria Gibson to contact me,' he said.

'Yeh have more neck than a giraffe, our Eamo.'

78

Ivy couldn't believe his gall.

'I cannot try to contact her myself — I cannot be seen to enter The Lane.' He grabbed hold of the pram's handle as she tried to move forward. 'It would be no bother for you to seek out Valeria and ask her to meet with me.'

'Ask yer ma to step into The Lane. I'm sure she wouldn't mind doing a favour for her beloved firstborn son.' She adopted a flat Dublin accent which her brother should have known was not her natural way of speaking. She saw him flinch back from her and didn't know whether to cry or kick him.

'I suppose it's not surprising you are jealous.' Richard sighed. 'After all, Mother and I have come up in the world while you are still wallowing in the gutter.'

He didn't add 'where you belong' but Ivy heard the words none the less.

'What makes you think I'd be willing to do anything for you?' She hadn't heard from him in years. He ignored her when he saw her in public and now here he stood, every inch the elegant gent, asking her for favours.

'You're my sister for goodness' sake.'

'No one would ever guess by the way you treat me.' She had to get away. She could feel her body beginning to shake at the shock of his nearness. She'd be deep-dipped and fried before she'd let him see how much seeing him like this had upset her.

'I'm simply asking you to carry a message to a dear friend of mine. Surely that isn't too much to ask of you?'

'Valeria married and moved away from The Lane before you ever left.' It was typical of him to think only of himself.

'Good Lord, I'd forgotten.' He pushed his soft hands through his beautifully coiffed black hair. 'Shay!' he barked out. 'You must have an address for our famous brother Shay. You two were always close.'

She stared deep into his blue eyes. There was only a year's difference in age between them. She'd once been able to read him like a book. 'You're looking for a hand-out.'

'I have need of liquid funds — yes.'

'There is this invention, Eamo,' she refused to call him by anything else. 'It's called work — you were never very fond of it as I recall — you get paid in liquid funds for hours worked. You should try it.' She grabbed her pram and walked quickly away, leaving him standing staring after her. She knew he'd keep after her until he'd achieved whatever devious plan he had in mind. She'd be prepared next time. She had to wonder though — what on earth could Valeria Gibson have to do with anything?

Ivy, still shaken by her encounter with her brother, parked her well-stuffed pram at the back of Ann Marie's house just off the Grand Canal. She stared at the pram for a moment. The amount of items she received on her round was both a blessing and a curse. Where was she going to store this lot? When would she get around to moving it along? She'd have gone straight home but she'd promised to drop in and visit Ann Marie.

80

She hit the back door with her knuckles before opening it and putting her head inside.

'It's only me, Sadie!' she called, pushing her pram inside the door. She set the brake before walking down the long dark hall into the spotlessly clean, glaringly white kitchen.

'In the name of God, Sadie, what's wrong?'

Her friend was hunched over the kitchen table, a picture of misery.

'Ivy!' Sadie's usual wide smile was missing. 'I'll put the kettle on.' She pushed herself to her feet.

'Where's Ann Marie?' Ivy looked around the kitchen as if expecting her friend to suddenly appear out of thin air.

'Upstairs resting.' Sadie kept her back to Ivy while filling the kettle.

'Where's your son?' Jamie — Sadie's adopted son would be two this year — was usually running wildly around the kitchen or pushing his latest toy along the floor, a mischievous grin on his face.

'Dora took him out to feed the ducks.' Sadie was referring to her youngest daughter.

'What's the matter, Sadie?'

'This isn't working for me anymore, Ivy.' She turned, waving her hand around the large modern kitchen. 'I can't keep up with everything.'

Sadie and her family had moved into Ann Marie's basement when her husband John Lawless started working for Jem. Ann Marie wanted to live without being surrounded by servants so the Lawless family took care of the

81

house. Sadie had kept the family's two tenement rooms like a little palace. She'd had no idea of the work involved when she'd agreed to see to the daily running of the big house in return for free housing. There was a cleaning crew, two women who did the rough work and a laundrywoman, but nonetheless the list of things needing to be done never seemed to end as far as Sadie was concerned.

'You put too much pressure on yourself.'

Sadie put her head in her hands, her blonde hair escaping from her bun. She raised sad blue eyes to Ivy. 'Ever since Ann Marie married Emmy's dad things have been different. I'm not saying anything against Edward O'Connor — he's a lovely man — but his being here has changed everything.'

'You serve up the tea.' Ivy stood. Something needed to be done and they could make no decisions without Ann Marie. 'I'll go upstairs and get Ann Marie.' She knew Edward was collecting Emmy from school today. The pair usually spent some time together around Dublin before returning home.

'Ivy — ' Sadie reached out as if to stop her friend before dropping her hand.

'*Ann Marie!*' Ivy shouted when she reached the main hall of the house. The place was so big Ann Marie could be anywhere.

'In here.' The voice came softly from the living room.

Ivy pushed open the door, surprised to see her friend stretched out on the leather couch, a soft blanket over her.

'What in the name of God is going on in this house? It's like the house of the living dead.' The silent film of *Dracula* had been shown at the local theatre recently and vampires were a source of conversation and fascination around Dublin.

'I don't feel at all well.' Ann Marie sat up, slowly lowering her feet to the floor.

Ivy inspected her friend. She did look pale, her creamy skin grey, the blue eyes without her usual gold-rimmed spectacles looked washed out. Oh, oh, Ivy thought, I know that look. With all the babies being born in The Lane this was a familiar sight. Ann Marie was in the puddin' club if she wasn't mistaken.

'I seem to be constantly nauseated. I've been feeling out of sorts for some time now.' Ann Marie pressed a trembling hand against her stomach. 'I shall have to consult a doctor. I should have done it sooner.'

'Do you feel well enough to come downstairs?'

'Of course!' Ann Marie snapped in a manner very unlike her calm, composed nature.

Ivy dropped to her knees and began to put Ann Marie's T-strap shoes on her feet.

'I'm not an invalid,' Ann Marie protested but made no effort to bend over and buckle her own shoes.

Ivy helped her friend to stand, waiting to be sure she was steady on her feet. The two women took the stairs down to the basement, Ivy keeping a careful eye on Ann Marie.

'Right!' Ivy slapped her hands together as soon as they walked through the door into the kitchen. 'Time for a kitchen-table conference

— I'm becoming very familiar with the bloody things. Sadie, is there e'er a biscuit?'

When the three women were seated around the kitchen table, tea and biscuits to hand, Ivy took control.

'First item on the agenda.' Ivy kept her eyes on the plate of biscuits, making her selection. 'Sadie, would you cast an eye over our dear friend here and tell me what you think?' Sadie's sister-in-law Patsy seemed to produce a baby or two every ten months. Her brother's home was bursting at the seams with snotty-nosed kids.

'Oh my God!' Sadie swiped the butter-cream-filled biscuit from Ann Marie's hand. Without another word she stepped over to the breadbin and with swift movements replaced the biscuit with a piece of dry bread. She sat back down and met Ann Marie's astonished gaze. She felt so guilty — she'd been drowning in her own problems and had paid no attention to the woman whose home she lived in — she felt like kicking herself.

'Right, if I could just ask you a few questions of an intimate nature,' she said.

Sadie didn't allow Ann Marie to refuse. She bit out a selection of questions about the workings of Ann Marie's body. The questions brought a blush to Ann Marie's cheeks and some of the answers she had to stop and think about but she answered them honestly.

'You're in the family way.' Sadie pronounced, 'and much further along than I would have supposed. If your memory serves you right you're about five months along.'

Ann Marie sat back in her chair, stunned. She felt extremely foolish — she had given no thought to the possibility of being enceinte — how could she have overlooked the obvious? She'd put down the changes in her body to being a married woman. She was thirty-two years old — was she not too old to have a first baby?

'The signs are all there,' Sadie said. 'I can't believe we all missed them.'

'Congratulations, Ann Marie, you and Edward have made a baby,' Ivy said. 'If you two make a baby as special as our Emmy you'll have done well.'

Ann Marie slapped a hand to her mouth. The colour drained from her face.

'Put your head between your knees!' Sadie almost shouted, jumping to her feet. She put her hand on the back of Ann Marie's head and gently pushed her head towards her knees. 'We don't want you fainting on this hard floor.' She met Ivy's eyes over the bowed head — misery in her gaze — how could she leave Ann Marie now?

'I should go to bed.' Ann Marie's voice was muffled. 'I must consult a doctor at once. I'll employ a nurse. I must begin to take care of myself.'

'Sit back up, Ann Marie,' Ivy said. 'What you should do is nibble on that chunk of bread in front of you and sip a cup of weak tea. You're expecting a baby, not dying.'

12

'I must say you are both taking this very calmly.'
Ann Marie was back on her leather sofa. She had
insisted on returning to her living room.

'My sister-in-law has given birth to ten babies
and counting.' Sadie had kicked off her shoes
and was sitting on one of the leather armchairs
with her legs bent underneath her. 'I've had two
babies meself. We are women, Ann Marie
— having babies is what we do.'

'You can't take to your bed like some rich
useless woman, Ann Marie,' Ivy said. Her friend
was suffering from what looked like an attack of
the vapours to her. 'Having a baby is a normal
part of a woman's life. You just have to be
sensible and look after yourself.'

'This from the woman who has never given
birth!' Ann Marie snapped.

'See!' Ivy laughed aloud. 'You're getting back
to your normal charming self.'

'It's your husband you have to worry about,'
Sadie said.

'*What!*' Ann Marie was indignant. She was the
one having the baby. She was the one who would
suffer the discomfort of constant nausea and
swelling. She deserved to be petted and cosseted.
Edward was the one who had put her in this
position.

'His first wife died in childbed,' Sadie said
softly.

There was silence in the room while the women considered the effect this might have on Ann Marie's husband.

'What is Patsy's eldest girl doing now?' Ivy had listened for years to Sadie bemoan the life her eldest niece was forced to live. The girl could be of some use to Ann Marie.

'What has that got to do with anything?' Ann Marie demanded. She looked closely at her friend. There was something going on behind Ivy's violet eyes — a darkness that she wasn't accustomed to seeing. Was something wrong? She'd have to wait until she had Ivy alone to delve into the matter.

'I'm just thinking.'

'Look out, as Jem Ryan would say.' Ann Marie lay her aching head back and closed her eyes. It was perhaps a mistake to take her eyes off her friend. When Ivy Rose Murphy Ryan got thinking she was dangerous.

'She's a lovely girl — Catherine,' Ivy said softly. 'She'd be a great help to you with the day-to-day care of Emmy.' Ivy believed Emmy needed someone to oversee her care. Ann Marie and Edward had been raised by nannies. They didn't seem to understand the companionship a young person needed. 'She'd be company for Emmy and you can't say the girl doesn't have experience with expecting women and child-birth.'

'I couldn't have Catherine here, Ivy,' Sadie protested. 'I'd have Patsy under me feet morning, noon and night.'

'You might not be here,' Ivy said. 'That was

the second item to be discussed on our agenda.' She pushed to her feet and strolled through the richly furnished room towards the window. She pulled the lace curtain to one side and stared out at the winter garden stretching down to a tall wall that hid the view of the Grand Canal. She couldn't settle and was finding it difficult to think about babies when she couldn't get the image of her brother out of her mind's eye. What was he up to? Why would he need cash? Surely the man her mother married gave him an allowance of some sort? Wasn't that how it was done in wealthy families?

'What are you talking about now, Ivy?' Ann Marie shared a concerned look with Sadie — something was not right with their friend.

'You should consult a doctor if you feel you must,' she said over her shoulder — that was what they were talking about, wasn't it?

'Thank you very much for your permission.' Ann Marie ignored the subject of Sadie's niece. There was much going on here that she didn't understand. She wanted to shake Ivy until she told them what was bothering her.

'If it were me . . . ' and it could be one day soon, Ivy thought. They were using birth control but nothing was perfect. They had been lucky the last time the contraption failed but what about next time? Her Jem was a passionate man. 'If it were me, I'd want Mrs Winthrop to attend me. She's the woman who has delivered all of the babies in The Lane and is often sent for by the gentry. She delivered me and my brothers.' The woman lived in the last house along the block Ivy's house sat in.

Sadie listened and said nothing. She'd heard of Mrs Winthrop. The woman was considered an angel and a devil both, by the women she'd attended. Was Ivy serious about asking her niece Catherine to work for Ann Marie?

'You should ask your Uncle Charles about Mrs Winthrop.' Ivy walked back to join the women around the fire. 'I'm sure, being a doctor, he knows the woman.'

'I'll do that,' Ann Marie agreed. If the woman was known by the medical profession that would be a point in her favour.

'Relax, Anne Marie — it's not like you're going to give birth tomorrow,' Ivy said.

Ann Marie pressed one hand to her stomach and smiled. A baby, how wonderful! 'Let us change the subject for the moment. What did you mean when you said Sadie might not be here?' She would wait until she was alone to wallow in this change and plan for the future.

Ivy waited to see if Sadie would say something but, when the other woman bowed her head and remained silent, she knew it was up to her.

'With the change in your circumstances, Ann Marie, this situation isn't working for Sadie and her family anymore.' She ignored Sadie's grunt of protest. She hadn't wanted to say anything before, so now she could sit there and listen. 'Truthfully, it isn't working for you and Edward either, is it, Ann Marie?'

'I refuse to even consider the idea of making Sadie and her family homeless,' Ann Marie protested. It had been her idea to have the

Lawless family live with her. The situation had been ideal when Ann Marie was learning to live an independent life. But it was true that since her marriage things had changed.

'You are not evicting the Lawless family.' Ivy again waited for Sadie to say something. When the woman remained huddled in her misery, she continued. 'You need trained household staff now, Ann Marie. Sadie knows that — in the name of God, Sadie Lawless, will you say something? This concerns you!'

'I know nothing about running a big house,' Sadie finally whispered, raising her eyes to the other women. 'But it seems to me you need a butler, housekeeper, cook and household maids. And now we know you're going to need a nanny and a nursery maid as well.'

'I so wanted to live a life unlike my peers,' Ann Marie moaned.

'It's your house — you can live how you bloody like.' Ivy had no room to pass comment. Her own house was becoming too much for her. She couldn't seem to get on top of the daily chores that came from being a married woman. Ann Marie had grown up surrounded by servants. She knew how to run a house but would have no idea how to handle the upkeep herself. She needed staff.

'I don't want to be the cause of undue suffering to your family, Sadie,' Ann Marie said. 'Living here is so convenient for John and your daughter Clare. They can just walk across the canal lock to work. It will be hard for you to find a house in this area to rent.' She knew the cost of rentals in the area would be far beyond the Lawless family purse.

Sadie had been wondering and worrying about the same thing for months. She had been driving her family crazy with her constant moaning. She wasn't fit to run the house of a member of the gentry.

'The carriage house might be a solution,' Ivy suggested.

Ann Marie had a carriage house at the back of her property. Jem parked his automobile in the space that used to house horse-drawn carriages. The upstairs had been fitted out as a three-bedroom flat.

'That might well be a possibility.' Ann Marie would need to talk to Edward about the changes in the household. There was no rush. They had time to plan. How would Emerald react to the thought of a sibling? There was so much to consider.

'What about your photographs?' Sadie objected. Ann Marie practically lived in the carriage house, spending hours developing the photographs she took incessantly.

'She won't be able to use the chemicals now,' Ivy put in, 'not in her condition.'

'Oh, I hadn't even thought that far ahead.' It saddened Ann Marie to think she would have to give up her obsession.

'You should think about allowing Sadie's family to live in the carriage house. You would have a woman friend close to hand. You could charge the family rent on those rooms.' Ivy knew that John and Sadie would not agree to live in the place rent free. They were a proud family. 'Jamie is old enough to walk up the stairs to the flat and, if you decide to employ Sadie's niece Catherine, she too could live in the carriage house.'

'Ivy Murphy, would you please stop running away with your wild ideas and suggestions!' Ann Marie could feel her blood quickening at the challenges ahead. 'Shouldn't we at least meet with Catherine before you arrange her entire life for the poor girl?'

'Yes, of course,' said Ivy. 'I think we should ask Catherine if she'd be interested in learning to become a nursery maid.'

'The girl would have plenty of experience to bring to the post.' Ann Marie wasn't sure of her own ability to raise a child. 'And I would be sincerely grateful for any advice you can give me on the matter of raising children, Sadie. Your own children are a credit to you and John.'

'Yes, Catherine would be ideal . . . except . . . ' Ivy squirmed with embarrassment but it had to be said, 'she'd have to learn about keeping her own person and her surroundings clean.'

'I can teach her that.' Sadie understood what Ivy meant and didn't bother to defend her sister-in-law. Patsy was a lazy cow and Catherine had never been taught cleanliness.

'You see, Ann Marie, she wouldn't be up to Mrs Winthrop's standards. The woman is a devil for cleanliness.' Ivy had had her knuckles rapped by the woman on more than one occasion. Mrs Winthrop demanded the highest level of hygiene possible when attending a lying-in. 'It would be a chance for the girl.'

'It's worth thinking about,' Sadie agreed. Although, she thought, God knows how I'll get the girl away from her mother. There would be wigs on the green, but it wasn't fair to have a young woman be a slave to her own family and that's what young Catherine was — a bloody slave.

'As I said, we'll need to speak to the girl before we decide her future,' Ann Marie insisted.

'It's just a thought,' Ivy murmured.

'I'll make a list of things we need to achieve.' Ann Marie yawned. She put her hand in front of her mouth and begged their pardon. 'I shall ask my Uncle Charles to recommend a doctor.' She gave an emphatic nod of her head, the bit well and truly between her teeth now. 'It will not do to drag our feet. There will be many changes that need to take place before this baby arrives on the scene.' Her blood fizzled at the challenges ahead.

Ivy saw her chance and took it. She had to get away. Her head was all over the place. She needed time alone to think about the meeting with her brother. She had to talk to Jem.

13

'Conn!' Ivy shoved her hands through her hair and stared when Jem walked into the kitchen with Conn following him. 'I forgot all about you coming over this evening.' She looked around as if expecting a meal to appear out of thin air.

'Ivy, will you for God's sake sit down.' Jem pushed her gently into one of their two easy chairs in front of the range. 'Conn,' he searched in the pocket of his work trousers for change, 'run to the chipper, will you, lad?' He passed over a silver florin. 'Get fish and chips for all of us.'

'I won't be long.' Conn ran from the kitchen. He could grab a bike from the livery.

Conn was glad of this chance to get away. He'd never been called to a meeting at the house before. He ran in and out of the place certainly — but to be invited! He was worried. Pete Reynolds was handling the day-to-day work of the livery. He'd seen Enda Reynolds around the place talking to Jem. He'd heard Jem tell the Reynolds brothers that he wanted a private meeting with Conn this evening. It scared the life out of him. Was he being laid off? He tried to think of anything he might have done to get himself into trouble.

Ivy dropped her head onto the chairback and closed her eyes. 'I didn't even think about cooking a meal.' She opened her eyes again and stared into the concerned face of her husband. Jem was hunched down in front of the chair, staring into her face. 'I'm a terrible wife.'

'You're the best wife I've ever had.' Jem leaned forward to press a kiss against her lips. He was worried about her.

'I'm the only wife you've ever had, Jem Ryan,' Ivy smiled. 'See you keep it that way.'

'You rest a minute.' He stood up. 'I'll make you a pot of tea. That will have you bouncing around the kitchen again. I'm giving you a mug of tea and I don't want to hear any complaints about it, woman. I'm not jumping up and down like a flea to fill those tiny cups of yours.' He smiled over his shoulder. 'I'll even butter a few slices of bread for chip butties while I'm about it.'

'I don't bounce.' Ivy was glad of the chance to sit.

When the tea was made and the bread cut and buttered they sat across the range from each other, content to rest in silence. There was so much she wanted to tell him but she needed this quiet time more than she'd realised.

The sound of Conn coming whistling down the hallway took them both by surprise.

Jem was pouring tea into enamel mugs when Conn, after a brief rap of his knuckles against the door, entered the kitchen.

'Do you need me to do anything?' Conn stood with the paper-wrapped fish and chips stuffed up his woollen jumper.

'No thanks, lad. Here, you can sit in Frank's chair. He's at the pub tonight.' Jem pulled the wooden soft-cushioned chair, which Frank had made for his own use when he visited, closer to the range. 'We'll eat the fish and chips out of the paper.'

'Thanks be to God!' Conn pulled the bulky packet from under his jumper and passed it to Jem. 'Whatever you want to talk to me about can't be too serious if we're having fish and chips out of the paper.' He knew Ivy preferred to serve the food up on plates and sit at the table.

'The talk we want to have with you is serious enough. We should have had it before now but time seems to be running away with us.' Ivy pushed herself straighter in the chair. She took a serving of fish and chips from Jem, making sure the paper kept all grease away from her clothing. She didn't even complain when he passed her an enamel mug of tea.

'Am I going to be laid off?' Conn couldn't wait any longer. He'd never get the chips past the lump in his throat.

'Of course not!' Jem punched his shoulder lightly and handed him a serving of fish and chips and a mug of tea. 'What would we do without you?' He carried the plate of buttered bread over to the fire and put it on the seat of a wooden kitchen chair he'd placed there. They could serve themselves.

They sat for a while eating the fish and chips with their fingers. They were all hungry.

'I wanted to talk to you about your future, Conn,' Jem said when the worst of the hunger had been appeased. He stood to refill the tea mugs. 'I suppose I could have talked to you over at the livery.' He laughed and winked at Conn. 'My missus though is a terrible nag. She'd have skinned me if she wasn't part of this meeting.'

'True.' Ivy toasted him with the mug he pressed into her hand.

'I wondered if you would prefer to work with me at the cinema.' Jem took his chair again.

'*What?*' That was the last thing Conn had expected.

'Conn.' Ivy leaned forward and shook his knee. 'You have been with us from the beginning. You've worked harder than anyone else to help us achieve our dreams. I know you've been worried since Pete Reynolds started work at the livery. You didn't say anything but I knew.' She waited a minute to see if Conn would say anything. When he remained silent she went on. 'What's your dream, Conn? It doesn't matter how crazy it seems to someone else. What do you dream?'

'I wasn't expecting this.' Conn gulped down the last of his fish. He used the newspaper to wipe his greasy fingers. 'Will yez give me a couple of minutes to get something from my place?' Conn lived with his family in one of the houses that formed the tenement block of The Lane.

'Certainly.' Jem gestured with his hands towards the door. He watched the young man jump from his chair and run from the room. He turned to Ivy. 'I wonder what that's all about.'

'We'll find out soon enough.' Ivy held out her mug for a refill. 'That lad never walks when he can run.'

Jem filled their mugs then gathered up the greasy newspaper. He opened the top of the range and forced the large ball of paper down. The blaze would help keep the long chimney clear of smut.

He was closing the top on the range when Conn almost exploded into the room. He was panting and had a familiar folder in his hands.

'I wasn't expecting homework.' Ivy nodded her head towards Conn's folder. Mr Clancy, a retired professor of economics, came to the livery three times a week to teach accounting skills to anyone who cared to learn. Conn's folder usually held his homework.

'The floor is yours,' said Jem, using a familiar phrase in Dublin pubs to encourage people to get up and perform.

Conn, however, sat down and leaning forward spoke earnestly. 'I admire the two of you more than I can ever say. I've watched you drag yourself out of the muck. I was proud to be part of that. I've learned so much from being part of the schemes you both come up with.'

He fell silent for a few moments, gathering his nerve.

'Ivy, I hope you don't think we've been talking about you behind your back,' he surprised them by saying, 'but me and our Mike have put our heads together about this. You need more help than you're getting from Mike. You need to employ someone full-time to help you keep order. Your business has grown so much. You can't do everything yourselves.'

'It's you we're here to discuss,' Ivy said.

'It's all part of the same thing. You asked me about my dream.' He took a deep breath and raised his chin. 'I'd like to be your right-hand man, Jem.'

'What?' Jem stared.

'The two of you are doing too much. You, each of you, need someone who can handle all the bits of your business. The two of you have your finger in so many pies. You need someone who can be by your side to help. It would be better if it were more than one person. You need people who can take some of the weight off your shoulders.'

'Begob, I wasn't expecting that.' Jem stared at Conn, amazed at the young man's insight.

'I've been on the outside looking in from the beginning.' Conn was feeling braver now that he hadn't been handed his head. 'I've watched the ball roll down the hill. If you two don't get out of the way you're going to be flattened.' He opened his folder. 'I've made notes.' He removed a sheaf of papers. After a quick glance at them, he passed one section to Jem before handing the remainder to Ivy. 'See, each of you think of your business as a single thing . . . ' He waited for their nods. 'But the business has grown arms and legs. Jem,' he leaned over to point at a line on the paper, 'you started with the livery. Then the taxi service — house clearances — removals — deliveries. These are all different businesses now and they're still growing. That's not even mentioning your talking-pictures business. You need to put someone in charge of each — ' he seemed to search for a word, 'arm, I suppose, of your business.'

'Well, now,' Ivy smiled at the young man she considered part of her family, 'you've been giving all of this a lot of thought, it seems.'

'Look at all the different things you do, Ivy.' Conn was on a roll now. He'd spent hours lying in his bed thinking about all of this. He hoped they wouldn't consider him an interfering so-and-so for stating his opinion. 'You've your round and I know that's important to you. You take things from servants to sell on — you launder and upgrade the clothes you take — you've your market dealers and then you've your doll business. You buy stuff from those warehouses down the docks to use or sell on. That's not even mentioning your work from the sheds out back. Then you have woman's work around the house. You can't do all that work yourself, Ivy. You need help.'

'Why haven't you shown this to us before, Conn?' Ivy shook the papers in her hand. She'd hate to feel Conn thought he couldn't talk to them — about anything.

'I suppose I was waiting for a moment like this.' Conn took a deep breath before stating his thoughts and wishes. 'I've said I want to be top dog under Jem. I know our Mike helps out but he's got a job.' He hoped his brother would forgive him — Mike hated working down the fish factory. 'I think my big sister Alison would be just the woman to help you handle your business, Ivy.'

'But your Ali is delicate.' Ivy thought of Conn's eldest sister. Alison had been born with a birth defect that left her with a hump over her left shoulder and stunted her growth. She looked like a china doll.

'No, she's not.' Conn loved his sister. He wanted to get her out from under her mother's shadow. 'Who do you think does all the work around our place? Ali has been mother and father to all my parents' many children. She's run the place ever since I was born.' There were six years between Conn and his big sister. She'd been far more of a mother to him than Lily Connelly. That poor woman was too busy having babies and trying to control a husband too fond of drink. 'And I've taught Ali everything I've learned from Mr Clancy about accounting. She's really smart.'

'I don't know what to say, Conn.' Ivy looked over at Jem, wondering if he'd say something but he simply smiled at her. The ball was in her court.

'Ali is amazing,' Conn said.

'I'll agree to meet with Alison and discuss the matter.' Ivy could see how much this meant to Conn. 'But it makes me nervous thinking of being someone's boss. Mike and me just get on with things. I've never ordered anyone about.'

'Oh, haven't you, missus?' Jem laughed aloud.

'Oh, hush, you!' Ivy tapped her laughing husband with the papers she still held in her hands.

'You've given us a great deal to think about, Conn,' Jem said. 'I'll need time to think about what you've said. Why don't we all agree to sleep on it and talk more about this another day?'

* * *

'It's been a day and a half,' Ivy said as she snuggled close in Jem's arms. The bed was warm and cosy and she had to fight sleep to say what she needed to say. She hadn't yet told Jem of the meeting with her brother. She'd waited until the end of that work day, thinking they would have time together to talk — but she'd completely forgotten Conn would be joining them. 'I'm that tired but I can't go to sleep until I tell yeh something.'

'That Conn has a bright young head on his shoulders.' Jem pulled the covers up to his ears. He was tired — not really listening.

'He does indeed but that's not what I want to talk about.' She rolled over, put her head on his chest and told him about the meeting with her brother.

'Well, that knocks the day into a cocked hat,' Jem was wide awake now — his blood boiling. 'We'll have to keep our eyes and ears open, that's for sure.' He tried not to say anything nasty about Ivy's family. He'd take great pleasure in giving young Mr Murphy, or whatever he was calling himself these days, a good thrashing.

14

'Name of God, where did you come from?' Ivy almost swallowed her tongue when she saw the man sitting at her kitchen table.

'It's too easy to get in here,' William Armstrong aka Billy Flint flashed his dare-devil smile at his niece. 'I came over that wasteland to the side of the house. It was easy to jump over that back wall. No one saw me.'

'Oh, I wouldn't say that.' Jem opened the kitchen door that led from the garden. He held a hunk of wood over one shoulder. 'You were seen all right.'

'Took both of you long enough to get here.'

'I don't expect anyone to creep around the place.' Ivy hadn't heard a thing and she'd been sitting in her workroom off the kitchen. She'd been using her sewing machine, trying to get stuff ready for shifting. It was too early for Mike to have arrived.

'You need to be more alert.'

'I'll put the kettle on.' Ivy shook her head and walked over to the kitchen sink. 'Are you staying, Jem? I was about to stop for something to eat. I could make you something if you've time.'

'I'm in the middle of something.' If he didn't know the man he'd have a hard time recognising his business partner, William Armstrong, in the shabbily dressed man sitting at his kitchen table. Billy Flint and William Armstrong were one and

103

the same man but sometimes it beggared belief. The man had made his mark in Dublin using the alias Billy Flint. He'd a finger in a great many unsavoury pies. 'I'll have something to eat with the lads later if you don't need me here now.'

'We'll be fine.' Ivy said.

Jem stepped back into the garden, pulling the kitchen door closed soundlessly.

'You need to put some class of a noise-maker on that door,' William said.

'So I see.' Ivy wouldn't turn down expert advice. She'd been only steps away and had heard nothing — lesson learned.

'I had one of my men speak to Hopalong — put a flea in his ear about Seb Walker and his missus Iris.'

'I could have done that myself.' Ivy spun around to stare down at her father's brother.

'My sister Betty came to me years ago seeking protection for you. You know that — God knows you moaned enough about it at the time. I gave Betty my word to keep an eye on you. I don't go back on my word.'

Ivy had grown up without ever knowing her father's family. It was after her father's death — when she started making a name for herself as the up-and-coming businesswoman Ivy Rose — that the pair had come into her life. She sometimes resented the fact that they had not helped her when she was really in need. She tried to tell herself that it had been her own da's decision to keep his family away from her. She was only human though and their interference in her life now bothered her.

'You need to put a spoke in Seb Walker's wheel, Ivy. The man has a bad reputation.' Billy Flint was spending a lot of his time on his legitimate business as William Armstrong these days. It gave some of the wild boys the idea that he was getting sloppy. 'The man will try to go around me. He'll use you — make no mistake. It would be quite the coup for him to hurt one of mine and get away with it. It would make him the big man in town.'

As if she didn't have enough to worry about.

William watched Ivy lay a pretty table for them. Here at least was one relative he could be proud of. 'That brother of yours — Eamo, the little shite — is opening his mouth where he shouldn't be opening it. He has been seen in Seb Walker's company — that can't be good for you.'

'I'm afraid I don't find that hard to believe,' Ivy said. 'He never did have a great deal of common sense, our Eamo.'

'At some point you will need to go see Seb Walker yourself, Ivy, and put him firmly in his place.' He'd keep his eye on things but eventually she would have to step out and make her place in the world known.

'Name of God, I couldn't do that!' she gasped.

'You will have to prove you can handle your own affairs sooner or later, Ivy.' He would think on how it could be done. They had time.

'If it's not one thing it's another,' she sighed.

They stared at each other for a while, each waiting for the other to look away. Ivy gave in first. She'd things to do. 'Would you like an omelette?'

'What kind?'

'I'm having a cheese omelette but there are mushrooms if you prefer.' She sliced the bread she'd made that morning and put it with curls of butter in a china dish onto the breadboard before putting the board on the table top.

'I'll have mushroom and cheese, thank you.'

They chatted politely about everyday events until Ivy had the meal served and joined him at the table. They ate in silence, both preferring to eat in peace without discussing the problem of their relatives.

'You're a fair hand in the kitchen,' he said when Ivy stood to remove their dirty plates. 'That bread is lovely. Have you any jam to go with it?'

'Of course.' She began to fill a pretty bowl from one of the glass jars which held the jam she made every autumn with the fruit she picked.

'Don't bother with that. I'm family. Just give us the jar.'

She plonked the jar of jam on the table. She'd leave the dishes until later. She poured fresh tea and sat back down at the table.

'Eamo came to see me.' She sipped her tea and watched him pile blackberry jam onto a slice of buttered bread. 'Like a bit of bread with your jam, do you?'

'Don't be cheeky.' He bit into the bread with pleasure. 'Blackberry is my favourite.'

'Eamo's up to something. I don't know what.' She gave him the details of her meeting with her brother while he made inroads into her supply of bread and jam. Where did the man put the food?

106

He was tall and slim, a well-set-up gent.

'Valeria Gibson.' He wiped his hands and lips on the napkin and leaned back. He'd enjoyed that. 'Who's she when she's at home?'

'You might have seen her about the place — a big lump of a woman with long white hair. She scurried around the place — wouldn't say boo to a goose.' Ivy had never really paid attention to Valeria — she'd been too busy trying to keep body and soul together. 'According to Frank,' she shook her head sadly, 'Eamo was a bit too friendly with her if you follow my meaning.'

'Wonder what he wants with her these days?' He'd give it some thought. 'If I know anything about the Williams family they'll be planning a suitable match for the lad. He's old enough and it will be up to him now to continue the old man's line. You think the lad might be trying to escape their plans for him, using this girl Valeria Gibson?'

'I doubt it. That whole family is strange. The grandmother is a great lump of a woman who never leaves the house. She sits in next door's window like a store dummy and watches the world go by. The father is out and about all the hours of the day and night on an old putt-putt with a sidecar. You've probably seen him around.'

'Is there any point in William Armstrong speaking with your brother?' He kept the two facets of his character separate even in his head.

'I honestly don't know. Maybe. Eamo looks like me da spit him,' Ivy said. 'It makes it hard to give him the kick up the arse he so desperately needs.'

'Something will have to be done about him.' He was illegitimate. He, his brother Ivy's father, and his sister were born to the long-time mistress of Franklin Williams. Ivy's mother had recently married the legitimate heir to Williams and given her sons the name their father had been denied. 'He's going places and saying things that could be a danger to both you and me.'

'I've never been able to do anything with him,' Ivy said. 'I thought, with him being all set up as a fancy gent, with expectations of a very nice inheritance, he'd be happy.'

'Maybe he's one of those who hate to see anyone else making something of their life. Some people hate to see others get on.' Billy had a team of trusted men at his back. 'You and Jem are making a name for yourselves. You've had your picture in the paper all done up like a dog's dinner, for goodness' sake. Your Shay is out in America making a name for himself in the talking pictures. Maybe young Eamo has a bad case of jealousy. He could well be one of those people who don't like to see one of their own make something of themselves — thinking they're getting above their station and need to be dragged back down into the gutter with everyone else.'

'Eamo always wanted what he had to be bigger and better than anyone else's. He just never understood that you have to earn what you have.' Ivy stood to fetch more tea.

'Your business is growing, so is Jem's.' He held

out his cup for more tea. 'You need to start putting trusted people in key positions. You need someone to watch your back.'

'I'm going to interview one of the Connellys this afternoon.' Ivy planned to meet with Alison and discuss her coming to work for her. She needed someone to take the bookkeeping off her hands at least.

'The Connelly family seem to be getting well in with you and Jem.' He checked his watch. He'd things to do — places to go — people to see. 'You know the father, Brian Connelly, lives up Leary's arse — don't you?' Father Leary, the Parish Priest, had been a thorn in Ivy's side all of her life.

'I don't think his children are as fond of the Parish Priest as he is,' Ivy said simply.

'On your own head be it, but you need to start being more aware of safety around here. It's too bloody easy to scale that wall out the back and walk into this place. There will be some watching the money coming in here and wondering where it goes. The kind of people who would never think you'd put your money in the bank.'

'You've given me a lot to think about.' Ivy had felt safe and secure in her little back-of-house flat but now her uncle had made her see the danger in taking her safety for granted. She'd have to think long and hard about making changes.

'I'm going to talk to Jem now.' He stood, stepped away from the table and shoved his chair back under it. He stood with his two hands on the chair back. 'I want to discuss closing up that scrubland beside your house or building on it.

It's a tempting place to hide.'

'Would you please go away now?' Ivy stood and stared into his eyes. They were a mirror image of her own da's. 'If you talk to me much longer I won't be able to sleep at night.' She couldn't live fearing her own shadow.

'Right, I'll go talk to Jem.' He left through the door leading into the garden without another word.

15

'Mike, I'll be inside waiting for your sister.' Ivy looked down at the long black skirt she wore with the slightly worn green jumper. She'd been hard at work in her sheds but now she had a possible employee to interview — if you wouldn't be minding. 'Let me know if there's anything you can't handle.'

'I'll be fine.' Mike loved being left in charge of the outdoor business. He wondered if he should say something about his sister and how much she wanted this job. He decided to keep his mouth shut. Least said, soonest mended.

'I'm going to change my clothes,' Ivy whispered, opening the door from the garden into her kitchen. 'If my uncle dresses down to be Billy Flint and like an elegant gent to be William Armstrong — then I'm going to do the same. I'm interviewing a potential employee. I need to look like a boss woman. I'll be Ivy Rose — no, I won't — I'll be Mrs Ryan.' She laughed aloud at her own silliness but, really, it was worth considering. She needed to create an impression and her old skirt and jumper wouldn't present the image she desired — simple as that. 'I'll have a quick bath.' She was excited about picking an outfit to wear. It wasn't often she dressed up to stay around the house. Perhaps she should — she was a married woman now and should make an effort to look well put together.

'Well, well, Ivy Rose, you clean up well.' She admired her image in the long mirror of the bathroom. She'd chosen one of the new-style slim black skirts that came inches above her ankles. The silk stockings she'd pulled up her legs gleamed and the black T-strap shoes flattered her slender feet.

She turned slowly and admired the white knitted twin set she wore. It was in the latest fashion — drop waist with a long pelmet around her hips — and it flattered her tall slim figure. 'I tell you what — that Molly Coyle can really knit.' The woman produced elegant garments that should have fetched a great deal of money for the maker. Sadly, there was not a great deal of money to be made from handcrafted items — not for the artist anyway — but the big shops made a lot of profit from something like the articles Ivy wore. She didn't have the clientele to pay for something like this. So she bought them for herself.

She had asked Conn to tell Alison to be here at three. It was nearly that now.

The knock on the bathroom door almost made her jump out of her shoes.

'Are yeh nearly done in there, missus?' Frank Wilson's gruff voice came through the wooden door. 'You've someone out here to see you — says how she has an appointment. Don't leave the poor girl waiting out here in the hallway.'

'I'll be right there!'

Ivy wanted to kick herself — she'd look lovely

walking out of the bathroom with her old clothes rolled up under her arm. Ah well, maybe they wouldn't notice. She smiled at her own image in the mirror. 'You look the business,' she whispered. She picked up her clothes, rolled them up tightly, opened the door and stepped out.

'Alison, I'm sorry to keep you waiting.' Her heart sank at the image the other woman presented. Those clothes would have to go. The blonde hair pulled tightly back in a bun did nothing to flatter the delicate face and her thickly lashed grey eyes seemed enormous in her pale little heart-shaped face.

'I was a bit early.' Alison was trying to stop her teeth from rattling. She'd never had a job interview before. She stared at the glamorous woman standing before her and wanted to slink away.

'Come through to the kitchen.' Ivy stared at Frank, hoping he'd get the message that this time he wasn't welcome. She wanted to talk to Alison in private.

Frank got the message. 'I'll leave you to it.'

'Sit down, Alison.' Ivy pointed to the chairs pulled up to the kitchen table. 'I'll just be a moment.' She hurried into her bedroom, threw her clothing in the corner, took a deep breath, plastered a smile on her face and stepped back into the kitchen.

'I'll put the kettle on,' she said to the shivering woman sitting there bolt upright.

'While the kettle is boiling . . . ' Ivy removed ink, pen and a notepad she had prepared earlier from one of her cupboards, 'will you please write your name, address and the names of your brothers and sisters on this pad?' She put everything on the kitchen table. 'I know it sounds silly but I want to see your handwriting. I've put a few sums on there for you to do as well, if you please.'

She occupied herself in getting the tea ready to serve. The sound of the pen scratching over the paper seemed overloud in the room.

'I'm finished, Mrs Ryan.' Conn had told Alison to call this woman Ivy but she couldn't. She was too elegant to be called by her first name by someone like her.

Ivy was at a loss. Alison looked like a tiny child dressed in her granny's old clothes. What on earth was she supposed to do with this woman-child? She didn't sit but set the table for tea, placing the Victoria sponge she'd prepared earlier in the middle.

'Alison, I'm going to speak to you in a very direct manner.'

'I prefer to be called Ali, Mrs Ryan.' Alison knew she'd lost the job before she'd ever got it. She didn't want tea and cake. She wanted to go home to cry her eyes out.

'Conn seems to believe you would be the ideal person to help me.' Ivy had seen the pain on the other woman's face. 'But it's not that simple.'

'He should never have asked you to give me a job,' Ali gulped.

'That's not it.' Ivy examined the writing on the pad. It was beautiful — far better than her own handwriting. The sums were all correct and had

114

been worked out at some speed. 'I'm going to come right out and ask you. It will be on my mind the whole time if I don't.' She took a nervous breath. She could be going to get herself into a lot of trouble. 'How do you feel about Father Leary?' She waited for the bolt of lightning to strike her.

Ali held the teacup in shaking hands, hoping it would stop her shivering. 'I know the man has been a problem for you.'

'That's not what I asked.'

'Father Leary told me da that the hump on my back was punishment for his sins.' Ali lifted her large grey eyes and stared across the table at Ivy. 'The man can't even look at me.'

'You still aren't answering my question.' Ivy couldn't afford to allow Ali to skate around the subject.

'Father Leary,' Ali put down her cup to bless herself frantically, 'is the most unholy man I've ever met in my life.'

'Merciful hour!' Ivy too blessed herself. 'I can't believe you said it.'

The two women stared at each other, both expecting a judgement from on high. When nothing happened, Ivy pulled her chair closer to the table.

'I had to ask, Ali.' Ivy gulped her tea. It was tepid. She emptied it with a grimace into the slop bowl on the table. She jumped up to pour a fresh cup. 'I know how close your family is to Father Leary but that man is no friend of mine. I couldn't have you here, Ali, if you thought the man hung the moon.'

115

'I can't be seen or heard to speak disrespect-fully of the man out of respect for me family, but I can think for myself.' Ali held out her cup for a fresh cup of tea. 'I have no intention of discussing anything that happens in your home with my family.'

'That might be very hard to do.' Ivy filled the cups before taking her seat again.

'Not really,' Ali said. 'There are so many of us and, to be truthful with you, Ivy,' she gulped, 'me da is fond of the sound of his own voice.' That was all she was willing to say about her family.

'Fair enough.' Ivy decided to take a chance. 'Conn said you know as much about keeping books as he does?'

'He taught me everything he learned from that Mr Clancy who comes to the livery to teach.'

'Why did you never join us in the lessons?'

'I didn't think I'd be welcome.' The truth was, her da would have done his nut if he'd thought one of his daughters was trying to get above herself.

'I need an office manager, Ali.' Ivy watched the shock on the other woman's face. 'I have so much to do and only two hands. Can you sew?'

'No, I'm useless.'

'Thank God for that!' Ivy laughed. 'If you'd been any good you'd have been pulled into helping me and that's the last thing I want you to do.'

'I know I might be talking myself out of a job, Ivy, but would our Mike not be of more help to you? I know he loves coming over here,'

'I have something else in mind for Mike and,

116

let's be honest, the poor fella would go mental locked inside most of the day. He's made for the outdoors, is Mike.'

'What would you need me to do, Ivy?'

'The biggest part of my need at the moment is for someone to take care of the books. I need someone to set up a system to keep account of what goes on around here. If you don't want to ask Mr Clancy for advice, Conn or I could ask him. Although I'd prefer you do it yourself. He can explain anything you might not understand. But, apart from the book-keeping, I'd want you to be willing to lend a hand wherever it was wanted.'

'I'm willing to turn me hand to anything. I can't sew but I can manage most other things. If I don't know how, I'll tell yeh, and I'm told I learn fast.'

'Ali,' Ivy stared at the other woman, 'I hate housework.' She jumped up, ashamed of herself, and grabbed a mug to fill with tea for Mike. 'I would be eternally grateful if you would take over keeping this place clean.'

She cut a slice of cake and put it on a piece of folded newspaper, then opened the kitchen door and shouted, '*Mike!*'

Mike hurried over to take the tea and cake. 'Thanks, that looks lovely, Ivy.' Then he put his head around the door to say, 'Hello, our Ali!' His poor sister looked shell-shocked. Ivy had that effect on people.

Ivy rejoined Ali at the table as Mike disappeared again.

'I'd love to take this place in hand,' Ali said.

The place was a little palace to her eyes. She'd love to make it shine.

'Right, the hours will be eight in the morning till eight at night. You'd get your meals provided. I do enjoy cooking and feeding people. I just hate cleaning up after meself. You might have to make meals from time to time yourself like but the food would be here. We'd work less hours on Saturday, and you would have Sunday off. Your start-off wage will be seven shillings and sixpence a week.'

'My da doesn't give my mother that much to support his home and children, Ivy!' Ali gasped. 'Are you sure?'

'I suggest you don't tell anyone what you're earning.' Ivy knew the amount was generous but there was a lot of work to be done. She didn't intend to cheat anyone. 'You should open a bank account and lodge the cheques I'll pay your wages with into the bank. I'll write your pay cheque on Friday. You can take time off to go to the bank in South King Street. I'll take you the first time to open your account.'

'People like me don't have bank accounts, Ivy!'

'That's where you're wrong, Ali,' Ivy said. 'If you get paid by cheque you won't have any money in your hand that someone can take.' They didn't need to discuss men who waited for their daughters with their hand out. Ivy's da had always removed every penny she earned from her as soon as she got home. 'I think you'll be giving me a lot of that money back because, Ali, you can't go around the place dressed like that.' She

118

waved a hand over the ill-fitting unattractive outfit Ali was wearing. 'I'll expect you to accompany me out and about to meet business people.'

'My Lord!' Ali laughed. 'It's outright mutiny you're talking.'

'I suppose it is,' Ivy agreed. 'What do you think, Ali? Are you ready to jump ship?'

'Yes,' Ali said simply. 'I'm twenty-seven years old — it's time and past I stood on my own two feet.' She looked down at the child's plimsolls on her feet. 'Even if my feet are in the ugliest shoes on earth.' She'd coveted Ivy's shoes as soon as she'd seen them.

'We'll be learning together, Ali.' Ivy said. 'I've never had an office manager before. I'm not sure what I'll be asking you to do. I promise I'll try not to ask you to do anything I wouldn't do myself.' She waited a moment. 'I notice you haven't sat back in that chair — does it hurt your back?'

'Yes.' Ali was going to be as honest as Ivy.

'I'll ask Frank to step in and measure your back if you don't mind. He can make you up a chair with a canvas back that will fit you better. You'll be spending a great deal of time writing in books — no point in you suffering. Anything else you need, tell me, and we'll work it out together.'

'I don't know what to say.' Ali's head was spinning. She had a job. She wanted to jump up and dance.

'We'll work it out as we go along,' Ivy said. 'I want to take your measurements before I get Frank. I'll have Mrs Bates in your building run up two dresses for you tonight. I'll pay for them and she'll be glad of the money.'

'I can't ask you to do that, Ivy.'

'You didn't ask. And I'll deduct the cost from your wages. I can't look at you like that every day. I'm sorry if that hurts your feelings.'

'You haven't hurt my feelings, Ivy. I've eyes in my head.'

'Right, let's get started!' Ivy jumped to her feet. 'We've a lot to do before you're ready to start working for me.'

16

'Yer ma and Ivy Murphy have been talking to me da,' Catherine O'Malley said.

'Mrs Ryan to you and me.' Dora Lawless knew her mother Sadie met with her brother — Catherine's da — a couple of times a week. She passed him money and food when she could.

'I don't care,' Catherine snapped. 'The two of them are causing ructions. There's been nothing but arguments in our place. I've never seen me ma and da like this.'

The two young women were strolling arm in arm around the People's Flower Garden — a Victorian floral wonder set inside the Parkgate entrance of the Phoenix Park. They were deep in discussion, uncaring about the extreme difference in their appearance. Catherine was dressed like an old woman in a threadbare black skirt that reached her ankles. Her worn boys' boots were letting in water but she was used to that. The black knitted jumper she wore had holes at the elbows and the cuffs were frayed. She'd covered her head and shoulders with a thin, torn grey blanket folded in two and worn like a shawl.

Dora was dressed like a young lady of fashion. A cloche hat covered her blonde hair and framed her pretty blue eyes and smiling face. Her navy-blue coat reached mid-calf, her stocking-covered legs gleamed, and her T-strap shoes were highly polished. They ignored the pointed stares of people passing by.

'Do we have to keep getting wet?' Dora didn't want to ruin her outfit. 'I'll treat you to a cup of tea at the teashop. We can sit in comfort and chat.'

'I'm not going into any teashop. The state of me and the price of fish!' Catherine was ashamed of her appearance. She didn't mind walking out with her cousin but she wasn't going to let strangers stare at her and whisper behind their hands.

'We're as good as anyone else.' Dora used the arm linked through her own to drag her cousin in the direction of the nearby tea rooms. 'They're not paying for us so they can all sod off.'

'Dora!' Catherine protested. She'd never been inside a tea room in her life.

'I'm serious, Catherine.' Dora continued to march towards the tea room. 'I want to talk to you and I'm not going to get me clothes ruined — so put that in your pipe and smoke it!'

Catherine's protests were in vain. In no time Dora had them both inside the tea room, sitting at a small round table, waiting for the waitress to take their order. Catherine was trying not to stare around with her mouth open. She was deeply impressed when Dora gave an order for tea, sandwiches and cake to the black-clad waitress. The cap and the shining white apron covering the black of the outfit the waitress wore were spotless. Catherine didn't know where to put herself.

Dora watched the waitress rushing about

— giving her cousin time to get comfortable. It was hard to look at her cousin sometimes. She looked so much like Dora's ma, Sadie, it was painful to see her in such a state. She sat back in the wooden chair and waited for the waitress to bring their food. She'd ordered the sandwiches for Catherine — the poor cow was always hungry. It was rare for the two cousins to be able to spend time like this without children hanging off them. Today when she'd stopped by to see Catherine, she'd almost dragged her out of the cluttered, smelly two rooms her uncle's family called home.

'So, what's all the shouting about at your place then?' Dora asked while pouring tea from the pot the waitress had left on their table. She'd waited to speak until the woman was out of earshot. 'Did it have anything to do with you coming to work for Ann Marie?' Dora's ma had asked her to see what Catherine thought about the idea.

'Me da had a word with me last night.' Catherine's mouth watered at the sight of the food sitting on the table. She didn't recognise any of the sandwich fillings. 'Me da's a lovely man, Dora — you know that.'

Catherine loved her da but she wished he'd stop making babies. The two rooms they lived in were overcrowded and it fell to her to try and keep some kind of order. Her ma seemed to live in a different world to everyone else. She didn't see the dirt, didn't hear the children crying with hunger. Sometimes it frightened Catherine. Her mother was like a ghost around the place. She only came alive when her da was home. The rest

123

of the time she was down at the church or sitting staring at nothing.

'Don't yeh want to get away from that place and all them kids?' Dora put a sandwich on a side plate that matched the design on the cup and saucer. She passed the tea and sandwich to Catherine.

Dora was glad her family were moving out of Ann Marie's house. She hadn't enjoyed being treated like a serving maid there. She'd never wanted to go into service.

'How can I?' Catherine almost wailed. 'If I leave, what's going to happen to the rest of them?'

The Parish Priest had found live-in jobs for each of the others as soon as they reached nine years of age. That left Catherine as the oldest of the six youngsters left at home. They'd never get anything to eat if she wasn't there to look after them.

'Your Delilah is almost nine years old.' Dora had spent more time with her cousin than with her own sister Clare. She'd helped her cousin care for the babies that were always underfoot. 'You were younger than that when you started taking care of everyone.'

'You know our Delilah will bow down to no one. There would be murder in the place with her in charge.' Catherine took another sandwich from the serving plate.

'Eat all them sandwiches,' Dora encouraged her. 'We have to pay for them anyway.' She thought it would serve Patsy right to have Delilah take over. The girl was very like her mother in nature — she thought only of herself. The two deserved each other in her opinion.

'You've been bursting with news all day.' Catherine wanted to change the subject. 'You may as well spit it out.'

'I got a job!' Dora almost danced on her seat. 'My elocution teacher gave me a reference. I start as a trainee in Woolworths on Grafton Street this Monday.'

'I'm made up for yeh!'

'I can't wait, I'm that excited,' Dora's grin almost split her face. 'I've got what I wanted now — we need to get you fixed up.'

'I can't leave me family, Dora.' Catherine could see only a lifetime of poverty and filth in her future. She didn't speak posh like her cousin. She'd never get a job in a fancy shop like Woolworths looking as she did. She could see the glares the waitress was giving her even if her cousin didn't. What chance did she have?

'Catherine, do you know what day it is?' Dora watched her cousin devour the dainty sand-wiches, all the time eyeing up the selection of tiny cakes on the three-tiered glass stand close to her hand.

'Course I do, it's Wednesday.'

'It's your birthday.' Dora was three months younger than Catherine. 'You're fifteen years old today.' She knew Catherine's family did not cel-ebrate special occasions but surely their daughter reaching her fifteenth birthday deserved a men-tion at least.

'Go way!' Catherine had to think about it for a minute.

'I think it's high time for change, cousin.'

Dora's family had insisted on giving her money to be spent on Catherine today. It would pay for this fancy tea and if they were lucky Pa Landers — a second-hand dealer with a shop close to Catherine's house — would have some clothes that would fit Catherine.

★   ★   ★

'I can't believe all of this is for me!' Catherine was almost dancing along the shabby street. She held tightly to the string of three large brown-paper-wrapped parcels. They had been lucky at Pa Lander's place. They'd bought two skirts, four blouses and a jacket that fit Catherine like a glove. They'd also bought two pairs of T-strap shoes. The old man had been very generous with them. Dora knew he'd knocked the price off several of the items they'd selected. It would have taken a very hard heart to ruin the joy practically glowing from Catherine as each item was selected.

Dora had to run to keep up with Catherine as she charged up the steps leading to their tenement building.

'*Ma! Da! Kids!*' Catherine yelled, pushing the door to their rooms open and almost falling through in her hurry to share her happy news. She couldn't wait to tell everyone about her first time in a tea shop. 'You're never going to believe — '

'*Where have you been until this hour, you little bitch?*'

Dora was in time to see the open-handed blow across the face that Catherine received from her mother.

'Them kids need feedin' and washin'! There's nothing to eat in the house! There's no shoppin' done! You should be ashamed of yourself leaving your family all day to go gallivantin' around the town. Do you ever even think about anyone but yourself?' Patsy was in fine form. 'As for *you*, Dora bloody Lawless — '

'Patsy!' Rory O'Malley said only the one word but the tone of his voice warned his wife she'd gone too far.

'What day is today, Ma, Da?' Catherine ignored the crying children calling out her name — begging to be fed — wanting to be picked up and cuddled. This was not her life. Her ma and da kept making babies — she had no say in the matter.

She looked around the room with fresh eyes and her heart sank. The slop bucket in the corner was overflowing, the smell overpowering. No one had taken it out to the WC in the back yard to empty its contents. That, it would seem, was her job. For some reason the sight of the turds floating on top of the bucket made her see her own life with new eyes.

'I can't,' she whispered under the noise around her. 'I won't live like this anymore.' Something inside of her had broken loose.

'It's a day you'll rue, my girl,' Patsy said pushing up the sleeves of her jumper.

'There will be none of that, Patsy.' Rory's heart was breaking. He'd watched the joy drain out of his daughter's face. The bright red imprint of her ma's hand stood out on her pale skin. She was the image of his mother and sister.

'Today is the day I leave here.' Catherine spoke softly then louder. 'I've been arguing with our Dora all day, it seems — finding reasons why I couldn't leave you to handle your own life, Ma.' Tears ran down her face as she looked at her brothers and sisters. She loved them so much but, if she stayed here, what could she do for them?

'You walk out that door,' Patsy gestured dramatically towards the still open door, 'and you'll never walk back in again. You'll be dead to me.'

'Patsy!' said Rory.

This time he was ignored.

'If that's the way you want it, Ma.' Catherine picked up the parcels she'd dropped when her mother attacked her. Her shoulders shaking with silent sobs, she turned her back on her family. 'Let's go, Dora,' she whispered and together the two girls walked out on the screaming children and shouting adults.

They closed the door gently behind them.

17

'I'll be sorry to lose you.'

'Truth be told I'll be sorry to go.' Ria looked at the woman who had all unknowingly offered her help at a time in her life when she'd desperately needed a bit of luck. 'I've never lived on a narrow boat before. I enjoyed the experience.'

'You're a hard worker, I'll give yeh that.' Midge Baxter stared at the strange youngster she'd taken on as a deckhand. 'It were a stroke of luck you being on that towpath when my fella turned his ankle.' She poured dark brown tea from a brightly decorated metal pot. The two were seated at a small pull-out bench in the cabin of the narrow boat.

'For both of us,' Ria said.

Ria had planned to stow away on one of the slow-moving barges that travelled from Dublin to Kildare and back. She'd removed and buried the black dress and bonnet she'd been wearing when she dropped Stanley off with Rowley. She'd slid down the high bank surrounding the canal towards the towpath. The large horses that pulled the barges along didn't walk very fast. She'd been sure she could jump on board a barge unnoticed. It hadn't been necessary. She'd been on the path when Midge's husband Bax slipped while leading their horse and his ankle had turned.

Ria had seen it all. She'd rushed to help, never

thinking she might profit from the situation. She'd offered to lead the horse along the towpath while Midge checked out the injury. She'd stayed with the couple for weeks and it had been a slice of life she'd never known. She'd stopped looking over her shoulder and settled down to enjoy the unexpected chance.

'Look here, young'un.' Midge needed to say something. This strange young person had been with her for weeks now. They had detoured down narrow rivers to pick up and drop off cargo with never a complaint. Her new deckhand had worked harder than most young men she knew and had been good company on top of it. 'It's obvious to me you're on the run.' She held up one wrinkled hand as Ria opened her mouth to protest. 'That is none of my never mind. It's just . . . ' she shrugged, 'you'll never pass for a lad if someone sees you in the light of day.'

'You knew!' Ria stared.

'I know nothing, nor do I want to.' Midge had taken a liking to the young woman. 'I can tell no one nothing if I know nothing. I was just letting you know you need to be careful.' Midge could guess what the young woman was running from. She hoped to God there were no children left motherless by what she was doing. 'Now, are you sure you'll be safe if we drop you off at the next lock?' They were travelling along the Grand Canal in Dublin. 'Only we have a load to pick up at the next lock. It's a busy place with lots of people about.'

'I'll be fine.' Ria knew exactly where she was. She was only steps from The Lane.

'I'm sorry I've no money to give you.'

'A roof over my head and food in my mouth was plenty.' Ria had been grateful for every kindness shown her. 'I'll be fine, I promise you.' She leaned over and gently touched the older woman's hand. 'Midge, I left no child of mine behind me.' The worry was almost written on the old woman's face. She thought of Stanley with great sadness but he wasn't hers to protect.

'Thanks be to God!' Midge was grateful for the reassurance.

'*Coming up to the lock!*' Bax shouted from above. '*Get up here if you're going!*'

'Thanks for everything, Midge,' Ria said with a lump in her throat.

'You take good care of yourself.'

'I'll do my best.' Ria had nothing to take with her. She'd only the clothes she stood up in. 'Goodbye.' She rushed from the cabin.

She jumped onto the towpath and waved towards the man and horse. 'Bye, Bax!' she called before stepping off the towpath.

She stood for a moment, trying to get her bearings. There was an opening in front of her that she'd never seen before. It looked as if it must lead into The Lane. She pulled her cap low on her head, hunched her shoulders and buried her nose in the scarf Midge had knit for her. She couldn't stand here, gaping like a tourist. She shoved her clenched fists in the pockets of her trousers. With her heart in her mouth she stepped towards the tunnel. If she was wrong she could always retrace her steps.

She walked slowly along the tunnel, astonished

to see there was another open tunnel directly across from her. What had happened in The Lane? In her time there had been only one entrance to The Lane and that had been beside a smelly public house. This was so much better. Now that she was actually here she was terrified. There was no point throwing herself on her father's mercy. The man had none.

She needed somewhere to hide until she'd got her ducks all in a row. Would she be safe coming back here? She hadn't been able to think of anywhere else to go. Frank Wilson, her old neighbour, had a reputation as a grumpy old man but he'd always been decent to her. Was she insane to think he might be willing to hide her until she could get herself organised? She needed to change the gold sovereigns into small change. The coins would attract too much attention if she tried to spend them locally. With her heart in her mouth she walked along the row of houses that were once so familiar to her. She stopped in front of Frank Wilson's door and, with her knees shaking, raised her hand to knock.

It was a shock to her when a bright-eyed child opened the door.

'I'm looking for Mr Wilson.'

'*Granddad!*' Emmy shouted towards the back of the house where her granddad was putting up a shelf for Auntie Ivy.

'May I step in?' Ria didn't want to risk someone seeing her.

'No,' Emmy said. 'I don't know you.' She knew she wasn't supposed to let strangers into the house.

'What is it, Emmy?' Frank Wilson stepped into the hallway from Ivy's kitchen.

'Mr Wilson,' Ria swallowed audibly, 'I'm sorry to disturb you — '

'In the name of God!' Frank Wilson almost ran down the hallway, recognising her face and voice. 'Come in,' he said while pulling the strangely dressed figure into the hallway and slamming the door. 'Emmy, run tell your auntie I'll be along later.' He opened the door to his own rooms and almost pushed Ria inside. He closed the door at his back and stood for a minute, staring at the trembling figure standing in front of him.

'I'm sorry to come here like this,' Ria bit her lip. 'I didn't know where else to go.'

'You look a mite different from how you used to,' he offered, waving a hand in the direction of one of his hand-carved easy chairs. 'Sit yerself down while I put the kettle on — have you eaten?' The young woman was skin and bone — it was a shock to his system to see her like this. They must have been starving her because Valeria had been a big, big girl when she'd left home. She was now a pale little thing but what in the name of goodness had happened to her hair? The wild tufts of white-blonde hair stuck up every which way when she removed her cap. There was a story to be told there but not today. The poor girl looked on the verge of collapse.

'I'm fine, thank you,' Ria croaked. She was so nervous her mouth felt like the Sahara Desert. 'I'd love a cup of tea.'

'I'm guessing from your appearance that

you've run away from your husband.' Frank knew it was a crime to protect a woman from her husband. He'd never understood that — some men treated women badly. The young woman in front of him looked like she'd been living rough for a while. The boys' clothes she wore would deceive no one in his opinion.

'I had to. I'm never going back there.' Ria had never been inside this house before. Would she have to tell him about her life with her husband? She was so ashamed.

'Well, you're here now.' Frank made the tea. 'I hardly recognised you. You're a shadow of yourself, woman.' He could understand why she hadn't knocked next door. The Gibsons would send her back where she came from without ever asking for an explanation. But what was he going to do with her? He'd have to talk to Ivy.

'I know.' She smiled gently.

'You can stay here for tonight at least.' Frank looked around the room as if seeing it for the first time. 'That chair you're sitting on pulls out into a bed.' He gave a nod of his head. 'You'll need clothes. Can you sew — are you any good at fixing things up?'

'What kind of things?' Ria was overwhelmed that, simply, she could stay — no questions asked.

'Dresses and stuff?' Frank didn't know what women wore. 'Ivy Murphy always has a load of stuff to hand. If you can sew you should be able to get yourself all fixed up.'

'Ivy Murphy?' Ria was lost. What had the local beggar to do with anything?

'She and her husband rent the back rooms from me.' Frank didn't feel it was his place to explain the situation here. He pulled his table out from its storage space under Ria's fascinated eyes. The room reminded her a little of the narrow boat. Everything seemed to serve a dual purpose.

'Was that her child who opened the door? No, it can't be,' she answered her own question. 'I'd have met her before — she must be about nine.'

'You have a lot of catching up to do,' Frank said simply. 'Here — ' He passed her a cup and saucer. 'Drink your tea and I'll step down and tell Ivy what's going on.'

'Must you?' Ria was hoping to keep her presence here a secret. She didn't want her family next door to know she was in the neighbourhood. They hadn't seen her in years. Her enormous weight loss since they had last seen her would help disguise her — she hoped.

'You'll need her help.' Frank didn't know anyone better at dealing with the unexpected blows of life than Ivy Murphy Ryan. 'You can't go about the place looking like that.' He waved a hand at her outfit.

'It seemed safer to travel as a lad,' Ria offered simply.

'Perhaps it was,' Frank said, 'but it will never hold up in the light of day around here. You'll need to get yourself sorted for something to wear. And we'll need to come up with a story to explain a strange woman living with me. You can't have forgotten what this place is like for gossip.' He waited till she nodded before adding,

135

'Ivy will be able to help you with all that. She might be able to pass you off as one of her workers. If you keep that white hair hidden I don't think anyone around here will recognise you.'

★ ★ ★

Ria lay on her chair-bed later that night, still reeling from the events of the day. She had never expected Frank Wilson to open his home to her. She didn't know quite what she expected when she knocked on his door but his immense kindness was certainly not it.

Ivy Ryan was another surprise. The woman was nothing like the shadowy figure she'd seen creeping around The Lane for years. Ivy Ryan was beautiful. She'd welcomed Ria with kindness, helped her choose garments from a veritable mountain of fine clothing she had stashed in one of her rooms. The garments would have to be adjusted to fit but she could do that in no time. Ivy had offered her the use of one of her two sewing machines but Ria preferred to keep to herself for the moment. She'd do the alterations by hand. She'd have to be careful but she was feeling far more optimistic than she'd thought possible this time yesterday.

The whole day had been a series of unexpected events. The images ran behind her closed eyelids like a kaleidoscope. Jem Ryan a charming, handsome and smiling gentleman, so much in love with 'his girls' as he referred to Ivy and Emmy. He'd welcomed her into their home without question.

Ria turned over, punching the pillow under her head. She had been accepted into their company without question or problem. She had never expected anything of the sort. She'd thought she'd have to pour out her life story and had expected little sympathy. She'd been proved wrong in the most wonderful fashion. She couldn't believe her luck.

She wasn't foolish enough to believe she'd escaped her husband's vengeful clutches. She'd be very surprised if he hadn't visited next door to demand her return. And he'd come again. She wasn't going back. It didn't matter what she had to do to make a life for herself. She would never return to the nightmare that was her marriage. She'd have to take each day as it came. There was no point fretting about something that hadn't happened yet.

She sighed deeply. She felt safe — she hadn't felt safe for so long she'd forgotten the sensation. She might not know what her future would bring but for this moment in time she felt safe. She was deeply grateful to everyone in this house who had made her feel this way.

18

'This is nice.' Ivy strolled along Grafton Street, her arm linked through Jem's. They were returning from first Mass at St. Teresa's Church. The streets of Dublin were almost deserted at this early hour.

'Where's the time going?' Jem looked down at Ivy's smiling face. 'Can you believe we've been married almost a year? It doesn't seem possible.' He tightened his arm, bringing her in closer to his body. 'It's a beautiful day. Why don't we take a leisurely stroll through Stephen's Green?' He didn't want to return to The Lane just yet. It seemed they never had a moment of privacy there. Someone always wanted to speak to one or the other of them.

'We're an old married couple now.' She nudged him. 'It seems to me that I saw more of you when I was dashing by the livery with me pram and you standing in the livery door waiting to make me a cup of tea. You don't do that anymore.'

Ivy matched her steps to his. She caught a glimpse of their image in Woolworths shop window. She looked elegant if she did say so herself. Her beige cashmere coat with matching cloche hat always looked a treat. Jem in his beautifully tailored grey pinstripe suit, cashmere overcoat and trilby hat looked a proper toff.

'The only time we ever seem to get to

ourselves these days is in bed,' Jem remarked. 'But I don't want to be talking when I get there.'

'I enjoy what we do in our bed,' she whispered with a fiery blush. 'We seem to be getting better at it all the time.' She giggled and nudged him, delighted with her life.

'Now, now, Mrs Ryan, no need to descend into vulgarity on this the Lord's Day.' Jem's smile almost split his face.

They strolled through the park, admiring the spring flowers that pushed their heads up along the verge and through the green of the grass.

Ivy stepped away from Jem to admire the ducks on the pond.

'Come on, missus, let's be havin' yeh!' Jem offered his bent arm, trying to mimic a Dublin accent — his slight Sligo accent making music of the words.

His efforts had Ivy laughing aloud. 'Thank you, kind sir,' she simpered, slipping her arm through his.

They walked along the pathways, breathing deeply of the fresh air and without comment turning from the gate that would lead to their home. They whispered and smiled — happy just to be together. Jem raised his trilby hat to the few people they passed. Ivy smiled graciously. A handsome couple out enjoying the beauty of the day.

'What's going to happen to Ria?' Jem said when they at last turned in the direction of home. 'She can't keep hiding out in Frank's place.'

'I had a confidential word with Garda Collins.'

Ivy sighed. Their little escape from the everyday world was over. 'I gave him chapter and verse of the situation without naming names.' She stopped speaking, needing to calm herself — otherwise she'd be screaming like a madwoman.

Jem continued to walk slowly along. He knew his Ivy needed time. The Gibson woman's story was a shocker.

'The good Garda said there was nothing we could do about the matter.' Ivy looked at her feet while fighting tears. 'I'm not being fair to the man. Garda Collins was horrified but the law is the law. *Robert Hunter*,' she almost spat the name, 'owns his wife body and soul. He can turn up any day and drag her back. He can do what he likes to her — short of murder — and no one can interfere.'

'Anyone who comes between husband and wife is breaking the law.' Jem knew Ivy had been afraid to commit her life to him and that was one of the reasons she had dragged her feet about marrying him. 'If you or Frank are caught helping Valeria Gibson you could go to jail. You would be the ones at fault.' He didn't think his words would make a blind bit of difference.

'Frank had a word with Billy Flint,' Ivy whispered as they strolled through the wrought-iron gates of the park.

'There's a man who knows how to duck and dance around the law.'

'I'm surprised Robert Hunter hasn't turned up on next door's doorstep — unless, of course, he's already been — but we would surely have heard about it,' Ivy said. 'Ria spends hours watching and wondering. All we can do is wait and see, I suppose.'

'Do you want to go directly to Ann Marie's?' Jem asked. They had been invited there for lunch — William Armstrong and his wife were also invited.

'No.' Ivy wasn't as comfortable in that house since Ann Marie had hired an army of staff. She could no longer walk into the kitchen and demand a pot of tea. There was a butler to open the door these days if you wouldn't be minding. 'We'll go home and have a bite to eat.'

They hadn't stopped to eat before leaving the house — force of habit after years of fasting before receiving Holy Communion. They no longer received the sacrament — Ivy had insisted they be married in a registry office so the laws of the Catholic Church prevented them from doing so.

Jem turned them in the direction of the Stephen's Lane tunnel.

Ivy fought the shiver of dread that crawled along her back when they entered the tunnel. The memory of the Parish Priest's attack on her was never far from her mind when she used this entrance to The Lane.

'Come on then,' she said. 'I'll put the kettle on.'

* * *

'He's a clever bastard, I'll give him that.' William Armstrong was giving a verbal report of his

141

findings concerning Robert Hunter.

The three couples, after a delicious midday meal cooked by Ann Marie's new chef and served by what to Ivy was an obscene amount of staff, were sitting in Ann Marie's drawing room where they had opted to take their coffee. Emmy was spending the day at the carriage house with the Lawless family.

William and his wife Thelma sat on one of the three green Chesterfield two-seat sofas arranged around a coffee table placed in front of a roaring fire. Edward O'Connor sat with his arm around Ann Marie, his hand resting on her distended stomach, and Ivy and Jem were seated across from them. Valeria Gibson would be astonished to know the number of people trying to help her.

William tried not to fidget. He'd rather have a cigar and a stiff drink after his meal but his wife would murder him if he asked for permission to smoke, so to please her he'd have to suffer and sip coffee from a china cup.

'I sent a couple of my men to Kildare to look into the situation,' he continued.

He had everyone's attention. No one moved or spoke.

' 'The Squire' as the man is called locally, runs his estate in a manner I thought went out with crinoline dresses.' He looked at the two couples hanging on his every word. Ivy was practically falling out of her seat. He knew if she could she'd pull the words out of his mouth. 'If I embarrass you, ladies, I apologise in advance but I was asked to investigate and that's what I've done. The Squire treats the females on the estate like his own private harem. The estate is staffed by a great number of the old man's bastards. His legitimate son is following in his father's footsteps.' William was glad of his wife's silent support. 'He pays his workers in his own currency. The bloody bastard is printing his own money. It can only be spent in his own shops, of course.'

'What has that to do with Valeria Gibson?' Ivy asked while Jem and Edward cursed under their breaths.

'We now know that her husband is one of the old man's bastards.'

'So?' Ivy demanded.

'From what my men were able to discover, this Robert Hunter is cock of the walk on that estate. He runs the old man's very successful racing stables. He can do no wrong. A lovely man, according to everyone,' William hated to tell them the rest of it. 'Valeria is his third wife.' He sat back and waited while everyone exclaimed, shouted and demanded.

'What happened to the man's first two wives?' Edward's voice cut through the noise.

'Suicides.' William took his wife's hand.

'And no one thinks it strange that two young women should kill themselves rather than live with this man?' Jem had his arm around Ivy, holding her in place.

'The women were of a nervous disposition apparently — just like the latest one.'

'Dear Lord,' Ivy whispered. 'I know what Ria told us but somehow I couldn't bring myself to believe it. Has there been any mention made of

Ria's disappearance? Surely someone would have noticed.'

'One of my men did approach a fellow Ria mentioned. This Rowley, yet another bastard son, said the boy Stanley was fretting for Ria but seemed to understand he should keep his mouth shut about her disappearance. Stanley is the son's bastard. They use the letters of the alphabet to keep the by-blows sorted apparently. 'R' is the old man's get with 'S' being the son's — very efficient of them.'

'I find myself horrified but not surprised,' Edward O'Connor said softly. 'I am curious as to what this chap is telling people about his wife's disappearance. Do we believe he will just let the matter drop? I find that hard to believe.'

'We can't know what he'll do,' William said. 'I have someone keeping their eye on the situation. That is all we can do at the moment.'

'Meanwhile Ria is living in hiding,' Ivy sighed. 'She doesn't leave the house. I'm grateful for her assistance with my work. She is an extremely skilled seamstress but the stress of living in hiding is bound to tell on her. It's no way to live.'

They agreed to keep an eye on the situation but really — what could they do? They were all waiting for Robert Hunter to make his move.

19

'Oh Lord, what now?' Ivy pushed her pram through the tunnel leading from the Grand Canal. She was tired and hungry, and her feet were killing her. Wednesday was a long day for her. She travelled around Fitzwilliam Square without a break, returning home only when she'd completed her round.

Frank and Alison were standing in the open doorway. She could hear their shouting and see their fists waving. She recognised Ruby Slaughter as the woman standing in front of her door. What was the small-time con-woman doing around The Lane?

Where was everyone? It wasn't like her Jem to ignore trouble, and there were usually a few barefoot lads cluttering up the courtyard. Her feet almost without conscious thought began to speed up. Ruby was a decoy. She was about to break into a run when someone grabbed the handle of her pram. She turned with her fist in the air.

'Your Jem asked me to watch out for you,' Augustina Winthrop said.

'What the — '

'He said not to worry. He has everything in hand. He wants you to act naturally.' She took the pram firmly in hand. 'I'll deliver this to your back gate.'

'Thank you.' Ivy walked at a brisk pace

towards home. 'Ruby Slaughter!' she called when she was still a few doors away from her own. 'What brings you to my door?' She walked until she was almost toe to toe with Ruby, then took a hasty step back when she saw the wildlife crawling around the sweaty dirt-corroded creases in the woman's neck. Her stomach heaved. She hated fleas. She had to stop herself scratching — imagining the things jumping from one hot body to another.

'I heard you was paying people to dress dolls.' Ruby smirked up into Ivy's face. She wasn't a tall woman. It was hard to judge her figure since she seemed to wear her entire wardrobe on her back. 'That humpback bitch won't give me no dolls.' She jerked her head in Alison's direction, unseating fleas which fell onto her chest and began crawling around searching for a new perch.

'Pull the other one, Ruby.' Ivy's stomach roiled. She wanted to clap a hand to her mouth and run. 'It has bells on.'

'I ain't pullin' yer leg. I got to thinking — I could be dressing them dolls while I were sitting in front of me fire of an evening.'

'The only fire you sit in front of in the evening is the one in the pub.' Ivy was afraid to move her eyes away from the woman's face. Where was Jem? 'I don't want my dolls smelling of cigarette smoke, piss and beer, thank you very much.'

'Yeh stuck-up cow!' Ruby raised her fat fist. 'Who do you think you are, talkin' to me like that? Yer no better than the rest of us, Ivy Murphy, for all yer fancy new ways — people are

146

saying yeh smell yerself these days.'

Ruby's attitude changed at the sound of shouts and curses coming from behind the house. She formed her hands into claws and threw her body at Ivy, her black-encrusted nails ready to gouge her eyes. Ivy turned her back to the attack. She brought her boot down on the woman's foot and without pause clasped one hand over her wrist, using the additional force to drive her elbow into the woman's stomach. She had three brothers after all. She knew how to defend herself. She swung her body around and clipped Ruby's chin with her elbow.

Jem appeared around the side of the house, dragging a man trussed up in ropes, with some of his livery lads wrestling and pushing three ragged, cursing, tow-headed boys along in front of them.

'Yeh rotten cow — you've done me a mischief!' Ruby Slaughter had thrown herself to the ground, groaning and moaning.

By now the women of The Lane stood in the square like a gathering of black crows, some clutching saucepans, others holding rolling pins. They all had one thing in common. A willingness to wade in and administer a few well-placed blows.

'Has anyone telephoned the Garda?' Ivy asked.

'We don't call the feckin' Garda,' someone muttered.

'I do,' Ivy stated, confident that Jem would have already done so. 'This shower didn't come in here to steal what they could carry. Has

147

anyone looked for their wagon?'

'Oh, they were braver than that!' Conn Connelly appeared from the side of the livery, pushing a youth before him. 'This boyo was trying to steal a horse and cart.'

'That's a hanging offence.' Marcella Wiggins held her rolling pin over her shoulder. 'You ought to be ashamed of yourself, Ruby Slaughter, putting your lads up to something like this — stealing from honest people trying to make a living.'

'She won't miss it.' Ruby tried to catch her eldest boy's eyes to tell him to run. How had the stupid git got himself caught? 'That bitch,' she spat towards Ivy, 'is making money hand over fist — everyone knows it. I have me man and lads to feed. What would a fancy piece like her know about struggling to put food on the table and keep a roof over yer family's heads?'

'Oh now, Ruby Slaughter,' Marcella caught sight of Garda Collins and a few of his men coming up behind the crowd, 'don't come that with us. You know Ivy had the raising of her brothers. Her da, God rest him, was a hard man to keep. She kept them all for years when she was little more than a child herself. You know that, Ruby, and so does everyone here.'

'What's going on here?' Garda Barney Collins jerked his head at his men, silently ordering them to remain alert. He recognised Ruby and her family.

'This man,' Jem shook the man he held, 'and his sons tried to break into my wife's storage units out the back. He gestured to one of his lads who walked over to the Garda and passed over the holdall of tools he'd been keeping safe.

'How were they planning to get the swag away?' Garda Collins had a good idea of the contents of the sheds out behind the Ryan's home. They were stuffed to the rafters. He looked around, searching for a handcart. 'Riley,' he called one of his men, 'see if you can find a horse and cart waiting in one of the side streets.' His man ran off.

No one in the crowd mentioned the attempted theft of a horse and cart. The punishment for that serious a crime made a shiver run down their backs.

'Mr Ryan,' Garda Collins said, 'I'd like to use your phone to call the convict wagon.'

Ruby and her family started cursing and shouting at the mention of the name.

'I'll need you to come down to the station and lodge an official complaint, Mr Ryan,' Garda Collins said. 'And I'll need a list of witnesses.'

'No better man.' Jem put his arm around Ivy's shaking shoulders. 'My wife wasn't a witness to what happened here,' he told the Garda. 'Alison, will you take her inside?' He didn't like how she was looking — her normal healthy skin-tone looked waxen.

'Ali, grab me a clean skirt and blouse, please,' Ivy said as soon as the door closed at their backs. She was scratching frantically at her skin. 'That woman was lousy. I'm going to have a bath. I'll throw what I'm wearing into the bathtub when I've finished. I don't want any of that woman's livestock in my house.'

Ali hurried away. The women of Dublin fought a constant battle against vermin. She was sure she'd seen a bottle of sassafras oil in the cupboard. Ivy was going to need it.

★ ★ ★

Alison was filling the battered metal teapot with hot water from the black kettle when Ivy came into the kitchen. Her skin gleamed from the scrubbing she'd subjected herself to. Her hair was wet and she smelled strongly of sassafras oil. She'd changed into the dress Ali had left for her. She was trying desperately not to scratch at imagined itching. She practically fell into the chair at the head of the kitchen table.

'It really is my fault, you know,' Ali said when the two women were sitting facing each other.

'What is?' Ivy had her eyes closed.

'That woman being here.'

'Why?'

'This isn't the first time she's been here.' Ali was drowning in guilt. 'She came around a few times asking about dressing the dolls. I kept putting her off — saying I couldn't make that decision.'

'Always on a day I wasn't here?'

Ali had to think for a minute. 'Yes.'

'Ali, Ruby was casing the joint.'

'No!'

'Yes, she's a well-known con-woman.' Ivy sighed. 'She doesn't usually work this side of the Liffey. I wonder what made her think of trying her luck here?'

'I can answer that,' said Jem, coming into the kitchen. 'Are you all right, love?'

'I'm still a bit shaky.' She smiled into his concerned green eyes. 'What did you find out about that woman?'

Jem had a crew of young tough lads that kept their ears and eyes open and brought him information from around the city. 'How did she know that Mike wouldn't be here this afternoon?' Ivy asked.

Mike and his sister Úna had gone to a matinee at a local theatre. They had been asked to see and judge Liam and Vera's new routine with the dogs.

'It was partly loose lips at the pub,' Jem sighed. Some men seemed to tell everything they knew as soon as they had a pint in their hands. 'A man with a wife and daughters working for you told anyone who would listen to him at his pub about the grand little business Eamonn Murphy's daughter was running.'

'Me da.' Ivy left it at that — even dead, her da was causing her trouble.

'That's not all, love.' He hated to be the bearer of bad news but she needed to know. 'According to the young lad we caught in the livery, your Eamo has given them inside information for a cut of the take.'

'Why?' Ivy was reeling. Her mother and two brothers were supposedly living the high life. Why would he need to steal from her?

'I don't know, love.' He intended to find out.

'How did you know what was going on over here anyway?'

'The lads know to keep their eyes open.' Jem accepted a mug of tea from Ali. 'Ruby is a well-known figure. We've been extra careful since the first time she was seen around here. I had to wait until she did something before I could call the Garda.'

'Why didn't you tell me?' Ivy didn't like to be kept out of something that concerned her.

'What could I have told you, love?'

Ali watched them, envying them their closeness. She didn't ask why she hadn't been told. She knew — she'd have told Ivy.

'Well, this won't get the baby a bonnet.' Ivy pushed away from the table. 'You have work to do, Mr Ryan, and so do I. On yer bike!'

'Augustina Winthrop brought your pram around to the back garden.' Jem stood.

'Right, you be about your business and we'll be about ours.' She pressed a quick kiss into Jem's cheek and almost pushed him in front of her towards the kitchen door.

'Talk about here's your hat what's your hurry!' Jem said. His Ivy was back to her old self. 'I have to go down to Pearse Street Garda Station. I don't know how long I'll be.'

'I'll expect yeh when I see yeh so.' Ivy pressed another kiss to his cheek and shut the kitchen door. Turning, she rolled up her sleeves. 'Let's get that pram into one of the sheds,' she said to the waiting Ali. 'I got some stuff I think we can cut down for you. We need to empty the pram and take stock of what we've got. I want to see for myself what damage, if any, that shower did to my security.

152

Those locks were bloody expensive.'

'I'm that sorry, Ivy.'

'We'll hear no more about it, Ali. I'd have had a hard time myself knowing what bloody Ruby Slaughter was up to. Now, come on — we've work to do. Grab your ledger. Have you got your keys?'

'In the pocket in me knickers like you showed me, Ivy.' Ali had the large ledger in her arms. She'd shoved a bottle of ink into her pocket — the pen was behind her ear.

Ivy's four stone-built whitewashed outbuildings had heavy locks on the wooden doors. The back gate into the garden was always kept locked. It was as much as she could do to keep her stuff safe. She did not intend to put barbed wire and broken glass on top of the stone wall that ran behind the house. She refused to live in a prison. She'd keep her eyes and ears open. She hoped that calling the Garda to Ruby and her boys would put others off trying their luck.

'Start unlocking those doors, Ali, while I empty the pram.'

The two women got to work in a routine that was becoming familiar. Ivy sometimes wondered how she'd managed without Alison's help.

'Here, I meant to tell you.' Ivy was bent over the pram, examining each article she removed. She passed the items to Ali who put them away after making a note in her ledger. 'I was talking to a cobbler today.' She didn't mention that she had sought out the man. Alison was tiny. It was difficult for her to find any adult shoes that would fit. 'Ali,' she turned and took the other woman by the shoulders, 'he told me that all the cobblers make sample shoes in tiny sizes because it makes the shoes look more attractive.'

'So?'

'Don't you see?' Ivy gently shook Ali's shoulders. 'You'll be able to buy ladies' shoes in your own size. This cobbler fella said they sold off the sample shoes cheap. Ali Connelly, your shoes are going to be the envy of every woman in The Lane!'

'Ivy!' Ali lunged and pulled Ivy into a tight hug. 'Real shoes, with a heel — can you imagine!'

20

'I have a house clearance today.' Jem sat at the kitchen table, a mug of tea in his hand. He watched Ivy carefully. His Ivy was indomitable but the last few weeks would knock the stuffing out of anyone. 'I had a look around the house yesterday.' He'd checked on the number of wagonloads for removal.

He was gaining a reputation around Dublin as an honest man, which delighted him, so he was often offered the contents of a house for a bulk price. If the house had been well cared for, he purchased everything. They used Ivy's knowledge and contacts to sell the items on.

'Did you see anything interesting in the place?' Ivy was standing with her back to him, stirring a pot of porridge on the gas cooker. She'd soaked the oats overnight — to make them cook faster. She didn't stop stirring — porridge could stick to the pot if you weren't careful.

'The house belonged to a woman in her nineties.' Jem stood to refill his mug of tea. 'She was a customer of mine for years.'

The old lady would send a lad to the livery whenever she needed a horse and carriage. He'd miss her — she'd been a lovely old dear. She'd often stopped by the livery to share a cup of tea and some of her home cooking with him. The last few years she hadn't been able to get around. He'd taken to paying her a quick visit several times a week, just to be sure she was alright.

'The family want the house cleared for a quick sale.' A family that never visited were eager to know how much she was worth to them now. He wondered if they'd go to her funeral. He'd make the effort himself. The old dear deserved his respect. 'She kept her house like a little palace.'

'Where is this house?' Ivy poured the porridge into two blue-and-white willow-pattern china bowls before joining Jem at the table.

'The house is on Percy Place, directly across the canal from us.' Jem spooned the rich porridge into his mouth.

'One of those lovely old terrace houses.' Ivy sipped her tea. 'I've never been inside those houses. I'd love a look around.'

'You're welcome to come with me.' Jem hated to be the one to dismantle the home of a woman he'd admired. He'd be glad of Ivy's company. 'I could wait until you're ready to leave?'

'I've things to do here.' She looked around her. 'I'll walk over to join you when Alison gets here. I'll get her started on the day's work. I'll be easy in me mind then and can enjoy spending time looking around.'

★   ★   ★

'Ivy Murphy, I want a word in your ear.'

Ivy had answered the knock on the front door, expecting to find Alison waiting. She hadn't expected Mrs Wiggins to be with her.

The woman pushed Ivy out of the way and

156

strolled into the hall. She pushed her sleeves up which almost frightened Ivy to death. The matter was serious when Mrs Wiggins started pushing her sleeves up her arms.

Alison smiled apologetically in Ivy's direction and whispered 'Good morning' before disappearing into the kitchen.

'I won't be keeping yeh. We are both busy women.'

While Marcella Wiggins spoke, her eyes were examining the hallway. Ivy half expected her to whip out white gloves and do an inspection.

'As you know, I do three days at your friend Ann Marie's place,' said Marcella. 'Today's not one of me days so I have a few minutes spare. Wouldn't you think, with all the staff she has to hand now, one of them could do the laundry — but no — I'm still taking care of it. Still, mustn't grumble — it's money in me pocket.'

'What can I help you with, Mrs Wiggins?'

'I'll have a cup of tea. I'm sure Alison put the kettle on as soon as she went through the door to your place.'

Ivy led the way into her private rooms.

'I'm glad to see she has yeh well trained, Alison.' Marcella looked at the table set for three. 'What do I smell?' she sniffed the air.

'I've a batch of soda scones in the oven.' Ivy rolled her eyes at Alison. 'Sit yerself down — the first batch should be almost ready.'

'How are you enjoying working here, Alison?' Marcella watched the two women bustle around. She'd heard nothing but moans from Lily Connelly about her 'delicate' child working.

157

'I love it.'

'I must say, yer looking good on it.' She'd never seen Alison looking better. The pretty cotton dress in a floral print fitted her well. The pale-yellow cardigan she wore over the dress was lovely. Someone must have made the clothes specially. Well for some people.

'Sit down, Ali, you're in me way.' Ivy was taking two trays of beautifully browned scones from the gas oven. She closed the oven door with a pleased smile. She removed the hot scones from the trays, putting them onto a cooling rack she had ready. 'We'll let them cool for a minute.'

She took three side plates from the dresser and put them on the table with three knifes. Then she joined the women at the table and poured the tea.

'Ivy, you're a credit to aul' Granny Grunt.' Marcella's mouth was watering at the thought of a hot scone with butter.

'Thank you.' Ivy smiled to remember the old woman who had mentored her in household matters. 'That means a great deal to me.' She stood to tend to the scones. They would still be hot but the smell was making her stomach rumble. She filled a large plate with hot scones and placed it on the table, then checked to make sure there was butter and jam on the table before sitting back down.

'Now, young lady,' Marcella snatched up a scone — nodding her head in approval when it separated easily in her hands, 'I want you to tell me what's been going on over here. What has old Frank Wilson walking around the place like a

158

dog with two tails?'

'These are delicious, Ivy.' Alison almost closed her eyes at the lovely taste. She was also trying to spare her friend and employer from the inquisition.

Marcella slapped the table-top with the flat of her hand. 'Now, while we're enjoying these little delights, tell me what I want to know — and while you're about it tell me why Valeria Gibson is living in Frank Wilson's house.'

'What?' Ivy almost choked on her scone. 'How . . . '

'I thought she looked familiar. It took me a while to figure out who she was, mind. The girl has changed a lot since the last time I saw her. Shouldn't she be living next door? Frank has some explaining to do.'

Alison turned her head from one woman to another. It was never boring coming to work here.

'I thought you and Frank kept away from each other and fought all the time when you didn't?' Ivy was trying to delay answering.

'That's just to keep his blood flowing.' Marcella helped herself to another scone. 'I'm not moving until you tell me what's going on. That young woman has a husband as far as I'm aware. I haven't heard she's been made a widow.'

Ivy gave up. Mrs Wiggins would sit here all day until she had answers. 'Ali, will you go talk to Ria?' she said. 'Ask her to come down here if she feels up to it.'

She waited until the door closed behind Ali before she filled Mrs Wiggins in on all she'd learned about Ria's married life.

'I've seen the scars from the cuts and bruises. There doesn't seem to be an inch on her body that hasn't been marked. It's a wonder to me he never broke her bones.'

'Some men need hanging.'

'She's terrified to set foot outside the house,' Ivy said. 'I'm surprised you saw her.'

'I was passing one day when she opened the front door for Emmy. It was the white colour of her hair.' Marcella accepted another cup of tea. 'It put me in mind of times past if the truth be told.'

'Ria said she'll be down,' Ali came into the kitchen. 'She's nervous.'

'No need to be,' said Marcella. 'I've known the girl since she was born.'

'Hello, Mrs Wiggins.' Ria stepped into the kitchen, her heart trying to beat its way out of her chest. This woman's opinion counted to the people of The Lane.

'Name of Jesus!' Marcella jumped up from the table to take the trembling young woman in her arms. They swayed together for a moment before she pushed Ria away to examine her with eyes that missed nothing. 'You may have had a hard time of it. But you've improved in appearance. Dear God, you take me back. You're the very image of your father. Lord knows he was a good-looking man.'

Alison and Ivy exchanged glances, wondering if Mrs Wiggins was cracking. Ria looked nothing like the miserable sod who lived next door.

Ria too was confused. What did Mrs Wiggins

160

mean? Was — had something happened to her father? Surely Ivy or Frank would have told her.

'Why are you all looking at me like I lost me marbles?' Marcella was once more seated at the table, reaching for another scone.

'I don't understand, Mrs Wiggins.' Ria was being served tea and a scone by Ali. 'I look nothing like my father.'

'Nonsense!' Marcella snapped. 'You're the spit and image of him.'

'I can't see it myself,' Ivy said. 'Ria looks nothing like Mr Gibson.'

'Mr Gibson? That aul' streak of misery? Why should she look like him?' Marcella looked from one young woman to another. 'That man next door has nothing to do with Valeria.'

'*What!*' Ria could actually feel the blood rush from her head.

'Why are you all looking at me like that?' Marcella looked from one shocked face to another.

'Mrs Wiggins,' Ria's head was spinning — she was holding herself together with spit and nerves, 'I have no idea what you're talking about. That man next door — Gibson — is my father.'

'That man next door,' Marcella jerked her head in the direction of the attached house, 'isn't even named Gibson. I don't remember what he called himself when your mother first employed him to value her antiques — but it wasn't Gibson.'

'My mother employed him?' Ria's voice was little louder than a whisper as she tried to keep

161

her body from shaking apart. 'What about his mother?'

'What mother?' Marcella hadn't had much to do with the people next door for years. She'd been busy bringing up her family. She'd had no reason to worry about what the people in that house were getting up to. 'The woman who lives next door is some kind of poor relation of your mother's as far as I remember. It's her that's called Gibson.'

'I'm losing my mind.' Ria stared with eyes that almost bugged out of her head.

'*Frank!*' Marcella yelled loud enough to wake the dead. '*Frank Wilson, get your auld derriere in here!*'

'In the name of Jesus, woman . . . ' Frank stepped into the kitchen. 'Oh, scones!' His eyes lit up.

'Yeh aul' fool!' said Marcella — and with that Frank and Marcella started yelling at each other.

Ivy felt in need of a breath of fresh air. She stood and walked over to open the kitchen door that led to the back garden.

'*How could you not know that man wasn't her father?*' Marcella was screaming into Frank's face.

'*How was I supposed to know?*' Frank was roaring. '*I mind my own business unlike some people!*'

'*That fat aul' cow next door is Gloria Gibson. She was paid to look after the child when the mother disappeared. How could you not know that?*' The veins in Marcella's neck were standing out, she was roaring that loud.

'I don't understand!' Ria jumped to her feet and started screaming like a banshee. The shocking sound stopped all motion in the kitchen. She looked like a madwoman when she started shouting, '*I was practically a house prisoner while I was growing up! I wasn't allowed friends! They wouldn't let me breathe. They married me off to that monster. You're telling me now they have fuck all to do with me?*'

Ivy wondered if Jem could hear the shouting over at the livery.

Ria's screams had frightened Ali so much she'd stepped out into the back garden to use the outside WC. She rushed back indoors, waving her hands about.

'*Everyone be quiet!*' she shouted.

In the silence the noise from next door could be heard — two people shouting. Everyone rushed out to stand in the back garden and stare at the house next door.

'*Huey, we're in trouble! Huey, are you listening to me?*' A woman's voice could be clearly heard.

'*Don't come up here, old woman!*' a man shouted. '*I'm warning you!*'

'*Huey, come and help me!*'

After a pause, a sudden and loud scream came from next door then an awful *bump, bump, bump* sound before silence fell once more. The people in Ivy's garden stood as if frozen.

'That was someone falling down the stairs.' Frank was as white as a sheet.

'Ria, do you have a key to next door?' Ivy asked.

163

'No.'

'We can look in the letterbox!' Marcella shouted as she ran through the house, everyone else following on her heels.

21

'I can't see nothin'.' Marcella, bent at the waist, her rear in the air, was looking through the letterbox. 'The vestibule door is closed.' She stood upright. 'Frank, Ali, look in the windows.' She started beating her fist against the door, shouting, '*Hello!*' loudly.

'Name of God, Ivy, what's going on?' Jem had returned to see what was delaying her, as she'd said she'd join him. 'What's Ria doing outside?'

'Jem Ryan,' Marcella said, 'use that machine of yours to telephone down to Pearse Street Garda Station. There's something funny going on here.' She kept beating at the door as she spoke.

'Better do as she says, love.' Ivy gave him a gentle push in the direction of the livery. 'The world's gone to hell in a hand-basket around here — we need the Garda.'

'Ivy — '

'Just tell them we think there's been an accident and we can't get a response from our neighbours.' Ivy shrugged. 'That's true enough. You'll know the rest when I do.' She watched him hurry towards the livery before she turned back to stand waiting for a reaction from the house.

Nothing happened.

'Frank,' Ivy said suddenly. 'Maggie Frost cleans this house — wouldn't she need a key to get in?'

'Worth asking.' Frank turned to go back into his own home.

'I don't think we should go in before the Garda get here,' Marcella said.

'If we have a key they won't have to break down the door.' Ivy looked over to where Ali was almost physically holding Ria upright. 'Ginger!' she shouted to one of Jem's stable lads. The carrot-top lad was watching the proceedings along with a gathering crowd. 'Run into the livery and grab a few chairs. Get some of the other lads to help you.' It looked like they were going to be here for some time.

Frank returned, panting. 'Maggie's not at home.'

'What's happening?' Lily Connelly rushed up. 'Alison, are you all right?'

'What's going on?' Maisie Reynolds hurried up.

'Stand back!' Marcella stopped banging on the door, pushed the sleeves of her jumper up and prepared to take charge. 'We've sent for the Garda.' She enjoyed the crowd's loud inhale. She hadn't expected this much excitement this morning. 'We won't know nothin' until they get here.'

'Here, you,' Lily Connelly snapped at Valeria, 'stand on your own two feet — you're big enough. Can't you see my daughter is delicate?' She tried to force the tall young woman hanging onto her daughter away.

'Relax, Ma.' Conn appeared with Jem, carrying wooden chairs.

Conn lowered the woman his sister was

supporting onto a seat.

'The Garda are on their way.' Jem put the chairs he carried on the cobbles.

Ali sat down on the chair Conn had placed right beside Ria's. The woman looked like a ghost. She wasn't reacting to anything going on around her. She just sat like a statue, staring at the closed door of what had been her home.

People continued to gather. Children ran home to get their mothers. No one would want to miss anything that was newsworthy. John Lawless put his daughter Clare in charge of the livery switchboard and stood, a mug of tea in one hand, a heel of fresh-buttered bread in the other, leaning against the livery wall. He too wanted to know what was going on. He'd been the one to place the call to the Garda station. It was a bright beautiful April day but chilly yet — hard to believe it was almost Easter.

The crowd grew as everyone in The Lane became aware that something unusual was happening. Dozens of children were screaming and running around.

A short while later Garda Collins arrived. He'd been ordered to present himself at this location.

'What's going on here?' he demanded, looking at the crowd and the seated figures. He pointed at Marcella Wiggins. 'Mrs Wiggins, what seems to be the problem?'

'There are a lot of strange things going on here, I can tell you.' Marcella walked over to stand by the tall officer. She kept her voice low. 'The main one for the moment,' she straightened her shoulders, 'is this. I was next door,' she jerked her head in the direction of Ivy's home, 'having a cup of tea with a neighbour when we heard raised voices — then an unmerciful sound coming from this house here. It sounded like a body falling down the stairs. We ran out into the street and knocked on the door. We called through the letterbox. We heard nothing. So I told Jem Ryan to call the Garda.' Marcella stepped back, report given.

'Do we know who should be in the house this morning?' Garda Collins asked.

'That's more of the strange tale to tell.' Marcella held her tongue about the mystery of the Gibsons. Now was not the time. 'A man and a woman should be in the house. He wasn't seen leaving today and you can't miss the sound of that old putt-putt of his. The woman never leaves the house.'

'Do you know if they leave a key with a neighbour in case of emergency?'

'Maggie Frost what does for them might have a key but she's not home,' Marcella said.

'And there has been no sound since you heard what you believe was an accident?' Garda Collins looked at the door of the house. He hated to break it down but there might well be people inside needing medical attention.

'Not a whisper but it's hard to tell with the vestibule door closed.' Marcella stepped out of the way.

'Jem Ryan — just the man — do you have something I can use to break open this door?' the Garda asked.

The crowd pushed in closer, not wanting to miss anything.

'I need to telephone the station for more men.' Garda Collins stepped towards the livery. 'I'd appreciate it, Mrs Wiggins, if you would keep this crowd away from the premises.'

John Lawless pushed himself upright and prepared to escort the Garda to the telephone switchboard.

The Lane had never seen anything like it. Garda Collins forced open the front door of the house and opened the vestibule door. Whatever he saw then made him stand tall in the doorway and refuse to allow anyone else entry. He stood there until more Gardaí arrived. Then there was much running back and forth to use the livery telephone. Then an ambulance and men in brown overalls arrived. The crowd had to be forced back to allow the men entry. No one wanted to miss a thing.

The arrival of two men in suits had the crowd at fever pitch. Those were detectives, it was whispered.

Inside the house the two men stood staring down at the entwined figures at the foot of the stairs. The unnatural angle of each head and the blood covering the tiled floor clearly pointed to the cause of death.

'How in the name of God are we going to shift her?' one of the junior Gardai gasped. The woman was enormous.

Detective Woodworth ignored the remark. He'd had the same thought himself. 'Do we know who they are?' He looked at the scene. If that woman had had a firm grip on the tall thin man when she'd lost her footing he wouldn't have had a chance of breaking free. His eyes travelled over the selection of expensive jewellery that spilled and sparkled over the floor. 'Who has this beat?'

'That would be me — Garda Barney Collins.' He stepped forward. 'I can't say I recognise the pair.'

'Do we have someone who can identify them?' Detective Caldecott looked towards the crowd still gathering in the square. 'Who are those people sitting outside?'

'You — ' Woodworth pointed to a young Garda officer, 'keep everyone away from the bodies.' He jerked his head towards the door. 'Collins, if you can select someone from that crowd who might have information, ask them to step in.' He walked back down the hall, stopping to look into one of the rooms opening off it. 'There's a good fire going in here,' he said, stepping into the room. 'We can bring the witnesses in here for questioning.'

'Mrs Wiggins!' Garda Collins stuck his head out the damaged door and called for the woman. He knew she'd be close by. 'Would you step inside for a moment?'

Marcella entered the house and walked into the drawing room, thrilled to be asked inside but disappointed that Barney Collins blocked her view of whatever lay at the foot of the stairs.

She was introduced to the two detectives and asked to sit. She walked over to a large chair pulled up to the window and pointed. 'She sat in that chair morning noon and night. She never waved, never said a word, but you knew she was there — watching.' She turned away from the chair and walked over to take a seat in one of the dark-brown chairs on either side of the fireplace. A matching sofa was pushed against the wall.

'Mrs Wiggins,' Caldecott leant against the chimney breast and smiled down at the woman, 'Garda Collins believes you may be able to help us with our enquiries.'

'I'll do what I can.' Marcella listened to the bustle and whispers going on outside the closed door of the room. 'Can yez tell me what happened? I was next door and we heard shouting, then a fierce noise like someone falling.'

'It seems they both fell. I'm afraid they're both dead, Mrs Wiggins,' Woodworth said. 'I'm sorry. Were you close?'

'No one was close to that pair.' She nodded her head in emphasis. She wouldn't pretend a sorrow she didn't feel.

'We need names for our report.' Caldecott didn't like the feel of this house — something smelled off to him.

'Yez might want to sit down while I tell yez what I know.' Marcella's head was spinning with what she knew and all she'd learned this morning.

The three men exchanged glances before taking a seat. Barney Collins took the chair across the fire from Marcella at a nod from Caldecott. The two detectives pulled the sofa closer to the fire before sitting — notebooks and pencils in hand.

171

'I'd like yez to just listen to me story. I've more questions than answers for yez.'

'We just need names, Mrs Wiggins.' Woodworth wanted to get on with it. They fell down the stairs — they were dead — end of the matter as far as he was concerned.

'That's just it.' Marcella glared at the detective. 'I can give yez her name but I can't remember what that long streak of misery is called. He was known as Mr Gibson but that was her name, not his.'

'Mrs Wiggins — ' Woodworth sat forward and stared at the woman.

'Would you just hold yer whisht?' Marcella didn't want this to take any longer than it needed either — she'd things to do.

'Mrs Wiggins, why don't you tell us what you know in your own way?' Barney Collins tried to signal with his eyes to the two detectives to allow him to handle this interview. He knew Marcella Wiggins — she was no time-waster.

'Right.' Marcella dropped her head into her work-roughened hands. She had to get this all in order. She owed it to Marsha.

'I grew up with Marsha Callaghan.' She held up one hand when the detectives looked like interrupting. 'My, she was beautiful — inside and out. That mountain of fat out there,' she jerked her chin towards the hallway, 'her name is Gloria Gibson. She was some kind of poor relation of Marsha's and the woman was always sorry for her.' She sniffed. 'One of them that'd live in your ear in my opinion but Marsha wouldn't hear a word against her.'

172

'Gloria Gibson.' Woodworth wrote in his notebook. 'And how do you know Gibson was not the man's name?'

'Will you wait?' Marcella slapped the arm of the chair. 'Yez need to know this and I don't know how to tell it any other way but me own. So whisht up for God's sake or we'll be here all day.'

Barney Collins bit back a smile. 'Go on, Mrs Wiggins — in your own way.'

'Marsha could have had any man she wanted.' Marcella was lost in visions of the past. 'She didn't run out to marry the first man who asked her. She waited and then she met Nat — he was Swedish — he had some kind of important job going back and forth to Sweden. He was on his way to visit his family when his ship went down — all aboard were lost.' She shook her head sadly, forcing her mind back to the matter at hand. 'But before that — I was married with young children around me feet when he bought this house for his wife.' She dropped her head into her chest.

Barney Collins waved the detectives to silence. The woman wasn't finished.

'I was that jealous,' Marcella whispered. 'I was a young woman without a pot to piss in and here was my friend being given a big fancy house. Marsha was going up in the world while I could hardly make ends meet. I kept out of her road when she moved into this house. May God forgive me.' She looked up with tears flowing down her face and stated with conviction, 'I think that pair out there murdered

173

Marsha and hid the body.'

'That's a serious accusation.' Caldecott wasn't surprised. He'd felt from the moment he'd stepped into this house that it hid secrets. His gut feeling might be a joke down at the station but it hadn't let him down yet.

'Yez will need to talk to Ria.'

'Who is Ria?' Caldecott was taking notes as he asked.

'Marsha's daughter.'

'The young woman with the white hair sitting outside,' said Barney Collins as he stood up, planning to fetch her.

'The poor love knows less than I do.' Marcella's words stopped Barney in his tracks. 'I only found out this morning that she thought that pair were her father and grandmother. She's been lied to all of her life. You see — Marsha disappeared — oh, years ago now. I asked and was told she'd left to travel after hearing of her husband's death. It struck me as strange at the time. But I'd a baby under me feet and another on the way and Dublin was in such a state — what with the British and all. I let it go — God forgive me — I let it go.'

Caldecott ignored the woman's comments for the moment. 'Was it usual to hear loud noises from this house?'

'You'd have to ask someone else,' Marcella said. 'I live across the way. I was visiting the neighbours next door when we all heard the noise in here.' She waited to see if they would ask anything else. 'Can I go now?' she asked when they remained silent, looking at one another. 'I'm only across the way. Garda Collins knows how to get me.'

'I'll walk you out.' Barney Collins led the woman from the room while the two detectives returned to the dead.

22

'Right.' Barney Collins hadn't removed his uniform hat, wanting everyone to realise this was an official occasion. He stood in the middle of Ivy's kitchen, notebook and pencil in hand. He had chosen the location with Ivy's permission, wanting to ask his questions out of the way of the team searching for answers in the house next door.

He'd asked Ivy, Jem, Ria, Frank, Marcella and the recently returned Maggie Frost to join him. He hoped one of them at least would be able to shine some kind of light on the happenings next door. His super would have his head for conducting interviews concerning two unexplained deaths in a kitchen. He didn't care. It was more efficient and gave them a degree of privacy away from the crowds still gathered around the two houses.

The medical people and the detectives could deal with the bodies. He had men on guard duty. There was little more he could do there. The kitchen he stood in held a group of people he considered persons of interest.

'Mrs Frost, is it?' he asked the dark-haired, dark-eyed woman who sat shivering in a chair pulled up to the kitchen table.

'Sit up there.' Marcella patted the woman's back. She was delighted to be part of this group. She could rest and gather her thoughts later.

'There's nothing to worry about.'

'I believe you are home help to the people next door?' Barney asked.

'That's right.' Maggie Frost sat up straight and looked at the officer. 'I go in every day to check on her. I was there this morning to light the fires and serve breakfast. I do the shopping and the cooking. I give the place a clean three times a week. They was both fine when I left for my next job.' She spoke her piece so quickly she was breathless.

'Jesus, Maggie, yeh said all of that so fast I was breathing for yeh!' Marcella pressed a hand to her chest.

'And you live at this address?' Barney continued, biting back a smile. You couldn't keep these people down.

'I rent rooms upstairs for me and me boys.' Maggie nodded her head frantically.

'It appears you are the person most familiar with the people next door.' He waited a moment to see if anyone would contradict him. 'I wonder if you could give me an idea of the kind of people they were?'

'They was strange. That's the best way I can put it and I don't think anyone here would disagree with me.' She had a cleaning job waiting but she didn't think old Mrs MacGuinness would mind when she told her the reason she was delayed. 'He lived upstairs. He has all kinds of weird objects sitting around the place. I were never allowed touch those. I just passed a duster from time to time. I swept and washed the upstairs hall and stairs — he'd allow me to do that. She lived downstairs. I never saw her go up those stairs although to be truthful I never saw her move at all. Only . . . ' Maggie was beginning to enjoy having everyone hanging on her words.

'Yes?' Barney Collins encouraged the woman.

'I heard how she was supposed to be his mother,' she looked around the kitchen table at the familiar faces, 'only she didn't look that old to me. Not old enough to be his mother any road. She were fat — liked to boast she were built like the old queen — you know, Victoria — bigger around than she was tall. That might have made her look old but she were never his mother.'

'Did you ever hear the woman call him by a different name?' Barney asked.

'No. I can't say as I have. I always called him Mr Gibson,' Maggie said. 'He never told me any different.'

'When you went into that house this morning did anything strike you as different?'

'It was the same as usual — her in her chair — him upstairs. They only talked to me to tell me what to do. They were never exactly chatty.'

'I see.' Barney thought he'd got all he could from her for the moment. 'I know you have a job to go to, Mrs Frost. I'll know where to find you if I need more information.'

They all watched the woman leave the room.

'Right.' Barney removed his hat. 'Put the kettle on, Ivy Mur — sorry, Mrs Ryan.' He took a seat at the table. 'Now which of you is going to tell me the rest of the story?' He looked at Jem.

'No point asking me.' Jem held his hands in the air. 'I'm a newcomer to the party.' He'd left

178

John Lawless in charge at the livery. He thanked God that his house clearance this morning had been cancelled. Mind you — he mightn't have some back if he'd known he'd be returning to this mess!

'Mrs Wiggins,' Ivy said as she filled her largest teapot, 'you should be the one to tell Garda Collins what went on here this morning.' She was glad Ali and Mike were in the sheds outside, taking care of business. This was one of the busiest times of the year for her second-hand goods. Everyone wanted to look their best at Easter.

Ria was sitting like a ghost in one of the soft chairs pulled close to the range. She didn't seem to be taking anything in of the fuss going on around her.

Barney Collins listened, taking copious notes as Mrs Wiggins gave him the details of what they had discovered that morning. He shook his head several times. Then sat back and stared at the people around the table.

'And you say you never knew they weren't your relations?' he asked Ria who had remained silent through the story. He had never seen her before to his knowledge but he must know her if she'd lived in The Lane. This was his beat but her face brought nothing to mind.

'Ria,' Ivy gently shook her arm, 'the man's talking to you.'

Barney repeated his question.

'No,' Ria answered. She felt as if she was floating above the room. She could hardly grasp a thought.

179

'Well,' Barney Collins said, 'this is above my pay grade. We'll have that cup of tea now, Mrs Ryan — and I wouldn't mind one of those scones if there is one going a-beggin'.'

He settled in to enjoy a cup of tea while the people around him muttered and wondered. He added nothing to the conversation but took careful mental note of anything that might help him with his enquiries. He'd have to inform the detectives of anything he discovered here.

★ ★ ★

'Where are the detectives?' Barney stepped into the organised chaos of the house next door.

'One of your lads ran in here,' a medical technician said from his place on the floor. 'They all ran off that way.' He pointed towards the rear of the building.

'Thanks.' Barney made his way to the back garden.

He found the detectives standing with their hands in their suit pockets in one of the garden sheds.

'What's going on?' he asked.

'Your men found this shed with a brand-new lock on the door but otherwise empty,' Caldecott said. 'Seems strange.'

Two young Garda had removed their uniform jackets and were carefully shovelling and shifting through the shed-floor dirt.

'*Stop!*' Barney shouted when he saw the first bones appear.

'Oh shit!' Caldecott cursed under his breath.

He'd seen enough human remains to know what he was looking at.

Woodworth left to get the medical officers.

'We were just going to call you in, Barney,' said Caldecott. 'There are a great many valuable objects stashed upstairs. They need to be checked against stolen and missing items.'

The technicians arrived and the three policemen stood silently watching while the body was exposed.

'I can't say for certain until I have the bones in my lab,' one of the technicians said, 'but judging by the pelvic bones and the items of clothing and jewellery I'd say this was a female. The back of the head has been bashed in.' He stood away from the grave. 'Whoever did this was bloody coldblooded — to bury the body in one of his own garden sheds, for God's sake!'

'If that's who I think it is,' Barney said, 'it's actually her garden shed.'

'You think it's this Marsha woman?' Caldecott asked.

Barney nodded.

'Remove that ring,' Caldecott instructed one of the digging Garda who bent and respectfully removed one of the dirt-encrusted rings from a fingerbone.

Caldecott pulled an evidence bag from his pocket and held it open while the ring was dropped inside. 'If someone recognises this, it will speed up the paperwork.' He turned the object over inside the bag. 'I'm no judge of jewels but it looks expensive.'

Barney noticed a barefoot lad jump down

181

from the top of the wall that ran along the back garden, into the lane outside. 'If I'm right about the identity of the remains, that woman's daughter is right next door. She shouldn't find out about her mother's murder from gossip.' He gestured towards the back gate. 'We'll take the back way — I've no doubt there's quite the crowd gathered out front.'

The three men stepped out the gate that led into the lane running along this row of houses. They turned in the direction of Ivy's home — stopping in shock when they saw the crowd of women gathered outside Ivy's garden gate.

Barney took control, practically pushing the two detectives in front of him. He ignored the questions shouted out from the crowd. He led the way through the gate and up the garden to the back door. He was glad to see Jem Ryan answer his knock. The men stepped inside at his invitation.

The three men stood almost to attention as Caldecott told Ria of the grisly discovery next door. They warned her it was too early to tell if the remains truly belonged to her mother but they thought it best she be prepared for the worst.

'I feel like my life has become a penny dreadful story.' Ria stared at the three men before dropping her aching head into her hands.

'Mrs Wiggins,' Barney gave Woodworth a nod, 'do you recognise this?' He watched the detective hold the evidence bag out to the woman.

Mrs Wiggins sobbed and pressed a shaking hand to her mouth. She nodded her head. 'It's

Marsha's — she wore it always. Her husband had it made for her. She always said it was unique.'

'Something of my mother's!' Ria reached for the bag.

'I'm sorry, miss, it's evidence — it will be returned to you at a later date.' Woodworth returned the bag to his pocket.

'The house next door is a crime scene, miss,' Caldecott put in. 'Do you have somewhere to stay? Is there anything you need from there?'

'I haven't lived there for years,' Ria said. 'I'm staying here — with friends — for the moment.'

'You will need to make yourself available for questioning,' Woodworth said to her bowed head.

'Officer,' Ria raised a ghostly white face, 'I'll make myself available but at this moment in time I know nothing.'

There was silence in the kitchen when the three officers of the law left. Nobody knew what to do — what to say.

'I'm going to take Ria into my place.' Frank stood as he spoke. 'Marcella, have you time to come in with us?'

'Of course I'll come,' Marcella stood like an old woman. This day had been a series of shocks.

'I have to get across to the livery.' Jem stood away from the table.

'I've work of me own to be getting on with.' Ivy would be glad to have her home to herself. She wasn't feeling the best. She really should go out and help Ali in the back garden but she wanted to sit in front of her range and close her eyes for five minutes.

23

'Ivy,' Ali's voice and the gentle shake she gave to her shoulder woke Ivy up. She couldn't believe she'd been that deeply asleep.

'Here.' Ali passed her a cup of tea. 'You look like you need it.' She'd already carried a mug of tea and a few scones out to her brother Mike who was working in the garden sheds. Ivy had slept through her comings and goings.

'I've made and wasted more tea today than ever before in my life,' Ivy said with a yawn.

'I've got the gist of what's been going on.' Ali dropped into the chair across the range from Ivy's. 'Me and Mike got to hear all about it. The women coming to pick up their goods at the back gate could talk of little else. Mike's outside putting a bit of order on the place. We've been really busy what with one thing and another.'

'What did I ever do without you, Ali?' Ivy gulped her tea. 'I'm having a hard time believing that the pair next door were hardened criminals. It beggars belief.'

'Poor Ria,' Ali said softly. 'It must all be so much of a shock to her. Imagine not knowing who you are!'

'I can think of some that would be a blessing for.' Ivy didn't want to discuss the horrors of the day. There was nothing she could do about the situation and she had her own life to run. 'Did you sell much today?'

'A lot of the jumpers and boys' shorts we had on hand have sold.' Ali leaned over to get the teapot. She'd left it and the milk close to hand. She'd never seen anyone drink tea like Ivy. She poured a fresh cup. 'Some women came by to finish off paying for the wool they'd put by.'

'They'll have their work cut out for them getting jumpers knit up by next week.'

There was a soft rap on the kitchen door. 'May I come in?' Ria appeared in the slowly opening door. 'I have the dresses you gave me to alter almost finished, Ivy.' She stepped into the room, her arms full of folded clothing. 'I only need to do a little hand-stitching.' She walked in and closed the door. 'Frank has gone down for a nap and Mrs Wiggins has gone home to lie down. Today really took it out of them.' She stood, holding the articles, and waited.

Ivy pushed to her feet. Ria had never asked to join them before. She probably wanted to get away from her own thoughts. 'I'll pour you a cup of tea.'

'I'd better get back outside and give Mike a hand.' Ali stood and with a shy smile left the room.

'I seem to have invaded your life with my problems, Ivy,' Ria said.

'Not to worry.' Ivy took the cups of tea over to the kitchen table. If she sat back down in those soft chairs she'd fall asleep again. She was exhausted. 'Sit down, Ria. Today has been one shock after another for you.'

'I don't know if I'm on my head or my heels.'

'The way I look at it,' Ivy sipped her tea, 'you

185

can collapse under all of the shocks you got today — or, you can give yourself a kick in the backside and start planning your new life.'

'I feel as if I've lost my mother all over again.'

'No, you got a present.' She leaned over to touch Ria's hands gently. 'You found out your mother didn't desert you — didn't leave you at the mercy of those two.' She jerked her head in the direction of next door. 'Your mother was taken from you. She loved you and wouldn't have left willingly, from what we learned today. You should try to think of that knowledge as a present. Take it from someone who knows.'

Ria would think about what Ivy had said later. There were many things to think about. She would have to consult a lawyer about her marriage. She was not going to hide away. It was past time to take control for her own life into her own hands.

'Don't mind me.' Ali stepped into the kitchen with a bulging leather bag.

Ali needed to get the money she'd taken for the sale of articles to the women outside stashed away somewhere safe. She hurried into the room they used as a workroom and stashed the shining coins away in a metal file-drawer. She'd count it later before taking it to the night safe at the bank.

'I was just thinking,' she said as she stepped back into the kitchen, 'do you own the house next door now, Ria?' She couldn't imagine the luxury of having a house to call your own.

'I don't know. Maybe I do.'

'Oh, that would be wonderful,' said Ali as she

sat down. 'If I had a house of my own I'd never leave it — I'd find it hard even to step outside the door!'

'I don't feel like that,' said Ria. 'If the house is mine I don't think I'd want to stay there all the time. I've always dreamed about travelling.'

'What?' Ivy said. 'Like my brothers? Leave home and never look back?'

'No,' Ria said slowly. 'I always dreamed of travelling — seeing the places I've read about — hearing the music I've dreamed about.' She was enjoying this time sitting and chatting with other women. She'd never done this before. 'I'd like to see Paris, Rome, Vienna and then return home to plan the next adventure. I'd like to be able to leave my treasures in a place that was my own. Oh, I'm just thinking out loud!'

'Maybe you're not.' Ivy shrugged. 'Maybe you'll be able to make your dreams come true.'

Ali listened to the others talking. What did she dream about? What did she want to do with her life?

'Well, at least sitting here talking about my dreams with you two is keeping my mind off my problems.' Ria smiled. 'At times I feel full of the joys of spring for some reason and then I think about my poor mother and feel guilty.'

'You shouldn't,' Ali said without thinking.

'Give yerself a kick in the arse,' Ivy added.

'I want to go shopping for new clothes.' Ria had told Ivy and Frank about her gold sovereigns. She'd insisted on giving them one each for her keep. 'I mean no insult to the clothes you've given me, Ivy.'

187

'No insult taken — but if you want to go shopping for fancy clothes it's my friend Ann Marie you need to talk to — she knows the best shops around Dublin.'

'Ann Marie's in the family way, Ivy,' Ali reminded her.

'Doesn't stop the woman being a devil around the shops.' Ivy grinned. 'She'd enjoy herself showing Ria around.'

'*Ali, any chance of you coming out here to give us a hand?*' a male voice shouted from the back garden.

'Oops!' Ali jumped to her feet and spun away. 'I forgot all about me brother Mike. He'll kill me.' She almost ran from the room.

'Am I keeping you from your work, Ivy?' Ria didn't want to get in the way.

'I'm being lazy, truth be told.' Ivy didn't want to go outside and face the crowd of women who would want to know every detail of what was going on. They would expect her to have inside information. She really didn't feel up to facing that. 'Having Alison on hand is a luxury I truly enjoy. I feel guilty sometimes — then I look at her smiling face and kick myself in the arse.'

'I don't think I've met Mike,' Ria said after a while.

Ivy stood to fetch more tea. They'd been sitting with empty cups in front of them for long enough. 'There's a whole shower of Connellys and every one a clever, bright individual. Lily Connelly can be proud of the children she's raised.'

'Thanks.' Ria accepted the tea. 'It's lovely to

sit and talk but I wanted to finish off those dresses I brought in.'

'Oh, you can do that later. Drink your tea and relax now.'

'I love the way you've added lace around the collar and cuffs to give the dresses a bit of a lift,' Ria said.

'I used to make the lace meself,' Ivy said. 'I buy it on a roll now. I don't think it looks as pretty but it's a lot less work for me and I know what to charge for the finished garment.'

'You certainly seem to have a good business going.' Ria sipped her tea. 'I never knew there was so much involved. I palled around with your Eamo for a while, you know. He never mentioned how busy you always are.'

'Eamo was never very interested in work.' Ivy didn't know if she should mention that Eamo was back in Dublin. 'He was more interested in the money it brought. He was quick to put his hand out for that.'

'I always thought you only made coppers.' Ria had listened to Eamo moan about his lot in life. She'd never heard him speak a word of praise of his sister. She wondered why.

'I supported four men with the money I made from me round.' Ivy had never really known how much money she took in on a given day. Her da had always been there to remove every copper coin from her hand when she stepped in the door. It had come as a shock to her to find, after his death, that her round was a nice little earner.

'Frank tells me you sell dressed dolls too.' Ria had been astonished when Frank told her of the many business ventures this woman had going. 'And he said you sell his dollhouses too. They're beautiful.'

'Frank is an artist.' Ivy laughed. 'He blushes when I call him that. What the man can produce from bits of wood he picks up down the docks is a marvel to me.'

The two women sat and chatted while the noise of Ivy's business went on outdoors. The police investigation was well underway in the house next door but neither woman mentioned it. Today had been a day of shocks and discoveries. The two women were escaping from the reality of the life going on around them. It wouldn't last but, while it did, they were determined to enjoy it.

24

'Does your husband know you have absconded with his horse?' a gentle cultured voice asked. 'They hang horse thieves, you know.'

'Mrs Winthrop!' Ivy grinned at the tall raw-boned woman standing on the path. The steel-grey colour of the woman's long dress matched the hair pulled back in a headache-inducing bun. She presented a severe figure but the smile on her face gave the lie to her appearance. 'I'm only borrowing Rosie.' She curled her bare toes in the grass verge.

'It is such a wonderful day — full of the promise of summer — I can see why you'd be tempted to play truant.' Augustina Winthrop enjoyed the picture Ivy presented. The dark-haired, violet-eyed beauty in her black skirt and beautifully embroidered white cashmere jumper, leading the black horse, backlit by the gently travelling water of the Grand Canal, was a vision of loveliness.

'Have you been to see Ann Marie?' Ivy's eyes travelled to the house sitting in its own grounds across the canal.

'I have indeed,' Augustina smiled. 'Mother and baby are doing very well.' She'd been surprised by the lady, expecting a bedridden attention-demanding whiner. She'd instead been presented with a dynamic female with no intention of taking to her bed. She'd been ashamed of her own assumption. 'Sending young Catherine to her was inspired thinking, Ivy.' She'd delivered Catherine O'Malley and several of her siblings.

'Catherine seems to be settling in well.' Ivy pulled Rosie off the towpath to allow a horse pulling a barge to pass. She waved to the people on board while Rosie calmly ate the daisy-dotted green grass.

'She's a very pleasant young girl and seems willing to learn.' Augustina decided to enjoy the day. A young lad would be sent running for her if she was needed. She took a large linen handkerchief from her pocket and covered the top of a dusty granite block standing upright in the grass with it before sitting.

With the horse on a long lead-rein Ivy sat on the grass beside the block. Both women stared at the water of the canal.

'You've been married almost a year, Ivy,' Augustina said carefully. 'Are you concerned that you're not with child?'

Ivy raised her eyes and stared into the older woman's pale-brown eyes. 'Not in the least.'

'I've known you since you were a small child, Ivy.' Augustina was feeling her way. 'I delivered you and your brothers.' She took a deep breath, ashamed at her own cowardice. 'Ivy, it's providential that I have met you today. You see, I have not only been to see Ann Marie. Father Leary demanded to see me.'

Ivy shrugged. 'Rather you than me.'

'Don't make light of this, Ivy.' Augustina put a blue-veined hand on Ivy's shoulder and shook it gently. She had no liking for the Parish Priest but had sense enough to know the man was dangerous — a rabid animal. 'I was questioned about ways you might be doing the devil's work in preventing conception.'

'Jesus!' Ivy prayed. 'Wouldn't you think, with all the work the man has to do as Parish Priest, he'd have better things to do with his time?'

'I don't know how to put into words what I observed today.' Augustina had been terrified. The man was unhealthily fixated on Ivy just as he'd been on her mother. It wasn't as a man of God he'd questioned her — the mere mention of Ivy had brought an increase in his breathing — he'd been visibly sweating. 'Father Leary said his parishioner Mrs Purcell had brought her concerns to him.'

'Honest to God,' Ivy dropped her head to her bent knees, 'with all the suffering and want in the world, wouldn't you think the pair of them would have something better to do?'

'We shouldn't be seen chatting on friendly terms.' Augustina stood. She removed her handkerchief from the block, shaking it vigorously before returning it to her pocket. 'I'm not brave, Ivy. I wish I were.' She had read about the women fighting for women's liberty. She corresponded with public figures supporting what they called birth control. She sent money but never dared to express her opinions aloud. She could not face public persecution as those brave women did. Just then she saw a familiar figure strolling from The Lane. 'I believe your husband wants his horse back.' She laughed and walked on.

She greeted Jem politely as she passed him.

She'd done everything she could for the moment. But she would keep watch. Ivy Murphy held out the hand of help to others without spouting religious fervour all around. She'd been a blessing to Augustina's friend and mentor Granny Grunt. In the old woman's memory, Augustina would watch over Ivy.

'Mrs Ryan, you've stolen my horse again.' Jem stepped onto the grass verge and dropped onto the grass beside Ivy. He had to take a moment to push Rosie's big head out of his face. The horse was demanding her own share of attention.

'She gets bored standing in her stall all day.' Ivy dropped her head to Jem's shoulder for a moment. She'd discuss what Mrs Winthrop had mentioned but not now. It was a beautiful day and she refused to spoil it. 'Want to go for a walk with me?'

'I'll feel a right eejit taking a horse for a walk.' Jem jumped to his feet and held out his hand. 'Where's your shoes?' He looked around the grass.

'In the house where they belong.' Ivy allowed Jem to pull her to her feet. 'I wanted to feel the earth under my feet.'

She walked on with her man and his horse. She took a deep breath of the refreshing air. She wouldn't borrow trouble. It would find her soon enough.

★ ★ ★

Augustina Winthrop's house was only steps from the tunnel leading from the Grand Canal. She was inside her own home now and still thinking of Ivy. She looked around the house that had been her home all of her life. She tried to help the women in her care. There were times when she was discouraged as she welcomed babies into a miserable existence. How many times had she wished she had someone to discuss her hopes and sorrows with? It seemed to her she'd been a coward all her life. Her mother and two older sisters had died in childbed. They were too narrow for easy births. She'd studied and learned all she could so she could help other women. She hadn't dared marry herself. She had no wish to die young.

'Oh, stop feeling sorry for yourself and put the kettle on, you old fool!'

Apart from the knocking on the front door when someone needed her service, her voice was the only sound ever heard in this house. She had briefly thought of asking Frank Wilson about changing the house from a private home to a boarding house, as he had done. The thought of strangers underfoot was not something she could countenance, however.

'There is only one way to fight the might of the Catholic Church.' Augustina was still fretting about Ivy. 'Money.'

★   ★   ★

'Ivy, are you about?'

The cultured voice of Ann Marie broke into Ivy's dreams.

'There's no rest for the wicked, it seems.' Ivy

had just put her head down for a nap. She'd been tired after her morning out in the fresh air. She didn't feel refreshed. What time was it?

'*I'm coming!*' she yelled.

She didn't want anyone coming in here and seeing the state of the place. She'd be the talk of the wash house — nothing worse than a dirty housekeeper.

'*Someone put the kettle on! I'm spitting feathers!*'

'*When are you not?*' Ann Marie shouted back.

'Good morning.' Ivy — bootlaces flapping, yawning hugely — entered the kitchen from her bedroom.

'It's closer to evening.' Ann Marie, pregnant belly pushed proudly out from her body, sat at the kitchen table while her companion Catherine O'Malley took care of making tea.

'What are you two doing here?' Ivy didn't have to be polite. She hadn't been expecting them.

'Gracious as always.' Ann Marie smirked.

'I haven't had a cup of tea yet, madam, so you be careful how you talk to me.' Ivy almost collapsed into the chair across the table from Ann Marie. She knew she could rely on Catherine to make a decent pot of tea. 'Seriously, what brings you here?' Thank God for Ali and Mike. The place was shining and she could hear the brother and sister talking outside.

'I was dropping off rolls of film to Milo.' The street photographer was training Ann Marie in the use of her camera. 'He has agreed to develop my photographs while I'm in this 'interesting condition' as my aunt refers to it.' She patted her bump gently.

'Ivy,' Catherine said, 'I was wondering if you'd got any more frocks?' She put a cup of tea on the table in front of Ivy.

'I have, as a matter of fact.' Ivy turned her attention to Sadie's niece. The change in the young girl was astonishing. She examined the drop-waist dress she'd sold to Catherine. 'I must say, someone's done a marvellous job of altering that dress.' She stood to examine the stitching in the flower-printed cotton dress she'd received on her rounds.

'I did it meself — me Aunty Sadie is teaching me to knit and sew.' Catherine was proud of her efforts. She didn't mind turning around and letting Ivy have a good look at her work.

'I have more dresses — you'll have to give me time to root them out though,' Ivy said. 'In the meantime, why don't you take tea and a few biscuits outside to Ali and Mike — stay and visit for a while?'

'I'll do that right now.' Catherine wanted to see that Mike Connelly. She thought he was gorgeous. 'I'll ask Ali about a dress while I'm there, will I?'

'You do that,' Ivy said.

'Very smoothly done, Mrs Ryan,' Ann Marie said with a grimace as she sipped at the ever-present tea.

'I want to know how things are going with you. We haven't been able to have a decent talk for ages.'

'I'm doing very well,' Ann Marie said. 'Edward

197

is a nervous wreck and if I listened to him I'd be a semi-invalid.'

'How is Catherine working out?' They really hadn't had a chance to gossip lately.

'The girl is a work in progress.' Ann Marie said. 'She has an incredible amount of knowledge on some things but is completely ignorant of others.' She ignored the tea in front of her and watched Ivy jump to refill her own cup. 'Having Catherine around at this time is ideal. If I have worries she will invariably have some wise-woman advice for me — and my efforts to improve her lot in life takes my mind off my own situation.'

'Are you worried?' Ivy returned to the table and stared at her friend.

'No, in fact I'm quite excited. But it's difficult for me watching Edward fret and worry. The poor man is terrified I'm going to die in childbed like his first wife.'

'There's not much we can do to help, I'm afraid.'

Ann Marie started laughing. She laughed so much tears came to her eyes, steaming up her gold-rimmed glasses. She reached into the deep pocket of her navy-silk dress to remove her lace-trimmed handkerchief. 'Oh dear,' she managed to mutter when she'd stopped laughing, 'your Jem took my Edward to see a woman in The Lane with twenty living children. He wanted to show him childbed wasn't necessarily dangerous — he frightened the life out of the poor man.'

'Mrs Riley.' Ivy nodded. 'That poor woman is

in a constant state of expectancy.'

The two women looked at each other and collapsed — and the sound of their shared laughter rang through the house.

25

'Yer mother would go spare if she knew you were out on me rounds with me.' Ivy looked over at Ali. She was dressed in the old-fashioned clothing her mother had bought for her. It was strange to see her so dowdy — nowadays Ali cut a fashionable figure — she'd changed so much since she'd been working for Ivy.

'You need someone who knows about your round, Ivy.' Ali was having the time of her life. 'If for whatever reason you can't get out and about, you need someone to step in. I plan to be that someone.'

'You and Conn don't plan to do away with me and Jem, do you?' Ivy pushed the goods in her pram down, getting ready for the next stop.

'Don't tempt me!' Ali almost skipped. It was a beautiful day. They had survived the madness of Easter and now she was out in the fresh air with Ivy. All was right with her world.

'How much cash do we have left?' Ivy at one time had taken goods from servants and sold them on, keeping a percentage for herself. These days she bought the goods outright. She had the money. 'I wasn't expecting that piece of jewellery at the last place. That cut into me stash.' Ivy never knew what the servants might have for sale. It could be anything from hair ribbons to a trinket they'd been given by their employers.

'I was shocked you paid so much.' Ali counted

the coins she'd stored in a purse Ivy had created for her. It went around her stomach under her coat.

'That was a nice piece of jewellery.' Ivy could guess what the pretty maid had done for the piece. Still, it was none of her business. The girl deserved to receive payment for services rendered. Many an employer treated his pretty young maids like his private harem. 'I'll make a good profit on the piece.'

'If we don't buy any more jewels we should be alright,' Ali said after counting her coins.

'Right, let's be getting on.' Ivy pushed her heavy pram forward. 'You'll be happy to know we're almost finished.'

Mondays she visited the back doors of Merrion Square. Its close proximity to The Lane meant she could make several trips back and forth to her home. This trip would be their last.

'Patricia Nugent!' Ali stared, shocked, at the maid who opened the door to them. 'I thought you went away to be a nun!' The girl had been a close friend of Ali's brother Liam who had planned on becoming a priest.

'That's what me ma wants everyone to think.' The young maid looked over her shoulder nervously. 'I never wanted to be a nun so she kicked me out.'

'Do you have anything for me today?' Ivy didn't like to interrupt but they could get the girl into trouble by keeping her chatting at the door.

'Here — ' Patricia picked up a newspaper-wrapped parcel from between her feet and passed it to Ivy. About to close the door, she stopped to ask: 'Is Liam still away, Ali?'

Ivy put the parcel in her pram and walked away. This seemed to be a private matter. She'd give Ali a few minutes to chat.

She stepped out into the lane that ran along the back entrances. She could wait here. Ali wouldn't be long. The maid wasn't free to stand and chat.

'*Miss, miss, can you help me?*'

Ivy caught the falling figure in her arms.

'Please, you have to help me!'

She couldn't see the young girl's face but she could see the torn and bloody back of her thin dress.

'What's going on?'

'Me ma!' the girl sobbed. She raised a bruised face.

She could only be about eleven or twelve, Ivy thought.

'She said as how I was looking at the boys. She's going to take me to the Maggies!' the girl wailed.

The Maggies was the common name for the Magdalene laundry. Once a girl entered there she was a slave for life. Ivy wouldn't wish it on her worse enemy.

'Let me help you.' Ivy looked around frantically. The girl's wounds needed to be washed and dressed. She'd take her home, then try and find somewhere for the girl to go.

'Mary Agnes Purcell!' Ali stepped out suddenly and grabbed the young girl by the elbow. 'What are you doing around here?'

'It's all your Conn's fault!' The girl's face

changed. No longer the face of a sweet young innocent, there was hatred in the eyes that stared at Alison. 'My mother said I was giving him the glad eye. She's going to send me to the Maggies!' The girl tried to assume her meek demeanour again.

'So the first person you thought to ask for help was Ivy?' Ali, like everyone else in The Lane, had heard Mrs Purcell call down the fires of hell onto Ivy's head many times. 'I don't believe you.'

Ivy felt her stomach turn. It was a trap and she'd almost fallen into it. Everyone in The Lane knew her routine. It wouldn't be hard for anyone to find her down these back lanes. If Ali hadn't been with her, she'd have brought the girl into her own home so she could tend her wounds.

'Come along,' she said softly to the child, for that's all she was. 'I know of somewhere safe.' Ivy's mind was working frantically. She knew every back road around here. The girl's wounds were real no matter how the situation had come about. She couldn't just abandon her here in this laneway. 'We'll have to take the back roads. Can you walk?' She was all tender concern. 'Here, lean on the pram.'

She led the way down the hidden laneways of Dublin. They hadn't far to go.

★ ★ ★

'Name of God, Ivy, name of God!' Ali was still shaking. She couldn't believe what had happened. 'If I hadn't been there, Ivy, if I hadn't been there!'

203

'But you were there.' Ivy, with Ali holding onto the side bar of the pram, was pushing along so fast she was practically pulling Ali along with her. 'We have to get home. We need to be home before the next part of this comedy of errors can take place.'

'But Mary Agnes was really hurt.' Ali felt she could faint for the first time in her life. 'Those were real cuts and bruises.'

'Ali, you need to calm yourself.' Ivy was relieved to see the entrance to The Lane just ahead. She had deliberately come to the Grand Canal side rather than the usual Stephen's Street side. Sheila Purcell would have someone watching, she had no doubt — sure Ivy would bring the injured child back to The Lane to treat her in her own home. She'd take the back entrances and go in through her own back gate.

'You need to go home, Ali,' Ivy said as soon as the back gate was closed behind them. 'I don't want you here.'

'I don't want to leave.'

'Go home, Ali,' Ivy said tiredly. 'And I'd consider it a kindness if on your way you would stop at the livery and ask my Jem to come home.'

'I want to help if I can,' Ali said.

Ivy unlocked one of the sheds and pushed her pram inside. 'Just go home, Ali. Your parents wouldn't want you mixed up in my problems.' She almost pushed the girl out the garden door.

Having locked the door, she walked toward the house. 'Father Leary!' she said aloud. She didn't know exactly what was going on but she knew in her bones the Parish Priest was behind this latest upset. Mrs Purcell wasn't capable of coming up with whatever this was on her own. She spat into the grass at her feet. 'I don't care if he is a priest, God,' she looked towards the sky as she prayed, 'if he's going to heaven I don't want to be there.' She was becoming hysterical. She was going to wash her face and hands and wait to see what happened next.

★ ★ ★

The pounding on the front door when it came was loud enough to shake the house. Someone had seen her return.

'It's okay, Frank.' Ivy stepped from her kitchen before Frank could open the door. 'That will be for me.'

'What's going on?' Ria stood at Frank's shoulder now.

'It might be best if you stayed out of this,' Ivy said.

She walked down the hall and opened the front door. She wasn't surprised to see Father Leary and Mrs Purcell but the presence of Garda Collins did surprise her. They really intended to do her a mischief.

'Mrs Ryan.' Barney Collins knew something of the history between these people but even he was surprised at the harm they appeared to wish on this woman.

'There's no need to be polite, officer.' Leary shook his silver-headed stick in the air. The lad he'd sent to keep an eye on Mary Agnes had run back to give his report as soon as the girl walked away with this one. 'Do your duty — arrest this woman!'

'Arrest me for what exactly?' Ivy crossed her arms and leaned against the door frame. It looked like a gesture of disdain but she needed the support. She stared into the priest's face. There was a limit to how much you could fear someone, she found.

'Do you hear how she speaks to me?'

Leary's stick was up again. Ivy was keeping close watch. She'd felt the sting of that stick before and wasn't willing to feel it again.

'I'm a man of God and this harlot stands before me without a sign of respect or devotion. Arrest her, I said!'

Ivy turned to Garda Collins but kept careful watch on Leary out of the corner of her eye. It seemed Mrs Purcell was content to stand and wail into her hankie. 'Again, I have to ask, arrest me for what?'

'Serious charges have been laid against you, Mrs Ryan.' Garda Collins was watching the priest. He didn't trust the man.

'What charges?' Jem came up behind them, pushing through them rudely in order to step to Ivy's side. He glared around at the gathering crowd. 'Have you people no home to go to?' The crowd disappeared. It was small of him but he wanted to demonstrate to Leary that he didn't hold all the power here. Jem and Ivy employed a great many of the people who lived in The Lane.

'Mr Ryan.' Barney Collins was relieved to see the man.

Jem glared at Leary. He refused to even think

of the man as a priest. 'What charges have been brought against my wife?' He didn't touch Ivy, afraid his touch might make her break down. She'd never forgive herself if she cried in front of this shower.

'She has estranged the emotions of a child from her mother!' Leary shouted, spittle flying from his mouth.

Jem removed a handkerchief from his pocket and wiped his face with an expression of disgust.

'She has removed a minor from the loving care of her mother. She has kidnapped one of my flock.' The cane came towards Ivy's face.

'I'm sure you were not intending to hit my wife with this,' Jem pulled the cane from the man's hand, 'again.' He passed the cane to Garda Collins who took it without a word.

'Mrs Ryan,' Barney Collins wanted to hit the fat priest with the stick himself, 'an accusation of child abduction has been made against you.'

'Who am I supposed to have abducted?' Ivy asked, still leaning against the doorway. She was aware of Frank and Ria at her back.

'*My Mary Agnes!*' Sheila Purcell screamed. 'You have her in your evil clutches. I know all about your evil ways. She is the purest of the pure and you would try to lead her from the path of righteousness — harlot!'

'I have no idea what this woman is talking about, Garda Collins,' Ivy said. 'Where is this child I'm supposed to have abducted? You are welcome to search my rooms if you like.'

'Liar, I know you have her! She never came home.'

207

'Why would you think your child is with Mrs Ryan?' Barney Collins was no fool.

'I did run into an injured child on my round,' Ivy said. This farce had gone on long enough as far as she was concerned.

'My Mary Agnes — you hurt her — I knew it. My poor, poor, girl to have fallen into your evil clutches!'

'What happened to the child, Mrs Ryan?' Barney Collins wanted to use the stick in his hand on the real villains of this piece.

'I delivered her to the Sisters of Charity,' Ivy answered.

She almost laughed at the look of shock on Leary's face. Everyone knew he and the Mother Superior couldn't abide each other. They had an icily polite ongoing war waging. Let them sort it out between themselves.

'I paid for the child's care and a Mass to be offered for her recovery. That's the last I've seen of her. I don't know if the child belongs to Mrs Purcell as her children are not allowed mix with the people of The Lane.'

'I'm sorry for bothering you, Mrs Ryan.' Barney had to hold back a smile. She'd turned the tables on the aul' besom. 'I'll check into the matter. I'll let you know the results. Good day.'

Ivy closed the door in their faces, collapsing into Jem's waiting embrace.

26

'I'll put the kettle on,' Frank almost whispered. 'You take care of our Ivy, Jem. I'll bring the tea down in a while.' He put his shaking hand on Ria's back. They both stepped into his rooms, leaving Jem in the hallway holding Ivy in his arms.

'Come on, love.' Jem could feel her shaking. He led her down the hallway into their kitchen. He kicked the kitchen door shut at his back and, bending, picked Ivy up in his arms. He crossed to the range, lowered his body into one of the easy chairs and settled Ivy on his lap. She snuggled into his chest without a word. They sat in silence, Jem running his hand down Ivy's back while they fought to compose themselves.

'That was nasty,' Jem grossly understated when he felt Ivy move to stand — he pulled her back to his chest. 'What happened?'

Ivy hid her face in his neck while she told him of meeting the injured child on her round. 'I'd have brought her home, Jem.' She shivered at the thought. 'If Ali hadn't recognised her, I'd have brought her home. She'd have been in here, in our kitchen, when they came with the Garda.'

'They hurt that little girl?' Jem was having a hard time wrapping his mind around injuring a child to seek revenge on another.

A brief rap sounded on the kitchen door and Ria appeared with a tray in her hands. 'Tea,' she said. She put the tray on the kitchen table. 'Enjoy it,' she said and stepped back out, closing the door without another word.

'She must have had to tie old Frank down to keep him out.' Ivy pushed herself to her feet, grateful for the gesture. She needed a cup of tea desperately. 'The tea cosy must be Ria's work.' She admired the knitted tea cosy with the pom-pom on top. The tray was fully stocked with everything they'd need. She filled the two pretty cups sitting on matching saucers. She carried the metal teapot, still wearing its cosy, over to the range. It would keep warmer that way.

Jem accepted a cup and saucer and reluctantly allowed his wife to sit across the range from him.

'Ivy, Leary will have to be stopped. To have injured a child and brought a Garda officer to the door — the man meant you real harm.'

He shuddered to think what might have happened if the child had been discovered in their kitchen. Ivy would have been arrested on the spot. Leary had the contacts to make her disappear onto one of the ships that sailed from Wexford to Canada. Had that been the man's plan? Jem's mind whirled. What was the Parish Priest's fixation on Ivy? He watched while Ivy almost visibly pulled herself together.

'I was so glad you were there with me.' Ivy was still shaking inside. 'I've never been more frightened in my life. When I saw that injured child — when Ali told me who she was — I swear my heart stopped.'

'That was quick thinking on your part to take her to Mother Columbanus.' Jem watched and waited. He knew Ivy needed the contents of the teapot to calm her system. 'But the child might still end up with the Maggies.'

'I don't think so.' Ivy stood to refresh her tea. 'I think that poor child is destined for a nunnery. She's been brainwashed. You could see it in her.'

They sat and drank tea while staring into the flames of the black range. Ivy didn't want to think about Leary. She had no idea what to do about the man.

Jem was watching and waiting. He took a deep breath and without warning said, 'Are you ever going to tell me?'

'Tell you what?' She looked over her teacup.

'Ivy,' Jem leaned over and took the cup and saucer from her hands, putting them on the floor beside him, 'I'm a farmer's son. I know livestock. You, missus, are expecting a baby.'

'Are you sure?' Ivy clutched his hands desperately. 'Really, Jem, are you sure? I suspected I might be but . . . ' The blush on her cheeks was almost painful.

'I'm sure, love.' He pulled her from her chair back onto his lap. He'd been keeping careful watch ever since they lost control and made love without precaution. She'd missed her monthly once and was late for this month. 'I'm sure. Are you mad at me?'

'We've been married all but a year, Jem.' Ivy raised a glowing face. 'I'd like to have your baby. It better look just like you though.' She was glad to leave the matter of Leary alone. This was a joyous occasion.

'Why?'

'I'll have two of you to love that way.'

'Ivy!' Jem pulled her into a tight embrace. He couldn't let anything happen to her. Leary had to be stopped.

They sat locked in a tight embrace, each lost in dreams of the future. 'A baby, Ivy . . . our baby,' he whispered into her hair, his hand laid on her flat stomach. 'If the poor thing's anything like you it'll be hell on wheels.' He grinned widely in anticipation.

'Here,' she pushed away to glare playfully up at him, 'I've just realised — *livestock* — the cheek of you, Jem Ryan! I'm no bloody cow.'

'No, love.' Jem laughed. 'You're a thoroughbred through and through.'

He sighed into her hair. They couldn't remain in this bubble of peace forever. The world was waiting for them. Leary would have to be taken care of. He needed advice — he knew the very men to ask too.

★ ★ ★

'I don't know why I have to come to this emergency business meeting,' Ivy grouched as she got herself primped for the evening. 'Honest to God, Jem, I've better things to do with me time than getting meself all dolled up like a dog's dinner.' The indoor bath with hot running water was always a treat but getting her glad rags on after a stressful day like today seemed the height of folly to her.

'I thought women liked to get dolled up.' Jem was only half listening to Ivy's grumbles. He'd telephoned his business partners as soon as he'd returned to the livery today. He was not going to let the grass grow under his feet with Leary out to harm his wife.

Ann Marie had taken the phone from Edward and demanded they meet at her house that very evening. She'd ordered a meal to be prepared. They would discuss Jem's concerns together.

'*I'm enceinte, not brain-damaged!*' she'd yelled down the telephone at Jem.

'Oh my God!' Ria, returning from a visit to the WC, stood open-mouthed staring at the glamorous couple walking down the gas-lamp-lit hallway. 'You two look like fillum stars! Frank! Get out here and have a look at these two.'

Frank, the evening paper clutched in his hand, glasses on top of his head, appeared in the doorway of his room. 'I've seen them before. They scrub up a treat, don't they?'

'I'm glad you approve.' Ivy was wearing a favourite outfit. Her brother Shay had brought it from London for her. The tightly fitted black skirt with a row of large white leather buttons marching down one side was matched with a white silk blouse with a row of black leather buttons. She always felt good when she wore the outfit. The black cloche hat with the white ostrich feather was the finishing touch. The silk stockings she wore flattered her calves and ankles. The black T-strap shoes gleamed. She'd draped a white lace shawl that Granny Grunt had made around her shoulders. She did look a treat, if she said so herself.

Jem's masculine attire flattered his long lean

213

figure. He wore a steel-grey tailored suit, white shirt and the green silk tie Ann Marie had bought for him that exactly matched his eyes. The suit was covered by an unbuttoned charcoal cashmere overcoat. His trilby hat was held in one hand as he stood smiling at his wife's side.

'You two are a picture of sartorial elegance,' Ria said.

'Them's guinea words to be using around here,' Frank said with a grin.

'We have to be on our way.' Jem took Ivy's elbow while placing his hat on his head.

Ria rushed to open the main door. 'You two have a wonderful time!' she said as they strolled through.

She closed the door at their backs and turned back towards the rooms she was sharing with Frank. 'They deserve to have some happy times,' she muttered.

★   ★   ★

'Let's take the Mount Street Bridge.' Jem walked proudly towards the Grand Canal exit. He loved nothing better than walking out with his Ivy on his arm. 'We're not dressed for crossing the lock.' They strolled out, a handsome couple admired by the people they passed.

Those two don't have a trouble in the world, one old dear thought as the gent tipped his hat to her.

★   ★   ★

214

'Ivy Rose Murphy Ryan!' Ann Marie, dressed in screaming red, stormed down the long hallway of her home, her stomach leading the way. She ignored the butler and footman who were standing to attention. She'd told them when she hired them that this would be an unusual household. She would not sit and wait for her guests to be announced — particularly when one guest needed her ears boxed.

'I could shake you until your brains rattle.' She did take Ivy's shoulders in her hands and shake. 'I have to read about a murder and gangsters in The Lane in the newspapers.' She was still shaking Ivy while she spoke.

'It is not considered polite to assassinate one's guests in one's hallway.' Edward strolled up to join his wife. He too was learning to live in an unusual household. He was enjoying the challenge.

'Auntie Ivy, Uncle Jem!' A nightgown-clad child ran down the central staircase and threw herself into Jem's waiting arms.

'Emerald, you should be in bed,' said Edward.

'I had to say hello, Papa,' She beamed around the company. 'It is only polite to do so.'

'Give your Auntie Ivy a kiss then up the stairs to Dreamland.' Jem tried to put the child down as she clung on.

'Can't I stay for a while?'

'No.' Jem was usually a pushover for Emmy but he needed to discuss adult business. There was a cold knot of fear in his stomach. 'You need your beauty sleep.' He grinned at the child. 'You, Miss Emmy, are looking a fright.'

215

She giggled as he put her down, then insisted on kissing both couples before allowing herself to be escorted back upstairs by Catherine O'Malley who had only taken her eyes off the little girl for a minute.

As they walked towards the lounge the door knocker sounded and they heard the butler greeting William Armstrong and his wife Thelma.

'We'll wait for them in the lounge,' Edward said.

'Give me a whiskey, Edward!' William Armstrong almost stormed into the room without waiting to be announced. He couldn't be doing with all that malarkey for an evening among friends.

'William, really!' His beautiful wife smiled around the room. 'Good evening.' She would not apologise for her husband's manners. This company knew him well.

'Murderers, abusers, kidnappers, liars, cheats!' William accepted the crystal tumbler of whiskey from Edward's hand. 'What kind of place is it you live in, Ivy bloody Murphy?'

'That's Mrs Ryan to the likes of you — now sit down and be quiet,' Ivy ordered.

'We need to discuss this matter right now.' William sat in one of the beautiful green-leather Chesterfield chairs. 'I can tell you I couldn't force food past my lips if we have to discuss Father bloody Leary over the meal.'

'William,' Thelma closed her eyes for a second before glaring at her spouse, 'you are not helping.'

'Is that what this business meeting is all about?' Ivy demanded of Jem.

'I asked them to meet with me.' Jem took one of her clenched fists in his hand. 'I need advice and help, Ivy. Leary is dangerous. The fact he tried to have you imprisoned frightens the life out of me. The man is insane.'

'He's been getting away with murder for years because he wears his collar back to front,' William muttered into his glass.

27

While Ivy and company were dining in style, the two rooms that the Connelly family called home were in an uproar.

'You are wrong, Ma, Da.' Conn pushed his bowl of blind stew to one of his little brothers sitting on the floor beside him. The meatless stew made up of damaged vegetables and barley was a familiar dish in this house. He usually enjoyed it but tonight he couldn't eat a thing through the lump in his throat.

'I'm the head of this household!' Brian Connelly slapped the arm of the only chair in the room. 'I'm telling yez right here and now.' He glared around at his children frantically shovelling food into their mouths. 'Yez will have nothing more to do with that bloody Ivy Murphy. That one is heading for a fall and I am not going to allow her to pull my family down with her.'

'What's this all about, Da?' Conn stood and walked over to lean against the wall nearest the door. 'What brought this on?'

'Father Leary had a word in my ear,' Brian muttered. 'That holy man told me that Ivy Murphy is the devil's spawn. He warned me to remove my children from her clutches. I'm a good god-fearing man. Would you expect me to go against the word of my Parish Priest? A man who has been nothing but a blessing to this family?'

'God, Da,' Conn had a pain in his chest — he'd swear he could literally hear his own heart break, 'you're a hypocrite.'

'Don't you talk to your father that way!' Lily Connelly was sitting on the floor by the fire. She'd removed the pot of potatoes and vegetables from the open flames to serve the family but hadn't bothered to pick herself up off the floor. She'd known Brian was spoiling for a fight. 'I don't understand what that fancy word means but I don't like your tone.'

'Show me what Father Leary has ever done for us!' Conn pressed his shoulders into the wall at his back and stared at the poverty around him. 'Go on, Da, point out one thing that your Parish Priest has ever done for us.'

'Father Leary,' Lily closed her eyes and rested her aching head against the chimney breast, 'is the man in charge of the parish funds.' She said softly, 'He has often saved you lot from starving.'

'Because me da gambled and drank away his wages!' Conn spat out. 'When our Liam came home from the monastery Ivy Murphy was the only one to hold out a helping hand to him. You threw him out, Da — your own son — you threw him to the wolves.'

'*He was supposed to be a priest!*' Brian Connelly shouted.

The children on the floor shovelled their food faster. Their da had been known to kick the bowls from their hands.

'He was to be me pride and joy. I could stick me chest out with a priest for a son.'

'Well, you should hang yer head for the way

you treated him.' Conn was shaking inside. His father could erupt at any moment. He was not willing to allow himself to be trounced anymore. 'It was Ivy Murphy who asked that Friar to help our Liam.'

'Father Leary said she'd been having unlawful relations with that Friar!' Brian roared. 'The man is going to be defrocked because of her. She led him into sin, the brazen hussy!'

'Name of God, Da, listen to yourself!' Conn looked around at the wide-eyed children clustered on the floor. 'Ivy Murphy holds out a helping hand to everyone who knows her. The spoons and bowls in yer childer's hands came from Ivy. It was Ivy who helped our Liam.' He waved towards a corner where Alison was sitting on one of the chests Ivy had found to hold Liam and Vera's props and costumes. 'Ivy found those chests and most of the clothes in them for our Liam and Vera. Look at our Alison. She looks a picture — now that's not all down to Ivy — Alison went looking for a job, I know — but Ivy has helped her look like a lovely young woman.' Conn was almost exhausted. He knew his da wouldn't take his defiance lying down.

'You're making a plaster saint out of the woman!' Brian roared and shook his large fist in the air. 'I won't have it. That woman laid hands on one of the Purcell children. She's leading me own children away from the teachings of their parents. Father Leary isn't going to let a sinner like that flourish amongst his flock. You need to get away from her before you're painted with the same brush of sin and sorrow.' He stood to remove the thick leather belt that held up his trousers.

'You try and hit me with that belt, Da, and I'll knock your lights out.' Conn wanted to throw up.

'Conn, honour thy father,' Lily moaned and buried her head in her hands.

'Conn, don't!' Alison cried, jumping to her feet.

'*Da, don't!*' the children screamed.

The two men stared at each other, each knowing they had reached a turning point. The sound of women and children weeping were the only sounds in the room while they stood frozen.

'I'm ashamed of yeh, Da.' Conn refused to cry. 'We haven't a chair to sit on because of yer drinking and gambling. The only reason those chests are still here is because our Liam threatened to leave and take his earnings with him. You think I don't know you've stopped giving me ma money since we went to work? I've been supporting this family the best I can but no more. You've made this hell, Da. You can live in it. I won't anymore.'

He turned his back on his spluttering parent and ran from the room. He knew where he was going. To the people his father had the barefaced gall to curse. He was moving in over the stables. He knew Jem would let him stay there.

'*Conn!*' Alison was pulling a woollen shawl over her shoulders while she chased her brother. '*Conn, wait!*'

'You won't change me mind, Ali.' Conn

hunched his shoulders against the chill of the evening.

'Where are you going?'

'To the livery.' Conn started walking across the cobbles.

'Will you wait up! I almost turned me ankle. I'm only learning to walk in high heels.'

He waited and she shoved her arm through his.

'Are you thinking of spending the night at the livery?' she asked as they walked on.

'I'll sleep in Jem's old room,' Conn was practically pulling her along with him.

'That's what I thought.' Alison used her grip on his elbow to pull him to a stop. 'Conn, you can't.'

'Jem won't mind.'

'Conn . . . ' Alison looked around the wide cobbled square. 'Look, it's cold out. Let's step into the livery tea room for a minute. With any luck we'll have the place to ourselves.'

'Never.' Conn allowed his sister to prod him along. 'The place is always packed. That's the only heat a lot of the youngsters around here have.'

'Who's in charge of the livery tonight?' Alison wanted somewhere warm where she could speak to her brother in private.

'Pete Reynolds.'

'Oh.' Ali pulled him towards Ivy and Jem's home. 'It will have to be Frank's place so.'

'What is this about, Ali?' Conn couldn't see the problem with him staying over the livery. He wouldn't be in the way. Jem had lived there for years.

Frank Wilson opened the door to their knock. 'Alison — Conn! Step in out of the cold.'

'Thanks, Mr Wilson.' Ali pulled her brother along with her. 'We need a place to talk.'

'Go on in,' Frank said, wondering what in God's name was happening now.

'Ali!' Ria jumped to her feet as they entered, letting her mending fall to the floor at her feet. She bent to pick it up.

'The youngsters need somewhere to talk.' Frank shut the door. 'I'll put the kettle on.' He began pulling his hidden table out from the deep cupboard. The youngsters could sit at the table on the folding chairs.

'Conn and our father had words,' Ali said simply. 'He was thinking of spending the night over the livery. I told him he couldn't.'

'Why not?' Frank had the kettle on the gas stove.

'I was with Ivy today when Mary Agnes Purcell tried to trick her.' Ali almost collapsed into one of the wooden chairs. 'I'm still having difficulty believing what I saw with my own eyes.'

'What's troubling you, Ali?' Ria had folded her work and pushed it down the side of the easy chair she was sitting in.

'Ivy told me to go home but I didn't. I couldn't just leave her.' She sobbed for a moment before wresting control of her emotions back.

'What's really troubling you?' Frank was busy with the tea things. He was getting good at this visitor stuff if he did say so himself.

'I hid nearby,' Ali said. 'I wanted to be on

hand in case I was needed. I heard Father Leary say to Mrs Purcell that Ivy would be punished for something called 'alienation of affection' between parent and child. I can only guess at what that means but it seems to me that if Conn goes under Jem's roof he'll be giving Father Leary more ammunition to use against Ivy and Jem — or am I wrong?'

'No, I don't think you are.' Frank had the table set, the tea served. He sat on another folding chair. 'Leary has a fixation on Ivy. I've seen that for myself.'

'Where am I going to sleep?' Conn didn't fancy sleeping rough. He'd been confident he had a place to go to when he stood up to his father.

'You can all sleep here,' said Frank. 'That's if you don't mind sleeping in a chair-bed, Conn?'

Conn grinned. 'That would be a luxury, Frank.'

'The ladies can take my bed,' Frank added.

They drank their tea, each trying to come to terms with the life-altering events of the evening.

'Someone needs to tell your mother what is happening, Alison,' Ria said. She didn't like to think of the woman fretting and worrying about her children. They might be considered adults but a mother worried.

'I'll go over to see Mrs Connelly,' Frank offered. 'I'll have a word in her ear.' He could do nothing about Brian Connelly. The man was just one of many who drank and gambled while their children went cold and hungry.

28

'Where's Conn?' Liam Connelly knelt on the floor to one side of the boys' mattress. He had a lit candle in a jam jar in his hand. The jar had a piece of string wrapped around the neck to use as a handle and a lid with holes punched through. He'd learned to have some kind of light to hand when he returned in the early-morning hours from his work in the nearby theatres. He shook his brother's shoulder gently. 'Mike,' he whispered. 'Where's our Conn?'

'Ali's not here either,' a voice from the girls' mattress across the room said.

'What's going on?' Vera was tired after a long stint of singing and dancing on stage. They'd had to tend to Liam's dogs before they could go to their own beds. The six dogs were a major part of their act. They had a kennel Liam and his brothers had built for them out on the tenement back yard.

The Connellys' two tenement rooms were set up for sleep. In the front room on the boys' mattress slept Conn, Liam, Mike and Malachi. The girl's mattress was for Vera, Úna, Alison and Carmel. The two youngest slept in the back room on a straw-stuffed mattress by their parents' bed. During the day, the mattresses were pushed into the back room.

'Keep your voices down, for God's sake.' Mike sat up on the ratty mattress. 'The last thing we need is the aul' man coming in here. You girls come over here. We can talk in whispers that way.'

'It was jigs and reels around here tonight,' Úna said softly while crawling across the floor from one mattress to the other.

'What happened to you?' Liam gasped when he caught sight of his sister's face in the light from his lamp.

'Me da.' Úna couldn't see the swelling on her face but she could feel it.

'What's going on?' Vera asked.

Úna filled her brother and sister in on the happenings of the day. She knew the other children were awake. They listened in silence. Too much talking could wake their parents. The last thing anyone wanted.

'I saw him, Liam.' Úna at nineteen was a year older than Liam. 'I saw Father Leary whip Mary Agnes. I was there.' She tried to sob silently. She'd been horrified by the scene she witnessed. She felt Vera's arm go around her shaking shoulders.

'What were you doing at the church?' Vera, a year older than Úna, hugged her sister close. It would soon be time for Úna and Mike to go to work at the fish factory but it didn't look like anyone was going to sleep tonight.

'It weren't at the church,' Úna said. 'It were in that room in the priest's house that he likes to call his atonement room.'

They all shivered now — each of them had unpleasant memories of that room.

'It were my turn to scrub the floors of the

226

parish house.' Brian Connelly was fond of offering his children's labour to others. 'I told me da what I'd seen.'

'Dear Lord!' Liam blessed himself. He may have decided the priesthood was not for him but he still had his belief.

'Me da leathered her.' Mike too had received his fair share of bruises when he'd stepped in to stop his father almost killing Úna.

'It were Father Leary what beat Mary Agnes.' Úna refused to be silent. The scene kept playing behind her eyes. It made her stomach turn. 'Mrs Purcell stood there and watched her daughter being scourged. She kept blessing herself and thanking God.'

'Where were Conn and Ali when Da was beating Úna?' Vera asked. The eldest two could usually stop their father from the worst of his excesses.

'They had already left,' Mike said. 'Conn said he's not coming back. Ali went after him then later Mr Wilson came and talked to me ma. Ali isn't coming back either.'

'Listen — ' Vera, as the oldest sibling present, felt she had to take charge. 'We can do nothing in the dark of night. Úna, you and Mike will have to go down the docks soon. Let's try and get some sleep. Liam and me will see what's what in the morning.'

'I'm not going to gut fish like this.' Úna held her hand to her aching face — her ribs hurt too. 'They can do without my money — see how they like it.' She always handed all of her earnings to her mother.

'It's mutiny,' Liam gasped. 'Honour thy father and thy mother, the Bible says.'

'You honour them, Liam!' Úna snapped. 'I've honoured them enough. It's time and past for me to leave home.'

'But where will you go?' Vera gasped.

'I don't know.' Úna turned to crawl back to the girls' mattress. 'I'll look for a live-in job in the morning.' She settled onto the mattress, and her sister Carmel cuddled into her for warmth without a word being spoken between them.

★   ★   ★

Frank woke as the first fingers of light touched his window. He wanted to be up and prepared for whatever might come. It had been long and many a year since he'd slept in a chair-bed fully dressed. It wasn't the best night's sleep he'd ever had.

'Conn!'

Conn forced gummy eyes open. 'What's the matter?' He pushed himself upright in the other chair-bed.

'We need to gather our troops.' Frank Wilson didn't think they'd seen the last of Father Leary. The Connelly children's rebellion would give that old goat another bullet to fire at Ivy. He couldn't allow that to happen. 'I'll be back in a minute to put the kettle on.' He walked towards the door leading into the hall. He needed the WC. 'Light the gas lamps and tidy up them chairs, lad.'

★   ★   ★

Augustina Winthrop, returning to The Lane after a difficult delivery, saw the lights go on in Frank Wilson's front room. It was unusual enough to have her stop. She took a deep breath and raised her chin. She had promised herself she'd stop hiding from the life around her. This was the first test of her conviction. She opened her own front door — stepped in only to leave her bags on the hallstand in the vestibule — stepped back out and walked towards Wilson's.

'Good Lord, Gussy, I wasn't expecting you,' Frank Wilson said when he opened the door at her knock. 'Come in.'

She stepped into the hall.

'Just a minute — ' Frank opened the door to his own room and stuck his head inside. The room had been returned to order. 'Come in, Gussy.' He opened the door wider.

'Conn!' Augustina stopped in her tracks. 'I wasn't expecting to see you here.'

'We are having a council of war, Gussy.' Frank hurried to fill his kettle. 'You can add your tuppence worth.'

Conn excused himself to use the bathroom and WC.

'Conn!' Jem Ryan, toothbrush and toothpaste in hand, was stepping out of the bathroom. 'What are you doing here?' The lad looked rough. He looked like he'd slept in the clothes he stood up in.

'Did I hear Jem Ryan?' Frank stuck his head out of his room while Conn slipped into the WC. 'Jem, go back into your own place and shove the bolt on the door,' he ordered. 'Don't let your Ivy move out of there. There is trouble brewing and it's best you two know nothing about it. Sit down and have a long breakfast with your missus.'

'Frank — '

'Do as I say, Jem.' Frank was watching the clock. The first Mass let out soon and he was betting they would have visitors. 'You'll know all soon enough.' He didn't wait to watch Jem obey him. He closed the door, leaving Jem staring in astonishment.

Jem stepped into the kitchen and shot the bolts at the top and bottom of the door home. He didn't know what was happening but if Frank wanted Ivy kept out of it that was good enough for him. The woman had enough on her plate.

'What's going on?' Ivy stood in the open doorway of their bedroom, staring at him. They never locked that door.

Jem walked over and took her in his arms. 'I thought I told you to stay in bed and I'd bring you a cup of tea.'

'It's early days yet to be spoiling me.' Ivy stepped out of his arms. She walked to the door, preparing to unlock it.

'Leave it locked, Ivy.' Jem was filling the kettle.

'I need to use the WC.'

'Use the outdoor one,' Jem said.

'It's freezing,' Ivy complained. They had got spoiled having an indoor WC.

'Pity about yeh!' Jem put the kettle on the gas stove. He saw the mulish look on his wife's face and said, 'I don't know what's going on, Ivy, but Frank asked that we stay in here behind that locked door. Now tend to your needs, woman. The sooner you go the sooner you'll get back.'

★　★　★

While Jem was keeping Ivy away, Frank had knocked on his bedroom door and asked the two women inside to get up and dressed. By the time everyone was decent and ready to start the day, Frank had enamel mugs of tea filled on his pull-out table.

'What's going on, Frank?' Augustina looked around the crowded room in surprise. She had thought Frank lived as lonely a life as she — obviously not.

'We need your help, Gussy.' Frank hadn't thought of asking the woman for help but her turning up like this was like divine intervention. 'Who do you know who knows the law of the land and is not afraid of a priest?'

'I beg your pardon?' Augustina gaped.

'Conn, you and Ali fill Gussy in on what went on yesterday.' He shoved his hands through his mussed grey hair. 'Dear God, was it only yesterday — it feels like a year ago.'

'I'll tell the first part, Conn,' Ali pushed to her feet. 'I was there.' She recounted the story of meeting the battered child without leaving out any detail.

'It's not tea you should be serving with this tale, Frank Wilson.' Augustina thought this was really jumping into the fire. 'It's whiskey.'

'I was there for the next part.' Ria too stood to deliver her account.

231

By the time Conn had also given his story Augustina's head was reeling. The Spanish Inquisition had nothing on it.

Augustina stared into the hopeful faces of the three young people sitting on wooden chairs at Frank's table. Frank had taken the easy chair by hers.

'As it happens, I do know someone who can help,' she said. 'He is usually to be found taking an early-morning stroll around the park at this hour. In fact, I'll go and fetch him right now.' She got to her feet.

'I knew you were a sign from God, Gussy.' Frank too stood.

'Do you really believe Father Leary will lead a lynch mob — like something out of the Wild West films — against Ivy?' Augustina enjoyed the Wild West films when they played at the local cinemas. She'd never expected to be deputised to protect the innocent however.

'I don't think he'll lead the charge himself,' Frank said. 'The man's a bit too fond of his own skin. But Brian Connelly, Sheila Purcell and some of their cronies attend first Mass every day. I wouldn't put it past Leary to egg them on to start something with Ivy.'

'Frank!' Augustina stared in horror. 'That's persecution.'

'I know,' Frank nodded, 'and it's gone on long enough.'

'I'll go ask my friend to join us,' Augustina said.

The man was part of the Jacob family and had a home on Merrion Square. She had delivered all four of his children. She knew he had a social conscience since he spoke often with her on the plight of the poor. The Jacobs, to her knowledge, were Quakers. There would be no fear of a Catholic priest to worry about.

'Hurry, Gussy, please.' Frank opened the door for her.

'Mr Wilson!' Ginger Cooper, his red hair flapping, his freckles standing out on his pale face, panted. 'Father Leary — he has a bunch of them Holy Marys back at his parish house. I don't know what they're planning but it's not good for Ivy or Jem.' The poor lad was fighting tears. His ma forced him to be an altar boy and he saw and heard a lot more than people realised.

Augustina took off. Frank sent Ginger home with orders to say nothing. Frank closed the door with a heavy heart. All they could do now was wait.

29

Jacob Kilbride Jacobs, known to his friends as JJ, enjoyed a brisk early morning walk every morning of his life. He was not, however, accustomed to being accosted by hysterical females on his walk around the enclosed park of Merrion Square.

'Thank you so much for coming with me,' Augustina said, her voice shaking, as they reached The Lane. She was terrified but felt more alive than ever before in her life. Finally, she thought, finally I'm doing something.

'I believed these entrances were used only for deliveries.' JJ stood to one side to allow a weary horse pull a carriage into the tunnel.

They followed the carriage, JJ's silver-headed walking stick tapping along with the ring of the horse's iron-shod hooves on the cobbles.

They emerged into the cobbled square and JJ stood open-mouthed, looking at the scene in front of him. He'd pulled off the walkway to stand on a small patch of wasteland well out of the way of returning carriages. He saw people — dockworkers to his eyes — hurry out of what were obviously tenement dwellings. Shawl-clad females hurried away. He supposed they were going to the surrounding factories. Some might even work in his family firm. Gangs of shabbily dressed youths swarmed the carriages, removing the tired horses from their traces while others led fresh horses out.

'Who are those men?' JJ asked when Augustina stepped to join him. He pointed with his cane towards the tramps sitting on the steps leading up to every tenement. They were being served tea by well-shrouded women.

'They're the homeless.' Augustina had seen the sight every day. 'They sleep on the wide stairs of the houses. The women give them tea and a chuck of bread before they go out looking for work.'

'Really?' JJ was fascinated. He wondered about stabling his own horse and carriage here. It would be far more convenient than the place he presently used. Although he supposed he was going to have to give in to progress and purchase a motor vehicle.

'Frank was right.' Augustina saw the crowd led by Sheila Purcell and Brian Connelly march into The Lane from the tunnel entrance across the courtyard from them. 'I didn't know whether to believe him.' There was no sign of Father Leary.

The five toughs at the back of the crowd saw the well-dressed gent and wondered what he was doing in here. Still, it was none of their never mind. They'd taken a few bob from the Parish Priest to drag some heathen female to him. He'd told them to enjoy themselves. They were looking forward to a bit of sport.

'I don't like the look of that lot,' JJ said as the small crowd stopped at the house steps away from where they stood.

'That is what I want you to see.' Augustina trembled but straightened her spine. She would not weaken now. She thought of the suffragette photographs she'd seen in the newspaper and newsreels at the picture house. Those brave women faced off against mounted armed men. She could and would do this.

'*What do you lot mean banging on a decent person's door at this hour of the morning?*' Frank Wilson shouted from the slightly raised sash window of his home.

'It's not you we want, Frank Wilson.' Brian Connelly felt brave with the crowd at his back. 'It's that harlot Ivy Murphy we want — get her out here or we'll come in and drag her out.'

'In the name of God,' Augustina whispered. 'They've run mad.'

'I'll not open me door until you step back.' Frank noted the men who drove Jem's horse-drawn taxis step up behind the toughs. It seemed Pete Reynolds had a good head on his shoulders. He'd sent his men to help. Those men were well muscled from handling horses all day.

Augustina raised her chin and stepped onto the path that ran along the row of terraced houses.

'It's a bit early to expect a lady in Mrs Ryan's delicate condition to be up and about,' she said.

She fervently hoped she wasn't telling tales out of school. Ivy's condition was obvious to her. She prayed the information she'd just revealed would make these people think twice about accosting Mrs Ryan.

'You people need to step back.' JJ didn't know what was going on but he feared what might take place here. 'You are blocking a public walkway

236

which is against the law.'

The crowd stilled at the richly cultured tones of the fancy gent. Unemployed men who had joined the crowd simply out of curiosity, and as a way to pass a few empty hours, drifted away.

'*Step back, I say!*' JJ waved his cane to move the crowd back.

He took Mrs Winthrop by the elbow and strolled forward. The crowd moved back further.

The toughs at the back found themselves being held in strong hands. They struggled as they were forcefully ejected from The Lane.

'Don't know what you're doing round here, Danny,' one carriage-driver said, recognising a face he knew well in the crowd, 'but you picked the wrong place to start a fight.'

'We was only having a bit of sport.' Danny spat into the dirt at his feet. 'It passes the day.'

'I'll tell Billy Flint you said that, will I?'

'*Here!*' someone shouted. 'No need to get him involved. We was just doing a favour for the Parish Priest. We wasn't doing any harm.'

'I'll take your names for Billy,' the driver said. 'Seeing as you were so interested in his niece. He takes care of his family, does Billy Flint.'

'Fuck that — we didn't know!'

The men turned and ran.

The drivers stood for a moment to be sure none of them felt brave enough to return.

JJ stared at the dwindling crowd. He faced two who stood in front and appeared to be the ringleaders.

'What is going on here?' he demanded in a voice that was not accustomed to being denied.

'Ivy Murphy has alienated me childer's affection,' Brian Connelly pushed his shoulders back to state. He was in the right of it. Father Leary had told him so.

'*My husband is leaving me and taking my childer with him, all because of that harlot!*' Sheila Purcell screamed.

'You did that all on your own, Da.' Úna Connelly allowed the shawl to fall on her shoulders. She walked forward from where she'd been hiding at the side of the livery. 'As for you, Mrs Purcell,' Úna raised her chin, 'you should hang your head in shame. I saw you. I saw you watch Father Leary lash your own daughter. Mrs Ryan had nothing to do with your husband leaving you. I'm surprised he stayed so long.'

'Why aren't you at your work, girl?' Brian Connelly felt sick when he got a look at his daughter's face. He didn't remember hitting her that hard — he'd just been so angry.

'Why aren't you, Da?' Úna leaned against the wall to one side of Frank Wilson's house.

JJ and Augustina stood to one side, a fascinated audience.

'I have to take care of me family,' Brian blustered. 'That Ivy Murphy has . . . ' He stopped when the door to Wilson's opened and his two eldest children stepped out.

'Mrs Ryan doesn't even know we are here,' Ali said.

Conn stepped to his injured sister's side. 'Is this how you take care of your family, Da?' He put his arm around Úna, pulling her gently to him.

'I believe you are all finished here,' JJ stepped forward to say. 'You should be about your own business.' He stood tall and stared down the crowd.

'Dear sweet Lord!' Augustina leaned suddenly against the side of the building, the strength gone from her knees. She watched through tear-filled eyes as the people, muttering unhappily, dispersed. 'That it should come to this.'

'I appear to need information about this situation,' said JJ. Things could have become very unpleasant. What was going on?

'Go home, Da,' Conn said when his father appeared unwilling to move.

'Mrs Purcell, you should not be here,' Ali said. 'You should tend to your own family without poking your nose into the affairs of others.'

The woman gasped at being spoken to so sharply. She'd go speak with Father Leary about all of this. Without a word, she turned and hurried towards the Canal exit. That good man would know what she should do.

'Gussy, are you going to introduce us to your companion?' Frank stood in his open doorway, feeling weak in the knees. He'd been afraid for the safety of his friends.

'I'm sorry.' Augustina pulled herself together and made the introductions.

JJ raised his hat to the company. 'I'd like to know more of the situation.'

'If you could all repeat your story,' Augustina suggested, 'just as you told it to me, I believe that would suffice.'

'Right!' Frank slapped his hands together.

239

'Everyone follow me.'

JJ stepped inside the house, fascinated by the unexpected events of his morning.

Frank insisted JJ and Augustina take the armchairs. He set out his four folding chairs for the others. Conn pressed a cold cloth to Úna's face while Ria went down the hall to fetch the Ryans. While they were waiting, they took it in turns to tell the story again. Úna was the only one with a story that hadn't yet been heard by this company. She listened to the others before pushing Conn away and standing to give her version of events.

'And where is the heroine or villain of the piece, depending on who is speaking?' JJ looked around. 'I think we need to speak with her.'

'She will be along in a minute,' Ria said, stepping into the room and looking around. It was getting pretty crowded in here. 'If everyone has told their story, why don't I take the Connelly family next door?'

'What?' Úna wanted to crawl into a dark space and hide.

'We'll explain everything,' Conn promised, helping his sister to her feet.

'I'll be able to contact you if necessary?' JJ asked as they began to walk towards the door.

'They'll be just next door,' Frank said.

Ivy, with Jem by her side, stepped into the room. 'I didn't mean to run everybody off,' she said.

Ivy had dressed to make an impression. She was wearing a slimline black skirt, silk stockings and fashionable buckled black shoes. For the first time she was wearing a twin set Molly Coyle had knit for her. The lacey hip-length jumper was of a shade of plum so dark it was almost black. The matching cardigan completed the fashionable outfit. Jem was dressed for work at the livery.

'I'll be in time for work, boss,' Ali said over her shoulder as she walked from the room.

'Same for me,' Conn added. It was still very early morning.

'I thought I was coming to my own hanging,' Ivy said to JJ. 'So I dressed up.'

'Mrs Ryan!' JJ jumped to his feet. He knew this woman. She advised his wife and their friend Ann Marie concerning charity work. Was this woman the cause of this morning's fiasco?

'Jem,' Ivy said, 'meet Mr Jacobs.' She turned to JJ. 'Mr Jacobs, this is my husband Jem Ryan.'

The civilities out of the way, the company sat — the women in the easy chairs, the men taking the wooden folding chairs.

'Mr Jacobs is here at my invitation,' Augustina said when everyone was seated. The others remained silent, not quite knowing what this toff was doing here.

'My area of expertise is business law,' JJ said. 'I was invited to observe this morning's activities by Mrs Winthrop.' He paused for a moment. 'I can, I believe, be an impartial witness. As such I advise you most sincerely, Mrs Ryan, to seek legal consultation.'

'We discussed this very thing last evening with Ann Marie and Edward O'Connor,' Jem said.

The five of them sat drinking tea and

discussing the events leading up to the morning's outrageous activities.

'If I hadn't been a witness to this morning's events I'm afraid I'd have a hard time believing a recounting of the situation.' JJ sipped his tea.

'My wife has a friend who is a Franciscan Friar.' Jem wanted to punch something. 'Brother Theo tried to remove the Parish Priest from his position of power — much to Brother Theo's detriment.'

'The amount of power being handed over to the Catholic Church is of great concern to me as an individual.' JJ looked around the company, hoping he wasn't causing offence. 'I fear where such unquestioning devotion may lead.'

The people around the table were silent. What could they say? It was a time of change in this new Ireland. They would have to watch what those changes would bring.

30

'Mrs Ryan, if you would be good enough to walk me home?' Augustina Winthrop said when everyone stood to leave. No decisions had been made. Nothing — it seemed to her — had been achieved.

'I'll catch you later, love.' Jem pressed a kiss into Ivy's cold cheek. He had to get away before his fury escaped his control. What good would it do his wife to have him rant and rave like a madman? He'd go shovel horseshit — that at least made sense. This bullshit the Parish Priest was shovelling was invisible to his eyes and deadly dangerous to his wife.

'I'll walk yez out.' Frank opened the door that led into the hallway. There was nothing more to say or add. They were all at a loss.

'I'll be on my way.' JJ put his hat back on his head and walked through the door being held open by Frank. 'I'll be in touch. Please do not hesitate to call on me if you believe I can be of further assistance.'

'Thank you for coming, JJ.' Ivy gave a ghost of a smile. 'It was good of you.'

The others whispered their agreement before dispersing to begin their own day.

★   ★   ★

'There were things went on this morning that I believe you are unaware of,' Augustina said as she and a smartly dressed Ivy walked along the terrace that housed both their homes. She nudged Ivy. 'The nets are twitching,' she said.

'The people in these houses have never truly been a part of the society of The Lane, it seems to me.' Ivy too was aware of eyes watching.

'I wasn't around in Georgian times when this square was built.' Augustina stood for a moment, examining the square. 'Like others in this row of two-storey houses, my family were in trade, my dear — quite frowned upon.' She gestured to the grander houses in the square. 'The four-storey houses facing the livery originally housed the gentry. The wide staircases, high ceilings and beautiful wall-details in those houses must have been beautiful once upon a time.' She wouldn't insult Ivy by bemoaning the current crumbling edifices and their occupants.

She walked to the end of the row and opened the door of her own home. 'Come in.'

'I've never been invited into one of these houses.' Ivy stepped into the vestibule. 'I mean, one that's been untouched.'

Augustina led the way through the stained-glass decorated door that opened out from the vestibule.

'Come through to my kitchen,' she said. 'You can have no idea how long it took me to begin living in the back of the house. We are creatures of habit, I fear. The back of the house was for the servants. I'd hardly set foot in the area until I was living here alone.'

'Your place is spotless for all you've no servants.' Ivy was admiring the elegant lines of the old house. It was a thing of beauty. So similar to her own home and yet so different.

'Ah, but Maggie Frost 'does' for me five mornings a week.' In the kitchen, Augustina moved the big black kettle from the back of the range to directly over the fire.

'Thankfully today is one of Maggie's days. The woman has left the range fire roaring. I'd be lost without her.'

Ivy had to put her hands behind her back to stop herself from opening the ceiling-height glass-fronted cabinets that lined the walls of the kitchen.

'I know you're addicted to tea, Ivy.' Augustina was pleased to notice Ivy's interest in the contents of her cabinets. She actually wanted to discuss the collection of silver her family kept in a bank vault. She needed information concerning buyers for the goods. It was time to liquidate some of the family assets. 'I'll have a pot on the go in no time — take a seat.'

'You've left this room untouched.' Ivy was trying to take everything in — the kitchen looked as if the servants had just stepped out for a moment. She took a seat in one of the comfortable chairs — lace antimacassars decorated the headrest and arms — pulled close to the range. She longed to have a rummage through the overstocked glass-fronted cabinets.

'The whole house is locked in the past, I'm afraid, like myself.' Augustina looked to see if there were any scones left in the large jar on the dresser. Empty. 'Did you hear what went on this morning while you were locked away in the back of the house?' Augustina was filling a large wooden tray with the needful for tea. The tray had a folding stand that would form a table by their chairs.

'I was too busy getting dressed up like a dog's dinner.' Ivy passed a hand down her own glamorous appearance.

'Mrs Purcell was one of those at your door,' Augustina said.

'She's usually around when trouble calls to me.'

'Ivy, she said her husband has left her, taking their children with him.'

'Thanks be to God,' Ivy said piously. 'The man should have done that years ago.' She moved her silk-stocking-covered legs out of the way as Augustina placed the stand for the tray on the floor between the two chairs. 'Are you about to warn me that she'll find some way to place the blame for his desertion at my door?'

'I'm frightened for you, Ivy.' Augustina placed the wooden tray on its stand and took a seat in the chair across from Ivy. She bent forward to stare intently into Ivy's eyes. 'This morning terrified me.'

'I'm sorry.'

'Why should you be?' Augustina poured tea into the eggshell-thin china cups. She'd leave Ivy to serve herself milk and sugar. 'You are the innocent victim in all of this.'

'It's very hard to accept that a lot of people appear to wish me ill.' Ivy poured milk into her tea.

'There are a great many more who wish you well.'

'That sounds like one of Granny Grunt's 'count your blessings, girl' sayings.' Ivy sipped her tea with a smile on her lips. She missed old Granny every day.

'Old Granny was a very special woman,' Augustina said. 'I learned so much from her. It was an honour to know her.'

'She was good to me. I don't know what I would have done without her wise advice,' Ivy laughed lightly, 'and her quick way of boxing my ears.'

'You were very good to her, Ivy.' Augustina couldn't believe this was the same little girl who had scurried around Granny's room tending to her needlework. 'Ivy, I'm afraid I was very indiscreet this morning. I did it with the best of intentions but now I fear you are going to be very angry with me. I must tell you what I've done although I dread it.'

'Missus, with everything that has gone on for the last few days nothing you could have done can be that bad.' Ivy was enjoying the oasis of peace to be found sitting in front of the fire with no one and nothing needing something from her. Ali would take care of cleaning up the kitchen and workroom before she started her book work.

'I'm afraid I let my tongue run away with me.' Augustina wanted to admit to her sin.

'Really?'

'I told that crowd of cowards that you were in an interesting condition.' She was heartily sorry she had. She knew some people were very superstitious about telling of the happy event for the first four months.

'How do you know?' Ivy carefully returned her teacup to its saucer. 'I really want to know. I don't even know for sure myself. Yet my Jem informs me I'm expecting a baby and now you — how in the name of goodness can you tell?'

'Perhaps my years of experience.' Augustina leaned forward, determined to get her point across. 'There are women who find becoming with child to be very difficult. Your mother was not one of them — I believe you will be the same. It is both a blessing and a curse. Do you understand what I am saying to you?'

'If I'm not careful I could end up with twenty childer under me feet?' Ivy remembered her mother's screams of anger when she discovered she was with child. The shouting and screaming had gone on for days before the tears started. She had no wish to end up like that. She would have to talk to Jem about this. He'd been careful but she was expecting a baby none the less. One or two would be fine but that was the extent of the family she wanted, thank you very much.

'Exactly.' Augustina was almost certain Ivy had been using some form of contraceptive. She preferred not to know for sure. There were women being pilloried for passing along information on what they were calling birth control. She didn't wish to be one of them.

'Have you told me everything I need to know now?' Ivy could see the woman was exhausted. She'd be better off in bed. The Good Lord knew when she'd be called out again to deliver a baby. 'You look like you're going to fall out of that chair.'

'There were several other things I wished to discuss with you — of a business nature — not anything that needs to be revealed at this precise moment.' She hid a yawn behind her hand. 'I must admit I am tired. Could we meet again to discuss business matters, please?'

'That's fine by me.' Ivy stood. 'You know where I live.' She had to get about her business. She'd a great deal to think about. She hated to walk out into the storm that seemed to be constantly whirling around her but needs must. 'Let me know when you have a little time free and we can have a chat.' She hoped the woman wanted to clear out some of the porcelain stashed in the glass-fronted cupboards all around this room.

'Thank you, Ivy.' Augustina pushed tiredly to her feet. 'I'll see you out and pray no one needs me for the next little while.'

'I understand that sentiment completely.'

Ivy walked along the long hallway, longing for a chance to poke her nose into some of the rooms. She kept her eyes front and stepped through the main door and out onto the cobbles of the courtyard.

It had been possible to forget for a while that they were surrounded by people.

31

'Ivy, would you step in a minute?' Ria stood in the open doorway of the house which was now hers. Frank had repaired the front door and put a new lock on it. 'I need your advice.'

The murder of Ria's mother was a closed case to the Garda and they had established she was the legal owner of her family home. Meanwhile, the Fraud Squad had taken over the investigation.

Ria hated to give up the company she'd found in Frank and Ivy's homes. She'd been spoiled and cosseted but it was time to move on. She had decided she would rent her downstairs back rooms and had mentioned that to Ali. She really didn't want to rent to strangers. She needed to talk to Ivy about the matter.

'Give me a minute.' Ivy bit back a sigh. 'I need to change out of this fancy outfit. Better come with me to my place.'

With Ria on her heels, she knocked on her own front door. She hadn't brought a key with her.

'I thought you were lost,' Frank said as he pulled open the door.

'Thanks for letting me in. I forgot me key.' She walked down the hallway.

With the other two following, she stepped into her kitchen.

'I have no idea what to do with this.' Alison

stood at the kitchen table staring at a blood-soaked parcel in horror. 'Jem said to tell you they've been hung — whatever that means!' she almost wailed.

The kitchen was spotless. The woman was a marvel at cleaning the place.

'Ria, Frank, sit down — yez are making the place look untidy.' Ivy took up the reins of her life. 'Ali, put the kettle on.'

She noticed Úna Connelly sitting in the workroom unpicking seams, a pile of clothing on the table in front of her. Her poor bruised face looked bad with the light streaming in the big windows.

'I've got to change me clothes.' Ivy walked towards her bedroom while asking over her shoulder, 'Did Jem say if that parcel was rabbits or birds?'

'Rabbits,' Alison answered.

'Right, put the kettle on and get me biggest pot out from under the sink. I won't be long.'

Ivy stood in her bedroom listening to the chatter coming from her kitchen. She missed the peace of Augustina's kitchen already. She changed into a long black skirt and lavender knitted jumper while trying to think what she had on hand to feed the people sitting around her table. She was starving. She pushed her feet into her work boots.

'Ali, is your Mike in the back garden?' She stepped out of her bedroom, closing the door at her back. The room was a mess, the bed unmade. Ali cleaned the kitchen and workroom but the bedroom was private.

'He's in the bathroom.'

'I'm here.' Mike, freshly scrubbed, stepped into the kitchen.

'I need you to grab a bike from the livery and do some shopping for me,' Ivy said. 'I've no food to feed this lot.'

'I'll pay.' Ria put a hand in her pocket. Ivy had changed two of the gold sovereigns for her.

'I'll let you.' Ivy stood for a moment, thinking what would be quickest to prepare. She didn't feel like standing over hot pans all morning. She wanted to get those rabbits into a stew.

'It'll be sausage sandwiches.' She began writing on a piece of paper. 'Mike, the butcher for two pounds of sausage and a tub of drippin', the baker for four large turnovers — my Jem loves a turnover.' The boot-shaped loaf was a Dublin favourite. 'I'll want fresh vegetables from the greengrocer. You'll have to go to the creamery too. I need milk and butter. Just this once get the milk in bottles — I haven't time to scrub out me milk can.' There was a charge for glass bottles that would be refunded upon their return. She passed the list to Mike.

Ria pressed two silver half crowns into his hand. She had no idea how much all that food would cost. He should have more than enough.

Mike put his hat on his head and left the kitchen with a smile. He had his orders.

'Úna, you may as well come out here!' Ivy took the bloody parcel from the table and carried it over to her sink.

Ali had put the big silver pot on the floor in front of the sink. Now she began to scrub down the oilcloth that covered the table. Ria and Frank pushed back out of her way. When the table was clean and dried, they sat down at it and Úna joined them.

Ali and Ivy danced around each other as they performed their chores. Ali made the tea and set the table. Ivy began removing covered jars from the cupboards under the tall freestanding dresser.

'I can't believe you Connelly girls can't cook stews. You'll have to learn, Ali, if you're going to leave home.' Ivy threw barley, lentils and the dried herbs she mixed herself into the water she'd put into the big pot.

Ali ignored Ivy's remark about cooking. Their mother cooked over an open fire — with children constantly under her feet she'd never had time to give lessons. In any case, stews would normally be meatless 'blind stews'.

Ivy got on her knees to search the back of the cupboard where she stored her vegetables to hunt out the remains of her celery. She preferred to use the fresh green leaves but in a pinch the stalks would do.

'Give us a hand with this pot, Frank,' she said as she got to her feet.

'That thing's like a witch's cauldron.' Frank walked over to take one handle of the overlarge pot — at his nod the two carried the pot over to the range.

'It does the job.' Ivy opened the paper-wrapped parcel in the sink, revealing three freshly skinned and cleaned rabbits. She added these to the stew pot, pressing its lid on top.

She'd leave the pot over the flame in the range until the water boiled then she'd move it to the back to simmer. She'd add fresh vegetables later.

'There's only enough milk for one cup of tea each until Mike gets here.' Ali began pouring the tea into the cups she had ready on the table.

'Have you thought about what I mentioned to you, Ali?' Ria asked as she reached for a cup. 'About the rooms?'

Ali sighed as she sat down at the table. 'I don't think Conn and me would be able to afford the rent on those rooms,' she said, looking around Ivy's home with envy.

'We have a tenant that gets a reduction in rent for keeping the public areas clean.' Ivy almost collapsed into one of her kitchen chairs. This morning had felt as long as a week already. 'Perhaps something like that would be of interest to you, Ria?'

'We have a lot of planning to do before we're ready to talk about rent and such.' Ria added milk to her tea from the jug sitting on the table.

Ivy's place appeared palatial to Úna's eyes, accustomed as she was to living in two rooms with a large family. 'Ali,' she said, 'if you rented a place like this, I think Liam and Vera would share the rent with you. Those sheds out the back would suit Liam's dogs. I'd love to live there meself but I've no work.'

'Look out, Ria, it will be the invasion of the Connellys!' Frank sipped from the china cup. He'd get a mug when the lad got back with the milk. 'Are you shaking in your boots?'

'I think I'd enjoy the company,' Ria said thoughtfully.

Ali looked at her hopefully. 'Would you really, Ria?'

'Yes — I would.'

Ali turned to her sister. 'But, Úna,' she said, 'what would happen to me ma if we all moved out?'

'Me da would have to become the man of the house. It might be the making of him.' Úna stood and walked over to stand behind her sister. She began to massage Ali's back. It was something all of the Connellys did without thought. 'Our Mike will want to be part of this too.' Úna had the bit between her teeth. She wanted to be part of this herself. If her brothers and sisters were going up in the world, she wouldn't be left out.

'Where would you all sleep though?' Ria asked. She couldn't imagine so many people living in her downstairs back rooms. 'So many beds would take up a lot of space.' She had no concept of sharing a mattress with siblings, being an only child.

'Frank could make yez cupboard beds if you're serious about moving,' Ivy added her tuppence worth. 'Emmy loves hers and it keeps her warm and cosy at night.' She pointed to where Emmy's cupboard bed stood against the kitchen wall. Ivy knew all about sleeping on any available surface under newspapers and old coats. She'd never seen or heard of cupboard beds until Jem had built one for Emmy.

'I've never seen one.' Úna didn't mention that they could just use mattresses on the floor. 'Can I look?' She pointed to the cupboard.

'Be my guest,' Ivy said.

'Frank can tell yez what's what.' Ivy knew it was only a pipe dream — they hadn't the money for fancy beds — but it did no harm to dream.

'That's a great idea.' Ali had often admired the clever design of the cupboard.

'They'd need to be a mite bigger with the beds one on top of the other,' Úna said. She wanted a cupboard bed. 'We could have one for the girls and one for the boys.' She stepped back to look at the drawer under the bed.

'What were you thinking of using for money, young Úna?' Frank asked.

'I haven't thought about that yet.' Úna grinned then winced when her cut lip stung. 'Ah, well, I may as well dream here as in bed.'

'If the cupboards are built into the rooms then the cost of them should be mine as the owner of the house,' Ria said.

'I could build them,' Frank said. 'But they won't come cheap.'

'What are you planning to do with the rest of the house, Ria?' Ivy asked.

'Like Úna — I haven't thought about that yet.'

'Well, you need to give it some thought,' Ivy said just as a knock sounded on the front door.

'That'll be Mike.' Frank stood and hurried from the kitchen.

Mike appeared with a brown-paper-covered parcel which he passed to Ivy. 'Here's the parcel of sausages from the butcher. I figured you'd

256

want that first since we're all starving.' He gave her a cheeky grin.

'You were right.' She opened the parcel and scooped dripping into the warm pans. She pricked the skin of the sausages — they wouldn't be pretty but they'd be fast. 'Ali, we need a fresh pot of tea. Úna, if you could cut the bread, please?'

Mike carried in the food he'd bought from the local shops. His stomach was rumbling with hunger. He didn't pay any attention to the conversation. He wanted to get the food in and the bike returned. His mouth was watering at the thought of a sausage sandwich and a mug of tea.

Ria began putting the bread Úna sliced onto a wooden breadboard. The butter could be served in its greaseproof paper sitting on a plate. There was no time to make fancy butter balls or curls.

'Úna, I was just thinking,' she said, 'I'm going to need someone to help me sort through the rooms next door. I'll need help around the place too. I have no idea where to shop for foodstuffs, for example. I could also use company while I'm walking out and about. Would something like that interest you?'

'Úna!' Ali gasped. 'Something like that would be ideal for you!' She knew her sister hated gutting fish.

'Don't be daft.' Úna kept her eyes lowered. 'Look at the state of me. I couldn't go walking around the fancy streets.'

'We can do something about your appearance,' Ali said. She knew Ivy would be willing to help and she herself had money in the bank. She felt

257

ashamed when she compared her own fashionable drop-waist dress to her sister's shabby long
skirt and frayed jumper. She'd been so busy
enjoying her own improved circumstances she'd
never given a thought to her sister.

'The first thing you need to do is talk with yer
mother,' Frank put in, staring at Ali and Úna.
'Yez can't make plans to move six of her childer
without talking to the woman.'

'You're right, Mr Wilson,' Ali said. 'We're
running before we've even started to crawl.'

'And I'll have to clear all of that stuff from
next door before I know where I am,' Ria said.

Mike slipped silently into the room and took a
seat at the table.

'You could hire my Jem to shift the stuff when
you're ready. I know an auctioneer who would
happily sell all of that fine art for you, Ria.' Ivy
turned the sausages. 'I'd have a look at it first
— give you a rough idea of what it's worth. The
man has an auction house on Stephen's Green.
He'll take a chunk of your money for his troubles
but it may be the answer to your problems.'

'Ivy, I can't thank you enough.' Ria needed all
the help she could get. 'That would be
wonderful.'

All conversation stopped while the food was
served. The only sound was from the movements
each person made as they put their sandwiches
together.

When the first cup of tea and the first
mouthfuls were consumed, it was Frank who
broke the contented silence.

'The postman's been, by the way. I got a letter

and the rent from Madame Beauchalet. She'll be here next week.'

'You'll enjoy meeting her, Ria,' Ivy said. 'She's a character.' She wondered if she should warn Ria that her brother Eamo was back in Dublin. She thought back to his questions about the woman that time she'd met him. Someone like Ria with a house of her own and the promise of money from the goods stocked in that house would be very attractive to a man like Eamo — he was always looking to make money the easy way.

32

Ivy stood with Ann Marie and Ria in one of the upstairs rooms of Ria's house.

'Well, there were no flies on Gibson, or whatever his name was.' Ivy moved more paintings forward so she could reach those behind. 'If you'll take my advice, you should give some paintings to the auctioneer. Gibson obviously bought some of these as investments. They are by unknown local artists — chances are he got the paintings for next to nothing — there are always starving artists who will trade a painting for a meal.'

'A great many of the items in the other rooms are valuable.' Ann Marie refused to be left out of the excitement.

'Name of God,' said Ria, 'I feel buried under all of this stuff. I want to feel as if this house is my own. There is so much to be done to clear up the mess that man left after himself.' She was feeling overpowered by all that needed to be done to claim her own life back. 'Is any of this even mine to get rid of?'

'The Fraud Squad said it was your money that bought these articles,' Ann Marie insisted. 'Gibson kept meticulous records of his dealings.'

'They must have been disappointed.' Ivy was still examining paintings. 'I think they thought they'd discovered a major crime ring in The Lane.'

'They could have removed all of this stuff as far as I'm concerned.' Ria hated to see the reminders of that pair of murdering bastards around her mother's house.

'If I'm not mistaken, this 'stuff' as you call it will finance those travels you talk about, Ria,' Ivy said.

Over the last two weeks, with the help of the Connellys, Ria had already boxed up a great many items to take to auction. She looked around to be sure they had the upstairs to themselves. 'Could I ask you to be an absolute angel, Ivy, and have a word with the Connellys? I don't think they are altogether happy with the arrangements.'

'I suppose it must be hard to learn to take care of yourself when you leave home,' Ivy remarked absently. She was glad to have her energy levels back up to something that felt like normal. That horrible feeling of tiredness was gone. She'd been afraid she was sickening for something. 'It's not my place to give them a lecture but if you think it would help . . . ' She stood back from the stacks of paintings and dusted her hands off. She felt as if she'd been eating dust.

'I don't know what to do to help them.' Ria had noticed the unhappiness of her tenants but she had no notion what their problem was.

'I know from experience how difficult it is to learn to be responsible for your own household,' said Ann Marie.

The three women left the upstairs rooms and walked down the stairs.

'You two go in and sit down,' Ivy said. 'And,

Ria, if you could make this one,' she nodded towards Ann Marie, 'put her feet up everyone would be grateful.'

'Just you wait, Ivy,' Ann Marie groaned. 'I'll get my own back!'

'Grand.' Ivy waved and made her way to the back of the house. 'Just so long as you do it sitting down.'

She walked into the kitchen and stared at the people gathered around the long kitchen table. It was early evening — the day's work was done for most of them. Liam and Vera were missing — they would be at the theatre. There was no smell of food.

'Úna, make a pot of tea, please,' she said.

'I can't — nobody lit the range.' A fashionably dressed Úna crossed her arms over her chest and glared. 'This lot think because I'm here all day I should be waiting on them hand and foot.'

'Yez can't go on like this,' Ivy sighed. What made her the boss — why did she have to tell them what to do? But she knew she should have kept an eye on them. She knew they had bought two mattresses from Jem but she hadn't thought to ask about anything else.

She stood over the big wooden table, her hands fisted on her hips. 'Now, you lot, there are six of you living in these three rooms.' She looked around at the space that was a copy of her own rooms in the house next door. 'If everyone does their own share of the work you'll be living like kings.' She stared at the two men sitting like lumps at the table. 'I've no time for useless men. I trained me brothers to share in the work of keeping house. You should all do the same. Start as you mean to go on.'

'Me da doesn't do any housework,' Mike dared to say.

'I don't have a great deal of respect for your da at this moment in time, Mike.' Ivy glared at him. 'I suggest you don't hold him up to me as an example of manhood.'

She waited for any more objections.

When none were forthcoming, she continued, 'Ali, you need to make a list of jobs to be done.' She pointed at the range. 'That range is the most important thing in the place. It will keep you warm and fed if you look after it. One person can be responsible for it every week. There will be no crying over who has to fetch coal and who has to clean it. Do I make myself clear?'

'Who is the boss?' Mike, the youngest, asked.

'There is no boss.' Ivy felt sorry for them. 'You are all adults. You just need to share responsibilities. You need to put someone in charge of the money. One of you needs to be in charge of the shopping, another in charge of the cooking, another the cleaning. That can be the same person all the time or it can change around — that's up to you. But I will be checking on you and, if I don't like what I see, ears will be boxed.'

'Edward arrived,' Ria said, coming into the kitchen. 'He has removed his wife. He offers his apologies for not stopping to greet you.'

'Thank God for that.' He'd make Ann Marie take it easy. 'I've got to be getting along. I've a husband to feed. Mike, if you'd come into mine at about seven I'd appreciate it — I want to talk to you.'

'I'll be there.' Mike didn't know what Ivy wanted to talk to him about but he'd listen.

'I'm off.' She left them arguing over who should run to the chipper and pick up chips. She walked next door and into the warmth of her kitchen with a grateful sigh.

★ ★ ★

'Well, Mike, what do you think?'

The evening meal had been eaten, Jem was away on cinema business, and Ivy had laid out her plan to a wide-eyed Mike.

'Name of God, Ivy!' Mike sat stunned. 'Name of God!'

'Do you think you can do it?' Ivy had thought carefully about her proposal.

'Take over your business?' Mike was gasping.

'Not quite.' Ivy laughed aloud. 'I want to train you to run the market-dealing part of the business. I don't plan to let you take over. I need another pair of hands and, as I said, it has to be someone who can wheel and deal with the best of them.'

'I've never had to wheel and deal. I don't know if I can do it.' Mike didn't want to talk himself out of a job but he wanted to be honest.

'You have the gift of the gab, Mike Connelly.' Ivy liked this young man. 'I know you have a good brain in your head. Your mother saw to it that you could all make your way in the world — more power to her.' Despite her harsh existence, Lily Connelly had made sure they all profited from the time they'd spent in school.

'I'd work me socks off for yeh, Ivy.' Mike couldn't believe the chance he was being offered. He'd have money coming in and a share in the profit on what he shifted. My God, he'd be made up.

33

'You're looking very glamorous this morning, missus.' Jem, returning from the bathroom, stopped to admire his wife. He'd returned from the livery to take a bath before changing. 'Where are you off to this morning?'

'I want to visit Geraldine in the toyshop in Grafton Street.' Ivy was wearing her pencil skirt with the purple twinset. She wanted to get her money's worth out of the clothes before her waist started to thicken.

'I have to change, myself.' He'd pulled his work clothes on after his bath. He stepped closer and pressed a kiss into her cheek. 'I've a meeting in the Hibernian Club.' He almost laughed to hear the words leaving his mouth. Who would have thought? 'Where is everyone?' It was unusual to find Ivy alone.

'Frank collects the rent today.' Ivy pulled a wraparound apron over her clothes. 'He's waiting in his own place until everyone has paid. Ali went to the bank for me and Mike's down the market.' She put the kettle on to boil. 'Do you have time to grab a bite to eat?'

'Any eggs?'

'The egg-man has been.' Ivy bought fresh eggs from a man who sold produce from his cart.

'I'll have a mug of tea and a sandwich after I've changed into one of my fancy suits.' He turned towards the bedroom.

She pushed her sleeves up her arms, not willing to risk getting grease on her pretty cardigan. The gold watch on her wrist caught her attention and she removed it. She wasn't accustomed to wearing jewellery.

'Armstrong wants us to start building on the plot of land beside us!' Jem called from the bedroom.

'Frank always claimed that land went with this house,' Ivy called back, 'but I saw no mention of it in the papers that came to me when I bought the house from him.'

Jem walked into the kitchen, tying his necktie. He'd left the waistcoat and jacket of his suit in the bedroom. 'Armstrong reckons it's better to ask pardon than permission.'

'You're going ahead with the automobile taxi service then?'

'It's a good time and Enda Reynolds has finally got his head out of his arse.' Jem hoped the man didn't take so long to think over every decision.

Ivy poured tea and brought the food to the table.

'This is nice.' Jem picked up his sandwich from the warm plate she'd put in front of him. 'Aren't you having any eggs?' He examined the lightly buttered bread in her hand. 'That's not much to start the day.'

'It's all I want.' She couldn't face a fried sandwich first thing.

'You should put that watch back on.' He picked up the watch from the table and passed it to her. 'You'll lose it if you keep taking it off.'

'I'm not used to wearing a watch.' Ivy held out her arm for him to fasten the gold buckle.

'Is yer woman,' he jerked his head towards the front of the house, 'still trying to pay her rent with jewellery?'

'I don't know what to do about that, Jem.'

The aging actress, Madame Beauchalet, was cash-strapped at the moment. She'd offered the watch to Frank in payment of arrears.

'I'm between a rock and a hard place. I can't help feeling I've taken advantage of her but what can I do?' She had made an offer for the watch, deducted the rent from the amount and given Frank the cash over and above to hand back to Madame Beauchalet. But she knew the watch was worth a great deal more than she paid for it.

'You can't eat jewellery.' Jem didn't see the problem. The woman was in need and Ivy gave her the going value. 'A thing is only worth what someone is willing to pay for it. You've told me that often enough.'

'I had another cheque from Betty Armstrong today.' Ivy's aunt lived in America. The woman had a factory that produced cosmetics. She used recipes Ivy had inherited from Granny Grunt for some of those cosmetics. She paid Ivy a very generous royalty on each item sold.

'There won't be much call for cosmetics if what we've been hearing about the American economy is true.'

'Perhaps for the general public but I can't see the film industry suffering.' But Ivy too was concerned about the rumours coming out of America. She didn't know how it would concern her but there was bound to be a knock-on effect if America began to have financial difficulties. 'Shay tells me there are long queues of people stretching around the studios trying to get what he calls 'extra' work.'

'We'll have to be careful.' Jem laughed, his teeth gleaming in his tanned face. 'We are among those with money these days.' He took her hand and kissed it. 'Who would ever have believed it?'

★   ★   ★

'That woman is driving me mad.' Frank pushed open the kitchen door after a quick rap of his knuckles against the wood. He had the ledger under his arm and a box in his hand.

'Come in, why don't yeh?' Ivy stood to fetch another enamel mug. The men in her life refused to use her pretty china.

'I'll finish getting dressed,' said Jem.

'Why are yez both dolled up?' Frank looked from one to the other as he sat down at the table.

'We've things to do,' Ivy answered while Jem went into the bedroom, closing the door at his back.

She placed the mug of tea in front of Frank and sat down opposite him. 'What's that you have?' She nodded towards the jeweller's case in his hand.

'The latest in that woman's loot.' He placed the case in front of her and picked up the mug of tea.

Ivy opened the case. 'Name of God!' She pushed it away from her, clasping her hands to her mouth. 'That thing is worth a bloody fortune if it's real!'

'What is?' Jem stepped from the bedroom, fully dressed in his business suit. He looked at the contents of the box, and whistled long and loud.

Ivy snapped the lid of the case closed, hiding the glittering necklace nestled in its velvet tray. She stared at the box on the table as if it were a snake. 'I'll have to talk to her, Frank. There is no way we can keep taking jewels instead of money.'

'I wish you would.' Frank rubbed the back of his neck. He was out of his depth dealing with pretty baubles.

'I'll talk to her when I get back from town.' Ivy got up and removed her apron. 'I'm going to walk out on my husband's arm.' She started to say more but a heavy rapping on the front door distracted her.

'Who in the name of God is that?' Frank barked, pushing to his feet. 'They'll break the door down banging like that.' He stormed down the hallway.

Jem closed the kitchen door but stood just inside in case he was needed. He held up his hand when Ivy went to speak, then stepped away from the door quickly.

'Mrs Ryan?' Frank didn't open the door after knocking politely. 'Mrs Ryan, there are some people out here wanting to talk to you.'

'I'll come with you,' Jem almost whispered. He opened the door and stepped out. 'What is it, Mr Wilson?'

'There are people here wanting to speak to

Mrs Ryan.' Frank kept his back to the front door and glared in warning.

Ivy stepped out and around the two men. She walked towards the open door.

'I am Mrs Ryan,' she said simply, staring at the two men standing there. The two men hastily took their hats off.

'Mrs Ryan,' the older of the two men said, 'we are from the St Vincent de Paul Society — may we step inside?'

'No.' Ivy delighted in the shock on their faces. These men were too accustomed to people almost licking their boots in the hope of receiving their aid. 'You can explain your business with me out here for all to hear.' If she brought them in there would be whispers running around The Lane in seconds.

'I think you would prefer to discuss our concerns in private,' the older man tried again.

'I have a great deal of business to conduct today.' Ivy delighted in pulling back her sleeve to consult her gold watch. 'To my knowledge I have no business with the Vincent de Paul. Please state your business so I may get about mine.'

'Mrs Ryan — ' the older man started to insist.

'My wife and I have matters to attend to.' Jem stepped to Ivy's side. 'Please state your business.'

The two men stared at the prosperous-looking couple in amazement before looking back at the barefoot children running screaming around the cobbled courtyard.

'We have reports from concerned members of our community,' the older man blustered while the younger man pulled at his necktie. 'It

271

appears that you, Mrs Ryan, have been leading impressionable minors into disrepute.' He consulted the notes in his hand.

'I beg your pardon?' Jem stood to his full height, towering over the men in front of him.

'I'm afraid you will have to explain.' Ivy was almost enjoying herself.

A crowd of interested people were gathering in the courtyard. It was probable many had had dealings with these men.

'Mrs Ryan, I really do think this matter would be better discussed inside.'

'And I've refused to allow you entrance,' Ivy said. 'Now state your business or allow me to go about mine.'

'Very well.' The man was becoming impatient. He was not accustomed to being treated in this fashion. These people came to his society for handouts. He was doing his Christian duty and didn't appreciate being treated like a door-to-door salesman. 'You have been accused of leading,' he consulted his notes and began reading off the six Connelly names, 'astray. We are here to remove these minors from your home.'

'I know the people you've named.' Ivy's blood was ice. 'They are none of them minors nor do they reside with me.' She pointed to the attached house. 'They live next door but I doubt they are home now. They are all gainfully employed.'

'I insist on your proving that.'

'I don't have to prove anything.' Ivy prepared to close the door. 'Their parents live over there.' She pointed to the tenement house across the way. 'I suggest you speak with them — good day, gentlemen.' She pushed Jem back with one hand while closing the door with the other.

'That — ' Frank began to say.

Ivy held her finger to her lips. She hadn't heard the men leaving yet.

They walked down the hall and into Ivy's kitchen.

'That Leary is really scraping the bottom of the barrel setting the Vincent de Paul on you.' Frank almost collapsed into a chair.

'It's a pity they don't protect the children really in danger.' Ivy pushed her hands through her hair. 'I don't want to deal with this now. I refuse to let that man and his cohorts ruin my plans for the day.'

'I'll bring all this in later.' Frank picked up the ledger and jewellery box. 'I'll tell yeh something for nothing. Lily Connelly looks like a new woman since her eldest children moved out. I don't think it was her or Brian that sent that lot after you.' It stood to reason the family were better off, he thought — it was easier to look after just four young children — and the six that left had been old enough to talk back to their parents. Brian Connelly wouldn't have liked that.

'I can't bring myself to care.' Ivy walked into the bedroom to fetch a jacket.

'Jem — ' Frank began.

'Leave it, Frank.' Jem agreed with Ivy. 'I'm going to walk out of here with my wife on my arm and my head held high.'

34

'He is a disgusting individual.' Violet Williams, once Burton, then Murphy, stated. Really, when she'd accepted this man's visiting card she had not expected the topic of conversation to drift to that disgusting lecherous windbag Father Leary. What on earth was Jacob Kilbride Jacobs doing questioning her about the man?

'I have been making discreet enquiries about him.'

JJ stared at the icy beauty across the small round table from him. He'd chosen to make an informal afternoon visit to his neighbour and enquire after his health. The man had been rumoured to be at death's door for some time. He'd been fortunate to find only the man's daughter-in-law at home to visitors. It had worked out better than he could have hoped.

'But I have been meeting with very little satisfaction,' he went on. 'Your name was mentioned in passing as someone who might be of assistance to me in my enquiries.' He'd been warned to tread carefully.

'I dare to suggest to you that the people who know that man best will not be found in polite society. He is a man of unsavoury appetites.' She'd made the mistake of commenting in company on his inappropriate behaviour when in her presence. If she had known what the results would be she'd have held her tongue. The man

274

had become fixated in his determination to bring her to her knees. He'd set out to destroy her — he'd almost succeeded.

'I've found many in polite society who support the Parish Priest in all of his endeavours.' JJ had been shocked to receive veiled warnings about the nature of his enquiry.

Violet was concerned about her own involvement in this matter. However, if she could do the good Father a disservice — well — she'd take the chance.

'Father Leary,' she hated to even say the man's name, 'uses — shall we call it 'intimate knowledge' of his acquaintances' vices to keep them donating generously to his church while at the same time keeping his reputation pristine.'

'You are speaking of blackmail, Mrs Williams?' JJ had suspected something of that nature but this was the first time he'd found someone brave enough to put it into words.

He wondered about the woman sitting so calmly sipping at her tea. She was dressed in the height of fashion, her blonde hair beautifully groomed. There was a brittle quality about her that he found unsettling. The violet eyes that should have been a startling feature in her high-cheeked, patrician face, were lifeless. She reminded him strongly of someone but he couldn't think who in his acquaintance that could be.

'I have made no such accusation.' Violet reached for the solid silver teapot to replenish her cup. She did not offer her guest more tea. She wanted the man gone from her presence. He had raised memories she preferred to leave buried.

JJ accepted the dismissal his hostess had indicated by not offering more tea. 'I have taken enough of your time, Mrs Williams.' He rested his bone-china teacup on its saucer and laid both on the large circular silver salver sitting so prominently on the table between them.

'I'm curious.' Violet felt she could question him now that he was making a move to leave. 'What is your interest in this man?'

'I hesitate to say.' JJ looked towards the closed doors of the withdrawing room. The colourful arrangements of flowers in the marble fireplace did not appear to lend any charm to this room. He was chilled by the atmosphere. 'I will say only that the man is guilty of persecuting an acquaintance of mine. I had hoped to discover a way to halt his endeavours or force the man to reveal his hand in such a way that he might be cautioned publicly.'

'Is your acquaintance male or female, may I enquire?'

'Female.' JJ stood.

'Then may I suggest she flee as far and as fast as she can.' The movement of Violet's mouth could not be called a smile. It was more of a grimace.

'Thank you for your time.' JJ didn't need details of how a man such as Leary could abuse a woman. The very thought made his flesh crawl. 'You have been most helpful.'

He waited for her to summon the footman to escort him out. He tried to walk slowly from the room when the footman opened the door. It wouldn't do to run as he so fervently wished.

'What an extraordinary encounter,' he muttered when he stood outside the closed door of the house on Merrion Square. He set his hat firmly on his head. I wish now I had agreed to my wife's company, he thought. I'd like her opinion of the situation — and that woman.

He set out walking in the direction of the Hibernian Club.

★   ★   ★

'Well met, gentlemen, may I join you?' JJ walked to a group of men who were acquaintances of his.

He received the expected response.

'Always welcome — certainly — be our guest.'

'We are discussing future investment in the Americas,' Edward O'Connor said while JJ stood waiting for a servant to carry another high-back leather chair towards the group.

JJ waited until the servant had placed the chair and withdrawn.

'I would not advise you to invest.' He tipped the crease in his pants to sit. 'I have some connections there. The news I'm receiving is unsettling.'

'I too have been told of dark whispering amongst the people in the know.' William Armstrong puffed on his cigar, a crystal tumbler of whiskey in his hand. His sister Betty lived in America. She had always had a man's head on her shoulders. She'd warned him to be careful

277

— it didn't do to ignore her advice.

Jem Ryan puffed on a cigar, wondering how in the name of God he'd ended up in this company. Ann Marie had begged him to remove Edward from under her feet. The man was driving her demented with his fussing. He'd thought a drink at the gentlemen's club would be just the ticket. He couldn't sit here like a tailor's dummy.

'My wife too has received word from her relations in America,' he said. 'They seem to think that the massive outlay of capital can only lead to disaster.'

'That is who she reminded me of!' JJ slapped the arm of his chair. 'It has been taxing my brain.' He accepted a cigar and a tumbler of whiskey from the servant standing silently at his elbow.

'It would help, old chap, if we knew what you were talking about,' William said when the servant left and JJ did not explain his comment.

'I have been making enquiries — ' JJ began.

'I know.' William had heard about this man's investigation and had been curious. 'You need to be more careful about whom you approach.'

'I had not thought my line of enquiry would be of interest to so many people.' JJ watched the men exchange glances.

'Dublin is a small tightly knit community — at every level of society.' William was aware of the listening servants.

'I am forced to admit that my lines of enquiry were not fruitful.' JJ watched, fascinated at the silent interaction between the men around the table. He had joined the group because of his

278

friendship with Ann Marie, the wife of Edward O'Connor. It was she who had pointed him in the direction of Mrs Williams, the lady he'd spoken with earlier in the day.

'The growing power of the Catholic Church and its followers was vividly portrayed for me in the recent elections,' William said. They had been forcefully controlled by the powerful men of the Church pulling strings. It had been a warning to all clear-thinking men in his opinion.

'Quite.' Edward too had been concerned by what he had observed during the canvassing.

'I'm surprised it came as a shock to you all.' Jem had feared the power-seeking members of the Church for some time.

'We digress.' William had noticed the sudden interest of the servants in their conversation. A man had to be careful of his words in public surroundings. 'You were about to tell us what caused you to exclaim when our friend Ryan here spoke about his wife's relations in America.' He pointed with his cigar, watching the servants carefully under lowered eyelashes.

'Oh, that!' JJ was content to change the subject. He did not like to discuss religion with others. 'I paid a visit to an ailing neighbour. The man is extremely frail. I simply called to express my sympathy and support.'

'Very civil of you.' William as Billy Flint had several urchins keeping an eye on this club and many other places around Dublin — information was power. You never knew what you might learn from the strangest places. He'd have a word with the lads watching this place.

'I was speaking with the lady of the house.' JJ allowed the servant to freshen his drink. 'And I was forcefully reminded of someone as we spoke.' He waited while the others were served. 'It wasn't until I saw Ryan here that the resemblance came to me.' The servants withdrew. 'The woman was the very image of your wife, Ryan. She had none of the warmth and charm of your good lady and the hair was of a different shade but they were as alike as two peas in a pod. It was uncanny.'

'Indeed?' Edward raised his whiskey.

'You would have been speaking with Mrs Williams, your close neighbour, I would suppose.' William liked nothing better than stirring trouble in that direction.

'You know her?' JJ was surprised. The lady had not been in residence for overlong at the Merrion Square address. He had not thought she would be acquainted with these men.

'Indeed.' A great word, William thought. It could cover so many things.

'The lady did provide me with the only solid information I've had so far in my investigation.' These men seemed to understand that he was making enquiries about the Parish Priest. There was no need to be more explicit.

'If anyone should know, she would.' William thought of the trouble that woman had brought to his wayward brother. She should never have married him. It had been the ruination of him.

'It is now I who am at a loss,' said JJ.

Jem had had enough. The poor man was only trying to help Ivy. They could not leave him floundering in the muck.

'The lady in question is my wife's mother.'

His words fell into the company like a rock. There was almost a physical sensation of movement under their feet. Almost like an earth shock.

Then the sound of Armstrong's loud laughter rang around the hushed room.

'That has put the cat among the canaries!' He wiped tears of mirth from his eyes and raised his glass to Jem.

'That's imposs — ' JJ snapped his teeth shut on the words wanting to pour from his lips. He pressed fingers to his throbbing temples, staring from one man to the other. Surely they were jesting — how could a girl from the slums be related to a woman from Dublin's highest echelon of society? It was impossible. He wasn't an innocent — he knew many men had by-blows running around the streets of Dublin — but the by-blow of a female — surely not!

'The lady — and I use the term loosely — was married to my brother.' Armstrong had nothing good to say about the woman.

'No!' JJ gasped.

'Ivy is the eldest of four — she has three younger brothers,' Jem stirred the pot. His Ivy's family had a lot to answer for in his opinion.

'The middle boy is the up-and-coming film star Douglas Joyce.' Edward was enjoying watching someone else reel in bewilderment at the conundrum that was Ivy Rose Murphy Ryan.

'But I watched her grow up,' JJ said. It was impossible not to see her running around the

281

Dublin streets in her ragged clothing, more often than not pushing a laden pram in front of her. She received goods from his own back door for goodness' sake! He'd believed her change in fortune had resulted from her marriage to Ryan — a man of property — but this — this was past believing.

35

Ivy was strolling along Grafton Street in the direction of Stephen's Green. The meeting with her buyer had been very satisfying. There was still demand for the Alice doll and the pre-Christmas orders for her baby dolls would keep her workers busy. The Ivy Rose dolls were more successful than she could ever have imagined when she'd first approached the shop in Grafton Street.

On the spur of the moment she turned right into a familiar lane. She'd visit Saint Teresa's church and light a few candles. She loved the peace to be found in an empty church. She'd have a chat with the people she'd lost — her da and old Granny Grunt. They didn't answer her but thinking through her problems as conversation helped her sort out her thoughts. She needed time to think about her life.

In the cool silent church she lit a candle and knelt down.

Granny, she prayed, I wish you could be here to enjoy the money being made by your wise-woman cures. The number of noughts on those cheques from Betty Armstrong is enough to make me dizzy. The money should be yours. You worked hard every day of your life for very little. I'm sorry about that. Do you know I'm going to have a baby? Wherever you are now — and I hope you're sitting on a big fat fluffy cloud in heaven — I hope you know about the baby. But I'm in a kind of a pickle, Granny.

Ivy looked at the flickering candle, thinking of the woman who had held her hand from the moment her own mother had deserted the family. She'd always carried her worries to Granny.

I'm surrounded by people, Granny. I don't know what to do. How do you ask people to leave you alone? Is that rude? I just want time on me own to think me own thoughts. If God is listening I'm not complaining — at least I don't think I am — I just want to be able to sit in peace with a cup of tea in me hand and gather me thoughts. Is that too much to ask?

She stood and lit another candle.

That's because I moaned so much — she sent the thought towards the heavens.

She lit another two candles. She was going to moan again.

Kneeling down, she spoke to her father.

Da, I'm having problems with our Eamo. He's got himself into some kind of trouble. I can tell by looking at him that he's been playing the big man around town. He's landed himself in hot water. I saw you do exactly the same thing many a time. Remember all those times I had to sell off some little treasure I had hidden from me round? How many times did I have to rescue you from your own folly, Da? If I refused to help, you usually pawned the bloomin' thing for less than it was worth. You were a hard man to keep, no offense, Da.

She could almost see him shaking his head at

284

her, his big blue eyes wide with innocence. He played innocent well, her da.

You're going to be a granda, Da. Ivy almost laughed aloud. The thought of that would kill yeh off right enough. Yeh'd tell me yeh were too young! But it's a fact. I'm going to have a baby. Maybe I should tell yer wife she's going to be a grandma. It'd be the death of her.

She blessed herself frantically. Imagine thinking something like that in the house of God. She stood quickly and lit two more candles — just in case — before returning to the bench to kneel and pray.

She raised her eyes to the heavens and thanked the Lord for her blessings. She had so much to be thankful for. She was eternally grateful for all the good in her life — but a bit of peace — was that really too much to ask for?

She remained on her knees for a while. She didn't know if lighting candles and talking to the deceased did any good. One thing she did know — it didn't do any harm. She stood, blessed herself, genuflected in the aisle — and with a smile on her face left the church.

She strolled in the direction of Stephen's Green, enjoying the sun on her face. She thought about going into the park to feed the ducks. She didn't feel like returning home just yet.

'Ivy! Ivy Murphy! I don't believe it. I was just at your place looking for you. They said you were out and about.'

Molly Coyle was distraught. Her little girl Jennifer was so unhappy. She hated working in the sweat shop. She was being picked on. Sally at the market had suggested she talk to Ivy Murphy. The woman was her last hope.

'Hello, Mrs Coyle.' Ivy looked at the drawn face of the other woman. Molly Coyle had once been a good-looking woman. You could see it in the bones of her face. But life had battered and bruised her.

Ivy looked back in the direction of the church she'd just left. It was almost as if Granny was standing at her shoulder. If she didn't do what she knew she must, she'd feel a phantom box around her ears. Jennifer Coyle was a lace-maker — just like Granny.

'I've been meaning to talk to you about your Jennifer.' There was no need to make the woman beg.

Ivy looked around. They couldn't stand in the middle of Grafton Street with the well-dressed toffs strolling past. It would embarrass Molly.

'Will you join me for a cup of tea in Bewley's?'

'In the name of Jesus, Ivy Murphy,' Molly Coyle was shocked at the suggestion, 'what would the likes of me be doing in a place like Bewley's, I ask yer sacred pardon?'

'I thought we could have a cup of tea and talk about Jennifer.' Ivy remembered when she'd been horrified at Ann Marie's invitation into that very place. It seemed a long time ago.

'There's a workman's caff down a side street.' Molly Coyle couldn't imagine paying for a cup of tea to be served to her. She was looking forward to the experience. 'We could go there if you're not too proud.'

'Lead the way, Mrs Coyle.'

'Call me Molly — every time you say 'Mrs Coyle' I look around for me mother-in-law.'

The café was in Clarendon Street within direct view of Saint Teresa's church. A poke around the ear from Granny to Ivy.

'I've seen Jennifer's work, Molly,' Ivy said when they had two heavy white mugs of tea in front of them. 'Sally at the market showed it to me. I'd have nothing that fine for her to do.'

'Ivy, I'm ready to get down and lick your boots if you'd give my Jennifer a chance.' Molly Coyle was shaking. 'Me man says how it's all my fault, that I babied the girl. I didn't really, Ivy, but she's me only girl. Her brothers are rough and tumble. They're not bad lads but they treat her a bit harsh. I've kept her close to me, you see.' She fought tears. It was all her fault her little girl was having such a hard time making it in the world.

'Molly,' Ivy leaned over and touched the other woman's hand, hating to see someone so upset, 'I've seen Jennifer's work — it is exquisite — and that's from someone who knows.' She used the word 'exquisite' deliberately, knowing it would be repeated in the Coyles' home that evening. 'Your daughter is very talented.'

'Oh Ivy, she is!' Molly beamed. 'She loves anything to do with colour and,' she paused for a moment, 'well, anything pretty. Not that there is much pretty around our place.'

'You live in George's Street, don't you?' The café they were sitting in was in a lane that divided Grafton Street and George's Street. They were steps away from Molly's home.

Molly nodded. 'We have a big room in one of

the places over the shops.'

'How much is Jennifer earning now?'

Ivy had some idea of the current wage but even she was shocked by the pittance the child earned for long hours of hard work.

'She's on good money because she's a fast little worker.'

'If I employed her, I'd also want her to lend a hand keeping the place clean and tidy. Is your Jennifer too proud to turn her hand to anything asked of her?'

'Indeed she is not!' Molly was highly indignant. 'Hasn't she been helping me scrub the place out almost from the minute she was born.'

'Molly, I know where you live.' Ivy was thinking hard. 'I know it won't take Jennifer long to get from your place to mine but I don't like to think of her walking along those streets on her own in the dark. It's not like going to a factory when there are loads of girls going in the same direction.'

'Her brother works in the Lyons factory on the other side of the canal. They could walk to work together.'

'Let me get more tea.' Ivy stood with the two heavy mugs in her hands. 'Are yeh sure you wouldn't like a cake or a meat pie or something?'

'Oh, go on then!' Molly felt the knot that had been in her stomach, ever since her girl started at that sweat shop, release. 'I'll have a meat pie, and thanks.'

Ivy returned with two brimming mugs. 'They'll bring the pie and mash when it's ready.' She sat down with a sigh. 'I should tell you,

Molly,' she hated to have to do this but it was only fair the woman knew, 'that I have problems not of my making with the Parish Priest. I don't know how he'll react if your Jennifer comes to work for me.'

Molly had heard all about the Parish Priest and Ivy Murphy. There weren't many that didn't have an opinion about the situation. All Father Leary had ever done for Molly was hold his hand out for money she didn't have. She didn't like the man, may God forgive her.

'Ivy,' she leaned forward to whisper, 'when that man pays me rent and puts food on me table, I'll listen to him then.'

Ivy wanted to jump up and kiss the woman. Someone with sense!

Molly sat back while the waitress served her the piping hot food.

'Enjoy that, Molly — I made it meself.' The waitress, a woman who lived in her building, smiled.

'Thanks, Tess.' Molly was almost licking her lips. 'I'll do that.'

'Fair enough, Molly,' Ivy said. 'Now, do you want Jennifer to come to mine and talk to me or can we arrange it between us?'

'Ivy, if I can tell my girl that she doesn't have to go back to that factory, she'll skip to your place.'

'What hours does your boy work in the factory?'

'He starts at five in the morning and works a fourteen-hour shift.'

'That seems a very long day.' Ivy felt guilty

about her eight to eight with Alison. 'I'm not even out of my bed that early in the morning.'

'They're out before the cock crows,' Molly agreed.

'Do you know Dai Griffiths?'

'Oh yes.' Molly was smacking her lips. What a rare pleasure to be served food someone else had prepared and she didn't even have to wash the dishes! 'He's a lovely man. He kept his horse down the back of our place until it took bad. I thought that would finish the old man off.'

'Dai works at the livery for my husband.' Ivy didn't know the man very well but Jem had nothing but good to say about him. 'Would you allow your Jennifer to walk over to my place with him?'

'But he doesn't start to work until nine in the morning on account of his age.' Molly was concerned. Jennifer needed to earn almost as much as she was bringing in now or her da would never let her leave the sweat shop.

'Jennifer will be able to give you a hand before she leaves for work then.' Ivy knew what the woman was thinking — every penny counted. 'She won't be on piece work with me. I'll pay her six shillings a week.'

'But that's how much a trained seamstress would earn,' Molly leaned forward to whisper.

'From what I've seen of her work she is well trained.'

'You are a blessing from above, Ivy Murphy.' Molly wouldn't tell her husband how much the child was earning. She'd say it was as much as the sweat shop and leave it at that. She'd put a

few pence aside each week and buy Jennifer a
decent outfit.

'Right, I have to get home and change out of
me glad rags,' Ivy said. 'I was coming from a
meeting when I ran into you. I'll pay for this lot
— I'll see Jennifer Monday morning.'

She walked towards the counter to pay for the
food, leaving Molly sitting stunned at the table.

36

'Is there nothing to eat in the house?' Brian Connelly stood in the open doorway of his two rooms and sniffed the air. 'A man needs something to eat when he comes in from work.'

Lily Connelly stood in front of the fire. She walked over to her husband with her hand out. She'd warned the four still living at home to stay away. Her husband was easier to handle without an audience.

'I thought you could treat yourself to fish and chips this evening,' she said with a smile. 'I know you'll be wanting to get to the pub — it being pay day and all.' She held her breath, praying he'd go along with her. 'The children and me will be fine.'

'That's the way it should be.' He slapped her housekeeping money into her hand without complaint. 'I'm the master of me own house. I'll not be gainsaid.' His was the only money coming in now.

'I've hot water ready if you want to have a quick wash.' She'd the kettle on the pulley over the fire.

'Nah.' He was hungry and he'd plenty in his pocket for the pub. He'd overtime pay to spend. 'I'll get fish and chips on me way to the pub.' He turned and left without another word.

'And the blessings of God on you too.' Lily's sigh came from deep in her heart.

292

She shook off her blue mood. She'd been invited out to dinner, if you wouldn't be minding. Her childer had invited them all over to their place.

'Is me da gone?' Carmel put her head around the door.

'He is. Get the others till I see if you've stayed clean.'

The three youngest children marched into the room with smiles on their faces. They were excited at being invited out to eat with their big brothers and sisters.

★ ★ ★

'Come on in, Mam.' Ali opened the door to their knock. 'We've the place to ourselves.'

Ria had taken Frank to see a play at the Gaiety.

'I've never been in one of these houses.' Malachi's eyes were everywhere. 'It's not half posh.'

'We don't live in this part of the house.' Ali led the way to the kitchen. 'We live in the back in the servants' rooms.' She didn't want the lad carrying tales to their da.

'Come on in.' Conn and Mike took their outdoor clothes from them. They threw them onto the mattress in the boys' room.

'I'm that nervous.' Úna stood in front of the range, rubbing her hands down the apron she'd made for herself. 'I've never cooked a proper meal for so many before.' She almost said Ivy had shown her how to cook the meal but thought better of it. No need to start the night on a sour note. 'Ma, you come sit in a soft chair.' She pointed to one of the chairs in front of the range. 'Our Ali will have the other. The rest of us can use the kitchen chairs. The meal won't be long.'

'I'll have a nose around first if you don't mind.' Lily had been consumed with curiosity about the living arrangements over here.

'Ma, look!' Carmel was playing with the tap. 'They have water inside — their very own tap!'

'I can see that,' Lily said. 'That range is a thing of beauty.' She was lost in admiration of the luxury in the room.

'We have two bedrooms,' Ali said quietly. 'One for the boys and one for the girls.' She was thankful they hadn't bought anything fancy for the bedrooms. There was no need to rub her mother's nose in their good fortune.

'I need the pot!' The youngest boy Rory was holding the front of his trousers.

'Conn, take him to the WC,' Ali said.

'Me too!' Amanda didn't want to be left out of anything.

'You can go to the outside bog or wait until Rory is back from the indoor one.' Úna didn't see why they should hide their advantages. She ignored the bull's looks she was getting from Ali.

'Imagine!' Lily wanted a look at these wonders herself.

By the time they all got back from the WC the food was ready.

'Will everyone sit down at the table, please?' Úna said.

She was positive she'd done everything just as Ivy had shown her. The potatoes were mashed and creamy. Conn and Mike had peeled them — complaining all the time. She'd boiled the onions in water before adding the smoked fish and making the white sauce. When Ivy made it, the food was delicious. She offered a prayer up to the heavens that she'd done everything right.

'Mam, you sit at the head of the table.' Ali pulled out the chair for her mother.

'I'll sit at the other end,' Úna said. 'I can jump up and down for food easier that way.'

'Right, the rest of yez!' Conn organised the family around the long wide kitchen table.

Úna had Conn carry the big heavy pots over to the table where they had placed two pieces of slate to protect the wood.

'With so many of us this was the best way we could figure out to do this,' Úna said. 'We'd spill too much if I filled the bowls at the stove to pass around. If everyone will pass me their bowls — one by one — I'll start filling them. Me mam first.'

The thick white bowls were passed along the table to the delight of the youngest children. They had never seen the like.

Úna put a big dollop of creamed potatoes into each bowl and a generous scoop of the fish to cover it.

'Help yerselves to the bread on the table,' Conn said, carrying the pots, the contents much diminished, back to the range.

'This is lovely.' Lily looked up to smile at Úna. 'I couldn't have done better myself.'

'Thanks, Mam.' Úna was almost faint with relief. 'I was so nervous. I didn't want to make a show of meself.'

Everyone tucked in. Compliments were paid to the cook from time to time but everyone concentrated on clearing their bowls.

'What's them funny balls in the dish?' Rory's eyes were almost bigger than his face. He'd never had so much food — it was lovely but it was all gone — but he could have bread too if he wanted, Conn said.

'That's butter, son.' Lily wanted to cry at having most of her family sitting around the table with her, tucking into the best meal they'd had in years. 'Who formed it into balls?'

'I did.' Úna blushed. Ivy had shown her how with two wooden paddles. She loved doing it.

Lily nodded. 'That Valeria Gibson is certainly training you well.'

'Valeria couldn't make a stew like this to save her life!' Mike laughed aloud. 'Ouch!' he yelled, staring at Conn across the table from him. 'Why did you kick me?'

Ali sighed. 'Mrs Ryan taught Úna to cook the food and make the butter balls,' she told her mother.

'Ivy is teaching me how to use the range,' Úna said.

Ali glared at her again. She didn't want to upset her mother. The poor woman had only an open fire to cook over. 'Would anyone like more food?' She asked the question that was sure to attract the attention of her young siblings.

'Can we?' Malachi asked.

'*Ma, can we?*' Rory shouted.

'*I want!*' Amanda yelled.

'You all quiet down now.' Lily rapped the handle of her spoon on the table. 'Answer your sister but in a nice polite way.'

'*Yes, please!*' they all yelled together.

Conn stood. 'I'll get the pots.'

'How am I going to do this?' Úna said as the four children thrust their bowls at her.

'*Put those bowls down!*' Lily ordered. 'Right, Úna — take one bowl at a time — return it to the person who gave it — then the next one is passed. Anyone who grabs gets nothing.'

'Thanks, Mam.' Úna began to refill the bowls, thrilled with the success of her first attempt at cooking. She'd be sure to tell Ivy how much everyone enjoyed it.

'Mam,' Conn looked down the table at his mother, 'Liam and Vera asked if you and our da would like to go see their show one evening. You could leave the youngsters with us one night while you and me da go out on the town.'

'Oh!' Lily held her hand to her heart. She hadn't been out on the town in years. 'I'll have to talk to your da.' She ignored the whining of the younger children who wanted to spend the night in this magical place.

'Of course,' Conn said.

'Can we see the rest of the house?' Carmel dared to ask.

'Afraid not,' Conn said. 'The place was left in a mess that hasn't been sorted yet. I'll ask Ria if she'll let you visit after the place has been cleared.'

'I've heard about that.' Lily and everyone else in The Lane had been talking about the goings-on in this house. 'Is it really that bad?'

'Mam, it's a nightmare.' Conn looked at the others who nodded in agreement.

'You know that old junk shop you used to take us to?' Ali remembered the visits to the shop long before all the babies started to arrive.

'Mr Hastlehoff — I haven't been there in years,' Lily smiled at the memory of holding a little Alison by the hand with a baby Conn in the pram. Where had the years gone?

'Well, upstairs looks a bit like that,' Ali said.

When the bowls had been licked clean — literally in the case of the younger ones — Conn stood to pull the black kettle that had been sitting on the back of the range over the fire. He took down a catering-size teapot and poured hot water inside to warm it.

Ali was aware of her mother's eyes following her son doing what would be called 'woman's work'. 'Mrs Ryan insists on everyone pulling their weight in a house,' she leaned forward to say.

'I'll make the tea if you clear the table, Mike,' Conn said.

Lily almost fell out of her chair when Mike stood without a word of complaint and began to clear the table of dirty dishes.

'We never realised how much you done for us, Mam,' Úna said softly.

'I'll set the table for the tea.' Ali stood to open the large cupboard standing against the wall.

The youngest children gathered around her to peek inside.

'Ooh, you've got lots of things!' Amanda's nose was almost in the cupboard.

'They came with the house.' Ali pulled her sister away before the child could be tempted to touch. 'I'll pass you the cups and saucers, Amanda, and you put each set carefully on the table when I tell you who it's for.'

'*Me, me!*' Rory bounced on his toes. 'What will I do?'

'I'll give you the mugs to put out.'

'Will you tell me who it's for and all?'

'The mugs are for the gentlemen.' Ali smiled down at his innocent face. She'd missed the youngsters.

'Ooh, am I a gentlemen?' Rory grinned widely in delight.

'You,' she bent to kiss his nose, 'are a gentleman.'

The setting of the table took twice as long with her helpers but she wouldn't have changed a thing.

Conn made the large pot of tea then refilled the kettle, placing it directly over the fire so they would have hot water to wash the dishes.

'Well,' Lily was taking it all in, 'I can see yez are getting on a treat.'

They all held their breath as Conn carried the huge teapot over to the table. Because of its size it had a handle directly over the spout to give the server additional support.

'Thanks, Mam,' he said. 'Like Úna said, we never realised all the work you did for us.' He smiled down at his mother. 'There was wigs on the green when we first moved in here.'

'Yeah.' Úna sat back to allow Conn to serve her tea. 'They all thought I should wait on them hand and foot just like you did.'

'I see you set them straight.' Lily watched Alison prepare milky sweet tea for the four youngest. Carmel was being served her tea in a fancy cup and saucer, much to her delight.

'I didn't.' Úna sipped her tea. 'Mrs Ryan did — all I did was moan and complain.'

Conn took his seat. 'Mam — ' he said, before jumping back up again. 'I forgot the biscuits.'

He pulled a brown-paper bag almost overflowing with biscuits from the cupboard. He emptied the bag under the watchful eye of the younger ones onto two large plates and set them on the table.

'Is that what you wanted to tell me?' Lily smiled at her eldest son. 'That you forgot the biscuits?'

'No.' Conn took his mug of tea in one hand and reached for a biscuit with the other. 'I wanted to tell you that we need help, Mam.' He prayed he could get this out without insulting his mother.

'I don't see how.' Lily looked around with pleasure. 'It seems to me you are all doing very well for yourselves.'

Ali decided to give her brother a hand. 'Mam, it's the laundry.'

'You know how fussy our Liam is,' Úna added her tuppence worth.

'You wouldn't know you were born doing

laundry in all this luxury.' Lily thought of the hours of hauling buckets of water — heating them over the fire — walking on the dirty clothes in the bathtub — trying desperately to get everything dry — putting the iron on the fire to heat. She eyed the drying rack that was tucked tightly against the ceiling. It was pulley-operated and could be dropped down in front of the range to dry the clothes. The iron could be put on the range top. Luxury indeed.

'Liam — ' Conn hoped his brother would forgive him for putting the blame on him — he wasn't here and hopefully their mother would have forgotten by the time she saw him, 'Liam wants to send the clothes out to the laundry.'

'Do you know how much those places charge?' Lily was shocked to think of giving anyone good money to wash clothes.

'Yes, we do, Mam.' Conn crossed his fingers under the table out of sight. 'We talked about it, Mam, and wondered if you'd do our laundry.' He leaned forward to stare at his mother. 'We'd pay you what we'd have to pay the laundry.'

'Would I do it here?' Lily couldn't imagine the luxury of having this big place to work in.

'If you would, Mam. When the youngsters are out at school. I'd put the big pots on the range in the morning to heat the water.' He knew his mother always sat in the cold. She lit the fire for the children coming home from school but never for herself.

'You'd have the place to yourself.' Úna too prayed her mother would accept. They'd be able to pay her and pass her little luxuries. 'I'd be somewhere around the house if you needed anything and Ali is only next door if I'm not here.'

'I'll have to think about it,' Lily said but she knew she would do it. Talk about having your cake and eating it too! She wouldn't know she was born.

37

In the house next door Ivy and Jem had eaten the same meal as the Connelly family and were now cuddled up in one of the soft chairs in front of the range.

'I had a cup of tea in a working man's caff today — in Clarendon Street.' She'd already told him about her decision to employ Jennifer Coyle.

'I know it well.' He rubbed his bristly chin over her head which was nestled in his neck. 'Before I married you, missus, I knew all the places a man could get a good cheap meal and a decent mug of tea.'

'I was a bit stupid though.' She'd wanted to kick herself all the way home. 'I was so intent on putting poor Molly's mind at ease that I told her to send Jennifer to me on Monday.' She hit his chest softly with her clenched fist. 'Sure, I forgot I won't be here. Monday I'm in and out the back garden and those sheds like a blue-arsed fly.' Monday was the day she did her round on Merrion Square.

'I'm surprised Leary has never tried to stop the wealthy from giving their discards to you.' Jem was wondering if he should shave before they went to bed. His Ivy's skin was so soft. He hated to mark it.

'He did,' Ivy laughed, 'don't you remember? He made the mistake of talking to the toffs who own the houses. Those people don't know I exist.

If he'd talked to the servants — not that he'd lower himself to do that — but if he had I'd be in a right pickle.'

'Just goes to show he's not all-knowing,' He was thinking about the conversation he'd had with JJ. The man was like a terrier hunting out facts.

Jem had come up against a brick wall when it came to a way of handling the good Father Leary. He wished he knew how to get the man to leave his wife alone. It was a sin what that man was trying to do to Ivy. Why couldn't he see that? He spouted lectures about sin and sinners often enough.

'I never found the time to talk to yer one,' she gestured with her hand towards the front of the house, 'about her bloody diamonds.'

'I wonder where she got them?'

'Let's not ask that!' Ivy laughed. 'We'd have Leary down on our necks for certain if she got them where I think she did.'

'That's none of our never mind,' he answered absently.

'I suppose I could get Ali to help Jennifer along.' She didn't really want another person under her feet all day but she could use the help of a skilled seamstress.

'You can set her some work to do.' He wasn't really listening, lost in his own thoughts. He was thinking of Conn in his new bespoke suit from Old Man Solomon. He'd looked a proper gent but there was something lacking. A bit of polish, he supposed you'd call it. He wondered how he could help there. He'd ask Ann Marie for her advice. 'Alison can show her what's what.'

'Jem Ryan, are you listening to me?' Ivy pushed away from his chest to glare into his eyes.

'Of course I am.' He wondered what he'd missed. He tried to pull her back into his arms. 'You were worrying about the young girl starting work with you Monday.' He hoped to heaven she'd still been talking about that.

She resisted the pull of his arms. 'I wanted to talk to the girl when she arrived.' She pushed further away from his chest to stare at him. 'I've never even clapped eyes on the girl. I don't want her to think she'll spend the rest of her days unpicking old dresses.' She began to settle back down, then suddenly pushed away again. 'And the state of me on a Monday — what will she think!' she almost wailed.

'You'll drill a hole in me chest if you're not careful.' He laughed. 'You're getting yourself into a state for nothing.'

'I suppose.' She snuggled in closer.

'Missus, will you stop wriggling or I'm going to throw you off and make you sit in your own chair!'

'I'm shaking in me boots.'

'You're not wearing any.'

They were silent for a while, then she asked, 'What did you do today — after you got dressed up all fancy — did you have a big important men-only meeting?'

'We talked about cleaners, would you believe?'

'Go way!'

'No, really. It's becoming a big problem for us at the cinema. The men leave melted toffee and

305

chocolate mashed into the carpet — and don't even get me started on mud from shoes. The place will be ruined if we don't do something about it — and soon.'

'There's your problem — right there.'

'What?'

'You said 'men'.'

'Yes, the men who work for us have to be able to turn their hand to whatever needs doing.'

'And when was the last time you saw a man pick up a bit of dirt?' Ivy pushed away to stare at him. The problem was easily solved.

'You'll have to explain it to me.' Jem knew he was missing something. He'd better pay attention.

'Employ women.'

'We couldn't do that.'

'I'll put the kettle on.' Ivy pushed to her feet.

Jem tried to grab her waist and pull her back down onto his knees. He missed: his Ivy wanted a pot of tea and she was fast.

'I must be the only man in the world who loses his wife's attention to a pot of tea.'

'I doubt that.' She occupied herself with preparing the tea. They hadn't had any after their meal. 'I've been thinking . . . '

'Oh Lord, spare me!' Jem groaned dramatically.

'Oh, whisht up!' she laughed. 'I've been meaning to talk to you about this for a while but I keep forgetting.'

'Right, lay it on me.' Jem stood to fetch the small table and carry it over to the range. He wasn't sitting on hard kitchen chairs. He liked a bit of comfort of an evening.

'Well, you have a man taking the money for the tickets — he's a disagreeable aul' bugger by the way — anyway, you know in the films at the speakeasy or whatever it's called, the people working in those places are pretty women with short skirts and a smile.'

'We couldn't have something like that, Ivy — Leary would lead the charge to break down the doors and burn the place around our ears.'

'I'm not explaining this right. You and the others — ARC — you're talking about having more than one cinema, right?'

She put everything she'd need close to hand on top of the small table and sat down in the chair opposite Jem. He was leaning forward in his chair, his expression intent. He was listening to her now. She knew he'd only been half listening before.

'We hope to have cinemas all over the country — in time.'

'Well, you should be selling the experience.' She poured the tea, searching for words to explain what she could see so clearly in her mind's eye. 'It's like the clothes we wear — what does Ann Marie call it — perception — that's the word I'm looking for.'

'You've lost me, love.' Jem accepted the mug of tea she handed him.

'Take this morning when those Vincent de Paul men knocked on the door.'

'I'd rather not think about that before bed — it will give me nightmares.'

'No, think about it, Jem.' Ivy leaned over to

307

shake his knee. 'We were all done up like the dog's dinner — it was only a fluke — but we looked the business. If we'd been wearing our work clothes those men would have pushed us out of the way and walked in — do you see what I'm saying?'

'I'm trailing behind as usual.'

'Right, I'm just going to spit it out — I'm getting meself into a muddle trying to spare your feelings.'

She jumped to her feet. She needed to pace to get her ideas across.

'Going to the cinema should be like going to the theatre. We got all dressed up when we went to see Shay on stage. You want to create that same feeling of specialness in your cinemas. You don't want hairy-handed men about the place. You want pretty smiling girls. You could even have elegant handsome young men. You can have security — that's a fact of life — but you can give the punters a feeling of stepping outside their own life into something glamorous.'

'Let me get a pad and pencil — I want to take notes.'

'Okay, I'll shut up.'

'No, I'm not being sarcastic, love.' Jem walked over and took her in his arms. They swayed together in front of the fire for a moment before he pressed a kiss onto her lips and let her go. 'I'm serious. I need to take notes.'

'You don't want to turn your cinemas into fleapits.' Ivy watched him take pad and pencil from the cupboard where she kept office supplies. 'You want going to an ARC cinema to be an evening out — a special occasion.'

'What else?' Jem had the pad on his knee, pencil at the ready.

'Stop selling loose sweets.' She hated listening to the rattle of paper bags when she was trying to hear her brother speak on the screen. 'Cadbury and Rowntree are selling those fancy little boxes of sweets. You should have a pretty girl selling those to the young men for their sweethearts. The girls would take the boxes home with them as a keepsake — cut down on the litter. As for the children, I'm sure a couple of lads from The Lane would pick up the litter after the matinee if you offered them free seats to see the picture — you can't stop kids making a mess.'

'Your mind never stops turning, does it?' Jem put his pad on the table and stood to take her elbow. 'But would you sit down, missus, or that little baby will come out of you running.' He pressed her gently into her seat. 'We men have been thinking too much about getting the films to Dublin and the machines we need for the new talking pictures. We haven't given a thought to what we're selling. Mind you, Armstrong's lad has been asking for pretty women to work in the place for a while now. We ignored him — thinking it was just a young man's fancy.' Jem shook his head. 'I never thought mentioning cleaning would bring all this about.'

'That's what started me off.' Ivy leaned forward to pour more tea. She was thirsty after all that talking. 'You need a team of women to give the place a good cleaning every morning when the place is closed. Those red-velvet

309

curtains that open and close over the screen have to look plush and gleam. They've been looking a little sad lately.'

'No sad curtains — got it.' Jem laughed.

'Talk to Mrs Wiggins.' Ivy would have a word with her herself. There was a business opportunity there for the woman. She'd have to think about that a bit more.

'I will.' Jem leaned back in his chair, his mind buzzing. He'd call a meeting with William and Edward. They needed to talk about this — he'd insist the women be present. It seemed to him that women noticed the small details more than men. He could be wrong — nevertheless, he wanted his Ivy there. The woman's mind was a maze. He'd never be able to think up half the things she did. Perhaps Conn and young Armstrong should be involved? He'd have to think about that.

'I don't know . . . ' Ivy removed the dishes. They'd finished the small pot of tea. 'You complain about losing me to tea. I've lost you to the cinema, haven't I?'

'You can get me back again.' He waited until she'd put the dishes on the sink and come back to him, then pulled her onto his knees. 'I'm easily led.' He pressed his lips to hers in a passionate kiss. 'One kiss and I'm all yours.'

38

'Madame Beauchalet, I wonder if I might have a word?' Ivy had never been past the door of these two rooms. The heavy scent of perfume wafting out into the hallway and the strange-smelling cigarette in the woman's hand had her fighting a sneeze.

'My dear, have you ever thought of going on the stage?' The woman's voice flowed, the well-rounded vowels a delight. The volume, however, was slightly overwhelming in close quarters. 'What I wouldn't give to have those cheekbones — and those eyes, my dear, they are simply divine!' She clasped her ring-bedecked fingers to her flat chest. 'What was it you wanted, my dear?'

'May I come in?'

Ivy wondered if she'd woken the woman up. Her eyes seemed sleepy-looking. It was ten o'clock on a Saturday morning. She'd have been out and about herself only she needed to talk to this woman. She supposed the woman was used to working nights in the theatre.

The clothes she was wearing were unlike anything Ivy had ever seen anyone wearing — flowing robes of eye-catching clashing colours. Those long red curls had to be a wig on a woman of her years. The woman had to be at least fifty. She must be really down on her luck if she was rolling her own cigarettes. She has to be

311

buying cheap tobacco, Ivy thought, because it stank.

'I need to have a word with you,' she said.

'The place is in a frightful mess, my dear. One simply can't find the servants these days.' The woman opened the door into her inner sanctum with reluctance. 'I had a marvellous manservant — stayed with me for years — but like all men he left to follow his own dreams. I do like to start my men off young — so much easier to train — can't have women around me — jealous, don't you know?'

'I'm sure.' Ivy hadn't a clue how to respond. She wondered if she could open the window and stick her head out. The smell in the room was overpowering. Her stomach objected violently.

'What was it you wanted again, my dear?'

Ivy showed the leather jewellery case she held in her hands. The woman hadn't seemed to notice it.

'Oh, I see.' The voice became slightly less dramatic and thankfully lowered in volume. 'Call me Felicia — Fliss for short, dear, if we're going to discuss filthy lucre.'

'Felicia.' Ivy held up the case. She'd examined the jewels. They were real. 'This thing is worth a small fortune. The price someone paid for this bauble would buy this terrace of houses. I haven't the kind of money to buy something like this. I'm sorry.'

'You were the one who purchased my watch from Frank.'

'Yes.' No point in telling the woman she was the landlady. But, with the amount of money she'd paid for the watch, how could the woman be short again so soon?

'I find myself in a financially embarrassing situation.' Fliss sucked on her kief-laced cigarette — so wonderfully calming for those of an artistic temperament. 'Never grow old, my dear — it's a fool's game.'

'I'd prefer it to the other option.' Ivy tried to find a clear surface to place the leather case. She finally just forced the case into Felicia's free hand.

Ivy wandered over to the window, desperate for a breath of fresh air. She jumped back when she almost hit her head off the stuffed bird in an oversized gilded birdcage that swung from the ceiling.

'Very droll, my dear.' Fliss shoved the case into the pocket of her robe. She waved her cigarette around wildly.

'May I open a window?' Ivy couldn't stay in this room. She couldn't breathe — the odour was cloying. The room was packed to the ceiling — there was barely room to walk around.

'Must you, my dear?' Fliss reclined on a velvet-covered fainting couch, displacing the stuffed toys already there. 'Fresh air is vastly overrated, don't you know? It blows everything around in a most unpleasant way.'

'Perhaps you would be more comfortable discussing your financial situation in my rooms?' Ivy had to get out of here before she fainted.

'How very civil of you!' Fliss's pale blue eyes glittered, her tongue reaching out to lick her lips. 'Would you have any food about the place?'

'Yes, I would,' Ivy said. Was the woman so short of money she couldn't eat? 'Come to my rooms when — ' She'd almost said 'when you're dressed' but had bitten the words back. The woman might consider the clothes she was wearing suitable to be seen in public. She didn't want to insult her. 'Eh, give me a while to prepare some food. I'll be expecting you.'

★　★　★

'Ivy?' Ali watched her boss almost run through the kitchen from one door to another. She looked sick. She stayed where she was, knowing Ivy hated being fussed over. Mike was out there — he'd call if she was needed.

Ivy stood in her back garden, gulping great breaths of fresh air. It was a beautiful day but, even if the rain had been bucketing down, she'd have stood here. How did the woman breathe in that funk?

'Mike!' Ivy shouted in the direction of the sheds — the lad could usually be found in one of the four — studying, he called it. 'I need you to come into the kitchen!' She bent from the waist, still sucking in air.

Mike stuck his head out. 'You all right, Ivy?'

'I'm fine — kitchen, please.' Feeling much better, she walked back into the kitchen and smiled into Ali's concerned face.

'What's up?' Mike stepped inside.

'I want you and Ali to get my weekend shopping.' She put the kettle on. 'I've my list ready. I'll note down the markets where you'll

314

find what I need. You both need to become familiar with the Dublin markets. Mike, you can get one of the bikes with a basket over the front wheel from the livery. The things I want will be heavy.' She was writing market addresses on top of her list as she spoke. 'I need these supplies. I also need you both out of the way.'

The other two exchanged glances but said nothing. It was obvious something was amiss but, if Ivy wanted them to know what, she'd tell them.

She finished writing as the kettle boiled. She passed the note to Ali saying, 'Check that you know where those places are. 'You should have enough in that.' She pressed coins into Ali's hand. 'When you come back, return the bike to the livery — I'll leave word with John when it's alright to return here. Now go!'

They hurried out.

She couldn't have these two innocents about — God knows what the Beauchalet woman would come out with. No need to give the pair wild stories that might get back to Brian Connelly.

She made a pot of tea. She didn't know what that woman wanted to eat. She'd ask her — save wasting food.

'Glad to see you've the tea made!' a male voice hissed.

'Heart of Jesus, will you stop creeping around the place?' Ivy whirled to glare at the figure standing in her open kitchen door. It was William Armstrong in his guise as Billy Flint.

'Pour tea for two more — ' The door started to close. 'I'll be back.'

315

'That's all I need!' Ivy pulled two mugs and a cup and saucer from the dresser. 'He'll have the bum's rush this morning. I must get rid of him before that woman comes.'

The door opened again as Billy pushed a battered and bruised Eamo into the kitchen.

'Yer little brother has things to tell yeh.'

'What did you do to him?' Ivy clasped her hands to her lips. She wanted to rush across and help her brother. He didn't look capable of walking across to the table. She stayed where she was. This brother had rejected her too many times.

'Not me.' Billy took Eamo by the elbow and pulled him towards the kitchen table. He pushed him — none too gently — into one of the kitchen chairs. 'One of my men found him huddled in the dirt down a back lane.' His man might have added a few bruises but the worst of the injuries had nothing to do with him.

'Jesus Christ, Eamo!' She had lotions and potions that would help with the bruising and pain but she didn't offer them. He'd sneered at Granny's potions in the past. 'It's me da all over again.'

'Don't dare say that, you bitch!' He raised a face swelling from the blows he'd taken. His two eyes were black, not yet swollen closed, his lip split. It was the malevolence in his blue eyes — her da's eyes — that broke her heart.

'You better not be calling your sister names in front of me.' Billy Flint didn't like this lad — he didn't like him at all. He slapped the back of his hand across the lad's head before he could spit

316

out the venom he could see trembling on his lips. 'You should be proud of her.'

'She's a beggar.' Eamo refused to groan at the pain that was racking his body. 'I can't bear to look at her. She's a disgrace.'

'You've learned well to land blows without using yer fists — haven't yeh, little man?' Billy Flint knew Ivy had worked almost from the moment she could toddle to support her three brothers. The lad should be down on the floor, licking her boots in gratitude. 'Yer mother must be proud.'

'You are not fit to mention her name!'

'Oh, for Christ's sake, Eamo, grow up!' Ivy had heard it all before. She slammed two mugs of tea down on the table.

'Having a meeting without inviting your husband?' Jem stepped into the kitchen. One of his lads had told him Billy Flint was here. 'Eamo Murphy, it's bright and well you're looking. Nice of you to finally visit the woman who fed, dressed and educated you.'

'The lad has something to tell us.' Billy Flint gave a jerk of his head towards the table. 'He's just searching for his courage.' He sat back, mug in hand, and smiled. They didn't see the kick he gave Eamo under the table.

'We'll need more tea.' Ivy put the kettle on to boil.

'There yeh go, lad!' Billy wanted to slap the sneer off the lad's face. 'See if you can find yer manhood anywhere about. They say confession is good for the soul. Tell yer big sister what you've been up to.'

Eamo sat with his head down, refusing to open his mouth.

'The brave lad has gone into business with Seb Walker,' Billy informed them. 'He's been fleecing people left, right and centre — making a name for himself as an enforcer — he likes to beat people up, it seems — has a special way with the women, so they say. A lad to be proud of, is Eamo Murphy.'

'It would appear someone gave you the 'talking to' that I would have.' Jem stared at his wife's stiff back. How this must be hurting her! He wanted to be the one to punch the little shite in the face.

Ivy took a seat at the head of the table. 'You, Eamo, are a disgrace.' She refused to reveal her feelings to the figure sitting with his head lowered at her table. 'I am heartily ashamed of you.'

'How dare you address me in that fashion!' Eamo's head jerked upright and he glared down the table.

'You, sir, are nothing but a guttersnipe.' Ivy knew exactly how to get to her brother. Sisters usually did. 'I am delighted that you cut me completely out of your life. I'd be ashamed to admit I was related to you.' She stood to attend to the bubbling kettle, giving him her back. Something she knew he hated.

'Oh, I wouldn't say he's cut you completely out of his life, Ivy.' Billy Flint was keeping an eye on the lad. He was one of those that would stab you in the back. 'He's been selling information about you left, right and centre. The lad's been

318

entertaining every low life he can find with details of your daily schedule — he has a lot to say about some of the valuable items you've managed to pick up on your round.' He smiled while administering another swift kick under the table.

Jem saw the movement but held his tongue. The lad deserved that and more.

'As if I've ever shared information about valuable finds with him!' Ivy hid her tears under cynical laughter. 'He was never trustworthy.'

A knock snapped everyone's attention to the slowly opening door.

Ivy groaned. In the thick of this Eamo drama, she had completely forgotten Felicia was coming.

'*Billy Flint!*' A delighted cry.

'Watch him,' Billy ordered Jem while jumping to his feet and opening his arms wide to the woman who was flinging herself at him. 'Fliss!' Billy swung her around.

Ivy was glad to see the woman had changed out of her fancy garments, though the black skirt she was wearing was perhaps a mite short and swung around her legs as she went spinning through the air in Billy's arms. She'd never seen so many frills, bangles and ropes of jewels worn all at once. It was theatrical, she supposed.

Jem forcefully held Eamo in place. The lad had thought to take this opportunity to run.

'I heard you were in town.' Billy set Fliss back on her feet. 'I can't believe you are still dumping your bits of rubbish here — are you still a pack rat?'

'I am,' Fliss flipped her long red hair, bangles rattling, 'and proud of it!' She looked around the others in the room. She did love an audience.

'Young Eamonn Murphy!' Fliss exclaimed. 'Look at you, all grown up.'

39

'You know my brother?' Ivy was reeling from the events of the morning.

'My dear,' Fliss laughed lightly, 'we were once intimately acquainted.'

She smiled at the lad who was desperately trying to escape from Jem's firm grip. He was in trouble — that much was obvious. She'd kept him for a short while — he'd been so pretty and willing to learn — but he'd proven to be a liar and a thief — and, that, in her book, was unforgivable.

'Jem Ryan, let me look at you!' She threw herself at him, aware that Billy Flint was replacing Jem's grip on Eamonn with his own.

'A gorgeous hunk of manhood!' Fliss pressed her lips firmly to Jem's. 'Shame you always resisted my allure!' she laughed. 'How is my lovely Rosie?' She'd taken a ride in Jem's carriage many times.

Ivy raised her eyebrow at this display of affection towards her husband — but she knew she'd nothing to worry about — Jem was her man.

'Hello, Fliss,' Jem smiled down at one of his favourite people. 'Rosie is fine, fat and sassy — eating her head off — when my wife isn't trying to take her out for a stroll.'

'Oh, whisht, Jem Ryan!' Ivy didn't know what to do with herself. These people all knew each other. Without any clear idea of what was going on — she put the kettle on.

'I believe food was mentioned, Mrs Ryan?' Fliss was almost weak with hunger.

'My niece makes a marvellous omelette, Fliss,' Billy said.

'Oh, so you're finally admitting the relationship?' Fliss crowed. 'It's not before time.'

'Let me take out the rubbish.' Billy hauled a struggling Eamo towards the door that opened onto the garden. He opened the door, put two fingers from his free hand in his mouth and whistled loudly. Two of his men who had been waiting outside appeared. He shoved Eamo towards them. 'You know what to do,' he said, closing the door on Eamo's shouts and curses.

'What's going to happen to him?' Ivy didn't think Billy was going to let Eamo stroll away this time. She couldn't bear to see the Garda called on her own brother but she did know in her heart of hearts that he couldn't be allowed to continue being a bully and a brute. He hadn't learned that from their da — at least she prayed to God he hadn't.

'I'm going to do to him what I should have done to your father.' Billy shook off the sorrow he felt at the disgrace that was his nephew. 'My men will stay with him until the tide turns. I've a boat sailing to the East Indies. The crew is mine. They'll help that young man develop a backbone.' The journey would either kill or cure him. At this moment in time he didn't care which. 'I should have done the same thing to my brother as soon as he started sniffing at

322

Violet Burton's skirts.'

'Some things you can't change.' Fliss was chewing on a hunk of the nutty soda bread baked that morning by Ivy. She'd investigated the kitchen while the little drama was being carried out. The bread was dry but she didn't care.

Ivy fought back tears. Eamo had earned his own punishment. She'd be lighting candles and praying that her wayward brother would finally grow up.

'Sit down, everyone. Yez are lucky the egg-man has been. I suppose you all want omelettes?'

'Please!' was heard from the men.

'Ladies first,' Fliss got in.

'Fliss Do-very-Little,' Billy shook his head, 'I can't believe you are still here. You don't usually stay in Dublin. What's keeping you here?'

'That is Madame Beauchalet to the likes of you, Billy Flint.' Fliss's stomach growled loudly.

Billy sat across the table from Fliss and stared. The woman didn't look her usual self. 'Seriously, Fliss, if I can help, you know I want to.'

'I've been forced to accept my own mortality,' Fliss said dramatically.

'Are you sick?' Jem was slicing the warm soda bread and putting it on a wooden breadboard. Ivy was beating eggs and had a pan on one of the gas burners of her stove. She hadn't been shopping yet, he knew, so it would be plain omelettes all around. Fliss was starving if the noises coming from her mid-section were anything to go by. He took the bowl of butter curls Ivy loved to make and put it on the board.

323

'I'm old,' Fliss moaned.

'Nonsense!' Billy buttered a slice of bread generously and passed it to her.

Jem put a delicate cup and saucer in front of her. He turned to fetch the teapot.

'Thank you, my dears.' Fliss caught Ivy's eye. 'Don't you love being served by tall, handsome men?'

'I can't say I've had much experience.'

'Oh, my dear!' Fliss leaned back to allow Ivy to put a plate holding a fluffy omelette in front of her. 'Stick with me. I'll teach you everything I know.'

They sat around the kitchen table, chatting politely about this and that while Ivy continued to serve up omelettes. There seemed to be a silent understanding to leave anything serious until after Fliss had eaten her fill.

'You have to try Ivy's blackberry jam, Fliss,' Billy said when she had almost inhaled the omelette. He hated to see such a good friend going hungry. What was happening in her life that had reduced her to this state?

Ivy grabbed a pot of jam and put it on the table. This was not the time to search for a fancy dish. The woman needed food.

'Why don't you tell us what's going on, Fliss?' Jem felt like putting the rest of his own omelette on the woman's plate. He watched her butter another slice of bread.

'I've told you all — I'm old.' Fliss added a good dollop of jam to her bread. She closed her eyes in bliss at the first taste. She did love sugar. She continued to eat eagerly as she spoke. 'I'm

324

getting too old to tour the country. The last couple of years have been very difficult. The parts are drying up for a woman of my advanced years. This last trip really took it out of me. My body is complaining of the abuse I subject it to. I don't want to sleep in any more damp beds. I can't be doing with all the grumpy landladies.' She looked around at the concerned faces. 'It's time for me to consider my options.'

'What are your options?' Billy buttered another slice of bread and passed it to her.

She took it from his hand with a smile and began to heap jam on it.

'I was speaking with,' she named a well-known Abbey actor, 'and he reckons there is work in America for people like him. His wife is refusing to make the trip.' She shrugged. 'I think that's a young man's dream.'

'Betty's in Hollywood.' Billy didn't mention Shay. The young lad wouldn't thank him for setting someone like Fliss on him.

'Betty Who?' Fliss held her teacup out towards Jem.

He jumped to his feet to oblige.

Ivy hid a smile as at last she joined them at the table with her own omelette. There was a lot she could learn from this woman.

'My sister Betty.'

'I thought your sister went down in the *Titanic*?' Fliss stared, amazed. She'd known the young Betty Armstrong very well.

'It turns out she didn't.'

'What is she doing in Hollywood?' Fliss said. 'Betty was never an actress.'

'Betty, if you wouldn't be minding, has a factory and a shop in New York that produces cosmetics.' Billy's smile held pride in his sister's success. 'She supplies the big studios.'

'More power to her elbow.' Fliss was thrilled for her. 'But I can't see me as a saleswoman.'

'You could teach them to speak,' Ivy put in.

'I beg your pardon?' Fliss had almost forgotten there were others in the room.

'You have a beautiful speaking voice.' Ivy could listen to the woman speak forever. Her voice was rich and musical. 'I believe the Americans are having a problem recording the accents of their stars. I've heard the American stars sound thin and tinny on the sound recordings. It is a big problem at the moment.' Her brother Shay had written and told her all about it. She'd noticed Billy hadn't mentioned Shay and, having seen Fliss's attitude towards beautiful young men, she hoped Betty would protect her gorgeous little brother. 'I've heard how they're seeking people from the Irish and English stage. You could set yourself up as a speech teacher or whatever it's called. You would be in at the beginning.' She accepted a fresh cup of tea from Jem with a smile. 'If you could teach people to speak as you do, they'd be lined up for miles trying to get to you.'

'My word, I had never thought of something of that nature.' Fliss had been reluctantly prepared to fade away. Perhaps she didn't have to — America, a whole new world to conquer.

'You could supply me with insider information,' Billy said.

'Wouldn't be the first time!' Fliss felt the old excitement stir.

'Betty tells me she has a big house with a swimming pool out there in California.' Billy was tempted to go out there for a look himself. 'She's invited me and the wife to visit any time. She has loads of bedrooms, she tells me. You could stay with her — at least until you've set yourself up.' Betty and Fliss got along well. He'd drop a line to his sister warning her to protect Shay from Fliss's more unfortunate habits.

'You've put images of dancing fairies in my head!'

Fliss was quite breathless thinking about the possibilities. The talk she'd had with her actor friend had frightened the life out of her. The man seemed to believe that the Catholic Church was about to take her beloved Ireland in a stranglehold. She could not survive in such a system. She avoided Dublin for that very reason. She needed to think long and hard about her options. She might prefer to present the image of a butterfly to the world but Fliss was no fool. 'Imagine me in America! I must re-invent myself.' She clapped her hands in delight. 'What image do I want to portray? Oh, this is exciting!'

'Don't go getting too excited,' Billy warned. 'How are you for the readies?' He rubbed his fingers together in a recognised manner. 'It's not cheap to travel to America and you don't want to travel in steerage.'

'Perish the thought!' Fliss said.

'I've got to get back to the livery.' Jem stood. It seemed all the excitement was over. He'd talk to

Billy later about Ivy's brother. He pressed a kiss into Ivy's cheek and, with a cheerful goodbye, left.

Ivy, feeling like an intruder in her own kitchen, stood to remove the used dishes from the table.

'You can't take all of that rubbish you've collected through the years with you, Fliss.' Billy had seen her rooms here. 'You'll have to have a clear-out. Ivy can help you with that.'

'Thanks for asking me!' Ivy snapped.

'You would make a few bob out of it and all.' Billy didn't mind Ivy's fire. He liked it.

'Don't you hate it when people try to organise your life?' Fliss said sweetly.

'You need help getting rid of your stuff, Fliss — and you can put business Ivy's way.' He clapped his hands together. 'You each get something out of the deal so no debt would be involved on either side.'

'Big of you to make work for me.' Ivy glared.

'See the thanks I get, Fliss,' Billy sighed. 'And after I took care of the problem of Eamo for her.'

'He was always jealous of Ivy,' Fliss said.

'*What?*' Ivy spun around from where she was stacking dishes.

'My dear,' Fliss shrugged, 'he was the eldest son — the man. You ran rings around him. You never needed or wanted his advice or support. Your father boasted to all who knew him about the great little daughter he had. Everyone could see that your father never did a day's work. It was obvious to all who supported that family. You were the example Eamo's father held up before him. He hated your guts.'

328

'Dear God!' Ivy leaned against the sink and stared at the two people making themselves comfortable at her kitchen table. The bread and jam was disappearing at an alarming rate. 'You learn something new every day,' she contented herself with saying.

40

On Monday morning Ivy pushed her pram around the back of the fancy Merrion Square houses. It was a relief to her to be out and about on her own, doing something that was so familiar to her she could almost do it in her sleep.

The last two days had almost been the death of her, she thought, pushing her pram in the direction of home. That Fliss — honest to God, the woman had more energy than twenty women. She floated around the downstairs of the house like a bumblebee. It seemed she never stopped eating. She'd drift from flat to flat with one of her stinky cigarettes burning in her hand while picking and almost licking at food. Her voice — thank God it was beautiful, because she never stopped talking.

Ivy had run out of her own home this morning like a coward. She hadn't been there to meet Jennifer Coyle. She'd left instructions for the girl to start unpicking a small mountain of old-fashioned garments. They could use the expensive fabric in the discards to fashion other garments. It was boring work but it gave the girl something to do until Ivy could sit down and talk to her.

She was anxious to get home now. She'd stayed out too long and the servants wouldn't appreciate anyone knocking at the back door at this time. She tried to time her visits to the rear of these houses when the servants were cleaning up after serving rather than when they were running around at the beck and call of their employers. Over the years she'd learned to time her visits when they'd cause the least disruption to the work of the house. She'd go out again later and finish her round.

She turned towards home, looking around her with wary eyes. She had that itchy feeling between her shoulder blades — the feeling of eyes on her back. She might well be mistaken but she'd be taking someone with her when she went out again. She had heard no more about that fella Walker but it didn't do to grow complacent. Billy Flint had warned her that she was becoming too successful — attracting the attention of the wrong kind of people. She'd be a fool not to heed his warning.

★　★　★

'Ivy, you're late.' Ali opened the door in the garden wall. She'd been watching out for Ivy. 'I've the arse burned out of the kettle I've had it on so long.'

'Where's Mike — is the new girl here?' Ivy pushed her pram through the gate, ignoring Ali's moaning.

'The new girl!' Ali shut and locked the garden door. 'Mike is making a fool of himself staring into her big golden eyes and sighing!'

'Golden eyes?' Ivy pushed her pram into the open door of one of the sheds. 'Ali, we need to

331

keep these doors locked when there is no one out here.' She gave a wave of her hand to the rest of the sheds. 'I'll have to make sure Mike is careful about that.'

She put the brake on the pram and took off her heavy coat to reveal a light floral drop-waist dress. She gave a sigh as the fresh air cooled her heated flesh. She took the money belt from her waist and rolled it in the coat.

Ali knew Mike kept the doors locked but nevertheless turned away to check. Ivy seemed all out of sorts.

Ivy kicked off her work boots and, with the coat in her arms, walked barefoot from the shed. 'Come on. I'm gasping for a cup of tea. And I've never seen golden eyes before.'

Ali, after locking the shed door, walked beside her without commenting on her strange behaviour.

'*Mike!*' Ivy hissed as she stepped through the door to her kitchen. The lad appeared from the workroom with a surprised look on his face. 'I want you to stroll around outside. Brush and wash down that bench Frank made for the garden — walk around like you have a plan — use the outside bog — anything — just make yourself seen.'

Mike didn't ask any questions. He stepped out of the kitchen.

'I'll call you when I have the tea on the table!' Ali shouted at his back.

Ivy put the coat and money belt in her bedroom before strolling into her workroom. She had an employee to meet.

'Hello!' Ivy smiled at the stunning-looking young girl sitting at the long work table. The girl's face belonged on a chocolate box, she thought. No wonder young Mike had been hanging around. The eyes, framed by long, thick, dark lashes, were brown but of such a light colour she could see why Ali called them golden. The light from the windows danced on her golden hair, creating a halo around her. 'I'm Mrs Ryan, but you can call me Ivy.'

'Oh, Mrs Ryan!' Jennifer jumped to her feet, almost knocking over the chair she'd been sitting on. She almost bobbed a knee.

She was so nervous. Her mam had found this job for her. She had no idea what to expect when she got here this morning, but this big bright workroom was the last thing she'd expected after working in that awful, airless, dark sweatshop. She wanted to keep this job even if it meant unpicking seams for the rest of her life.

'I'm pleasured to meet you.' Her mam had told her to say that. 'I brought some of me work for you to see.' Her mam had suggested that and all. Her heart was in her mouth.

'Take a deep breath, Jennifer!' Ali said, laughing, from the open doorway of the workroom. 'Ivy, the tea's up.'

'Thank God, I'm parched.'

Ivy was pleased with her new employee so far. The long dark skirt, white blouse and knitted cardigan the girl wore were neat and tidy. The girl had an honest face and seemed eager to please. She cast an eye over the unpicked garments sitting off to one side on the table. She was fast too if she'd done all of that by herself. 'Come into the kitchen, Jennifer. You can show me your work while we have a cup of tea.'

Jennifer picked up the cloth bag from the floor at her feet and followed along. She was in a daze. She'd only been here an hour or so and already they were offering her a cup of tea. She'd worked fourteen hours in the factory without anyone offering her a sip of water.

'Let me have me first cup of tea.' Ivy sat at the head of the kitchen table, a cup of tea in her hand. She was sipping from the cup as she spoke. 'I'll be human then.' She turned to Ali. 'Give Mike a shout.' She waved a hand towards the table. 'Sit down, Jennifer, until we organise ourselves.'

'Ginger jumped up on the back wall.' Mike stepped into the kitchen in his stocking feet. He'd been digging in the muck and his boots were dirty. 'He said Jem said to tell you that you were right. I hope that means something to you because I haven't a notion.'

'It does, thanks.'

She'd seen Ginger hanging around when she came through the tunnel leading into The Lane. She'd taken a chance and whispered at him to watch and see if someone was following her. A lot of people would underestimate the redheaded lad with the big blue innocent eyes and freckles — Ginger saw a lot more than people thought and had the sense to keep his opinions to himself. It would appear that Billy Flint was right — someone was keeping an eye on her. She'd have to discuss this with Jem — but later

334

— she had other things to attend to now.

'Ali, I made a batch of scones earlier, are there any left?'

'I hid them,' Ali laughed. 'I put them in the range oven.' She opened the heavy cast-iron door of the oven and pulled a tray of golden-brown scones from its depths. 'It won't take me and Mike a minute to serve these up.'

Ivy sat back and allowed herself to be waited upon. Under Jennifer's fascinated eyes brother and sister moved around the room. The table was laid with pretty matching dishes. There was butter and jam to go with the scones arranged on a wooden breadboard. She watched fascinated as Ivy's cup was filled and refilled. She'd never seen anyone drink tea that fast.

'I've put the kettle on for more tea, Ivy.' Ali took her chair with a smile. 'You almost inhaled that last pot.'

'Did you walk over with Dai this morning, Jennifer?' Ivy split a scone, pleased with the texture. She hoped to God Frank and Fliss didn't smell the tea. The pair had been in and out of the kitchen until she was thinking of putting a swinging door in.

'I did.' Jennifer blushed when Mike, after washing his hands at the indoor sink — a marvel she'd silently admired — passed her a scone. 'I could have walked over on me own. It was light out. The streets were well aired by the time we left.'

'It won't always be that way.' Ivy put butter and jam on one half of her warm scone. 'I'd prefer you walk to work with Dai — if you don't

335

mind. It's better to be safe than sorry.' She finished her scone and pushed the side plate away. That was enough for her. She wasn't really hungry — just thirsty.

'If your hands are clean, pass me your workbag, Jennifer.' Ivy pushed her chair to the side. She'd seen the girl's lacework at the market — she was eager to see more of her needlework. 'I'll have a look while you're having something to eat.'

'Oh!' The girl blushed at her greasy hands.

She jumped to her feet and daringly used the tap in the kitchen. Ali had shown her how this morning. Hands clean, she picked her bag up from the floor and carried it over to her new boss. 'Here you are.' She put the bulging bag on the floor before returning to her seat. She didn't know if she could manage to eat while her work was being examined. She hoped and prayed she'd brought a good enough selection. Her mam had helped her pick stuff out.

'This bag is lovely.' Ivy examined the cloth sack. She knew how much work was involved in putting the bits of this bag together. She examined the seams — all handstitched. The patchwork of flowers and bees was stunning. 'Did you make this?'

'Me mam showed me how.' Jennifer's heart was in her mouth. 'I covered a bucket in the cloth to get the shape.'

'I do the same with bottles.' Ivy opened the fabric ribbon that held the wide mouth of the bag closed. She began to remove the contents then stopped. 'Mike, pass us that small table.'

She had the bag on her lap. 'I don't want to put these things on the big table in case I get them dirty.' She was tempted to sit in one of the soft chairs but if she did that she'd never want to move.

Mike jumped to his feet. He washed his hands before he touched anything. Ivy was a devil for washing her hands all the time. She insisted he did too. He carried the small table over to her side before sitting again.

'Thanks,' Ivy said absently. She was busy removing the beautifully stitched items from the bag. 'You can chat amongst yourselves.' She was examining every stitch minutely. The girl really was an excellent seamstress for one so young.

'Do you sew all the time?' Mike asked. He didn't know what half the things Ivy was taking out of the bag were but they were pretty.

'I love to sew.' Jennifer blushed at the attention being paid her by the handsome lad. 'Me mam always has something she's working on close to hand.' She smiled. 'I think she taught me to sew to stop me pestering her — but I love it.'

'Your work is exquisite,' Ivy said. 'Jennifer, I'm afraid I can't spend much time with you this morning. I'll be in and out. That's why I asked Ali to give you unpicking work to do.' She looked at the anxious young girl. 'I'll have more time this afternoon to talk with you.'

'Yes, Mrs Ryan.'

'Ali, I'll leave Jennifer in your hands. If there's something she can help you with, that is fine. Otherwise, Jennifer, if you'd keep unpicking for the moment. The work needs to be done. If you have any ideas for using the fabric make a note of it and we can talk about it when I've more time.' She returned the items to the bag. 'I'll want to examine these in more detail later.' She stood and carried the bag into the workroom.

Jennifer jumped to her feet and stood there, wondering if she should go with her new employer.

Ivy returned to the kitchen and smiled at the girl. She'd settle down eventually.

★ ★ ★

'Two of my lads had a word with the one following you,' Jem said. 'Iris Walker ordered him to keep an eye on you.'

'Iris, not Seb?' Ivy was sitting soaking her feet in an enamel bowl. It had been a long day.

'Iris.' Jem, sitting across the range from her, watched while she pulled her feet from the water and dried them on the towel she'd had on her lap.

Ivy picked up the bowl, opened the back door and threw the water along the pathway. 'Well, then, it seems it's woman to woman.'

'I know that look on your face.' Jem watched her clean the bowl and put it back under the sink. 'What are you going to do?'

'I'm going to send her a polite note, of course.' She dropped into her chair.

Billy Flint had provided them with the Walkers' address. They lived in the Iveagh Trust buildings — a much sought-after Dublin address for those trying to improve their lives.

'I'm going to thank her for her interest in me and mention how much I enjoy piano music.'

'That is evil!' Jem laughed.

'Well, if the man is stupid enough to store paper money in a wooden piano!' Ivy had been horrified when Flint told her of Walker's habit of stashing his ill-gotten gains in the upright piano in his flat. How Flint had discovered that little fact she neither knew nor cared.

'Listen . . . there's something else . . . ' Jem said when Ivy had been silent for a while. He waited a moment, then told her. 'Flint has taken two of my lads to train. He's going to see they are trained as bodyguards — for you.'

'Name of God!' Ivy's mouth gaped. 'What's the world coming to?'

41

'*Where's Mike?*' Ivy shouted, walking out the back of her house into the garden. She needed a break from sewing.

Ali put her head out of one of the sheds. 'He's away selling more of yer woman's stuff!'

'Fliss,' Ivy sighed. 'She'll be the death of me. What are you doing?'

'I'm counting little rubber dolls and I'm going blind doing it.' Ali was comfortable enough with Ivy to grumble.

'I'm going to put the kettle on. I'm spitting feathers. We'll have the tea in the garden and pretend it's summer.' She turned to go back inside.

'It *is* summer!' Ali shouted.

'Not so as you'd notice.' Ivy wanted sunshine. 'It's not raining at least.'

'*Hey, missus!*' a male voice was heard from over the wall. '*E'er a chance of a cup of tea for us poor working folk?*'

'*Yez can bugger off!*' Ivy shouted back.

The building of the garage for the automobile taxi service had been going on for months. It felt like a lifetime sometimes. The noise from mallets, saws and hammers was enough to drive a person crazy. The bloody Taj Mahal must have gone up faster. She'd said that to Jem and he told her the Taj Mahal had taken twenty-two years to build. She hoped to Jesus this didn't take as long.

'Yez have a tea lad — let him make yer bloody tea — cheeky beggar!'

'Aah now, missus, don't be that way!' The male voice sounded amused.

She ignored him. 'Jennifer, we're taking a break!' she called as she entered the house. The young girl was a hard worker but Ivy wasn't running a sweat shop. They could take a deep breath from time to time.

'Yes, Mrs Ryan?'

'Jennifer, I want you to set the garden bench up for a snack.' The girl was never called Jenny — she'd tell you quick enough her ma said Jenny was a donkey. 'You may as well go ahead and set up for Fliss and Frank as well. You know as soon as they smell food they appear.'

She didn't begrudge them a bite. Frank was always doing something for her around the place and he wouldn't take a penny for all of his work. He was cheap to keep. And she'd made enough money off the sale of Fliss's goods that the woman was welcome to a cup of tea and a feed. Although what she did with the money Ivy paid her was a mystery. The woman never seemed to have a ha'penny.

'Did I hear someone take my name in vain?' Fliss appeared in the open door of the kitchen.

'Honest to God, woman, I'd swear you have a way of knowing the minute I turn on the stove.' Ivy was putting eggs on to boil. 'Get in, yer letting the heat out.'

'Ah yes, the Irish summer!' Fliss too was heartily sick of rain and grey skies. 'Should I call Frank?'

341

'There's no need. The man will smell the food just like you.' Ivy watched Jennifer out of the corner of her eye. The poor girl didn't know what to do with herself when Fliss floated into the kitchen in her trailing robes. She was finally remembering to remove her starched white apron when she left the workroom. Ivy had learned the value of a clean work apron and hand-care from Granny Grunt — lessons she was passing on.

'I'll be seeing those dolls in my sleep.' Ali stepped into the kitchen. 'Morning, Fliss, it's fresh and well yer looking.'

Ali took the black kettle from the range and filled a bowl with hot water. She put the bowl in the sink and cooled the hot water with water from the tap. She stuck her hands in the bowl. She didn't shave the Ivory soap but used the large bar to scrub her hands, paying special attention to her nails. They were black from dusting those blessed dolls. She took the towel Jennifer held out to her with a smile and dried her hands, then stepped away from the sink saying, 'Your turn'.

'You have them well trained.' Fliss had watched everything through sleepy eyes.

'We're dining outside, Fliss, so if you'd get out from under me feet I'd appreciate it.' Ivy sliced bread. They could have egg-salad sandwiches — they could make them themselves — she wasn't the maid.

'I'll get Frank.' Fliss wanted to get one of her kief-laced cigarettes if they were dining outdoors.

'I don't care what anyone does as long as the

table is set outside and a pot of tea is on the range.'

When the table was set they gathered around to eat and chat. If worried glances were directed at the sky from time to time, no one dared mention the weather.

Jennifer, without a word, jumped up to go and fetch the tea. She returned carrying the large catering teapot. She was taking note of everything going on around her and how things were done. She loved to tell her mother all about what went on here. They had a good laugh and a chat while they cleaned up their own rooms after the men left for work of a morning, before she had to leave herself. Her mother couldn't get enough of her stories.

'I could build a little fire out here.' Frank sat back, mug of tea in hand, and smiled. 'You could keep your teapot on top of it. Save all that jumping up and down.'

'I don't mind jumping up and down, Mr Wilson.' Jennifer poured the tea carefully.

'Ah, but you're young yet, little Jennifer.' Frank appreciated the young woman's beauty and her constantly smiling face.

'I'm not exactly in me dotage meself, Frank Wilson,' said Ivy. She had been served her tea first. By the time everyone else was served she was ready for another cup.

'That baby of yours must be swimming in tea.' Frank had said it time and again — she needed to cut down on the amount of tea she drank — but he might as well be talking to a brick wall.

'I'll get back to making up those summer

dresses,' Jennifer said, her tea drunk.

'And I'll start clearing up.' Ali reached for the dirty dishes.

'I've run them off!' Fliss blew a stream of smoke through her nose.

Ivy rolled her eyes. 'They have work to do, Fliss!' She turned to call out to Frank who was now pacing the garden. 'How's your workshop coming along, Frank?' He was to have a workshop built onto the back of Jem's garage.

'It will take as long as it takes.' He had his tape measure and notebook in his pocket and a pencil behind his ear. He wanted to think about putting a fire out here. 'Some of us are not as impatient as others.'

'I've been writing to your Aunt Betty, Ivy.' Fliss nibbled on another sandwich. 'I've been thinking of the image I want to present when I arrive in America.' She sucked in smoke and held it.

Ivy said nothing.

'Betty advises me to present a business-like appearance.' Fliss closed her eyes to enjoy the buzz. 'She tells me they take their business very seriously out there in Hollywood. Can you imagine it?' She pressed a well-manicured hand to her flat chest and sighed. 'Me, in a business suit!'

'What you do in the privacy of your own home will be up to you. It might be a good idea to have a few business suits to hand. I imagine it will make it easier to get in to see studio heads. Your beautiful speaking voice will do the rest.'

'I'm scared, Ivy,' Fliss leaned forward to

whisper. 'The price of a first-class ticket to America is outrageous. Perhaps I should reconsider and travel steerage?'

'As soon as you step onto that ship you'll be selling yourself.' Ivy waved the sickly-smelling smoke away from her face. 'I've shown you the pictures my brother sent back. That lounge place where he sang was full of the money people, he said. That's the kind of people you want to meet. If you travel steerage you'll be meeting the cleaners. That's a fact of life, Fliss.' There was no point in trying to keep Shay a secret — Betty had told Fliss all about him in her letters. 'We have to be sensible — if you fail and are coming home then you can travel steerage. But I can't imagine you'll fail.'

'But the cost of the ticket!' Fliss didn't have that kind of money. 'I suppose I'll have to sell more jewellery.'

'I've been thinking about that,' Ivy said slowly. She received a great deal of information from her brother Shay who was proving to be a skilled and informative letter writer. Who knew where he got that skill from? She was entertained and educated by his long frequent letters home. She'd advised him to start keeping a journal. She hadn't believed in this great wonder of talking pictures but he did. If Shay was right, he was in at the start of something amazing. His notes would be of interest to future generations. She thought things like that, now that she was expecting a baby.

'How good a friend of yours is Betty Armstrong, Fliss?' she asked.

'Why?' There were things about her friendship with Betty that Fliss would never divulge.

'I was wondering if you could borrow the cost of the ticket from her.'

'What!'

'Hear me out,' Ivy sat forward to say. 'That jewellery you have screams money and lots of it.'

'And?'

'If you get rid of it for a fraction of the value — and that's all you'll get from a dealer — it's gone. If, however,' she took a deep breath, 'you wear that jewellery when you are on board ship, you are clearly stating that you are a woman of means. That's the kind of impression you want to create.'

'I'm not trying to catch a husband, Ivy.' Fliss squinted through the smoke from her cigarette. 'Men with that kind of money usually prefer lovely young things.'

'That's not the point, Fliss. The point is that the items of jewellery you've shown me — and I know you have more — scream class.'

'There is no class system in America, Ivy.'

'Of course there is — the same one as everywhere else: money!'

'You are very cynical for one so young.'

'Will you be serious for five minutes, missus!' Ivy practically hissed. 'Betty and you will be two women of a certain age, alone in a country not your own. You talk about the image you want to present. Well, wearing that jewellery and the dresses Jennifer will design and make for you, you will be seen as society leaders — you can lead from the front instead of being followers of fashion. I think that's something you and Betty need to think about.'

'Lord above, Ivy!' Fliss sucked the last of her cigarette into her lungs. 'That is either evil or genius and I can't tell which.'

'Start as you mean to go on, I always say.'

42

Ivy was running away from the noise of the workmen. They were putting the final touches to the garage, according to Jem. She'd never considered what it would be like to endure the noise of engines and the men working on them — why couldn't people be content with horses?

She was sitting with Ann Marie on a bench in her garden, trying to persuade her friend to remove her shoes and stockings. It was late July and this was the first true summer day they'd had — why not take advantage of it?

Catherine was sitting on the grass with Emmy, making daisy chains.

'I do wish Edward had agreed to our moving to the Dalkey estate.'

Ann Marie's family estate overlooked the sea. The family withdrew to the estate for the summer months. This year Edward had put his foot down. The estate was too remote, he argued. With his wife in the family way he wished to remain close to the medical professionals in the city.

'Well, he didn't agree. Honest to God, Ann Marie, this garden is completely enclosed by that bloomin' great wall that blocks your view and any stray breezes that might come from the canal.'

Ivy too was overwarm. She loved the sun but the additional weight she was carrying was making her cranky. She was four months with child but Ann Marie, at more than eight months, felt she had the better cause for complaint.

'Catherine, would you be a love and take your boss in to change her clothes? I'm sure there are one or two lightweight cotton dresses in her vast wardrobe.'

The white cotton dress Catherine wore could never be called a uniform. Emmy too was dressed all in white.

'You can be such a bossy-boots at times, Ivy.'

'While you're about it, ask one of that horde of servants to bring iced lemonade out here. We may as well make ourselves comfortable.'

'You, madam, are getting above your station.' Ann Marie allowed Catherine to take her elbow.

'I know,' Ivy grinned. 'It's a curse.' She stood for a moment watching them walk away then walked over to join Emmy on the grass. The little girl lay on her front, knees bent, ankles crossed, elbows bent as she rested her face on her hands.

'Your feet are black as the hob, Emmy.'

'I know.' Emmy loved walking in her bare feet like her Auntie Ivy. 'Papa says you are a bad influence on me.'

'A little bit of dirt never hurt anyone.'

A joyous childish shout and the demanding voice of a woman sounded, moments before Jamie dropped onto Emmy's back. The little boy chortled in delight.

Sadie, running breathlessly across the grass in hot pursuit, looked less than delighted.

'Honest to goodness,' she panted and dropped down to join Ivy, 'I need eyes in the back of me head and four legs to keep up with this young fella! He refuses to wear his leading reins.' She had tried and tried to get the child to accept the reins but to no avail.

The two youngsters ignored the adults and wrestled madly on the lush grass.

'Catherine will never get the grass stains out of that white dress, Emmy,' Sadie sighed.

'Oh Lord, we're being invaded!' Ivy watched the small army of servants carry tables, chairs and all other manner of rubbish into the garden. Why couldn't they sit on the grass? The poor servants must be sweating cobs in those uniforms buttoned up to the neck, she thought.

'Emerald, I have instructed the servants to carry your dollhouse into the garden.' Ann Marie was feeling considerably cooler in the cotton dress that did nothing to conceal her condition. The pleasant feel of the grass under her naked feet was a surprise. 'I thought you might enjoy playing with it out here in the sunshine.'

'Thank you.' Emmy didn't want to play quietly with her dollhouse. She wanted to run around screaming and laughing like she did when she was in The Lane.

But Jamie clapped his hands when he saw the large dollhouse being placed on a low sturdy table the servants had placed securely in the grass. He loved to throw the furniture out of the house and have Catherine and Emmy try to catch.

'Ivy, Sadie, come join me!' Ann Marie was seated at a table the servants had set with ice-filled goblets and a jug of freshly made

350

lemonade. A three-tiered stand of dainty cakes and sandwiches sat proudly in the centre of the table. Ivy rolled her eyes but said nothing as she surveyed the long, pressed, lace tablecloth that draped to the grass.

'I don't want to be an adult,' Ivy muttered under her breath as she walked over to the table. She took the chair the waiting footman held for her. Really, it was ridiculous, she thought.

'Thank you.' Sadie took her seat more graciously.

Catherine held Jamie by the back of his shirt. The little boy, who had just celebrated his second birthday, was trying to climb on top of the table to reach the dollhouse. She shyly passed a cloth bag to Emmy. She needed both hands to handle young Master Jamie.

'What is this?'

Emmy's voice attracted the attention of the three women. They watched while Catherine blushed and stuttered that the bag contained a small gift. Emmy opened the drawstring of the bag and squealed in delight. She emptied the contents carefully on top of the wide table that held her precious dollhouse.

'Oh!' she exclaimed. 'It's a granddad, a grandma and babies — cloth people to live in my house! Did you make these, Catherine?' She didn't wait for an answer. 'They're wonderful!'

'Let us see, please?' Ivy held out her hand.

'Look!' Emmy carried the precious items over to the table to be admired.

Catherine wished the ground would open up and swallow her. She made those little dolls all

351

the time for her family. It was nothing special. She was finding it difficult to fill her time. She spent all day with the mistress and Emmy but had her evenings free when Emmy was in bed. She slept in a room off the nursery which she was still having difficulty believing was all hers. It was all bewildering. She missed her family — making the little dolls had made them seem closer.

'Catherine, come here, please!' Ivy was examining the dolls with a gleam in her eye. 'Did you make these?'

Catherine stood, keeping a careful eye on Jamie while she answered Ivy's questions. Yes, she'd made the dolls. No, it was nothing special. Yes, she'd made the cloth bag.

'Where did you learn to do this?' Sadie was astonished at the skill involved.

'It was just something I always did with the children.' Catherine had needed something to entertain the children when they were all inside one room with no food and no heat. Since she'd learned to sew properly the dolls were a lot neater — she'd been pleased with how they turned out. She wouldn't have offered them to Emmy otherwise.

'I can get you money for these.' Ivy admired the painted cloth faces of the dolls — the clever use of string to make hair.

'Those are mine, Auntie Ivy!' Emmy made to grab the dolls.

'Of course they are,' Ivy said.

Ivy and Sadie exchanged glances. There might be a way for Sadie's brother's children to make extra money — making tiny dolls could be a cottage industry. They'd discuss it later.

'I was told I would find you out here!' a male voice called out, startling the company.

'Uncle Charles!' Ann Marie exclaimed as a distinguished gentleman dressed all in white strolled across the grass, followed by a servant carrying an additional chair.

'Dr Gannon!' Sadie greeted the man.

'I hope I may join you?' He waited for the servant to place the chair, sure of his welcome.

'You're welcome,' said Ivy.

Catherine shyly offered a greeting before stepping away from the table with a sigh of relief. If she'd known there would be so much bother about the dolls she'd never have made them.

'Jamie, no!' Emmy shouted.

Catherine rushed to stop the boy running with a big grin on his face, grubby hands outstretched, as he raced for the only male in the group. She caught the boy and swung him up in the air. She twirled around with him, laughing, then settled him on her hip and strolled over to join Emmy.

Dr Charles Gannon observed the scene with a smile. The child reminded him forcefully of his own youth running wild with his brother. He sighed deeply. He still missed his brother — Ann Marie's father — with a constant ache. He must be getting old because he fancied the boy resembled his brother and himself.

'May I pour you a glass of lemonade, Uncle?' Ann Marie leaned forward to grab the sweating glass jug. She too could see Jamie's family resemblance. It brought her pleasure and pain. She would tell the boy about his family connection and his roots when he was older. Her uncle had never expressed a desire to know what had happened to his son's indiscretion. His son had no interest in knowing the whereabouts of his child. He paid a weekly amount grudgingly. Sadie and John banked the money for the child's future.

'You shouldn't be lifting heavy objects.' Charles returned his attention to his niece. 'I have instructed the servants to serve me iced Pimm's — ' he broke off when he noticed the footman carrying a fresh jug of iced liquid in their direction. 'Here it is now. I hope you don't mind, my dear?' He smiled at his niece. She was looking well for a woman in her condition.

The gathering settled down to polite chit-chat. The children ran around under Catherine's watchful eye.

'That young man needs male company,' said Charles. He had watched the boy run rings around his companions. It seemed to him the boy was being spoiled. But what did he know of raising a boy? His own son was a great disappointment to him. Young Charles slept all day and chased women all night. What a waste of time and money! Charles wondered if it was too late to do something about that — watching this young lad smile and charm his way around the females had given him a lot to think about.

'His father is of the same opinion.' Sadie had no idea that the distinguished visitor was her son's biological grandfather. If she had, she'd have worried.

Ann Marie and Ivy, both aware of young Jamie's blood ties, said nothing.

Dr Gannon enjoyed the relaxed atmosphere. It was vastly different to any social event his dear wife would have organised. He sat in the sunshine, his straw boater protecting his head, his mind whirling with plans and ideas for his son's future — while he visited with his niece and this pleasant company.

43

'You'd never believe we were into August.' Ivy strolled along Grafton Street, arm and arm with Jem. They were returning from first Mass. 'I suppose I shouldn't complain. Poor Ann Marie is ready to drop any day now. She's probably glad of this cool weather. They invited us to lunch today but I refused.'

'I have to admit that it's not very relaxing to visit them at home, with the servants and Edward jumping every time the poor woman takes a deep breath. Still, it will be all over any day now.' Jem raised his hat to a passing couple. 'You're carrying our little bundle well yourself, missus. Do you want to step into the green and feed the ducks?'

'I won't today.' She wanted to get home. It was her birthday. She planned to cook a special Sunday lunch for herself and her husband to enjoy. She'd bought a lovely piece of beef from the butcher yesterday. She would put out a meal that would put Ann Marie's fancy chef to shame, she thought smugly to herself.

'You must have Fliss's rooms nearly cleared now?' Jem strolled slowly along, enjoying the peace of the morning. The woman would pop up like a genie as soon as Ivy put the meal on the table, he thought with an inward sigh.

'Honest to God, Jem, how can one woman have so much rubbish?'

'Mike will have muscles on his muscles from carrying all that stuff around town to shift.'

'I have more beads, bangles and ribbons than I've ever had before in me life.'

Ivy had spent weeks clearing out Fliss's two rooms. The woman was a menace. The goods had to be almost forcefully removed from her grip. Mike had made a fair bit of money from his share in the sale of all of the unusual items the woman had picked up in her travels.

'The summer dresses Jennifer made from some of Fliss's stuff are amazing. Shame we haven't had the weather for them. Still, I have to say, with Jennifer's help my sheds have more space in them. That's a blessing.'

'We can't really complain, can we, love?' Jem waved to a carriage driver picking up a fare from the Shelbourne Hotel. Business was good and the extra men he'd taken on had shifted some of the load from his shoulders.

'The Connellys have been a great help to Ria, shifting the mountain of goods in her house. You can almost see the floor in the rooms upstairs now.'

They strolled along in this fashion, talking idly about this and that, happy to spend time together, until they reached The Lane.

'Name of God, Jem, is that Ann Marie?' Ivy dropped his arm, preparing to run towards the figure in the tunnel directly across from the tunnel they stood in.

'Don't you dare run across there!' Jem stopped her. 'I'll get her.'

Ivy walked swiftly after the running figure of

her husband. What was Ann Marie thinking of, coming across that lock on her own? She could have lost her footing and fallen into the canal. She wouldn't have been the first.

'I can't bear it, Ivy,' Ann Marie said as soon as Ivy reached her side. 'I feel as if everyone is counting my heartbeats — the servants are always underfoot — and my own husband is the worst of all.' Her voice echoed around the tunnel.

'Does yer mother know yer out?' Ivy asked, using an old humorous expression, as she took her friend by the arm.

'I didn't tell anyone I was coming here.'

Ivy couldn't really blame the woman for running away. She'd have been up for murder herself if she'd been in Ann Marie's position. She was having a hard time herself finding a bit of peace and quiet.

'I'll let Edward know you're here.' Jem wasn't fool enough to get between two expecting women.

'Ivy,' Ann Marie whispered as soon as Jem left them, 'I've wet myself.' She started to cry. 'I haven't done that since I was a baby.'

'*For goodness' sake, woman!*' Ivy practically yelled.

She took her friend's elbow and towed her towards Mrs Winthrop's house, praying the woman was home. She felt her knees sag when the woman answered her door.

'She's having the baby.'

'Come in.' Augustina didn't bother asking questions. She'd noticed how irate the woman was becoming with the constantly hovering servants. The birth would be a nightmare if they couldn't get the woman to relax — not that giving birth induced relaxation — however, they had to do something to calm her down.

'I'm not going back there!' Ann Marie bent forward, clutching at her stomach.

'Lean her up against the wall and rub her back, Ivy.'

Augustina looked around frantically. This was most unusual — she was always called out to a birth, not confronted by women in labour at her own front door. She had a birthing chair in one of her front rooms. The item was considered an antique by the medical profession but Augustina thought it was one of the best inventions for labouring women she had ever come across. The chair was kept highly polished and like the rest of the furniture in that room was covered by a dust sheet. She'd need help preparing the room but she was going to use that chair.

'You shouldn't be here, Ivy,' Ann Marie panted. 'It isn't fitting or fair.' She had no idea what to expect. Would she be one of those women who died screaming? She had to be strong. Ivy had all of this ahead of her. She had to set an example. Ivy shouldn't be here.

'I've helped at many a birth.' Ivy rubbed Ann Marie's back. The woman was too tense. She needed to relax into the pain. 'There's no privacy for anyone having a baby in The Lane.' They lived on top of each other, for heaven's sake.

Augustina returned, having uncovered and

checked the chair. 'How long have you been having pains?'

'I beg your pardon?' How was she supposed to think or speak over this pain?

'She's too tense.' Ivy exchanged a worried look with Augustina.

'Do you want me to telephone the doctor?' Augustina asked. Ann Marie had told her that the man had been constantly underfoot as of late.

'*No!*' Ann Marie screamed. 'I don't want anyone around me. I want to be left alone.' She tensed up again. 'I'll have my baby without anyone telling me what to do.'

'Right, come into the kitchen.' Augustina had seen it before. The animalistic instinct to make a nest and hide. 'I'll put the kettle on.'

'*I don't want any flaming tea!*' Ann Marie screamed.

'I do, you ungrateful heifer!' Ivy snapped in an effort to make Ann Marie focus on something else.

'How dare you speak to me in that fashion?'

'I'll dare what I like.' Ivy noticed she'd relaxed from her tense position. 'Take my arm. We'll go into the kitchen and you can watch me drink a pot of tea.'

'Honest to goodness, Ivy Murphy!' Ann Marie allowed Ivy to take her arm to lead her down into the back of the house. 'Is there any occasion when you don't want a pot of tea?'

'I haven't found it yet.' Ivy's hand was gently rubbing Ann Marie's back. 'Why don't we step to the WC and get your wet undergarments off?'

They set off but had to stop while Ann Marie suffered another labour pain. Ivy noticed she'd tensed up again. Something had to be done. She was fighting her own body.

'She can do that here, Ivy.' Augustina was putting water on to sterilise instruments she prayed wouldn't be necessary. She filled large pots and put those on the range top. 'We are all women together.' She stared at Ivy and jerked her head towards the front door. 'Get Marcella,' she mouthed.

Ivy hurried from the room without Ann Marie noticing.

'How long have you been experiencing pain?' Augustina asked Ann Marie again — she needed the answer to that question.

'I've had a bad backache since yesterday afternoon.' Ann Marie blushed as the woman helped her remove her soiled undergarments.

Augustina visually examined Ann Marie while removing her shoes and stockings. She slipped a pair of knitted socks with leather soles, which she took from a pocket in her smock, onto her feet.

'My dear, having a baby is not something we women do neatly and tidily.' Augustina stood with the garments in her hands. She took a bucket from under the sink and put the garments in to soak before scrubbing her own hands again. She was mentally running through a checklist. 'We were fashioned to bring babies into the world. The Good Lord doesn't make mistakes.'

'I want Edward to have it,' Ann Marie said through gritted teeth.

'I'm sure you do!' Augustina laughed. 'Are you comfortable standing or would you rather lie down?'

'I want to walk.'

'By all means, walk. All that I ask is that you walk around my kitchen and when a pain strikes grab hold of the nearest object and hang on. We don't want you falling. Can you do that?'

'Of course.' Ann Marie slowly circled the room. She paused for a moment to examine the stocked kitchen cabinets.

Ivy returned with Marcella Wiggins on her heels. She'd caught the woman just as she and her family were leaving for Mass.

'Right!' Marcella summed up the situation in seconds. She pushed up her sleeves. 'Ivy, you take Ann Marie into the front rooms for a stroll. Gussy and me will get organised.'

Ivy was happy to obey. Ignoring the noise coming from the rest of the house, she entertained Ann Marie with tales of Fliss and her eccentricities — anything to stop the woman from stiffening at each approaching labour pain. The tales of Fliss's hot-and-cold running stream of pretty young men was a particular favourite of Ann Marie's, Ivy noticed. She searched her mind for any little titbit of gossip or humour.

★   ★   ★

Hours had passed as Ann Marie's labour pains gathered strength. Eventually Augustina settled her on the birthing-chair. This, she believed, would speed up the process and facilitate

362

pushing when the time came.

'You are doing really well, Ann Marie,' she said from her position on the floor in front of the birthing chair. 'It won't be long now.'

Ann Marie, naked but for a loose bleached linen robe, leaned her head back tiredly — her hands were clenched around the wooden balls set into the arms of the chair. 'I feel another one coming . . .'

'Relax, Ann Marie, it's nearly over — you're doing well.' Ivy leaned in to wipe the sweat from the labouring woman's brow. There was little she could do but be there for her friend.

At last Augustina said, 'I can see the head now. Ann Marie, when I say 'push' *push* as hard as you can — but stop immediately I tell you. Do you understand?'

In what seemed a very short space of time after the hours of labour, Augustina triumphantly held a squealing baby aloft.

'It's a boy!' said Ivy.

'Is he alright? Is he healthy?' Ann Marie panted, welcoming the support of the chair at her back.

'He's perfect,' said Augustina.

'Started complaining before he was all the way out! The poor child is obviously related to you, Ann Marie.'

'Don't make me laugh, Ivy Murphy!'

'Actually, that helps.'

Augustina laid him on a towel and cut the umbilical cord. Then she wrapped him up and laid him in Ann Marie's arms, ordering Ivy to watch over the pair of them as she prepared to deliver the afterbirth. It wasn't over yet.

Ann Marie looked at the child — her child — with tears streaming down her face. She gazed at the dear little face, lost to the world around her, but automatically obeying Augustina's commands as the woman tended to her aching body.

After Augustina had dealt with the afterbirth, Ivy walked to the door. 'I'll tell Edward,' she said.

'He shouldn't see me like this!' said Ann Marie.

'Ann Marie, that man has been going slowly out of his mind. You had the choice to have the baby in a nice clean hospital with nurses jumping to your command. You could even have had it in your lovely bedroom at home. You decided to come here so now you can deal with our rough and ready ways.'

'No, wait, Ivy,' said Augustina. 'I need to wash Ann Marie and tidy her up. Don't let him in yet.'

'Right — I'll just tell him the good news.' Ivy slipped out the door.

Edward was right outside.

'Oh God, tell me quickly — is my wife alright — did she come through the birth?'

'Yes — she's — '

The strength went from Edward's legs and he swayed on his feet.

'Edward!' Ivy didn't fancy having the man fall on top of her. '*Jem!*'

Jem was there immediately, grabbing hold of Edward from behind.

Marcella appeared behind them, looking

alarmed. 'What's happened, Ivy? What's wrong?'

'Nothing!' said Ivy. 'Mother and child fine! In the name of God, what a carry-on!' She shook her head. 'You'd think they were the first people ever to have a baby!' She opened the door a crack. 'Augustina, can we come in?'

'No, not yet!'

'Just drop him, Jem.' Ivy had had enough.

'There's a fainting couch in that room.' Marcella pointed to the room across the hall. 'Drop him close to it, Jem. We can put his wife and child on that couch when they're all cleaned up.'

Augustina was finishing up with Ann Marie. She had washed, changed and tidied her. The baby was washed and wrapped in a fresh towel.

Jem carried Ann Marie into the other room and laid her on the fainting couch as Marcella carried in the baby.

So the newest O'Connor was born in The Lane. He didn't seem to mind, content to rest on his mother's breast being much admired by both his parents.

Everyone else went into the kitchen for a well-deserved pot of tea. There was more to be done but it could wait.

44

'Honest to God, Jem,' Ivy fell into one of the easy chairs in front of her range. 'What a palaver!' She was exhausted. 'Mind you, I have to say those beef sandwiches Ann Marie's cook sent over were delicious.'

'And very welcome.' Jem too was tired. It had been difficult trying to keep Edward from losing his mind. 'I wouldn't want to live through another day like today.'

'I've never seen so many people running around like headless chickens in my life.' Ivy closed her eyes. She'd think about getting up in a minute. 'Thank God for Marcella Wiggins.'

'Young Catherine proved she had her wits about her when she pushed the pram across with all manner of things for the baby packed inside.'

'Did you see that pram?' Ivy had almost salivated at the beautiful baby-carriage.

'All those people running around and worrying — and Ann Marie and Edward cuddling close without a worry in the world — must be nice.' Jem had marvelled at the way the staff had jumped through hoops in order to insure their employers had no worries.

'I wouldn't fancy it meself.' Ivy thought she was almost ready to stand when the familiar sound of Frank's knuckles rapping against the door sounded.

Frank stepped in. 'I'll put the kettle on.'

'If I had the energy, Mister, I'd get up and kiss you.' She let her head fall back.

'I'd let her.' Jem too leaned back.

'What a carry-on!' Frank busied himself around the kitchen. 'I hope to goodness the pair of you are not going to put us all through something like that.'

'It was like something from the fillums!' Ivy laughed. 'I didn't know where to look half the time. The Keystone Cops had nothing on the goings-on in The Lane today.'

'It livened up a Sunday, that's for sure,' Frank agreed.

'I thought I'd collapse laughing when Conn and Pete Reynolds turned up with one of my old carriages all polished and beribboned to drive the mother and baby home.' Jem laughed. 'I thought the horses pulling the big old heavy thing were practically prancing.'

'It was good of Edward to gushie the children,' Ivy said.

'The children?' Frank objected. 'The man was throwing thrupenny bits — there were adults trying to get some of those! It was a sight for sore eyes right enough!' He laughed at the memory. 'I saw Milo out there with his camera recording the big moment.'

'It was nice of the lad to be born on the same day as yourself, Ivy.' Jem grinned slyly across at his wife. She'd made no mention of her birthday today. 'It will make it easy to remember his birthday.'

'Won't it though?' Ivy contented herself with saying — birthdays weren't a big thing. She was

367

sad about her lovely roast though. She'd never got to make her special dinner. She was too tired now to fuss with all that. She'd have to put it on top of the range tomorrow and make a slow pot roast while she did her round.

'I don't know what yez are going to eat.' Frank looked at the pair. It was so unusual to see both of them sitting still like this. He wasn't much of a hand at cooking. But they needed something in their bellies.

'I'll settle for a pot of tea just now, Frank.' Ivy wanted to change out of her soiled Sunday go-to-Mass clothes. She wanted a bath. She'd think about something for them to eat — later.

There was a knock on the kitchen door. Before it could open Ivy shouted: 'Tough luck, Fliss! It's duck under the table all around tonight!'

'Now, is that nice, Ivy?' Fliss stuck her head in the kitchen door. 'When I bring glad tidings?' She laughed and stepped into the kitchen. 'A charming young footman was approaching our door as I arrived.' She fluttered her eyelashes and threw her red curls over her shoulders. 'I, of course, asked if I could help him.'

'Nice of you.' Frank served the tea. 'I suppose you want a cup of tea and all.'

'I wouldn't say no,' Fliss fluttered.

'When do you ever?' Ivy sipped her tea. Fliss would get around to telling them her news in her own time.

'What did the footman want?' Jem couldn't be bothered waiting.

'The charming young man informed me that Mrs Craven — I believe that is Ann Marie's cook

— has assembled her world-famous steam puddings. The woman will send one of these meat puddings — which I am informed are delicious beyond words — for your meal this evening, Mr and Mrs Ryan.'

'Bless the woman and the horse she rode in on!' Ivy said.

'That takes care of that.' Jem too was pleased. 'I thought we'd be sending out for fish and chips.'

'On a Sunday?' Frank said. 'I don't think so!'

There was a small silence. Ivy looked from one person to another — there was something going on here. They all looked shifty. She was about to open her mouth and ask, when Fliss spoke up.

'Do you need me to sing?' Fliss looked from one man to the other.

'Hold your fire,' Jem said.

'I need a hand, Jem.' Frank cleared his throat in a nervous manner most unlike himself.

'Lead the way.' Jem stood with a smile.

Ivy turned to look as the two men walked out of the kitchen into the main body of the house. 'Should I ask?' she said to Fliss.

'I wouldn't.' Fliss moved to sit in the chair Jem had vacated. 'Just enjoy.'

The two men were soon back, carrying a long low table with leonine legs and claw feet which she recognised as Frank's work. It was beautiful. They placed it in front of her.

'You made me a table, Frank!' Ivy was delighted and went to push to her feet to examine her gift.

'Sit where you are, woman,' Jem said, 'and

close your eyes.' He stood waiting until she'd obeyed his instructions. She wasn't too fond of surprises, his Ivy.

'Keep them closed.' Fliss watched the men carry the gift into the kitchen and place it on the table. She'd be prepared to swear that their chests had swollen with pride. She began to sing.

'*Happy Birthday to you! Happy Birthday to you! Happy Birthday, dear Ivy . . .* '

She was joined by Frank and Jem: '*Happy Birthday to you!*'

'You can open your eyes now.' Jem was nervous.

Ivy's reaction was everything he could have wished for. She stared, her big violet eyes wide. Her hands flew to cover her trembling lips as tears filled her eyes.

'My own dollhouse,' she whispered, her gaze moving between the two men. 'You've made me my very own dollhouse.' How had they known how much she envied Emmy her fabulous dollhouse? She'd been ashamed of her own feelings. Imagine being envious of a child!

She pushed to her feet, all thought of tiredness gone. She stood before the three-storey Victorian, gabled, arched and porch-wrapped wonder of a dollhouse, afraid to touch. Jem had to lean forward and open the front of the house to reveal the fully furnished rooms hidden inside.

'It's a marvel.' Ivy was deeply touched. She recognised the handwork of so many people in the interior of the house. Catherine had even fashioned little people to live in it.

She turned to press a deep kiss into Jem's lips.

There were tears running down her face when she turned to Frank.

'Thank you,' she whispered as she hugged the old man, and kissed his cheek. 'It is the most beautiful gift I have ever received.' It was also one of the few but there was no need to mention that.

Frank blushed, thrilled with the success of their gift. 'Your husband had a fair hand in making it. If he ever gives up his other businesses he has a career in dollhouse-making in front of him.'

'Really?' Ivy spun around to stare at Jem.

'The staircase — ' He pointed to the elaborately carved staircase that went up through the house. 'The wraparound verandas and other little bits and pieces — all my own work.' His smile was wide as he pointed a thumb at his own chest.

'Don't be shy!' Frank laughed at Jem's discomfort. 'He made the tiny tea set on the kitchen table and all.'

Ivy immediately dropped to her knees to examine this marvel. She was almost afraid to touch the delicate fine porcelain cups and saucers. She removed the dainty items from the hand-carved table and cradled them on the palm of her hand. She was almost afraid to breathe in case she broke them — still on her knees, she looked up at Jem with a big smile almost cracking her face.

'It is fabulous — wonderful — the most beautiful tea set I've ever seen.'

'I wouldn't want you to be too impressed. It

came in a kit. I turned the air blue with curses, I can tell you, when I was trying to put the blessed thing together.' Jem was thrilled with her beaming delight.

Ivy carefully replaced the tea set, tempted to remain on her knees and ignore everything else while she touched and examined each little detail. She accepted Jem's hand to get up. She stood gazing down at the dollhouse, thrilled beyond words.

'It just needs one other thing,' she said.

'What's missing?' the two men said together, both turning to look at the dollhouse. They'd been so careful to put everything they could imagine into it.

'A *bloody big sign saying* Hands Off!' she shouted.

'I can't believe it, gentlemen. She's forgotten her tea!' Fliss exclaimed dramatically. 'Truly your gift has been a great success — almost up there with the Wonders of the World.'

Their laughter was interrupted by a loud knocking on the main door.

'I'll see who it is,' Frank said and hurried to the front door.

Jem and Ivy stood in the open kitchen doorway, curious to see who had come calling.

'*If you would clear your table, missus!*' one of the two male servants, revealed when the front door was opened, shouted down the hall.

The men were carrying the biggest wicker basket Ivy had ever seen, struggling to carry it between them. They stepped into the kitchen with relieved smiles.

'We've been given detailed instructions by Mrs Craven on how we should serve this meal,' one of them said. 'If everyone would be seated we'll serve the food. It's more than our jobs' worth to disobey.'

'Allow me!' Fliss jumped to her feet to clear the table of tea things. 'It's your birthday after all, Ivy.'

'It must be if you're doing housework,' Ivy said with a laugh.

'Allow me to seat you, madam,' Jem took her elbow and led her over to their kitchen table. He pulled out the chair at the head of the table for her.

Ivy sat and watched the two men remove items from the basket as mouth-watering aromas escaped from the food being placed on the table before her. There were even dishes and cutlery in the hamper. She need do nothing but sit back and wait to be served.

'Mrs Craven said that you should replace the dirty dishes in the basket, sir,' the quietest of the two servants said shyly. 'The basket will be picked up in the morning.'

'No need for that.' Jem was almost salivating at the aromas that wafted around the room. He wanted the two servants to leave so he could dig in. 'I'll have two of the lads carry it over tomorrow.'

'Very good, sir.'

The two men served the meal — then stood back to be certain they'd forgotten nothing.

'That's fine, thank you,' Jem said. 'We can help ourselves now.'

'We wish you a pleasant meal, sir.'

'I'll see yez out.' Frank led the two men through the house and out the front door. He couldn't wait to get his teeth around that lot.

Ivy looked down at the gravy-rich meat pie on her plate. She put the linen napkin placed close to hand on her lap, then picked up the gleaming silver utensils. But she waited until Frank returned and took his place at the table before saying, 'I don't think I'd like servants under me feet all day every day but, by God, tonight they were very welcome — dig in!'

There was silence as everyone ate the delicious meal.

Ivy smiled down the table at Jem. What a day!

45

Fliss walked around the polished wooden floors of her rooms with a pain in her heart. All of her treasures — gone. She'd spent a lifetime amassing the items she'd stashed in these two rooms. She'd carried it to extremes perhaps but she'd never planned to actually live here. This had been somewhere cheap she could use to store her items and visit them from time to time.

How had it all gone so drastically wrong? How had the years flown past so quickly, leaving her an aging woman? Why hadn't she seen it coming and been prepared? How did other people do it? She paced out her problems, her heels tapping out a background rhythm to her disturbed breathing.

She walked over to the full-length mirror screwed to the wall. She'd forgotten it was there. It had been revealed when the mountain of her treasures had been removed.

'Madame Beauchalet.' She sucked on her kief-laced cigarette and stared at her reflected image. 'Fliss Do-very-Little. Fliss — everyone's friend. Who the fuck are you?' She took a deep drag of her cigarette — raised her chin — pulled off her long red wig.

The image revealed frightened her. Her mother stared back at her. She'd never wanted to see that face again as long as she lived. The gleam of manic hatred in the reflected eyes was oh so familiar.

'I hope you're dead!' she hissed, turning away.

She looked at the wig swinging from her hand. 'I paid a lot of money for you,' she said to it.

She sucked on her cigarette, throwing the wig in the direction of where the fainting couch had once stood. The wig spread obscenely on the beautiful bare wood of the floor.

'Real human hair, cost a bloody fortune, nothing but the best for our Fliss.'

She turned towards the window, tears leaking from her eyes.

'I don't want to grow up!' she hissed against the glass. 'Growing up — growing old — that's for other people — not for me.'

She stared out into the courtyard at the barefoot children kicking a newspaper-and-twine ball around in the wind and rain. What did they have to laugh about? Their little stomachs were swollen with hunger but they still managed to run screaming and laughing over the wet cobblestones.

A sudden clatter of hooves had the children shouting and racing towards the area in front of her window. They pointed and called to the elegant carriages being driven from the livery. Shouts, whistles and the sound of whips being swung over driver's heads had the children enthralled. It took so little to please them — why had she never been that innocent?

Always thought you were better than everyone else — always wanted more than was good for you — nothing but trouble every day of your life, my girl.

She swung towards the mirror and shouted at the image. '*Those are your words — not mine — never mine!*'

She walked over and collapsed onto the highbacked cane throne-chair she'd refused to part with.

'Am I going mad?' She was scaring herself.

She pushed trembling hands through the soft strands of silver hair on her head. She cut it short herself. It made wearing a wig so much easier.

The sound of Ivy and her workers talking and laughing carried up from the back of the house. She could pick up her wig and join them. Fliss could entertain and amuse them. She could cadge something to eat. She could keep the memories and ghosts at bay for one more day.

'No.' She closed her eyes, raising the cigarette to her trembling lips. 'You have to do this. That medium I consulted said it was time and past to lay the ghosts to rest. You have to get on with the rest of your life. You have to — or she wins.' The cigarette burned her fingers. She was tempted to throw it dramatically onto the floor but she'd hate to burn Frank's beautiful wooden floor.

'Right, Fliss, my girl.'

She pushed herself to her feet and, mentally grabbing her courage with both hands, walked back over to the mirror.

'This is me. This is what I look like. I'm not her. I've never been her.'

She carefully studied her mirror image. She wore no cosmetics and was wearing a subdued outfit of navy straight skirt and pale-blue blouse. She didn't recognise the person in the mirror as her. Despite the up-to-date clothing it was still her mother staring back at her.

The lips of the mirror-image moved. 'Time to take stock.'

She almost jerked away but forced herself to stand still and look.

'Betty has promised to purchase the steamer ticket for me. I won't be sorry to leave this weather behind. Betty writes that the weather in California is sunny and bright. Dear Lord, I want sunlight on my skin. We've had no summer — storms blowing over the trees in the Phoenix Park. What is the world coming to?'

She took a deep breath, forcing her thoughts back to the matter at hand.

'I've had my professional outfits tailormade.' She waved a hand down her body, forcing herself to step closer to the mirror. She was an expert at examining her own image before going on stage. She'd apply the same rules here.

'I'm good-looking, some have said beautiful.' She raised a hand to her shorn hair. 'I need to be brave enough to visit a beautician and have something done with this hair. I won't dye it. The silver shade is beautiful and suitable for a woman of my years.' She took a deep breath, 'God, I look old!' She almost wailed.

'Fliss, you okay in there?' Ivy rapped on the door and waited. Frank had said there were strange noises coming from inside. She prayed to

God that Fliss didn't have some young stud in there doing things she didn't want to know about.

'Showtime,' Fliss whispered to her image before turning towards the door.

She pulled the door open and simply stood there.

'Name of Jesus!' Ivy stared. 'Fliss, is that yerself?'

'The real me.' Fliss stepped back. 'What do you think?'

'Give me a minute.' Ivy stepped inside.

She walked slowly around Fliss's stiff figure, taking in every detail.

'I think you are a stunningly beautiful woman.' Ivy shrugged. 'I love your hair. The cut is almost manly but it suits you. The colour is gorgeous — it's almost as white as Ria's.'

She was having a hard time taking in the change in the woman. She recognised the outfit Fliss was wearing. Jennifer had made it for Fliss's travel to America — there was a fitted jacket to match the skirt.

'Ah, but Ria's hair is a shade of blonde — mine is simply grey.' It had turned silver overnight on her twelfth birthday.

'It's beautiful and suits you, believe it or not.'

Ivy didn't like the wild look in Fliss's eyes. Frank had said he'd heard shouting and screaming coming from these rooms.

'Why don't you come down to my place for a cup of tea?' she offered. 'I'll be glad of a break. It's been all hands on deck today, dressing baby dolls. I've even got Frank and Mike at it. I'm sure the rest of them would be glad of a break too.'

The largest order of dolls had been delivered in July for the Christmas market. The pre-sales orders had everyone demanding more dolls. No bad thing as far as business was concerned. The women she employed had produced beautiful garments and doll blankets. She'd almost had to sit on Ann Marie to stop her buying all of the outfits for her son to wear.

'I won't, thank you, Ivy.'

Fliss had to finish what she started. It was tempting to run away from her problems but she'd been doing that for years. She was not taking them with her to America. She'd leave all of her ghosts here and start afresh. She was determined.

'Tell Frank to ignore any noises he might hear coming from here. I'm working on re-inventing myself.' She forced a gay laugh. 'I work better when I can hear myself think.'

'Fair enough.' Ivy had to accept that. 'You know where we are if you need us.'

She walked back to inform the concerned people waiting for her that everything was alright — even if she had her doubts.

★ ★ ★

Fliss closed the door when Ivy left and leaned against it, needing the support. She had one more thing to do. Her stomach heaved at the thought but it had to be done.

She walked very slowly over to a beautifully

crafted small leather chest. Her hands shook as she undid the straps. She reluctantly raised the lid, biting back the cry that came to her lips at the phantom odour that crept out.

She stripped quickly and pulled the outfit concealed in the chest over her shaking limbs.

'You can do this.' She turned towards the mirror, her fists clenched as tightly as her jaw.

She stood in front of the mirror, the tears she'd refused to shed in front of her mother streaming down her ashen face.

'I used these clothes to run away.' Her eyes glittered strangely. The slender figure in the mirror was dressed entirely in black. The clothes were outdated but they proudly proclaimed the expense of the fabric, fit and design. She wasn't seeing her own image.

'Did you miss them? The servants never noticed me slipping from that great barn of a house. They thought it was you — probably thought you were off to commune with the moon or sacrifice a villager.' Fliss closed her eyes, remembering the fear, the pain, the humiliation she'd suffered at her family's hands. 'I wore them whenever I had to play a bitter old witch on stage. It entertained me to think how horrified you would be.' She sobbed.

She turned like a marionette, as if someone controlled her with strings, and walked over to the chest. She bent and removed the last item, her entire body shaking so hard she feared she'd break bones. She carried the item over to the mirror and held it aloft.

'I bet you missed *this*!' She shook the plaited

leather crop she held in her trembling hand. 'Didn't you, Mother? It was your favourite toy.' In her mind's eye the crop was blood-encrusted.

She fell to the floor weeping, allowing the tears she'd never shed then to flow now. She couldn't continue to carry these memories around with her — and keep her sanity.

She lay on the floor, lost in visions of the past. She'd been suppressing these images for years — refusing to examine them in the light of day. No more. She had to cleanse herself of these nightmares or go insane. She lay on the hard floor, sobbing, the force of her sobs carrying her body across the polished wooden floor. It seemed she had oceans of tears to shed. She didn't know how long she cried until sleep eventually overtook her.

The nightmares were merciful. They did not follow her into her dreams.

46

'I can't believe we got all of those dolls dressed.' Ivy put her hands to her back and pressed down, pushing her swollen stomach forward. 'The smell of that soup has been tormenting me for hours, it seems.'

Ali, Ria, Úna, Jennifer, Mike and Frank groaned in united relief. They were all glad to see the back of that lot.

Ivy looked around at the tired faces. She'd been determined to finish dressing the baby dolls she had in stock.

'Jennifer, you may as well eat here,' she said. 'Anything your mother might have prepared must be stuck to the pot.'

'Me mam knew not to keep dinner back for me.' Jennifer stretched. They'd been dressing dolls all afternoon and into the evening. 'You sent Mike around to tell her I'd be late after all.'

'Yes,' Mike said. 'Mrs Coyle said Jennifer could pick up fish and chips for herself if she was going to be late.'

'Sounds good to me,' Ria groaned. She'd been roped into helping. She'd enjoyed the laughter and chat but she was tired — too tired to think of planning anything to eat.

'I've probably got enough in the pot for everyone.' Ivy had put the meaty ham bone and split peas onto the range before they'd started work. 'It's only split pea soup but, with chunks of the crusty bread Mike got at the bakery, it'll taste like heaven.'

'We won't stop, thanks, Ivy.' Ali groaned when her sister began to massage her back. 'Vera and Liam will have grabbed something but Conn needs feeding when he comes in from work.'

'We need to check on the range too.' Úna continued to apply pressure to her sister's back. 'I'm nervous because I forgot to run in and check it after we got started on this lot.' She gestured towards the long line of stacked blanket-wrapped baby dolls that covered the long counter in the workroom. The sight was a little disturbing to her eyes.

'Someone needs to put a stew on top of the range first thing in the morning — if you don't mind me saying.' Ivy sighed. 'It's not like we've had a bloody summer where we could let the fire go out.' She put her hands in the air. 'Sorry if I'm stepping out of my place.'

'No, you've told us before, Ivy.' Ali stepped away from her sister with a smile of thanks. 'We know you're right — it's just finding the time.'

'We could pick up Conn and walk over to the chipper together,' Mike said. 'It might be miserable out but I'd enjoy a walk in the fresh air. Then we'll walk you home, Jennifer. We don't want you walking through the dark streets on your own.'

Ivy walked out of her workroom, leaving the others to make their plans. She was glad they'd refused her offer. She was tired and would be glad of a chance to sit down. She was hungry. Jem should be home soon. She had a nice piece of ham she could slice and make into sandwiches with their soup.

'There hasn't been a sound out of Fliss since you went up there, Ivy.' Frank had followed her out of the room. He fancied a fish and chip supper on his own tonight. He'd been around people enough for one day. The chatter and laughter of the young people had worn him out.

Ivy checked the watch on her wrist. 'Fliss doesn't usually stay in of an evening.' She knew Fliss liked to see and be seen around the Dublin theatre scene. 'She's probably getting her war paint on before she goes out.'

'I suppose. I'll love yeh and leave yeh, Ivy.'

He made his way to his own rooms. He'd put the kettle on low while he walked over to fetch his fish and chips. Might have to pick up a bottle of milk from the back of the creamery while he was about it, he thought as he opened his door.

★   ★   ★

'Ivy, don't take this the wrong way but I'll be heartily glad to see the back of you today,' Ali said as the crowd of workers walked laughing down the long hallway.

Ivy stood in her open doorway at the bottom of the hall, waving them off. Truth be told, she was glad to see the back of them too. She closed her door with a grateful sigh. She walked over and pulled the pot of split-pea soup to a warmer part of the range top.

'I'm not going to wait for Jem.' She rubbed her distended stomach as the baby complained by kicking her. 'I know you're as hungry as me,' she whispered. She took a crusty turnover from the breadbin and sliced the toe of the boot shape into slices. She buttered the bread, unable to resist biting into the heel. Lord, she hadn't realised she was that hungry. She poured a bowl of soup and carried it and the ham sandwich she'd made over to the table. She settled in to enjoy her solitary meal. There was a lot of noise from outside but she ignored it. It had nothing to do with her.

'Ivy!' Jem almost exploded into the kitchen. 'Thank God you're here! Stay in here, for God's sake. There's murder going on outside.' He dropped into a chair at the table, relieved to see his wife sitting calmly enjoying her meal. He'd been terrified she was in the crowd outside. 'I put in a call to the Garda.'

'What's going on?' It wouldn't be the first time a fight had broken out in The Lane.

'There are a lot of angry people shoving and shouting out there. I don't want you getting mixed up in that.' Jem stared at his wife, astonished she wasn't rushing out to get involved in the action.

'I won't endanger our child, Jem,' She rubbed her stomach gently. 'Whatever's going on outside they can handle it without me. I'm not as quick on me feet as I used to be.'

'I'm going back out there. The crowd is too close to my livery and this house for my liking.' Jem stood and pressed a kiss into her hair. 'I'll keep you informed.'

'You do that.' Ivy watched him slip out the

back way. She'd eat something first — she had to take care of the baby after all — then she'd go into Frank's room and watch the goings-on from his window.

Outside, Jem walked along the lane by the side of his house. He was glad to see Enda Reynolds standing in front of the closed doors of the garage. He didn't want anyone damaging his motor vehicles.

'What's going on?' he asked Enda.

'It's Father Leary and Mrs Purcell,' Conn answered him, appearing seemingly out of nowhere. 'And they have a big fella with them I've never seen before.'

Jem hurried around the front, Conn and Enda at his heels. As the crowd shifted, he saw that Mike, Ali and Jennifer were trapped against his closed front door. Their passage was blocked by the Parish Priest in all his fury and his company.

'Oh Christ!' Jem saw the silver head of Leary's walking stick shine in the gas light when he waved it over his head. 'Stay here, you two — no point all of us getting into trouble.'

Jem pushed his way through the crowd. He caught the stick raised on high and lowered it slowly without comment.

'I have business to conduct here.' Father Leary was unhealthily flushed, sweat pouring off his face and staining his suit. The tight collar he wore so proudly bit into his jowls. 'This fine man came to me for counsel. We are here to right a great wrong. I am an instrument of the Lord and I will see His will be done.'

Mrs Purcell stood by the priest, clutching her

rosary beads, her lips moving in frantic prayer.

Jem didn't recognise the big man with them. 'What business could you possibly have at this door?' he demanded.

'I've been informed Frank Wilson has a tenant leaving,' Leary waved his free hand in Mrs Purcell's direction without ever looking at the woman. 'I have a member of my flock needing accommodation.'

'I beg your pardon?' Jem started to laugh. He couldn't help it. It was so ridiculous.

Leary ignored Jem's amusement. 'I tend to the needs of my flock as a shepherd of the Lord. Frank Wilson is unemployed. He can't afford to be out the money a good tenant would bring in and Mrs Purcell, a good god-fearing woman, would be a good tenant.'

'You've run mad.' Jem shook his head, unable to believe what he was hearing.

'My name is Robert Hunter — I've come for my wife,' the stranger with Leary said. 'This matter doesn't concern me.' He'd been laid up after a kick from a horse or he'd have been here sooner. He'd been promised the money that white-haired bitch stood to inherit. He was not willing to be cheated out of what he'd earned.

⋆ ⋆ ⋆

The noise outside woke Fliss from her coma-like sleep. She pushed to her feet and stumbled towards the window. The sight that met her eyes almost stopped her heart. It seemed all of her ghosts were coming to visit today. She bent slowly and picked up the crop from the floor.

Almost in a trance she opened her door and stepped into the hallway. When she opened the main door a wall of humans blocked her view.

'Everyone into my place!' she tapped Ali on the back and jerked her head in the direction of her rooms when the young woman turned. The young people almost flowed around where she stood in the open doorway.

Fliss stepped forward onto the cobbles until she confronted Leary.

'Aloysius.' Fliss raised the crop and tapped the Parish Priest forcefully on the face. She knew exactly how to do it. She adopted her mother's soft seductive slight French accent as she lisped. 'What has upset Mummy's darling boy?'

'Mama?'

The effect was startling. Leary stiffened for a moment before the strength left his legs. He crumbled to the pavement whimpering. His body started to jerk and gyrate. He lost control of his bladder and bowels.

Mrs Purcell started screaming like a banshee before flinging herself to lie by his side on the street. She fought off all efforts to assist the priest, biting and scratching at all who came near while wailing almost loud enough to crack glass.

'Conn, telephone for an ambulance!' Jem shouted over to the men still standing watching the unfolding drama. 'Tell them the man's having some class of a seizure!'

Leary's left side was pulling in on itself in a shocking manner. The arm and leg twisted. The left side of his face pulled up and froze.

Fliss stood for a moment looking down at her brother's twitching body.

Aloysius, the brother who had whipped her bloody on the eve of her twelfth birthday. Her punishment — his twenty-first birthday gift. He'd laughed while whipping her under the watching eyes of their insane mother.

She bent to lean over the gyrating figure.

'Hello, brother dear.'

She watched his eyes roll in his frozen face. He struggled to force words past his lips.

'It would appear my God got you,' she whispered before standing and walking back into the house.

She closed the door at her back.

47

Detective Caldecott jumped onto the back of the purring Garda motorbike. He was on his own time. The scene that met his eyes when he arrived in The Lane looked almost theatrical.

He walked over to join Barney Collins in the ring of Garda surrounding an ambulance crew who were working on some figures on the ground.

'What's going on?' He couldn't make head nor tail of the scene. 'What's that noise?'

'The Parish Priest has had some class of a seizure. They are working on him here before he can be moved.'

The loud wailing was abruptly cut off.

'Thanks be to God.' Barney raised his hat to wipe his forehead. 'The medicine the doctor gave that woman has finally worked.'

'Why did you send for me?' Caldecott looked at the crowds pushing and shoving to get the best view. The whispers going through the crowd sounded like frantic bees to his ears. The noise wasn't helped by the circle of shabbily dressed people off to one side, loudly proclaiming a decade of the Rosary.

'I thought you might like to talk to your man over there,' he jerked his head in the direction of Robert Hunter. 'It seems to me he'd be a person of interest in this case that has you so fascinated.' He lowered his chin and, barely moving his lips, said: 'He's the daughter's supposed husband.'

'Is that a fact?' Caldecott resisted the urge to rub his hands together. 'I'll borrow a couple of your officers and take him down to the station for you — out of the goodness of my heart, of course.'

'What's the charge?'

'Unlawful imprisonment.'

'Is that a fact?'

'Oh, indeed.' Caldecott had spent time deciphering the journal of the dead man claiming to be Gibson. 'The daughter was part payment for blackmail.'

'Take him down.' Barney pointed to two of his officers. 'Those two will help. They've the new handcuffs on them. I have to deal with this situation here.'

Caldecott took a card from his breast pocket and handed it to Barney. 'Can you deliver a message for me?' he said.

★ ★ ★

'I've the best seat in the house.' Ivy had slipped outside to watch the carry-on in front of her door. She was sitting on a blanket folded over Frank's windowsill, her back to the open window of Frank's front room.

Frank and Ria were inside the house, away from the open window. Ria had recognised the figure of her husband through the slight gap of the open doorway — she'd hidden behind the door while the others stepped outside. She'd been hiding in Frank's place, her heart thumping

392

in fright, her mind frantically seeking a means of escape. She would not be returned to that man's untender care. She'd die first. She had to force herself to remain inside with Frank. It would serve no purpose to run screaming into the streets as her frantically whirling thoughts were urging her to do.

★   ★   ★

'It's a bit ghoulish of us, I suppose,' Ivy said as she watched the medical people work on Father Leary. She didn't envy the people dragging Mrs Purcell out of the bodily waste that surrounded Leary's body. The smell even from here was enough to knock you out. 'I can't believe you lot are eating fish and chips to watch this. It's not a bloody fillum.'

'Shame to waste food,' Frank said. 'You worked us all like dogs today and we deserve a feed.'

Mike and Jennifer had hotfooted it to the chipper. They'd picked up Molly Coyle on the way. No one wanted to miss a minute of the drama surrounding the Parish Priest — each had their own reason for their interest.

Brian Connelly was leading some of the onlookers in prayer.

'Ria!' Ivy leaned back against the window so her lowered voice would carry. 'The Garda are going up to yer supposed husband.'

Robert Hunter tried to escape the two Garda officers. In a flash they had him face first on the cobbles and cuffed in a practised move under the riveted stares of the people inside Ivy's house.

Ria was standing to the side of the window watching. 'Would a round of applause be inappropriate?' she said.

Fliss had been waiting for her moment. She stepped out of the house. 'Doctor, a moment!' she called in her beautiful voice. The crowd stilled — no one had ever seen anything like her before. She was wearing one of the beautifully tailored suits Jennifer had created but it was the sparkle of diamonds at her ears, wrists and in the opening of her blouse that held the crowd enthralled.

'Lady Arabella Wilkinson.' Fliss offered her real name and a hand sparkling with diamond rings to the bemused doctor. 'The afflicted man is my brother. What is his prognosis?' She waited, clearly expecting an immediate answer.

'I couldn't . . . ' The junior doctor looked around as if seeking help from the gathered crowd.

'I shan't hold you to it, of course,' Fliss shrugged delicately, 'but there are family matters to attend to.' Her smile held steel, her gaze almost pinned the young doctor in place. 'What, in your opinion, is his prognosis?'

The doctor stepped in to murmur for Fliss's ears only. 'I think he's suffered a brain bleed.'

'How very tragic.' Fliss dropped her eyes. She wanted no one to see her emotions at that moment. She had seen men have seizures before. If God was in his heaven and answering her prayers, her brother would never recover.

'Would you care to accompany your brother in

the ambulance?' The doctor watched the heavy figure being moved with great difficulty into the open mouth of the waiting ambulance. Mrs Purcell was already inside. No one had been willing to offer to care for the woman.

'Thank you, no.' Fliss stepped back.

The world of The Lane began to move again. The ambulance pulled away, bell clanging. The Garda moved the crowd along. A group of Jem's lads carried hot soapy water and strong brushes out to wash the cobbles outside Ivy's house.

'Lady Arabella Wilkinson?' Ivy pushed herself upright from her position on the window ledge. 'Fact or fiction?'

'Fact, my dear Ivy.' Fliss walked tiredly towards the open door of the house. 'Fact.'

'Is Ria around?' Garda Collins stopped in front of Ivy. He watched the older woman walk back into the house, wondering if he had the most interesting beat in Dublin.

'I'm here.' Ria stepped from Frank's room into the hallway.

'Detective Caldecott has found your father's people, the Vandemans,' Barney said. 'They are eager to contact you. He left his card for you if you want to get in touch.' He passed the card to her, tipped his hat and walked away.

Astonished, Ria looked after him as he walked through the thinning crowd.

'*Stanley!*' she screamed suddenly, dashing out into the courtyard towards a couple that had been hidden by the crowd.

Ivy watched Ria almost pull the couple and

child into her own house. She knew the name Stanley — Ria talked and worried about the boy all the time.

★ ★ ★

'I'm so glad to see you, Stanley.' Ria smiled at the young boy digging into the newspaper-wrapped fish and chips. 'I worried about you.'

'Me mam and Rowley brought me to see you.' Stan was having the time of his life. He was sitting in a big comfortable chair pulled up to a blazing fire, surrounded by smiling people.

Ria stared at the bruised and battered face of Stanley's mother. She'd never had a great deal to do with the woman for all they had been neighbours for years.

'The boy was fretting.' Rowley's beard moved, indicating he'd spoken. The man's black hair fell to his shoulders — the heavy moustache and long beard he wore practically covered his entire face. The ragged cuff of his old tweed jacket fell back to expose a delicate wrist when he raised his hand to carry chips to his lips.

'We've come to Dublin to find jobs,' Nora, Stanley's mother, stared at Ria out of haunted eyes. 'I'm not going back there.'

'It's very late.' Ria looked over at the little boy who had finished his fish and chips and was yawning in his chair. 'I know you won't mind roughing it here for tonight. We'll talk in the morning.'

★ ★ ★

While Ria was entertaining her company, Ivy and Jem were sitting by their range, Ivy on her husband's knee. She was still trying to come to terms with the events of the evening.

'My God, Jem, I don't think I'll be able to close my eyes tonight.'

'It's been a right old drama alright.' Jem caressed her bump while staring into the flames. 'I wonder if this is what that shellshock they talk about feels like.'

'Well, our world certainly exploded in front of our very eyes.'

They remained silent for a while. Jem hadn't been joking when he said he felt shell-shocked. He wasn't ready to discuss Father Leary's fate or that of Mrs Purcell. The two people who had persecuted his wife were out of the picture for the moment at least by the looks of things.

'Fliss looked a picture stepping out of our door,' Jem's voice broke the comfortable silence. 'They'll be talking about that till the cows come home.'

'Lady Arabella Wilkinson if you wouldn't be minding.'

'I telephoned Edward and Armstrong.'

'Did you?' She was lost in her own thoughts.

'I thought Edward was going to come through the telephone wires when I told him about our Fliss,' Jem said slowly.

'Why?' She wasn't really paying attention.

'It seems Lady Arabella Wilkinson is of great interest to Galway society.'

'Go way!' Today had been so full of shocks what was one more?

'He's coming now to talk to her.'

Ivy snorted inelegantly. 'I hope you warned Ann Marie to hold onto her man.'

What could he say?

'Who were those people with Ria?' Jem had seen her talking to them. 'Did you find out?'

'I think that's the lad Stanley she was worrying about. I don't know who the couple were. We'll find out tomorrow no doubt.'

'Did you ever discover why they took that fella Hunter away?' He'd been glad to see the man being taken from The Lane in handcuffs. Ria didn't need to have him anywhere close to her. She was only learning to live her own life.

'Conn was close.' Ivy smiled against Jem's chest. 'He heard the charges being read. It seems the fella is being accused of false imprisonment — illegal earnings — abuse of power and several more things I can't remember.'

'All of that!' Jem clicked his tongue against his teeth. 'He'll be away for a long time.'

'He was shouting for them to contact The Squire, according to Conn. Seems he believes the man will have him out in the morning.'

'I hope to Christ he doesn't.' Jem didn't want to have to deal with the man.

'All we can do is wait and see.' She yawned into his chest.

'Ready for bed?' he whispered.

'I'm afraid to close my eyes,' she said. 'Let's just sit here for a while.'

'You need your rest and so does the little one.' He pushed her to her feet. 'I'll be just a minute.'

'I don't know what to think or feel about

Father Leary,' she said, walking towards the bedroom.

'I'm just glad he didn't drop dead on our doorstep.' Jem said as he raked the coals of the range.

48

'I've come to examine your new abode and catch up on all the latest gossip.' Ann Marie, with Catherine proudly standing by the baby-carriage, stood in the open doorway of Ivy's house. 'I've heard your rooms are finished and open for viewing.'

'Would yeh get in out of that — it's perishing!' Ivy shifted her balance to unblock the doorway. She was so big these days. It was a race now to see if Christmas or her child would get here first. 'I can feel me husband's hand in this.'

'So gracious.' Ann Marie stepped aside to allow Catherine to push the large pram into the hallway.

'You can leave the baby in here with me.' Frank opened the door to his front room. 'I've the fire lit and the poor lad must be sick of the sound of women's voices.'

Master Gannon O'Connor knew that voice. His little legs started to kick at the navy covering of his pram — his mitten-covered fists waved.

Ann Marie was learning to let her child out of her sight but it was difficult. She was fascinated by her son, his every breath a treasure. At only four months old she thought he was the smartest child ever born. The gummy smile he bestowed upon her lightened her heart. She undid the waterproof cover of the pram, peeling back the nest of blankets. She unbuckled the safety straps and with loving hands removed her son from his nest.

'Come to yer granddad!' Frank stepped forward to scoop the baby into his arms.

'Is that the baby?' Ali opened the kitchen door, other heads peeking over her shoulders.

'I have him.' Frank stepped quickly into his room, closing the door at his back.

'Everyone wants to hold the baby.' Catherine laughed, walking down the hall into the kitchen.

'So,' Ann Marie had restored order to the pram and set the brake, 'I want to see it.'

Ivy opened the door to what had been Fliss's rooms and stood back.

Ann Marie stepped inside, followed closely by Ivy.

'Oh, you've done a marvellous job!' Ann Marie didn't know where to look first. 'What a great idea to take Fliss's rooms for yourself!'

'Jem insisted. He thought with the baby and all we needed somewhere to call our own — our back rooms are overrun with people from morning till night it seems to me. I'm going to use our old bedroom to store the expensive items I pick up from time to time on my round.' Ivy was becoming more conscious of the need for security.

'The dollhouse looks wonderful.' Ann Marie walked over to admire the beautifully carved table with the dollhouse sitting on top, tucked into one of the alcoves created by the chimney. 'I do love these old fireplaces.' She put her hand on the tiled mantelpiece. 'They make such a statement in a room. This room is certainly very different from when Fliss lived here.' Ann Marie dropped into one of the two tubular armchairs on either side of the fire.

'You couldn't see this room when Fliss lived here.'

'So, what news of the travellers?'

'Lady Arabella Wilkinson — our friend Fliss — is taking Hollywood by storm.' Ivy began to pull over a chair that Frank had made for her.

'I'll do that!' Ann Marie jumped to her feet.

'Oh, not you too!' Ivy stood back and let her move the chair closer to the burning fire.

'Everyone's concern getting on your nerves?' Ann Marie understood but found it impossible to stand back and let Ivy struggle.

Ivy opened her mouth to reply but the door to the room was pushed open after a brief tattoo of knuckles on the wood.

'I thought you'd enjoy a pot of tea in here.' Ali pushed a wheeled trolley into the room. The top held cups, saucers, milk and sugar. The bottom held utensils and a plate of scones, butter and jam. 'I'll bring in that teapot thing Jem got you and you can relax.' She glared at Ivy. 'Sitting down.'

'I give in.' Ivy lowered herself carefully into the chair.

'Oh, that's clever!' Ann Marie admired the heavy wooden chair that tilted forward to allow Ivy to sit. She didn't comment on Ali's manner. She'd heard enough of that sort of thing herself when she was with child — and resented it.

'Frank made it.' Ivy fell silent when Ali bustled in with a tall teapot that stood on a stand. The stand was a burner which, when lit, kept the tea warm. She waited while Ali poured the tea and fussed with lighting the burner under the pot.

'I'll take over now, Ali.' Ann Marie could see that Ivy was only moments from throwing something at the fussing Ali's head. 'Thank you.' She waited until Ali had closed the door behind her and passed Ivy her tea before saying, 'You were telling me about the travellers,'

'Ria, as you know, is in Stockholm.' Ivy sipped her tea. 'She has met with her father's family. Her letters home are not very informative. I suppose she's never had much practice sharing her news. Maybe I'm spoiled because Shay's letters make his world come alive on the page. Úna, on the other hand, is having the time of her life. She sends very colourful postcards home but not a lot of newsy letters.' It had been a surprise to everyone when Ria asked Úna Connelly to accompany her. 'Fliss, however, is a vivid and entertaining letter writer. The woman is loving Hollywood. Her letters are full of the famous students she has and their tragic speaking voices.'

'My Edward is quite the celebrity in Galway these days. Galway society is positively agog at what they see as his solving of the mystery that was Lady Arabella Wilkinson.'

'Fliss never talks about it, you know.' Ivy allowed Ann Marie to serve her more tea, biting back the words on the tip of her tongue.

'One can only imagine the life the poor woman must have led with Father Leary as a brother.' Ann Marie watched her friend carefully. The tales of the priest's perversions had run around Dublin like wildfire once the man was incapable of retaliation. Ivy's mother was dining out on her 'I told you so' stories. 'Lord Wilkinson was an old man when he married a very young Fliss, it seems.'

'I wouldn't have thought that was so strange for the times.'

'Ah, but there were already three Wilkinson sons.' Ann Marie had got some of the story from Edward. 'There was also the matter of a lack of dowry.'

'Fliss will go to her grave with her secrets.' Ivy had tried to get the woman to tell her story but she'd refused. 'Some things, my dear Ivy,' she had said, 'you are better off not knowing.' She'd had to be content with that.

'It's maddening.'

A loud cry echoed. Ann Marie felt milk fill her breasts. 'My master's voice.' She looked towards the door. 'Frank won't be able to take that noise for long.' She was feeding the baby herself, much to the horror of her peers.

'Someone wants his mammy.' Frank came in, passed the baby to Ann Marie and hurried from the room.

Ann Marie laughed softly and prepared to enjoy this time with her son. She arranged her clothing and settled back with her baby at her breast.

'I notice you have Emerald's cupboard bed in this room.' She pressed a gentle kiss to her son's head.

'She insisted.' Ivy tried to find a comfortable sitting position.

'I'm sure.' Ann Marie glanced around the room. 'Did all of these pieces come from Jem's storage space? Some of these I wouldn't mind for my own home.'

'There are advantages to being married to the owner of a house-contents resale business,' Ivy said with a grin.

'I found it unbelievable to hear that Robert Hunter was walking free in Kildare.' Ann Marie hated the fact that she had missed the fascinating events that had taken place in The Lane on the evening Father Leary collapsed.

'Money talks and criminals walk.' Ivy hadn't been surprised. 'I believe that is why Ria decided to travel. The poor woman didn't want to be here if that man comes looking for her again.'

'What about Stanley? You will have to procure an invitation for me to visit.' Ann Marie was watching Ivy closely. 'I'm simply fascinated by the whole affair.'

'The lad's mother has taken control of the house next door while Ria is away. She has practically cleared out Jem's supply of household furnishings to deck the house out.' Nora had taken on the role of housekeeper with a vengeance. 'You would not believe the changes in that house. Nora has moved the Connolly family out of the back rooms and into the main house.'

'No!'

'The woman is at home all day and insists she should have charge of the kitchen.' Ivy winced. 'A new gas cooker has been installed and I've been giving Nora advice about the use of the range. It seems that Rowley is actually Nora's brother — they share a mother. He and Stanley have one bedroom off the kitchen and Nora the other. I think it's working out for all concerned.'

'How are Frank and Rowley getting along?' Now, that had been a surprise. When the man had removed all of that unsightly hair from his person he'd been truly beautiful. 'I thought at one time Rowley would leave with Fliss.'

Ivy laughed at the memory of Fliss's reaction to the cleanshaven male. She'd purred every time she'd seen him, much to Rowley's horrified embarrassment. 'Rowley has practically moved into Frank's new workshop. The poor man is pestered by swooning females. I can see why he hid behind all of that hair. He seems to have a very creative mind. He and Frank discuss inventions until the stars shine. And young Stan is like a dog with two tails. He loves school.'

'Yes, I know,' Ann Marie smiled. 'He and Emerald are practically joined at the hip these days.'

'So many changes.' Ivy watched Ann Marie put her son on her shoulder. A very masculine burp was her reward. Both women smiled and Ann Marie changed breasts.

'Not only in our world, Ivy,' Ann Marie said. 'I'm worried about the news coming out of America. If their economy fails it will affect the rest of the world. How will that affect our husbands' business? They are investing a great deal in their cinemas.'

'Jem has consulted with Mr Clancy on this subject. The man is a retired professor of economics after all.' Brother Theo had found that teacher for them. 'Brother Theo too is deeply concerned.'

'You must be glad to have the Friar's counsel once more.'

'Leary made an awful lot of problems for Theo because of me. It's hard to believe that one man could have so much influence.' Ivy winced a little. She sat back in her chair and tried to find a comfortable position. 'Fliss said the family estate had been promised to the church. I said to Brother Theo that that explained a lot but he only gave me one of his looks.' The two women fell silent once more.

'I'm worried people won't have money to spend on going to the cinema,' Ann Marie said.

'I think you're wrong and Mr Clancy agrees with me. The cinema, like the theatre, is an escape from reality. I never had time to enjoy it myself growing up but I know several women who take their children to the cinema weekly. The cinema is out of the weather with comfortable seats. The world on the big screen is bright and beautiful — people are going to need all of that.'

'I hope you are right.'

'It's no use worrying about something that hasn't happened yet.' Ivy was philosophical about the matter. She'd been poor before. She didn't want to return to those days but she'd get by if she had to.

'It's getting very noisy outside,' Ann Marie remarked.

Ivy could put an action to every sound she heard. 'The automobile taxis are very popular.

Some people are hiring the cars just to drive in a circle so they can say they've experienced automobile travel. And I can hear the women pulling my place apart trying to find something for Christmas.' Ivy was delighted with the increase in business. She didn't know what she'd have done without her helpers.

'You must find it hard to rest,' Ann Marie said.

'Ann Marie, the only time I get to myself is when I do my round.' Ivy let out a long low breath. 'I've had to fight to be allowed to do that.' She put her hand on her hardening stomach.

Finally.

'Now, I need you to do something for me,' she said.

'Anything.'

'Sneak me out of here and down to Mrs Winthrop.'

49

'Where's Ivy?' Jem stood in the workroom doorway.

'Ask Ali.' Jennifer didn't look up from her sewing machine. The answer to most questions asked of her was 'Ask Ali'.

'She's still out back,' Molly Coyle at the second machine said. She had been taken on to help with the Christmas rush. Mother and daughter were crafting outfits from discards that working women were buying for 'best' outfits. They couldn't keep up with the demand.

'It's late for her to be out and shouldn't you two have left by now?' Jem was bloody glad he'd insisted they move — living in these rooms had been like sleeping on the factory floor — there was always someone underfoot.

'Have yeh seen the queue out the back?' Molly Coyle pulled a brown skirt in the new style from her machine. She'd been able — under Ivy's instruction — to get three skirts out of an old gown.

Jem backed away. This was Ivy's business. He pulled open the kitchen door and almost jumped back. The back garden was bedlam.

'*Ali!*' he shouted, standing with the door closed at his back.

'What?' The voice came from one of the sheds.

'Have you seen my wife?' He ignored the lewd jests some of the gathered women shouted.

'She's been sitting in with Ann Marie for hours.' Ali's head appeared over the top half of the split doors Frank and Rowley had insisted on installing in the sheds. She'd had cause to bless their name these days. The women weren't shy about pushing their way into the sheds and pulling the place apart. The bottom half of the split doors could be locked and business conducted from the open top half. She felt like a horse sometimes but it made doing business a lot easier.

'If someone could give us a cup of tea we'd be thankful.' Mike's head appeared over the half-door of one of the sheds.

Catherine's head then appeared. She'd been forced into service. 'I'll second that!'

How in the name of God does Ivy manage this madness? Jem asked himself.

'If you could ask me ma and Carmel to come over?' Ali's voice suggested. The woman herself was hidden by the crowd of women pushing forward. 'That would be a great help.' They'd enjoy the chance to sit in the warm kitchen.

'I'll do that but I'm sending some of my men to move these women out — it's long past business hours.' He ignored the screams of abuse — enough was enough.

He stepped back into the kitchen, locking the door behind him. He'd check on Ivy then deal with the mess outside.

'Ivy!' He pushed open the door to their living room. It was empty.

He rapped on Frank's door. He received no answer.

'Woman,' he pushed his hands through his hair, 'where the hell are you?' He opened the front door and yelled *'Conn!'*

'Boss?'

'Get over here.' He stepped back inside and held the door open for Conn. He gave his instructions for dealing with Ivy's business in short sharp commands. He didn't wait for Conn's nod before running out the door. He knew where his wife was and he was going to wring her neck for not sending for him.

⋆   ⋆   ⋆

'Do not bang on that door.' Augustina Winthrop pulled open her front door before Jem could batter it down. 'I saw you running past the window. I've enough to do with your wife without bothering with you.' She stepped back. 'Get inside. You can make yourself useful by tending my range and boiling water. It won't be long now.' She turned to walk away then paused for a moment to smile over her shoulder. 'You know your Ivy — the first thing that woman is going to demand is a cup of tea.' She stepped into what she was now calling her birthing room and closed the door.

'Oh, good, you're here!' Ann Marie was sitting in front of the range, her baby on her shoulder. 'Master Gannon,' she pressed a kiss onto the baby's rosy cheek, 'picked the worst time possible to turn demanding — just like a man.'

Jem opened his mouth. 'What — '

'No time.' Ann Marie stood and practically

shoved her son at Jem. 'I've fed and changed him. He needs to be cuddled. You can do that while I help your wife.' She hurried from the kitchen, calling over her shoulder. 'It will be good practice for you!'

'Well, little man, it looks like it's just us men.' Jem cradled the baby in his left arm while using his right to open the door of the range. 'We've been exiled to the kitchen. There's something wrong with that but at this moment in time I can't think what it is.'

He looked around for the coal. The fire in the range needed tending. It was almost out. There were large pots of hot water steaming on top.

'That wife of mine!' He smiled down at the big-eyed baby in his arms.

He went into the hall and pushed the fancy baby-carriage into the kitchen.

'I thought I knew what I was getting into when I married Ivy Murphy. Let me tell you something, little one — no man knows what he's getting into with women. These are pearls of wisdom you're getting from your Uncle Jem.'

He looked towards the hallway. Was his Ivy safe — did she need him?

He put the baby into his fancy carriage, ignoring the little whimper of objection. He had work to do.

Ann Marie, wrapped in a white smock, hurried into the kitchen, beads of sweat on her brow. She nudged Jem out of her way with her hip. She emptied the enamel bowl of water she was carrying and, with swift efficient movements, rinsed it before refilling it with hot water from the stove. With a quick glance at her complaining son she hurried from the room.

'When do I get to see my wife?' Jem shouted to her back and was ignored.

'Looks like we're on our own again,' he muttered to the baby, rocking the baby-pram.

He had the fire burning brightly and the pots refilled. He stood for a moment trying to think what else to do.

'Right, that's done. When that fire is blazing I'd better make a pot of tea. This is one time I'd love to hear Ivy demanding a pot of tea because she's spitting feathers.'

He felt useless. He wanted to be at his wife's side, not on the sidelines. He looked down at the baby in the pram, his green eyes glittering with tears.

'I'm bloody terrified,' he whispered to the baby and lifted him out of the pram.

It felt like a lifetime passed as he paced the kitchen, the baby on his shoulder, while he worried.

An infant cry had him removing the baby from his shoulder to check if something was wrong. When he saw the baby's sleeping face the strength went from his knees. He fell into one of the chairs in front of the range. That cry came from his child — his and Ivy's.

★ ★ ★

'Jem Ryan — ' An exhausted Ann Marie finally appeared in the kitchen. She'd removed the soiled smock and left it in the birthing room as ordered by Augustina. 'Give me my child. You have one of your own.' She took the baby from the silently weeping man and with a moan of relief collapsed into the chair across from his. It wasn't her place to tell him. She'd leave that to Ivy.

'Ivy?' Jem looked up, unashamed of the tears pouring from his eyes.

'She is — ' Ann Marie started.

'Jem Ryan!'

Ivy's voice was music to Jem's ears. His tear-streaked face split into a huge smile.

'I hope to God you've made that tea!'

'That's my woman!' Jem jumped to his feet. *'I've the arse boiled out of the kettle!'* he shouted back. He turned to look down at Ann Marie. 'I love her, Ann Marie, but I have to tell you — I'm going to wring her neck.'

'This would be a good time for it.' Ann Marie rested back with her eyes closed, her baby held close. 'She's too weak to fight back.'

Jem had the tea brewing, cups and saucers at the ready, when Augustina stepped into the kitchen.

'I'd consider it a great favour if you'd pour me a cup of tea.' Augustina sat down with a sigh of relief. 'Your woman is on the fainting couch — you know the one — she's waiting for you.' She'd call Marcella Wiggins to clean the birthing room. She herself was exhausted.

'I can't believe I'm saying this!' Ann Marie laughed. 'Tea all round!'

'I'm waiting!' was shouted down the hall.

'She's a very demanding woman, your wife,' Augustina accepted the cup of tea Jem passed to her. 'Better get down there or your name will be mud.'

★ ★ ★

'I'll swap yeh, missus.' Jem, tea in hand, stepped into the front room. His Ivy was stretched out on the sheet-covered fainting couch, her short dark hair almost stuck to her head, her violet eyes lowered to the bundle in her arms.

'It's a good deal.' His heart was in his mouth as he looked at his wife and child. 'A cup of tea for a baby.'

'Come and meet your son.' Ivy raised tired violet eyes to his. 'I'm not letting go of him but I've earned that bloody tea.' She licked dry lips. Augustina had given her a wet cloth to suck on but she wanted tea.

Jem put the tray he held on a side table and dropped to his knees. 'Show me my son.' He gazed at the baby. 'He's beautiful,' he choked.

Ivy put her head back for a moment and closed her eyes. This giving birth business was hard work.

Jem remained on his knees, admiring the two most important people in his life, his heart almost beating out of his chest.

'I want to go home.' Ivy's voice broke into Jem's fascination with his son.

'I'll go and get something to wrap you in.' He knew there was no point arguing with Ivy.

'I can walk,' Ivy objected.

415

Jem ignored her, going into the kitchen to ask Augustina's advice.

'I thought I'd carry Ivy and the baby home,' he said when he'd explained Ivy's desire to leave. He looked at Augustina. 'Will that be alright?'

Augustina walked in to talk to Ivy. 'It's so cold out,' she objected.

'It's December,' Ivy groused.

'I'll put the baby in the pram with Gannon,' Ann Marie suggested. 'We won't be going far.'

'*The Prince and The Pauper*.' Ivy didn't care how she got there — she just wanted to go home.

The deed was done.

★   ★   ★

A crowd of people had started gathering in the hallway outside the bedroom door. Ivy could hear them. She lay in her big brass bed, her son in her arms, resting back against the pillows.

'You may as well let them in,' Ivy said to the hovering Jem. 'You'd think they'd no homes to go to.'

Frank was first in the door. He had a beautiful wooden cradle in his arms. He was followed in a steady stream by more and more gift-carrying people. Ivy didn't think the room would hold any more when Edward O'Connor pushed his way to his wife's side by the bed. There was much oohing and aahing over the baby until Augustina, with Frank's help, ushered the crowd from the room.

'What are you going to call him?' Edward, with his son in his arms, was sitting on one side at the foot of the big bed with Ann Marie almost stretched across the end of it, her head close to his side.

Jem sat at the head of the bed beside Ivy. He looked down at her before saying, 'I had thought to call the child 'Trouble' with Ivy for a mother,' he said to their amusement. 'But . . . he coughed to clear his throat, 'we are naming our son Connor.'

They had thought about it long and hard. Without Edward O'Connor Jem would never have found the courage to court Ivy. They would never have met Emmy, never had the funds to start their business. The man had all unknowingly been their benefactor long before they met him. It was fitting they should name their child in his honour.

'What an honour, darling!' Ann Marie looked at the couple with delight. They meant so much to her. What would she have become without them?

'I am undeserving of that honour.' Edward felt quite choked up.

'Can I come back in now?' Emmy's little head appeared around the slowly opening door. 'I want to kiss my new brother.' She walked over and climbed up onto the large bed. 'I couldn't before with everyone here.'

'It's late.' Ivy smiled at the child who had changed everything. 'You should be in bed.'

Emmy snuggled into a familiar place between Jem and Ivy. 'I'm so lucky having two brothers,' she whispered before sleep claimed her. No one contradicted her.

We do hope that you have enjoyed reading
this large print book.

Did you know that all of our titles
are available for purchase?

We publish a wide range of high quality
large print books including:
**Romances, Mysteries, Classics
General Fiction
Non Fiction and Westerns**

Special interest titles available in
large print are:
**The Little Oxford Dictionary
Music Book
Song Book
Hymn Book
Service Book**

Also available from us courtesy of
Oxford University Press:
**Young Readers' Dictionary
(large print edition)
Young Readers' Thesaurus
(large print edition)**

For further information or a free
brochure, please contact us at:
**Ulverscroft Large Print Books Ltd.,
The Green, Bradgate Road, Anstey,
Leicester, LE7 7FU, England.
Tel:** (00 44) 0116 236 4325
Fax: (00 44) 0116 234 0205

THE HA'PENNY PLACE

Gemma Jackson

Ivy Rose Murphy has come up in the world. She still begs for discards from the homes of the wealthy which lie only a stone's throw from The Lane, the poverty-ridden tenements where she lives. These discards she repairs and sells around the Dublin markets. But she is fast turning herself into 'Miss Ivy Rose', successful businesswoman. With her talent for needlework, she has begun to supply an upmarket shop in Grafton Street with beautifully-dressed dolls. Then Ivy's wealthy friend with her beloved camera spends a day at the airport photographing planes. Little does she know that her visit can destroy all Ivy's hopes for the future.

HA'PENNY CHANCE

Gemma Jackson

Ivy Rose Murphy dreams of a better future. For years she has set out daily from the tenements known as 'The Lane' to beg for discards from the homes of the wealthy. Her fortunes take a turn for the better, but there are eyes on Ivy and she is vulnerable as she carries her earnings through the dark winter streets. Jem Ryan, who owns the local livery, longs to make Ivy his wife, but she is reluctant to give up her fierce independence. Then a sudden astonishing event turns Ivy's world upside down. A dazzling future beckons and she must decide where her loyalties lie.

THROUGH STREETS BROAD AND NARROW

Gemma Jackson

On New Year's Day 1925 Ivy Rose Murphy awakes to find her world changed forever. Her irresponsible Da is dead. She is grief-stricken and alone but for the first time in her life free to please herself. After her mother deserted the family, Ivy became the sole provider for her Da and three brothers. As she visits the morgue to pay her respects to her Da, a chance meeting introduces Ivy to a new world of money and privilege, her mother's world. Ivy is suddenly a woman on a mission to improve herself and her lot in life.